THE RED FRAME

DAVE PITT

TIME WILL NEVER FORGIVE

THE RED FRAME

For Meghan Sandra

With special thanks to Rosaline for helping me with every step of this journey.

DAVE PITT

Authors Introduction

Well here we are at the final part of the trilogy. I can only presume you have read the other two books and that is what has brought you to this page. Of course if you haven't then this book could be a little confusing, also you will have missed out on my growing tale, so many twists and turns to appreciate.

From the bottom of my heart thank you for following this story, for giving me your time, the most precious of life's commodities.

It was during the lockdown of 2020 that I was suddenly given four months of that rare commodity. I chose to eat it up by sitting down and writing the Life Machine, perhaps as my way of coping with an uncertain world, as it was certainly an escape from the rolling news feeds. So for me Hands-Face-Space became Sit-Imagine-Write, which I found to be just a useful in the fight against the spread of the disease.

Of course I was far from unique in doing this as millions of other people took advantage of this opportunity to write their children's stories, adult books, memoirs, diaries, or poetry, therefore with the publishing market saturated when the world reopened my original manuscript got lost in the swell. Traditional publishers, to whom I was often only allowed to send the first three chapters, told me after months of hoping for a positive reply that their waiting lists were too long. During that time I received literally dozens of offers to publish with companies using either a vanity or hybrid contract, but I had no intention of paying money to see my work in print, also I had little cash to pay anyone. So I self-published and in doing so learned all the mistakes and pitfalls along the way. I don't believe it would be particularly helpful to list them here because everyone's journey will be different. Suffice to say, I learned from my first book, that one should never trust self-editing; your eyes will deceive you so always get someone to help, to judge and critique. For me that gracious and generous soul was Lorraine Gomersall, who gave her time to read then reread my work, spotting typos and problems with my writing, sometimes suggesting whole rewrites of paragraphs and chapters, but always with a loving care for the characters and the story. I know how lucky I am to have a friend like this, someone willing to spend hours and hours sitting with me at her kitchen table, or even longer periods on the phone talking into the middle of the night; Thank you Lorraine for all your precious time and for making me a better writer.

THE RED FRAME

The story that developed into the Life Machine was an idea born over twenty years earlier. I was living in Edinburgh at the time in Leith on Dalmeny Street where a lot of the action takes place in the original novel. In that beautiful city the millennium celebrations were imminent, the countdown was on with some people believing it could be the end of the world, certainly the end of computers as we knew them, something to do with their system clocks being unable to handle the change from 1999 to 2000. Anyway that didn't happen.

I remember looking out of the window of the tenement flat I shared with my fiancée and seeing the four inch ledge outside. For me it held no purpose in the construction of the building and wasn't present on any other floors, so I guess my mind gave it a purpose and thought of it as a suicide ledge, a narrow precipice that one could stand upon to privately prepare their farewells before plummeting to the cobbles below. Immediately I gave my fictional suicide victim a name and it has never changed from the first short story to now. He'd be called Alex and would be thirty one when he jumped, roughly my age at the time, but he wouldn't simply die, if only because that would be the shortest and most unsatisfying of stories ever put to paper.

From that simple setting I knocked up, I won't say wrote because I still have the original version and it's awfully written, a three page draft which I called ALEX. In that version he fell to the cobbles but his soul passed through and entered a world of blue goo, before being born again, his memories wiped out as he was forced through the birth canal. Let's not waste time with the ins and outs of that tale, but what it did was make me think about the concept of death and the afterlife. Questions; What if everyone experienced their passing in numerous different ways?

I imagined at the exact moment of a life ending some may leave their bodies and float out upon an ocean, before slowly breaking apart allowing their molecules to once more return to the universe. Perhaps others went off like a firework with their souls flying up to explode in the heavens, while some experienced it as white world where they could ask questions forever.

Soon I decided to write another two short stories with two different characters. The first was called OSCAR concerning an imprisoned serial killer who didn't know where he was or why he was there, but with a voice screaming in his head, condemning him for what he'd done. At the end of that story he killed himself with a pen through the ear and floated away in a blue ocean. The other was entitled CHARLIE about a young woman who paid a friend for some unusual sexual favour. I'm reticent to say anymore on that story for now because I may revisit its set up one day; I will only add that she ended up passing over as a glorious firework exploding into the heavens.

So back to 2020 where after two weeks of furlough and finding myself unable to make decent banana bread, having twice watched the series where the king of tigers got his comeuppance, and while struggling to keep up with all the advice for physical and mental wellbeing, I pulled out those old stories from a folder I'd carried with me for almost a quarter of a century. Time does fly.

That was how it started, I began to focus on my writing and since then I sit down at every opportunity to let my imagination have its say.

Oh if only it really was that easy, which brings me to my biggest acknowledgment, the friend who supported me through the whole process and still does to this day. Rosaline Webb (I took her surname and gave it to Alex as a thank you.) who gave me both the belief to begin and the drive to continue. She has listened to literally every word I've written for this trilogy, that's roughly 450,000 of them, she has picked me up when I've thought the task too big and wanted to give in, she asks the questions that need to be asked to clarify scenes and characters, and is always there night or day to help me thrive as an author and a human being. On top of that weighty commitment to the cause she has also formatted and uploaded my work for others to see, sorting out parameters, orientations, page breaks, spacing and indents, amongst a hundred other things that have to be done. These are all time consuming and attention to detail undertakings for which I have no proficiency, but ones that she performs with a saintly patience while asking for nothing in return, again making my life as a writer and a human easier

The covers to my books have received many plaudits, people commenting on the use of colours, the details hidden within the images, the striking stand out designs that tempt the browser to become a buyer. They were all laid out and done by Rosaline who took my, at best, sketchy ideas and returned them back to me with interesting and incredible work.

So that's my story and here's the final part of my written one, The Red Frame, which follows on directly from The Snakes Tale, no time slips to see here, ruthlessly bringing all of my characters and plots to their conclusion. Three years is a long time to spend with souls who you literally know inside and out. It has been far more emotional to write and finish this series than

I expected, but I have tried my best and worked so very hard to give you a believable and enjoyable ending.

This is a sincere thank you to all my readers for letting me show you the inside of my head. Many more thanks go to all my family and friends who over the years have helped in making my head this way, plus finally the greatest thank you to whoever takes responsibility for this messy and ridiculous universe.

I wouldn't want to be anywhere else.

D Xx

1

Let us fall steeply from the emptiest of heavens where, if we can feel such sensations, dust particles brush over our skin. Far away in the distance a miniscule white pinprick appears in the blackness. Is that a hole we can see through? Most certainly not, that tiny dot is a centre of this Universe, although given our fresh acceptance of quantum theory as a solid science, perhaps one day we shall discover it is both, after all to be observable or not to be observable, isn't that the question of theoretical science.

Now moving faster and faster we tear on through its outer reaches towards places where other scattered luminosities shine bright. Finally we begin to feel some warmth from the lights because whatever exploded here isn't done yet, it is continuing with its affect, infinitely spreading outwards and causing rippling sheets of time and space, all pegged out on a washing line of reality, with the essence of life no more than sparkling flickering embers rolling round inside a blast furnace. Ever more matter is crushed and mixed until sparks slowly break free from the clouds of dust and dreams, these tiny lights travel away from their nursery and we can see it all with our miraculous eyes, marvel at their expansion, but never where they're heading.

Onwards we go falling towards the light, towards the heat, towards the heart like a seed pushing up towards the sun. We hurtle uncontrollably towards the centre, ignoring the innumerable lives and deaths of stars around us because there is somewhere we need to be.

Surely every soul must have learned by now that time is vitally important, it is truly in essence a dangerous sin to waste. So we keep moving forward as we now begin to spiral within a spiral, funnelling down fast towards a rare blue dot. The azure sphere that is all we've ever had, an average sized orb mostly covered in water, the only place we call home.

The searing flames of atmospheric re-entry won't affect us, we are supposed to be here, invited to hurtle faster still, we scream through the layers of cloud towards something solid, and God don't we all need something solid in our predominantly gaseous existence. With our descent slowing we find the final few thousand feet are to be enjoyed and appreciated, looking out across the hills and lochs of nature's perfection. Finally we are home, over the City, and the Castle, and Arthur's Seat.

Now let us float down silently together for the last ten feet, listening to the sounds of the backstreets, until finally coming to rest on a rusting corrugated roof on top of a deserted lock up. Inside this ten foot by six foot space sits a man with three voices in his head, but he only has one human heart, which right now is experiencing a raging beat. Within his blue eyes both pupils are shockingly dilated, while his murdering hands clench into fists tightly, because these rushes feel so damn good. Everything about this sensation was wonderful and new, the rushing thrill an unexpected perfection they never dreamed of, in fact so astounding that they instantly crave another line for their studies.

One soundless voice then spoke to the other inside the mind of a mute.
We want more
Yes we do
Take us there vessel
Take us there now!!!

The teenage boy, unable to resist their cries and shrieks, rewraps a rag around his scarred and damaged face. By hiding his injuries he can sneak through the streets unseen, unhindered to do their bidding, to find, kill and steal from the men who sell the powder.

DAVE PITT

The previous day

The injured vessel carrying the Glitch had been faltering on through the morning streets in broad daylight, feeling and looking like a horror show, until a line of washing hung out to dry had proved to be useful, although far from perfect. As it struggled its body back out of the garden there was no doubt that sartorially the physique of Snake Hornblower had lost a great deal of its previously held panache. It limped away down the street in a pair of large blue workman overalls over the top of its bloodstained grey suit, the look completed with a blue baseball cap emblazoned with the word Benidorm and a happy palm tree. It was a horrible looking ensemble but enough to avert prying eyes and avoid unwanted attention, incredibly useful because this body's physical movements weren't up to speed yet.

On entering the skull the bullet appeared to have caused damage in the primary motor cortex of the Snake's brain. It was this heavy jolt to the system that had made it appear dead to Emma, allowing it to make an escape through the window, but leaving this body unable to move in a straight or controlled manner.

The shocking injustice of this situation was deeply puzzling to the Glitch as it kept replaying the scene over and over, wondering where it had gone wrong. After all as she'd fired it had moved. On seeing the flash of the muzzle it instinctively turned to avoid the bullet and could only reason the close proximity had caught it out. At the moment it was the most workable theory for allowing itself to be shot in the head and decidedly preferable to the other option. That it had naively delayed because it didn't believe she would actually shoot, that somehow the night they'd spent together had meant something? Well if that were the case then it had been fooled, fatally deceived by a woman's promise, by her proposal of a trusting intimacy and that hurt far more deeply than the bleeding hole in its skull.

Snake's body stiffly avoided the busy thoroughfares and progressed through quieter backstreets. This alternative route was taking it the long way round but the Glitch cared little for that inconvenience, it just wanted to get back to the lock up safely then use the privacy and time to heal. It believed it was already feeling the green shoots of recovery, the brain being rerouted around the bullet lodged in it, as it forced its feet to keep moving forward. Stumbling through the pain it mused again on Emma and her deceit. That woman was just about the luckiest soul it could ever imagine even with all the history of the Angels book in its head, where there were literally billions of tales and escapades where blind luck had saved someone's life, yet the timing and reasons for her good fortune had been quite exceptional.

Last night there had been no intention on its behalf other than to kill the woman after making her talk. It was to be the death of Emma Oxtoby, Harvey's secretary, and it was a definite plan. Yet somehow to save herself she'd found a way of unlocking emotions deep within it, feelings it was blissfully unaware it owned, then she took savage advantage of that tiny window of chance. It had been a cruel lesson and one which wouldn't be repeated as long as it drew breath, of that there was no doubt, because their once in a lifetime parleying was over. When fully recovered and back in the position to do so, the Glitch's vengeance would be sweet, drawn out and pitiless, but first it needed to get back, rest and recover from the shock of being shot in the face.

This Snake vessel had almost been lost to it, a dangerous warning that it was only just surviving, but the lesson had been learned. From now on the Glitch would avoid all emotions, the heartbreak and damage they can cause, setting itself to only move forward cold and callously to wage its heartless war, to fulfil its purpose.

Meanwhile, not too far away in a decrepit lock up, a teenager was sitting on an upturned bucket talking to no one visible. 'What exactly do you want me to do...?'

I need you to stop asking so many questions

Jay Cleaver couldn't help but think the chances of that happening were very low at best. He'd hundreds of more questions and best of all a Demon in his head to answer them. God damn it for his whole short life he'd fantasised about having a super power. The closest he ever got was bullying kids half his age. Now not only did he have this gift, but he could speak again, even if it was only in his mind. All the words he wanted to say came across clear and concise. There was no need to use speech cards or struggle with a worthless tongue which made him sound like a moaning ghost. Not anymore, now he had something to talk to, something with the same interests, although clearly not something with infinite patience towards his curiosity. But even though Jay understood the voice in his head was getting pissed off he couldn't stop himself. 'Can we kill anyone? Can I choose some of them?'

You have been warned and still you defy me. I believe you are lined up for lesson two.

'What's lesson two? Lesson one was the screaming right...?'

....
'Hello...?'

....

Oh so you're just gonna fuck off and ignore me then...that's lesson two is it...hello...?'

....

'...Piece of shit!'

The Demon remained silent and unprovoked to whatever filthy insults Jay called out. It was far too busy taking stock inside the teenager's skull, seeing what was available, because there was a new mind here to be sifted through and studied.

During its time residing inside Oscars head it had often discovered many layers of facts and figures, emotions and dreams, in all honesty nothing of much use to a Demon, however distinct proof the small man had been both a thinker and a learner. Yet here it turned out after only a brief search of Jay's memories and intelligence things were a little different. During the search it soon became abundantly clear this boy did not attend the same school of thought as Mr Downes.

In this boy's addled brain there were no titbits of information scattered around, no secret corridors leading to interesting subsections, nothing more than a barren landscape unsullied by even the most basic forms of creativity or imagination. It appeared to the Demon this boy lacked basic skills or discipline to make any lasting progress with his life. In fact Jay's only obsession appeared to be proving he'd been hard done by and then blaming everyone else. It was a cheap and nasty mind, immature and self-absorbed, yet for all this shallowness the Demon was finding a genuine affinity within its new home.

Getting closer to the lockup the Glitch scurried awkwardly across the bridge, its hand on the stone rail for balance, all due to a growing stiffness in Snakes joints. The effort of this limping sprint was causing a surprising shortness of breath so it chose to stop halfway, just for a minute, to peer over the edge. Down to the right it recognised the carpark and the watery place where it had first discovered this body. All of that seemed like a lifetime ago now and in this instance it almost certainly had been, or still could be. Gasping to refill the struggling lungs the Glitch looked around at the familiar skyline and couldn't help but question why it was still here. Surely it should be a billion miles away by now with its purpose duly served, returned to its slumber, this universe destroyed, yet here it was casting its eyes over the exact location where it first became a real boy. Seeing the place again was disappointing for the Glitch, knowing that after achieving the almost impossible objective of ensuring a physical presence in this realm, it had failed in becoming a superior being. It had failed so abjectly it was now diminishing rapidly into frailty, to the point of death, without leaving any significant marker that it had ever existed. Its wish to be chaos incarnate had caused the death of a few dozen souls so far, but really was that it? Its purpose and journey complete? No, no it couldn't be. There must be higher levels to attain, another evolutionary step to take.

A low whirring sound disturbed the Glitch's thoughts as a man on a bicycle came along the bridge. It turned Snake's face away in an attempt to look casual, hoping to be mistaken for a tourist out for a stroll, but then its knees buckled and it grabbed onto the wall.

The cyclist stopped 'Are you alright mate...you need a hand?' He enquired. His lime green Lycra shorts offended the Glitch even more than the spatial intrusion.

'Leave me alone...!' Snakes voice crackled at the Good Samaritan.

'...Okay mate I was only offering to help. Just thought you were looking a bit wobbly that's all.'

The Glitch looked over its shoulder in the hope the offending man would accept everything was fine. However, honest human reactions are rarely as straightforward or predictable, especially when the cyclist recognised the face under the baseball cap as the bomber from the news. Instantly the startled man began peddling hard to get away, leaving the Glitch stricken, mostly by the fact there was no way of physically stopping his escape. Leaving it with no other choice, it had to move quickly before the man phoned the police, but where and how in this condition? The end of the bridge looked a lifetime away through these eyes.

The strangest absurdity about this anomalous physical condition was the fact it was fine, the Glitch itself was more than fine, alive and healthy but trapped in a broken frame, within a dying man's skin.

No doubt the interfering cyclist was already contacting the police; who would soon surely arrive and probably in great numbers because this was the bomber. This was a major problem as it had neither the strength nor the mobility to fight them, or to run, so it must find somewhere to hide.

With some considerable effort of concentration it turned Snakes body to face forward then began to walk, with slow stuttering steps, forging ahead in search of survival until gradually the muscles relaxed a little allowing it to stride more freely. The momentum certainly wasn't fast but there was a chance it could get off the bridge and down to comparative safety if the police dallied too long. From within Snakes fading eyes the Glitch spotted a gap. It was where the stone of the bridge ended and met the steel railings, a steep grassy hill on the other side, but if push came to shove it would jump and risk bouncing dangerously down the slope to the car park some fifty feet below.

Abruptly a siren began to wail its threat in the distance so the Glitch focused all its efforts on escape. There was no time left to think or reason, this was flight or fight in all its glory, even though it could do neither of them comfortably. So suppressing any cries into a silent agony it forced itself forwards to the gap and threw itself over. Snakes body already badly injured rolled and bumped down the greasy grassy bank, strewn with litter and larger, sharper, dumped rubbish. During the unforgiving descent the Glitch had a moment to summarise its condition, but it was only when it reached the bottom and came to rest on the broken glass and fast food cartons that it accepted the terrible truth; the body it occupied, this skin of a Snake it had worn with such deep pride was dying, leaving only the consciousness of the Glitch to keep it breathing.

It laid there accepting the bullet that Emma had placed in Snakes brain was catastrophic in its impact. So ruinous that even a new species with apparent godlike powers found it was unable to fix the broken plates, nor reassemble the scattered cortex, and it had tried so very hard to do so.

The Glitch desperately attempted to stand the body upright but the signals were blocked. It looked out through the blackened eyes to see the legs twitching in spasm; whatever had been wrong with it up on the bridge was now far worse after the fall. If the Glitch had teeth they were now gritted in a monumental effort to roll the body over, to get to the deeper grass, to hide...there was really nothing else it could do.

The sirens reached the bridge above and stopped. Even though it was a sunny morning this body had never felt such cold. Along with the deathly chill and while feeling Snakes blood beginning to thicken, a new concept came into view, one it had never expected...fear.

The Glitch was immortal, that was a stone cold fact, but fully realising the body it occupied was not had awakened the most terrifying of thoughts. The horror of the situation flashed bright as it predicted the fate waiting, because if it were destined to live forever, then that time would now be spent inside a corpse. Whether they burned or buried this vessel for the funeral the Glitch would remain within it, trapped frozen in time, with no choice but to scream its anguish for eternity.

THE RED FRAME

***

The police car rolled slowly down into the car park and drove around the perimeter before stopping less than fifteen feet away. Two young officers got out.

Another sickening twist of chaotic fate began to claw at the Glitch. This was a mistake. It had hidden the body low in the grass, laying it flat using an effort that exhausted it physically, but if it could move again and get their attention it would be caught. In this position that was a good thing, the policemen would have no choice but to take this body to a hospital. Surely once there, with medical attention, they could fix this problem, resuscitate the Snake, which offered a chink of hope to this lost situation.

The two officers took opposite routes to search the area, but both of them were heading away from where the helpless Glitch lay. It was unable to move or speak to give up its concealed position as much as it strained. Finally one of the uniformed men turned back and came over towards the body. This was perfect, everything it needed, if the policeman took two more steps it would surely be seen and saved.

'I bet it's another crank call mate...!' The officer furthest away shouted over. '...We've done nine of these since yesterday and haven't even come close to catching a bomber. I'll tell you what the problem is, that Inspector Cooper! He shouldn't have gone public with that picture of the guy's face, all the weirdos in the city are calling in now.'

The officer nearest to the Glitch, its only real chance of survival, turned back towards his partner. 'You're right mate. He's a slippery bastard.'

'Who is...Inspector Cooper?'

Both men laughed at the joke because it satisfied a sense of injustice, after all Inspector Harvey Cooper wasn't the one traipsing around car parks looking for invisible men. So fuck him for causing them all this unnecessary work.

'Come on mate lets go. We'll have another look up top...if there's no sign of anything I reckon it's time for an early lunch.'

'That's a great call.' The officer nearest the Glitch replied while miming running back towards the car.

Of course that *great call* meant the body of Snake remained hidden and helpless, lost and trapped, much like the occupant inside it.

A ferocious need for nicotine was growing bad for Jay Cleaver, only now it was being double teamed with hunger pangs beginning to growl. With no instructions from the Demon in his head he took an independent decision to head to the city centre, at least up there he might be able to bum a smoke, could even beg a few quid for some food. There was nothing negative about the idea, but in the process of leaving the lock up the Demon woke up in a bad mood.

What the hell are you doing Jay?

'I'm going to get some fags and food. I'm starving.'

Food is essential, cigarettes are not.

'Fuck you!'

Do you believe that attitude will help?

'Look I'm happy to do this yeah. I'll carry you around to kill people but it's my body...and I know what it needs.'

Huh...if you could see what I can see you wouldn't be so confident in your care.

'What does that mean...what the fuck's wrong with me?'

Too much to list!

'Oh yeah you're funny...I get it now, I see what you're doing. Oscar might have been an idiot but I'm not. This is going to be by my rules or...'

...Or what Jay! The voice bellowed.

It sounded to Jay like the growl of a real Demon which shook him a little. 'I'm going up to the city.'

No. Everything we need can be found down here. There are others like you sleeping under the streets. We will take from them...let us go.

'But...' Then Jay fell silent as he began to walk away from the lock up. He wasn't in control of this momentum, merely an obedient passenger.

Try and calm down Jay. You have to understand a few simple things. I'm here rooted inside your head. I know everything that you know...so if you try to fight back it will always be in vain.

The scarred teenager spent a few moments looking down at his own striding feet. 'Where are we going...?'

I've told you, to find the others of your kind, now be quiet.

Jay tried to follow the request but instantly failed. '...That's not easy. I haven't been able to speak for months. To be able to talk again...it's kind of amazing for me...'

Well perhaps you shouldn't have allowed yourself to be cornered. Held on to your tongue a little tighter, but of course if you had done so, we wouldn't be having this conversation.

'Oh man...what the fuck are you?'

I have requested you stop asking questions.

'I've said I can't do that...how about I slow down on asking questions?'
That would be a step in the right direction.
'Okay but just answer this one. I need to know...exactly who, or what are you? You can tell me while we walk.'
Or I could never tell you at all, or I may choose to lie and create a fictitious character, or even fall silent and ignore any of your investigations. I beg you to understand Jay that those are some of my options, while you only have one...do as I say.
'You're an awkward shit aren't you?'
......
No answer. '...Fucking dickhead...!'

Deep down in the long dry grass the Glitch had no one to talk to. Its host body was plainly dying, leaving it with no option but to slowly recover a little sensibility about this life threatening situation. It still believed it could physically move this dying frame with just a little more rest and a great deal of focused concentration, because this couldn't be the end, it made no sense. This Glitch was supposed to be the next generational leap, the perfect being formed from the wish of an Angel and the touch of a mortal, yet here it was down in the dirt, thinking that all this self-carnage had been caused by a desire to experience deep emotions.

Even now it was still struggling to conclude whether Emma had been outrageously smart or just plain lucky. Either way she'd skilfully played on a weakness during the only period it had showed its hand, before trapping it in short cycle of what can only be described as soul searching. She'd even used its body for sexual intercourse, almost convincing it to believe pleasurable physical contact constituted the same thing as some deep emotional bond, but of course it didn't, doesn't and never will. The Glitch understood that heartless fact now, because to a human or an apocalypse, love is love and sex is sex...and they will always be two altogether different beasts.

Why hadn't it simply killed her when it had the chance?

When it finally found the answer to that question it had to regretfully agree and admit the reason had been ego. A rather humiliating motive for such an entity, but proof the Glitch had been younger then, a fact which apparently a group of mortals were also aware of. They seemed to understand it was growing and learning all the time, hoping it could even be vulnerable at this stage, but their knowing made little difference as no lifeform can change its age. There's no skipping ahead to a good bit. Every life must be lived in stages and because of such truths the Glitch faced up to its biggest mistake, one it had still messed up even after realising its true purpose should be to survive and grow, live its life to the full. Yet it had failed that simple task miserably whilst barely in its teens, bullishly approaching its new found freedom with a fearless headstrong attitude, with wild and careless abandon, based on an unfounded belief that it was immortal in this body. There was an annoying irony in the ego theory. It had naturally behaved exactly like human teenagers do, believing they will live forever, seeing death as a lifetime away only to find that tragically sometimes it isn't always the case.

Stranded at the bottom of a grassy bank next to a car park the Glitch was still trying to fight back. With a mournful groan of concerted effort it battled to lift Snakes body from the ground, to force it to stand up on two feet and walk away. Perhaps this mournful groan, this anguished cry, accompanies any death that comes on with a slow inevitability. The kind that lets you know it's the end before you're actually gone, so you have time to think about every aspect of your passing, to appreciate the imminent arrival of your demise, a death within a death.

If there had been a witness to this moment they would have reported seeing a young man dressed in overalls and a Benidorm baseball cap sitting upright before trying to stand, may even have suggested in their imaginary statement to the fictitious police that the man was either drunk or partially paralysed to describe his pitiful efforts. Watching his buckling legs fail to support his weight they could even make comparisons to Bambi or other such wobbly fawns, but from such reports no would guess the mayhem erupting within his head. Instead they would highly likely advocate he stay where he is, sleep it off, but of course it's impossible to know what goes on in another dimension...isn't it?

Jay Cleaver couldn't comprehend why the Demon was walking him back to this place, although what he found even more confusing was the lack of homeless here. Almost any time of the week, on any given day, someone lost could come down here and find another someone in the same hole. It was a magnet for the down and outs, a mecca they would visit to share their meagre supplies and confess their hard luck stories. Always in the same vein, being better to suggest any failings were down to misfortune rather than admit to anyone you were a victim of the very real struggle of modern living, the struggle of simply trying to keep up.

As he walked along the water's edge Jay looked up at the arches coming into view. There were tens of thousands of bricks fixed in perilous positions for decades. They had seen millions of lives pass over and under, although it could be safely said that what they were about to witness was utterly unique.

There is no one here.

'Yeah I noticed. Can we go up to the city now?'

No.

'Why not…? I want food and fags.'

Far too risky, you are wanted by the authorities and I have no intention of being locked up again.

'Fuck that, I was up there yesterday with no problems.'

Yes…and since then we have slaughtered your parents. I think we can safely presume they will link you to the crime when the bodies are discovered. There will be no more daytime trips. We shall sleep during the light and go out after dark…and that is how it shall be.

'Because of my face…?

Your face is a significant part of it…but everything about you is a risk to our freedom.

Jay's body was walked forward, close to the base of the arches when the Demon spoke in a scheming tone.

Would you like to see a secret?

'Yeah…' The boy replied with little enthusiasm. '…Why the fuck not…?'

Just as the Demon was about to reveal the secret of Oscar's graffiti scratched into the wall, Jay eyes noticed the figure of a man sitting low in the grass.

So instead they walked their shared body over to the bottom of the bank for a closer look. Above them the fallen man in his overalls and baseball cap didn't react to them. Jay decided he'd better handle this and called out to the stranger. 'Moooowahhhh…!'

Stop that disgusting mewling. He can't understand you.

'Fuck it! I forgot, I thought I could talk again!'

Not to anyone else. To them you're a horribly scarred freak without a tongue in your head. Do you understand now why you need me?

The Glitch was struggling to see, the eyes of Snake's body were milking over as death neared its conclusion, but there was definitely a figure looking up here. It had been found, it could be saved, perhaps with proper care it could continue on with its purpose forever. The man appeared to be shouting, but all the Glitch could hear was a horrible guttural moan.

2

Harvey Cooper wanted everyone to know he wasn't proud of his actions over the past week or so, during in which time he'd failed to capture the Glitch, had been unable to ascertain the whereabouts of Jay Cleaver; in fact he'd only succeeded in one line of investigation, the rather distasteful act of imprisoning his own secretary. Someone he'd trusted.

Today was Emma's first official interview about the theft of his gun and its alleged discharge into the head of a wanted murderer. Of course Harvey would be present, but he wouldn't be the officer conducting the interview, far too close to the accused being the official line. So instead the big man himself was coming downstairs.

Superintendent Jeff Shilling had of course done this hundreds of times before, although not a great deal in the last five years. Looking back most witnesses to those sessions would likely suggest his interview technique could be brusque, flying extremely close to full on bullying and because of that style not always successful. Harvey had been his equal partner back then and just about able to save most of the carnage his ham fisted colleague caused. Worryingly those days were gone now. Jeff Shilling was now his direct superior not to be second guessed, so Harvey feared for Emma under that man's particular technique of questioning.

Although he had no regrets over arresting her, believing it was the bare minimum he could have done under such circumstances, the theft of a police issue Glock from his office drawer being a serious class A offence on its own. There was no denying the last two days had seen a serious softening of his anger towards her. Emma's excuse that she'd simply been trying to extract more information for their ragtag group of Glitch hunters had been honourable enough, however the fact she'd told the beast all about them in an exchange of knowledge was what had pushed him to act.

The evening after her arrest and the Glitch's escape had been one of the most nerve-racking of his life, waiting at home in the dark for the monster to arrive, after sending Flo and Alex away to a hotel for the night for their own safety, only for the damn thing to not show. To be doubly sure he'd repeated the plan a second night, once more holding the loaded gun as he lightly dozed, but still nothing. In his head he prayed the thing was dead in a darkened corner somewhere but his heart screamed differently. Wherever the Glitch was holed up was a mystery but there was no more time to waste, so Harvey called a meeting at his house for this evening. Alex Webb the one armed man who had inadvertently started this deadly quest would be there as would Harvey's wonderfully patient and understanding wife Flo. Rhian Sanger and her possessed son Sammy would also be in attendance. This little group of humanity were the only ones on earth who knew the gravity of the danger closing in. The Glitch wasn't dead and Harvey was sure of that, it was coming back to continue its killing. Dozens had died at its whim in the city centre bombing while others who crossed its path were in the morgue, some dug up from the garden of an old lady who had tried to help it on its way.

Harvey checked his watch. It was eight minutes until the beginning of Emma's interview. Police protocol demanded he wasn't allowed to see her beforehand to ascertain or censor anything she may say. So the worry of what could come to light was clearly shown through the trembling in his fingers. If she admitted the truth to the Superintendent then Harvey was up for the fall with everyone else, as surreptitious investigations, even done in your own time were never going to be taken lightly by a man as serious as Shilling, especially after he'd told Harvey his prime objective should be to apprehend teenage tearaway Jay Cleaver.

The Inspector clenched his fists to control the adrenalin as he stood up, then released them a little to straighten his tie, before making his way down to interview room four. As he opened his office door his eyes fell on Emma's empty desk, with her chair pushed up neatly underneath. It saddened him to think it would remain that way for a long time to come, and that he'd played such a major part in her uncertain future.

There was another secondary level to his current anxiety, caused when Emma had been first taken down to the cells and the panic attack she'd experienced on being locked in the confined space. It was unforgiveable that Harvey could have forgotten about her claustrophobia, especially after experiencing it first-hand less than two months ago, when the two of them had been locked in a cell at the facility as a security measure. He'd never forget his helplessness at her suffering and actually believed at that time she might die, such was her reaction, but this latest episode had been far worse. The poor girl having pulled a handful of hair from her own skull such was the fear she displayed. In the end a doctor had been called to calm her down with soft words, some medium strength medication, and the strict instruction her door was to be left slightly ajar with an officer situated in the corridor.

Harvey was now walking that same hallway with Emma as she was lead before him to the interview room. Superintendent Shilling sat waiting at the table and didn't lift his bulk to greet anyone. She was placed in the seat opposite the cantankerous beast of a man while Harvey was left outside just over the big man's right shoulder. Through the two way glass he could see the confusion in Emma's eyes; forcing him to look away in some wretched display of embarrassment or shame, difficult to choose which regret carried the most weight.

A fat finger pressed the record button. 'Interview under caution with Miss Emma Oxtoby...' Shilling began and he wasn't waiting around. '...I must advise you are allowed legal representation at this time but you have declined that option. Would you like to continue now or would you prefer for us to contact your preferred legal representation, or have one assigned for you?'

Emma faltered for a moment before replying. 'I'm happy to continue.'

Shilling tapped his biro on the desk. 'The interviewee has asked for no legal representation to be present at this initial interview. Very well Miss Oxtoby we shall begin...'

Harvey looked down at the scuffed floor then up at the ceiling, anywhere but into her eyes, as Shilling began his heavy handed search for the truth.

Forty three minutes later the excruciating experience was over, Harvey's secret investigations were unmentioned by Emma so his career remained safe, for now. On the other hand hers was done for completely as she was led back down to the cell in silence.

The Superintendent waved him in. 'There you go Harv, that's how you do it...' Shilling pronounced proudly. '...The deceitful cow gave it all away. I'd forgotten how much I enjoyed making them crack. I should do this more often...speak up if you get any stubborn ones again and pass them on to me...' He raised his hands behind his head sitting back in the creaking chair.

Harvey was still trying his best to process the situation. Emma, his friend and ally for over four years, had given up nothing of the group hunting the Glitch. On the contrary she'd taken the blame for everything and protected them all.

'You can organise yourself a new Secretary can't you...or do you need me to sort that out for you as well?' Shilling was enjoying this moment way too much for Harvey's liking.

'Is that sort of comment necessary Jeff...?'

'...Oh come on Harvey I'm just yanking your chain. This has been a good morning. The two of us sorting out troubles again, old team back together, and in one pincer movement we've removed a bad egg from this station. She won't be dropping you in it anymore...'

'...Dropping me in it...?' Harvey asked.

'...It was your bloody gun Harvey, taken from your desk, where it was clearly unsecured, that's a six month suspension at least if I chose to follow it up...'

'...It wasn't secured Sir because I trusted her.' Harvey replied but there was so much more he wanted to say.

Shilling took this opportunity to puff out his flabby chest once more. '...And look where that got you. The world has changed Harvey. Trust isn't what it used to be. I blame the internet myself, all that social media bull, nowadays good old faithful dependence has been replaced by tolerance.

'With all due respect Sir I don't do social media...'

'You don't have to, it's still altered the way the world turns, how you're judged, more importantly how tolerated you are by friends and colleagues. Look at Emma for example, years ago she wouldn't have dared gone rogue on you, there would have been real trust, now everyone does whatever they please and breaking a friends trust is no big deal.'

'I believe she thought she was doing the right thing.' Harvey countered in defence of his lost friend.

'Yeah I'm sure you do, but it doesn't really matter what you believe...' Shilling wasn't for turning. '...That young lady could very easily have got you suspended and from what I've just heard didn't even have the decency to apologise for it. Stop being a mug Cooper...try and keep up...'

That comment stung but Harvey had to take the pain as his superior continued his admonishment.

'...You have to learn to focus on number one and keep your caring for your wife. It's a snake pit out there my old friend. In our positions we can't afford to relax for a second.'

'Sorry to interrupt Sir...but I've grasped the point you're making.'

'Good, then don't forget it, now get back to work and for Christ's sake find that Cleaver kid. I'm sure we'll locate Emma's mystery victim soon enough, because if what she says is true, then a bullet to the head should slow him down.'

Harvey stood and moved to the door as he'd had enough. 'Very good, Sir...I'll keep you updated.'

'Updated? That's my minimum requirement from now on. I need to know everything...oh and Harvey...'

Inwardly sighing 'Yes Sir...?'

'Lock your gun away...securely.' Jeff said with a wink.

Harvey left the room, forever thankful his thoughts couldn't be read. Back in his office he focused on plans to be made, leads to be followed up, only there was no one to share the burden with now, and it hurt like a savage burn to think Emma was gone from his life.

3

The Bulgarian man already had the goods set out on a table, ready to do business. He raised his head to see the scruffy scarred mute boy standing by the door. After asking him in no uncertain terms what the fuck he was doing, Jay approached without hesitation and the dealer asked nothing more…ever.

Shortly afterwards a teenager, a Demon and a Glitch, walked out of the grimy flat of a drug dealer, their one set of pockets filled with cocaine.

The mesolimbic conduit is a wonderful route, your minds reward pathway, but right now Jay Cleavers dopamine road was being overrun, torn apart from within. In this place where the system governing desire and craving is controlled, his life was rapidly becoming a nightmare as his usually singular insatiability for stimulus, had suddenly became part of a three way cocaine circus. Meaning his self-control of mental and bodily functions, in all truth never the strongest in the first place, were being stripped away since the other voice arrived.

Thinking back to yesterday he could remember feeling contented for the Demon to walk him down to the arches under the bridge. Their plan had been to find some homeless unfortunates rob them; most likely murder them and then remain hidden until nightfall before walking the streets to see who else they could pick off.

The Demon living in Jay's mind had been transitioned from the serial killer Oscar Downes, quite accidently, through a cut on his finger, which meant he now fully appreciated why the taxi driver had killed so wantonly and frequently. The little guy never stood a chance of winning this battle of wills, the war within his own conscience, because whatever this voice was it feared nothing.

Now it was partnered with a teenage murderer there seemed no limits on their future bloodlust. However a quite unspoken incongruity to such a description was the simple fact that Jay really wasn't much of a murderer. Yes, people had died at his hands but he'd always claim it was fateful timing or intrusive geographical positioning, if he knew what those words actually meant, but he didn't so instead he categorised those deadly events as the direct result of people giving him shit! He had never walked the streets hunting victims, never set out to kill anyone, not even his parents, even though he bore pure hatred towards them.

THE RED FRAME

His disgust towards them was forged over a resentful fire for years by the longing and disappointment that they never believed in him, or liked him particularly. Even then their horrible demise really wasn't his fault.

He vaguely recalled their murders starting with a burnt out car. It was coming back to him now in bits and pieces; he'd lost his shit because it was towed away, then stormed off back towards the only place he had left, the last place on earth he wanted to go, home.

Shortly after arrival his father had laid dead from the dreadful blow to the skull, but his mother was an altogether different story.

The Demon had taken its time with her, cutting, ripping and tearing pieces away. The last image Jay had of his mother was her bloodied face looking out from behind a greasy glass door. Her mouth, which never once stood up for her son's right to be happy, was open, slack jawed, hanging down where her breastbone used to be. Yet all of that disgusting violence had been the Demons doing, the removal of her head, the putting it in the oven. Although it couldn't have been sitting there at two hundred and twenty degrees for more than ten minutes, it was easily enough time to frazzle and blacken her hair, to make the skin on her cheeks turn pink and blister. Then the oven unexpectedly clicked off because the electric top up meter ran dry. Jay did remember having a thought about asking a neighbour to lend him ten pounds, so he could run to the shop and get more, but it wasn't worth the hassle.

So with the Demon calling the shots Jay Cleaver was now weaponised and further dehumanised by the presence in his brain, the exact same outcome which had caused Oscar's rampage, only this time the Demons human vessel wasn't resisting as hard. This boy more accepting of a fresh chance to be someone, believing it would somehow gain him respect in the world, the only thing he'd yearned for his whole short pointless life.

What happened under the arches however had changed everything.

For a time having the Demon in situ returned to him the gift of speech, even if it were only communicating through his thoughts. It was such an amazing by product of his possession he almost felt normal again, being able to ask questions, voice his feelings, even considering that he might have finally found a friend in this world. All of that ended however when they discovered the dying man on the grassy bank, not just any fucking man either, Snake Hornblower! The bastard somehow reanimated after a previous death from a beating with burning clubs, followed by drowning. Jay had been told all about it, yet there he was, sitting in the grass.

Jay recognised him instantly even though his dreadlocks were gone. Replaced with a modern short slick cut and dressed in a pair of baggy work overalls. Snake's eyes were milked over and his shallow breathing almost imperceptible as they approached. Jay was first sickened by what he saw as a black slug above Snakes eye, but on closer inspection it was where a bullet had penetrated his forehead. Even to this kid's untrained eye in forensic ballistics he could tell this man was dying...again.

Jay would have been content to leave the piece of shit to die alone in the dirt but he wasn't in control. The voice in his head forced him to kneel next to the body, moved his hand to the bullet wound, seeming to clasp at something before putting it into Jays mouth. Forcing it open to accept its offering the boy felt nothing solid ingest, but a foul taste rose up from his gut immediately, filling his cheeks with an overwhelming urge to vomit. He tried to move away but the Demon kept him fixed there until Snake's body gave one final gurgling rattle, then nothing more.

The next thing Jay remembered was his body being walked back to the lock up. The Demon had said nothing to him for the twenty minutes they travelled, but that wasn't the major problem concerning the young man. All his fears and anxieties were being caused by the whispering in his skull. Unseen in the darkness were the sounds of two voices, colluding quietly, furtively, but he couldn't hear what they were saying and at that moment he knew the rules of the game had changed.

Back at the lockup, feeling once more voiceless and powerless, he snorted the chopped lines knowing he was bottom of the pile again, while the other two seemed happy with this feeling...this few, this happy few, this band of others.

THE RED FRAME

4

Late afternoon was dropping over the city under laden oppressive clouds rolling in from the sea.

Harvey finally had a duty to undertake that gave him some sense of wellbeing. Although strictly speaking he hadn't skipped down the stairs to the cells, happy to concede his skipping days were far behind him, it could be said his jaunty footfalls were considerably lighter than his usual latter day plodding, while the reason for this unexpected gracefulness lay behind the steel door he was unlocking.

'Good afternoon.' Harvey offered as he opened it wide.

The face looking up from the bunk was non-committal on its feelings towards the surprise visit. 'Inspector Cooper...' A deep voice replied.

'Would you like some good news?' Harvey asked then entered without locking the door behind him.

'Are you joking...?'

'Not at all...I'm here to pass on the order that you're free to go.' Harvey was smiling as he spoke, a little through natural politeness, but mostly because he was genuinely happy to be giving this lump of a man a much needed boost.

Allan Kosminsky stood up, towering over Harvey's five foot ten with his broad shouldered six foot four. The Inspector unsurprisingly lifted his chin to face the man and waited for some cheerful or relieved response, but it didn't come.

'What happened?' Kosminsky asked disdainfully.

'Well you'll be relieved to know Oscar Downes is fine. The blood loss he suffered was caused by an injury from the rubbing of the large motorbike helmet. You should have got him a new one rather than put him in your oversized spare.'

'Being on the run we didn't have much chance to go for a fitting.'

Harvey nodded at the unexpected sarcasm. 'Of course, I understand that.'

'I'm not too sure you do Mister Cooper.'

'You know you can call me Harvey.'

'Yes I do...so Oscars doing okay and cleared my name has he...?' Kosminsky strolled over to the tiny window, one that a man of his height could see out of, whereas most would only see sky.

'Yes...he said you were only doing as he requested.'

Harvey moved towards Kosminsky who unexpectedly turned causing him to stop his approach. With no intended threat on either side they were suddenly in a face off position, full eye contact, when the big guard broke the spell. 'It's all lies again, just more lies, when is it going to stop...Mister Cooper?'

'I'm not lying...'

'Not you...Oscar! Why do you keep pandering to him...?'

Of all the scenarios Harvey imagined for this situation not one of them had looked like this. Kosminsky was annoyed by the Inspectors presence and wasn't responding predictably to the good news. '...Do you have a problem with me Mister Kosminsky...?'

The big guard smiled at Harvey's quid pro quo, because although this resulting formal mirroring was unintended he was pleased to hear he had the policeman's full attention. '...I've had a lot of time to think since I was thrown in here, seeing as I spent all my working life on the other side of that door. It's surprising what goes through your head when you're locked away.'

'Are you telling me you've had a revelation of some sort in the past few days?' Harvey was willing to go along with this uncomfortable moment for now.

'Not a revelation no, more of a simple realisation telling me that Oscar could be no more than a pathological liar who manipulates everything to his advantage, cleverly playing the little man victim card. It's only by going through his actions that it comes to light.'

Harvey was intrigued but didn't fully understand where Kosminsky was going with this or to what end. After all it wasn't as if Oscar was going to be set free again. Downes was to be locked up long term when released from the hospital. 'Is this sudden resentment based on anything...?' Harvey asked. '...I was under the impression you were friends.'

'We were never friends. He isn't capable of friendship, but like you, I wanted to see if I could scratch the surface.'

'Did you find out anything that could be useful?' Harvey asked.

'No. He sort of tells you everything and nothing all at the same time.'

'I see...well look Allan, this door is wide open for you to leave. We can have this conversation another time. I have to get on.' Harvey stood aside to let the big man past but he didn't budge.

Instead he spoke calmly. 'Where am I going to go?'

'Back home I presume.' Harvey really wanted to get back to the office.

'And do what? I've lost my job Inspector. When future employers read I spent days in a cell for the suspected kidnapping of an inmate...I don't think it will help me with my job prospects.'

'There won't be anything on your record.' Harvey countered.

'I'm not an idiot Cooper...there is always something on your record. An accusation is still an accusation whatever the outcome. It's written down somewhere. I know how the system works Harvey.'

'Oh we're back on first name terms now? I'm pleased to hear that.'

Kosminsky glanced at the open door. Harvey followed his eye line then turned to leave. Hence his surprise when he looked back to see the man still stubbornly sat down on the bunk.

'What the hell are you doing now?' Harvey curtly enquired.

'I don't know...I really don't know.'

Harvey was about to tell Kosminsky he couldn't stay here when they were rather rudely interrupted.

'I'm sorry Sir but the Superintendent wants to see you right away.' The untimely interrupter was Officer Bob Jenkins, the guard who looked after the detainees down here in the cells. Harvey hadn't heard him approach.

'Thank you Jenkins but I'm a little busy with...'

'...Right now, Sir...!' Jenkins demanded with a sharp interruption, which was a little above his post, but one that had to be done '...I'm to take care of Mr Kosminsky's release.' Then stepped aside to let Harvey understand the request was none negotiable.

Around three minutes later a slightly out of breath and confused Inspector Cooper stood facing the seated Superintendent in the top floor office.

'What's...?' He caught his breath before continuing. '...going on?'

'We've found the body of our bomber.' Shilling said with a smile.

'You reckon?'

Shilling's eye twitched at that response before producing four high definition A4 photographs of a dead man in blue overalls and baseball cap. The body lay on its back in scrubby grass, the detailed images capturing the stiffness of the dead hands. The right one raised slightly, frozen claw like as if trying to reach out, maybe to grab at someone or to cling onto its life.

'That's our man isn't it...?' The Superintendent asked matter of factly.

There was no doubt in Harvey's mind that it was. Snake Hornblower was now an ex-bomber, but what of the other thing, the Glitch that possessed and used this body, was that dead?

'...Yes Sir...that's him.'

If Harvey was expecting this to be the end of the chat he was sorely mistaken. Shillings next comment blew that option straight out of the water. '..So there you are we can now charge your secretary with murder. I thought you might like...well perhaps not like...but want to know.'

It would be perfectly natural and acceptable for Harvey to swear loudly at this juncture with the Superintendent's brusque attitude sounding so extremely harsh, but profanity wasn't his style, also he knew Shilling wouldn't appreciate it, so in the end he went with a gentler but ill-fitting exclamation. 'Crikey!'

'My thought's exactly.' Shilling replied straight-faced.

Harvey then took a few more seconds to calm down and digest the information before asking earnestly. 'When can I inspect the body?'

'That won't be necessary Harvey. You've already given it a positive ID.'

'But Sir I think you'll find...

'...You just concentrate on finding Cleaver!'

After another pause Harvey tried again. 'I would very much like to see the body Sir...'

'...And I'd very much like you to understand the word no! The matter is out of our hands. Trust me when I tell you the bomber is dead, bullet to the temple...it will do it every time.'

As horribly frustrating as it felt there was nowhere for Harvey to go on this with Shilling, who was currently being both his most officious and belligerent best. It left little room for negotiation so the Inspectors options were scarce, but if Jeff was telling the truth then surely by default that meant the Glitch was also dead.

Harvey looked up and out the window, past Shillings large balding head, taking in the view of the rooftops, while his logical and ordered mind whipped up a tornado of details and feelings. If the Glitch was dead or at least trapped in some lifeless limbo then all hope for their survival wasn't lost. However countering these positive thoughts were the emotions he had towards Emma; she'd let him down, broken the law, but who knew if that girl may have just saved this world, for which she was going to prison.

As he took the stairs down to his own office, the heavy steps reflected the mood of his heart.

5

The young boy knew he was in big trouble. Fighting and brawling weren't allowed in the schoolyard no matter what the provocation. So it was that a helpless fear of oncoming punishment came trembling through his veins.

The door next to him opened sharply and a horribly serious voice spoke. 'Get in here Sanger, sit in that chair!'

Sammy dutifully obliged finding himself face to face with the head of the school, Mr Wilmot.

'Would you like to tell me what happened?' The scary man asked from underneath his overly large greying moustache.

Sammy was fascinated by the facial fur on Mr Wilmot's top lip, in fairness every kid was, its thickness was frightening. To craft and wear such a facial adornment displayed an inner manly confidence to be admired, even if no one could understand how it worked in practical terms such as drinking or eating, but at this exact moment Sammy wasn't considering the problems of the moustache, he was a little preoccupied with being scared.

Mr Wilmot waited patiently at first giving the boy every opportunity to respond to his question. This kid gloves approach having been learned through thirty five years of running schools, dealing with disruptive pupils, complaining teachers and the worst of all, irritating parents who believed they always knew better.

'Your mother is on her way here to the school. I can tell you she's not too pleased at having to leave her place of work. So I think it would be helpful if you were to tell me what provoked the incident so we are ready for when she arrives. Then I can deal with this behaviour and ensure it isn't repeated. Do you understand that Samuel?'

The snivelling boy imperceptibly nodded his head, but all the fears he'd been feeling were now being overtaken by thoughts of the disappointment he would see in his mother's eyes. He wanted to speak and explain what happened but it was pointless, the words wouldn't come out.

There was a knock on the office door. With a glare Mr Wilmot went out into the corridor, speaking in whispers with someone, before returning to his chair from where he eyed up the boy. 'I'm afraid you have broken young Adam's nose...' Mr Wilmot paused for effect to let that news sink in before continuing. '...You understand Samuel that we can't tolerate that behaviour in this school or anywhere for that matter, vicious assaults have no place in this world.'

'He started it...!' Sam finally blurted out.

'I'm sure you believe he did...but that doesn't explain away your violent reaction. There are many ways of dealing with provocation Samuel but punching another pupil is never the answer.'

'He...he...he was saying...horrible things...!' His pleading words were broken up and coming out in breathless bursts.

Mr Wilmot remained unmoved by the boy's emotional response, being well versed in such panicky explanations, of which this appeared to be just another textbook scenario. Clearly the young man had overreacted in blind fury as a peer took an insult too far, after all the mind of a ten year old isn't the healthiest field for understanding, rather one that ignites and burns itself out in a flash of fury, doing whatever it takes to get rid of the hurt.

The door was knocked again, only this time Sammy turned round on hearing his mother's voice. All he wanted was for her to rush over and pull him to her chest, but instead she sat down next to Mr Wilmot, the two of them staring at him.

'What's happened now...?' She asked Sammy but it was the head teacher who answered.

'...Allow me...there appears to have been an altercation between your son and Adam McNeill. I haven't been able to ascertain exactly what it was about, but it ended when Samuel punched the boy in the face...breaking his nose.'

'Oh my god...!' Rhian cried. '...What the hell were you thinking Sam...?'

'...I doubt there was much reasoning going on Miss Sanger.' Mr Wilmot interjected again. 'Quite clearly Sam was upset by what he perceived to be cruel jibes...but we can't have such wanton violence in our school. It must be dealt with and that is why I have called you in.'

'Okay.' She replied with a nod of her shocked face.

'We have a protocol in place for such situations and I will have to ask certain uncomfortable questions. Some of them may be difficult to answer, but I need you to understand I am only trying to get to the root, so that we can fix it together.'

'Go on then...' Rhian replied with a quick glance at her boy whose tears appeared to be drying on their own.

Mr Wilmot sat back then cleared his throat and interlinked his fingers like some hack psychologist. '...Well the obvious first step is to enquire how things are at home...are there any fresh problems we should know about?'

Rhian didn't appreciate the use of the word 'fresh', almost causing her to overreact, but she held herself in check, after all her boy had been in the wrong. '...What kind of problems are you suggesting...?' She asked calmly.

THE RED FRAME

'...I have no idea. I'm not suggesting anything in particular Miss Sanger, just enquiring so we can tick things off the list I have to fill. You may find yourself surprised how even the slightest change to a child's surroundings or routine can affect their behaviour...'

'...Let me tell you his home life is very settled and we share a lovely relationship.' Rhi wanted to put any suggestion of a broken home to bed straight away.

'I hear what you're saying...erm is there anyone else there?' Mr Wilmot asked.

'Sorry...?'

'Boyfriends, lovers...'

'No...!' She bristled as she answered this hurtful assumption. '...There's just me and Sammy.' The question was cutting because there really wasn't a man in her life, just a fucking Angel that she couldn't tell a head teacher with his stupidly thick moustache about.

'I see...and he's a well behaved boy at home normally?'

'Yes...'

'Go on...' Mr Wilmot said.

'...What?'

'I thought you were going to add something to your answer...'

Rhian took a second as she rolled her tongue round her teeth thinking hard on how to manage this crazy situation. Were there any reasonable options left open to her? She soon decided there weren't which meant explaining her son's behaviour away as something unexpected, surprising or hormonal, instead of a celestial possession residing inside his body. 'Don't worry Mr Wilmot I'll have a stern word with Sammy when I get him home. I don't really want to embarrass him any further in this room, he's a growing boy and sometimes those changes as we get closer to teenage can be overwhelming, can't they?'

'That is true...' Mr Wilmot acceded. '...though not always to the point of extremely violent reactions...'

Rhian would later think this was the moment she should have walked away, taken that remark on the chin and led her boy home, but that wasn't how she was made. '...It was hardly *extreme* violence Mr Wilmot. My son punched another boy in the face yes, but surely these things happen in every school all over the country every day. It's just boys playing isn't it, growing up, working out the pecking order.'

'I must say you have a very forgiving way of looking at it....'

'...Of course it's forgiving...he's my son...but don't worry I will be having words when he gets home later.' Rhi kept the serious look on her face and was about to stand up when a sporting phrase came to mind. Game, set, and match, because surely that was the end of it, she could get back work and finish her shift now. The meagre wage she earned there was becoming even more essential with the tarot card enterprise out of business.

Mr Wilmot got up from his chair and Rhi went to follow suit.

'If you could just remain where you are for now Miss Sanger, I need to speak to a colleague. I won't be a moment.'

As he closed the door Rhi huffed loudly then spoke directly to Sammy for the first time. 'Why did you punch Adam in the face?'

'I didn't.' The boy sounded much calmer with the head master gone.

'Well Mr Wilmot seems to believe you did.'

'It wasn't me!'

'So who punch...?' She stopped the question before it came out of her mouth fully formed, she didn't want to hear the answer. '...Oh I see...don't worry sweetheart we'll get you help. It won't always be like this.'

He looked up at her, his eyes sorrowful and confused and without a second thought she held him close.

Mr Wilmot re-entered the room and witnessed their embrace, which really didn't make his next task any easier. He waited politely until they'd released before telling them the news. '...Miss Sanger, after discussions with the appropriate authorities we have agreed on a course of action. We believe it to be fair to everyone involved and to hopefully put this kind of behaviour to rest. So with that in mind, I must inform you that Samuel is to be expelled from this school for one week. His expulsion is immediate and he may not return before next Wednesday. I sincerely hope that you agree this is both an understandable and satisfactory punishment in response to his ferocious outburst.'

But Rhian really did not agree. Her mouth, at first agape on hearing this decision, reengaged and she began to fight their corner. Sammy observed his mother's reaction with a certain pride, watching her efforts in trying to change the ruling, because at first her voice was calm, only beginning to rise as she realised Mr Wilmot was never going to reconsider it.

Therefore in the end it turned out the boy began his week's suspension by having to drag his own mother out of the office, her final words towards the headmaster still ringing in his ears, an angry yell demanding that Mr Wilmot could just go 'Fuck himself and his stupid moustache!'

THE RED FRAME

When the two of them were finally sat in the car he leaned across and gave her hand a squeeze of support. It was a heart-warming moment that managed to calm her down enough to begin the drive home.

'I'm going to kill that Angel.' Rhi said determinedly as she turned out onto the main road.

Neither the boy nor the Angel responded, but the both of them clearly heard that threat.

6

Florence 'Flo' Cooper waited patiently as the kitchen clock ticked away to six thirty in the pm. She had to keep her phone close at this time every day because Harvey would call, either to tell her he was on his way home, or he was working late again. She hoped it wouldn't be the latter this evening because she needed him.

Today had turned out to be an uncomfortable experience, one in her own home after having a first disagreement with their one armed lodger. She checked the clock again, using her husband's imminent arrival to help take her mind off replaying their conversation over in her head, but it wasn't working.

The awkward moment had begun mid-morning when Alex complained about being unable to find a particular report. It was one that Harvey had procured from work and involving the gruesome details of the murders at the old lady's house. Flo had simply explained to their houseguest that it wasn't actually her responsibility to keep all the papers he chose to leave scattered around refiled and on hand for whenever he needed them. Alex had responded by suggesting, well if not suggesting then heavily inferring, that she seemed to be losing a little interest in helping to solve the ongoing mystery, also if that were the case she should just leave him to it. He'd then commenced to turn her living room upside down searching for the lost paperwork before locating it in his jacket pocket.

Afterwards there had been not so much as an attempted apology; this had irked her usually generous and giving soul and the two of them hadn't spoken since. She'd sat down at the kitchen table with her phone while listening to Alex walking around in her living room. What the heck else was she supposed to do?

She'd tried to help him with finding an answer to the Glitch, but he knew a lot more about it than her, always leaving her feeling a little stupid when she got a detail wrong. Then on top of that she'd fed the man and cleaned up after him, visited the shops to buy particulars he'd requested, washed his old clothes, brought him new clothes and generally tried to assist in every way possible.

Finally, and with no little relief, her phone rang. A sunny picture of Harvey appeared on the screen; a candid shot of him in flowered shorts taken on their last foreign holiday three years ago, which made her sigh because another week away like that would be perfect right now.

'Hi Harveypud...' She announced to make herself feel better.

'Hey darling...is Alex there? He isn't answering his phone...'

Well that was sky high on the list of last things she wanted to hear right now, but somehow she pushed down the annoyance. 'He's here...well he's probably lost it.' She said with a hint of private joke amusement.

'Okay...err can you get him for me please?'

A slight pause before 'Of course I can dear.' Flo had engaged her self-control to maximum on entering the living room, where she found Alex settled down on her sofa, reading Juliet's dream journal. Her eyes scanned round to see every surface of the room suitable enough to hold piles of paper now performing that duty. Even the window sills were displaying police photos of bloodied victims, her mantelpiece apparently a makeshift altar to Alex's story about meeting an Angel. There were reproductions of pages from the very book he was reading now, the one his Nurse compiled surreptitiously, lined up in front of, on top of and behind Flo's ornaments. She was struggling to remember how spacious and calming this room used to be. 'Alex...?'

'Huh...?' He replied without looking up.

'...It's Harvey. He'd like a word with you.' She offered her mobile phone towards his only hand.

'Fantastic...!' He took the phone before enthusiastically greeting her husband. '...Hi Harvey...what...are you serious...why won't they let you see it...?'

Alex's lack of gratitude was the final straw. Flo didn't want to hear anything of whatever the hell they were talking about and walked out the back door. Admiring her beautifully curated little piece of garden almost brought her to tears, as she realised how much she missed her normal life, how much she wanted it back, but most of all how much she needed her husband to understand this couldn't go on. Whatever the hell was happening in this world, or the next, really wasn't her problem. She'd tried to understand, to get a full grasp of it all, but there seemed to be no end in sight. In her mind what had started out as a new exciting project, involving a secret team of amateur investigators, was now becoming nothing more than a tedious bog of frustrating inactivity, one where it appeared every fresh lead they picked up only led them blindly round to another dead end.

Flo wasn't wholly without sentiment. Of course she had sympathy for Alex and everything he'd been through, who wouldn't, the poor soul had been to hell and back if all of this was true, and the loss of his arm certainly attested to that fact. She understood everything about his life had changed on the day he'd decided to commit suicide. Perhaps he hadn't been truly serious about the attempt, but he still ended up falling from the fourth floor of a building regardless, putting his body in a six month coma and causing the amputation of the limb.

She recognised that was an awful situation, but in all honesty it wasn't the real problem, it was the story of what happened after his fall that Flo was a smidge doubtful of, the parts about meeting an Angel who released a Demon upon the earth. How Alex had believed he'd defeated them both until he'd awoken from his medical slumber. It was at that time Alex would have you believe, that some curvature in the timeline of life itself occurred and we split off, rewinding us to start again from just before his fall. So everything from that moment in this world had worked out a bit differently; where another life was being lived...apparently.

The splitting of the timeline was created by it having to move around a new entity known as the Glitch, which was now on earth controlling an unsavoury character named Snake, who recently bombed the city centre killing dozens. This was the foe that the group meetings in her house were focused on finding, so yes he was right with his heavy inference. She was losing a bit of interest.

Of course Flo wouldn't have given Alex's story any credence at all if it weren't for her husband's acceptance of it as true. She trusted Harvey's instincts implicitly, after watching his logical and methodical process bear fruit on many occasions. In all truth she would love and trust him until the end of time, but on this occasion she was going to make a stand, as this ongoing private investigation was getting her down.

It didn't help her mood that he'd already let her know there was to be another meeting this evening, which meant another houseful, when all she wanted was some feet up on the sofa time, a small glass of red in hand and some mindless TV while warmly snuggled up next to her soulmate.

Then Alex appeared in the kitchen doorway to take her away from any tranquillity of her calming thought.

'You won't believe this...' He spoke as if they'd never shared a crossed word, or he didn't remember, or didn't care. Flo took a deep breath but chose not to reply, she just faced him nonchalantly as he joined her on the stepping stone path that threaded through the lawn. '...They've found the body of Snake Hornblower...the Glitch...!' Flo was about to respond with something witty and cutting when he placed a blood red cherry on top of his statement. '...Emma shot it...at her flat...it was trying to get to us.'

Her first and only thought was for the poor girl. Admittedly she and dear Emma had started off on the wrong foot, but that was behind them and none of this sounded right. Flo suggested that surely the case could be closed then and Emma proclaimed the heroine who saved the day.

Alex immediately put her straight on that. 'You know she's committed a murder and admitted to doing so. I don't think she'll just walk away from this.'

'But surely it can be proven now it was self-defence?' Flo stated firmly.

'But it wasn't Mrs Cooper, it was premeditated...and there's something else...she used your husband's gun.'

'Harvey's involved?' Flo was becoming increasingly alarmed.

Alex noted her concern and tried his best to calm her back down. 'Not directly...she stole the gun...his gun...from his unlocked office drawer...and acted independently...but in the eyes of the law she still killed a man in cold blood.'

'He was a wanted murderer!' She snapped.

'An unproven one...and now a dead one...'

'Then surely that means we can go public now...tell them what's been happening...what we've been doing here?' her reasoning felt sound.

'Of course we can't...we still need to deal with this under the radar, find actual solid evidence of what's happened. I agree that Emma's actions could have saved a lot of unnecessary deaths, maybe this and a billion other universes are safe now because of what she's done, but she may also have ended our only chance of ever returning to normality...'

Flo raised her voice sharply. '...Normality!'

'In case you've forgotten we are still on the wrong timeline.'

'...And in case you've forgotten I was almost killed on that one.' Flo harshly reminding him of the Demon's attack in her bedroom; an event that she'd never experienced, only read about in his dream book. '...At least that's what you claim!'

Their mounting rat a tat discourse abruptly became a furious silence.

Alex felt the full force of the meaning behind her veiled accusation. For a fleeting moment under the fading evening sun he considered, but then resisted, an unnatural and unbecoming urge to shake her by the shoulders. How could she doubt him about any of this; people had died, real people had really died, yet here she was packing all of that up as something he 'claimed' to be true? What in hell was she thinking? Fair enough he could understand if she hadn't believed any of this from the start but she'd been helping him, the two of them working closely together for over a week. Flo had seen all the evidence, listened to his story, even held him when he'd become upset through exhausted frustration...now this.

'I see...' It was all Alex could manage to say in response.

On the other hand Flo's natural motherly instincts meant she wanted to immediately apologise to him, to smooth the situation over, because it's what she always did but no, not this time. This was different and she felt strongly about no longer being seen as second class, seen as someone who didn't understand his problems and never would. So instead of following him indoors she walked to the bottom of the garden and felt contented in doing so. She'd stood her ground because in her mind, all of this was about time.

7

During that evenings meeting at the Coopers house the latest happenings were discussed. Obviously it mainly centred on the death of Simon 'Snake' Hornblower and therefore hopefully the Glitch as well. They also spoke of Emma's decisive action and then her wholly unjustified arrest on murder charges, before they considered Harvey's unanticipated submission that Allan Kosminsky should be allowed to join their little group for any future meetings.

After deciding to discuss the possibility of allowing a new member at a later date, it would be accurate to describe the mood of the attendees as being relatively calm but confused. Obviously they were pleased the threat of the Glitch was seemingly over with, although no one would admit they fully believed that option. All of their doubts centred on the simple fact it seemed too easy somehow, despite it having cost them one of their own, so almost as if in honour of her actions, the rest of the meeting was spent deliberating over what they could do for Emma's plight.

It was Flo who had the room's attention now with her always honest opinion. '...I suggested we tell the Superintendent everything we know. He can only be as stubborn and disbelieving as Harvey would have been at first...and he's been swayed.'

Alex was the first to respond.

No surprise there, thought Flo.

'The problem is we don't have anything concrete...' He suggested. '...It's not as if we have confessions or any physical evidence...'

'...No, we don't...' Flo enjoyed interrupting her lodger again because it was exactly her point. '...All we have is a narrative from you and a painting of a red square which shouldn't exist...and again that's only because you say so.'

'I don't think that's very helpful.' Harvey said, realising he was speaking in his Inspectors voice even though they were in his own living room.

'And what about the Angel...?' The room went quiet as Rhian spoke for the first time in ten minutes, during which she'd been listening intently while remaining focused on her son who was fussing Goldie. '...Aren't you forgetting it spoke to us through Sammy?'

Flo couldn't deny that event had occurred, but time can smooth even the sharpest memories, up to the point where she was now only willing to concede it had been odd.

'Odd...!' Rhi replied, controlling her annoyance at the description, while also feeling that Mrs Cooper needed reminding of a few things. She made sure Sammy was fully occupied with the Labrador before speaking to Flo tight lipped.

'...My son's behaviour is changing and don't tell me it's just because he's growing up. I know him and there's something wrong in his head. I don't know if it's a real Angel in there or not but somethings going on. He's started lashing out at school and is now serving a week's suspension. So if it's not too much trouble can we focus some of this meeting on that particular problem?'

'The Angel's actions are often unpredictable.' Alex offered, because it was all he could think to say.

'No shit!' Rhi said with a grimace.

'Or...total shit...' Flo responded.

'What is going on here...?' Harvey crackled into the conversation making sure he caught his wife's eye.

Flo looked back over at her husband before requesting. '...Can I have a private word with you in the kitchen?'

'No you cannot...' He replied instantly.

Flo was stunned by this. '...And why not?'

'Because when we talk at these meetings it involves everyone, it has to otherwise it will fall apart...' His tone was serious enough for everyone to take notice, even the boy and the dog. '...We have to stay together on this. I'm sorry Flo but if you have something to say about our investigation then it's for everyone to hear.'

'Very well...if that's the way you want it.' Flo began her confession as the eyes of the group slid over to her. 'I think we need to, or maybe I need to, understand why we're following this man's claims which are certainly questionable, definitely unprovable and alarmingly dangerous...certainly for our friend Emma who at this moment is sitting in a police cell charged with killing a man. I don't know if anyone else here apart from my husband knows what sentence you can receive for premeditated murder. No? I'd suggest we start at thirty years and hope for mitigating circumstances to bring that down.'

'Flo please...!' Harvey was trying to gently subdue his wife, but of all the people in the room he should have known better than to choose such a path.

'...Oh please nothing Harvey! We aren't having these meetings for our bloody health. This isn't us sharing a warm social get-together where we bring cake and play bridge. This is our house where we gather and blindly believe the tales of a man we hardly know, one who I might add has suffered a serious head trauma for the last year. Now I've worked very closely with Alex for the past week and I have no doubt that he more than considers he's telling the truth, so I'm not calling him a liar or doubting his intentions, but what I am doing...is beginning to doubt my own.'

Rhian continued to stand shoulder to shoulder with Alex. 'Please Mrs Cooper, why are you doing this?'

'Isn't it obvious...poor Emma. A young woman's life is ruined because she got involved with this man's story.'

'She killed the Glitch before it could murder anyone else...!' Alex stated firmly but Flo was ready for it.

'...No Alex she didn't, she killed a suspected bomber with no genuine proof but what you tell us. I'm sorry if that upsets anyone but I don't want to give this any more of my time unless I can see something tangible and undeniable.'

There followed an awkward pause before Sammy surprisingly spoke '...Precisely what kind of proof do you require Mrs Cooper?'

The boy's young voice sounded clipped and cold, the living room walls seeming to close in at his words, until even Goldie slunk away from the sofa to what she considered a much safer position by Harvey's feet.

Every sense in the room was centred on the kid who sat upright and straight backed, not unlike a choirboy keen to be noticed, his unclouded eyes staring straight ahead, before slowly turning to focus on Flo. '...Would you'd like to see a magical illusion? Perhaps a minor miracle would feed your pessimism, turning water into wine used to do the trick.' Sammy's stare was set unblinking as he spoke with a voice of an Angel. 'Come here Florence. Come closer to me...I want to convince you.'

Flo didn't move an inch toward the chilling invite. 'I don't want to...'

'...Why not? If you believe all of this is no more than a fantasy created in Alex's tortured mind, that it's all fake and your friend has killed a man for no reason...then come here...because surely if you're correct, then I'm just a young boy and nothing to be scared of.'

Rhian took her attention from Sammy for a moment, waiting for Flo's response, but when none came back, and after another uncomfortable pause she proceeded to back up her son, or the Angel, or whatever was currently at her side on the sofa. 'He's right Mrs Cooper, if you don't believe in any of this then you can approach him.'

'I said I don't want to…' Flo was feeling as uncomfortable as she could ever recall. '…I've said no. Do not try and tell me what to do under my own roof. But while we're being brutally honest do you mind telling me why you're even here? As far as I was told you're a crooked psychic who made money through devious methods, a self-confessed hack who preyed on the vulnerable. For all I know you could be trying to continue with this charade to justify your questionable behaviour.'

Harvey tried his best to save the situation. 'Please Flo this really isn't necessary.'

'Be quiet Harvey. If I'm going to be pressured and put on the spot I'm going to respond with the truth as I see it…'

'…Explain it to me then…!' The boy shouted. '…Respond with your truth about me.'

And with one simple step forward, using words that would never be forgotten in Harvey's eternal pride for his wife, he watched and listened as Flo advanced and explained clearly to the boy's face.

'…I don't know what you are or how you're doing this. I think there are two possible explanations. Either this is a parlour trick being played out for Rhian's and Sammy's entertainment, if so then well done because he's a fine actor for such a young boy. My other opinion is perhaps you're a lost spirit wandering aimlessly with no true purpose…how would I know? But that's what I'm not seeing here…the problem I have with believing any of this…what's the purpose of it all…the purpose of you? I'm hearing and reading all the stories about the end of the universe, a lost timeline, the empty heaven above us, or how great and powerful the Angel Metatron is…but let's be right about this, that apart from putting on a deeper voice, what have you actually done?'

Sammy didn't flinch as he stood face to face Flo, his young frame only coming to three quarters of her height, meaning there was no threat from his strength or physicality at the moment, but that was about to change, when the boy began first to tremble, then violently shake. His head started to judder and twisted down toward his right shoulder as he began to speak once more, only this time the sound of his words savagely changed the mood of the captivated group.

The boy was transformed, not of this world, as the mortals in the room heard the genuine voice of the Angel explode forth.

Not from the boys mouth, but its own.

THE RED FRAME

8

Across the city, at the exact same time a seven foot Angel appeared inside an Edinburgh living room, an extortionately expensive private jet landed at an equally exclusive private airfield.

It slowly taxied to a halt then its only passenger disembarked, calmly making a phone call.

'Hello?' A grumpy voice answered at the other end, unappreciative at being disturbed so late in the evening, but when recognising the caller his demeanour changed, listening intently to its demands.

'Good evening old friend...' A softly confident voice began. '...I've just landed and I'm going to need your assistance immediately.' He spoke while entering the airport's main building.

'What for...why...? I thought you were gone for good...or at least for the foreseeable.'

'Please be so kind as to never try and predict my actions. Just follow my orders. It's a simple enough arrangement that has worked perfectly well so far.'

'Alright I've got it. I just thought you had what you wanted...' The fat man said while rolling himself awkwardly over his sofa to sit upright. '...I don't know what else I can do for you.'

'Let's say that after our previous business I ended up being deceived somewhat...I would like very much to put the incident right.'

'I see.'

'I very much doubt that.'

The line and tone was a little condescending but the large man let it go, he knew better than to upset his old 'friend' and paymaster. '...So what do you need me to do?'

'To collect them together again...'

'What...?' came the fat man's shocked reply.

'...I need all three because one of them still has it.'

The fat man measured his answer carefully. '...I can look into it but I can't make promises. It won't be easy, the last I heard Oscar Downes was hospitalised and under armed guard. He tried to escape the city with your ex-employee Kosminsky. Reports tell me a guard's sudden unemployment caused by your departure and closing down of the facility left him close to clinically depressed. As for the slippery swine Jay Cleaver, he's still being slippery, we've been trying to locate him but no one knows where he's disappeared to.'

'Shush! And accept my apologies because I have stopped listening...' It was a cold interruption which the recipient felt keenly. '...I have no time for excuses. I'm already aware of their predicaments. All I need is for you and your resources to find them, there's really nothing more to it than that, do as I say and get them detained for me. I'm giving you two days. On Thursday evening I want the three of them together at the facility. I'll take care of all my other requirements from there...and I assure you I will make no mistakes this time.'

'Listen, Marcus. It's not going to be as simple as...'

'No listen to me...!' Kirby's dense growl instantly convinced the other man to both shut up and listen. '...Just do precisely as I say and you will find our arrangement stays in its current format, I may even consider increasing your fare, but if you don't, if you fail me...then God help you.'

A tiny smile slithered over his thin lips as he rolled out the icy threat, Marcus loving the power he wielded over such poor and greedy souls, but he also knew there was greater power he could yet attain. A precious gift shown to him clearly when he'd witnessed first-hand the Demon back at the facility. He'd watched it kill in intimate detail before speaking to it at length, learning what it could do, what it needed, but too impressed by its power he'd allowed the beast to play him for a fool.

This time he was better prepared, he'd get what he desired. Or they would all die. 'Expect my call tomorrow evening for a progress report!'

'Like I said Marc...' But his desperate excuses were spurned into silence as the line went dead.

He knew there'd be no reply if he attempted to call Kirby back so placed the phone down. It was with a heavy sigh that he lifted his bulk off the sofa and poured a drink. His usual routine of following the two finger rule as a healthy measure didn't come into action tonight; it was a special occasion, albeit not a happy or needed one, so instead he filled the glass to the rim before sinking the single malt in one.

A full ten minutes passed before he realised he hadn't moved an inch, stuck as he was in a world of conflicting emotions, still stood at the side table holding his empty glass. Maybe a thousand thoughts had breezed across his minds horizon in that time but none were of any use, he was back where he started, meaning there were calls to be made, nefarious plans to be actioned and followed through to the letter, if he was going to please his imposing benefactor.

He read the engraving on his personalised whisky glass, 'World's best Grandad', which brought home the risk of what he was about to do again.

THE RED FRAME

Stupidly, somewhat naively, but most certainly hopefully, this overweight anxious man had briefly entertained a belief that his dealings with the rich weirdo were at end. It had been a warm comfort for a little while to think Kirby was gone from his life, perhaps he could try and return to a life and career of normality, be true to himself and his privileged position, to make up for previous misdemeanours. Hearing that voice whisper its orders down the phone once more he had to accept a bitter truth, nothing had changed and it was back to business or...God help him.

Those had been the exact words, delivered crystal clear and with full intent, that intention being to remind his 'friend' of a simple fact. Marcus Kirby could not be refused, having so much money and power allowed one to stride unhindered between the raindrops, a man who never got wet or dirty, a man who had killed before, many times, one who thought nothing of taking such actions. To men like Marcus it was merely a quicker route to achieving their next goal, the shortest of cuts if you will, always with the safety net that whatever dreadful deed he committed, such acts could easily be covered up with generous payments to immoral idiots.

Kirby was particularly fond of those who sat in the right places, who greased the wheels of the city to turn smoothly and there were plenty of those around. The type who allow the rules to be bent for their benefit, the sort who would stay quiet to keep on giving and taking, the ones who answer his phone calls without hesitation, a certain class of immoral idiot, people like Superintendent Jeff Shilling.

9

It was midnight if the church bells were to be believed. Sitting in the lockup Jay Cleaver listened intently to the boisterous tolling while thinking of how he'd never understood the point of them. As far as he could fathom they only rang for people who went to church anyway, so didn't those faithful believers already know what time their sermons started? Why are they so fucking loud, why do they chime on the hour, on the half hour and sometimes on the quarter? It was a repetitive ding-dong madness that even this twisted young man couldn't comprehend.

For sure a hundred years ago he could have appreciated their updates, timely and constant reminders of where people should be, but why hadn't things changed. Nowadays everyone had a watch for fucks sake and surely nobody enjoyed being woken up by massive steel bells clanging out of sync.

He had covered his ears in the end, the noise had been deafening, and even when they ceased he could still hear, or at least imagined he could, the squeaking of the screws that held the bells settling back down as they came to a silent rest. Of course he knew that couldn't really be happening, the church was half a mile away, it was impossible.

Fully awake his eyes carefully opened but he didn't get up, instead he stared at the abandoned cobwebs hanging from the underside of the rusty roof. It was pitch black outside with an angry wind whipping against the ill-fitting metal door. The twelve bongs that pissed him off could only mean it was midnight, but there was something else concerning his addled mind, a feeling that even though he'd all the evidence he needed, he strongly doubted the chime was telling the truth. It didn't feel like the right time, it was different somehow, but more than that why they'd been so fucking loud? After all he'd crashed down in this place many times before, back in the days when he'd believed Snake Hornblower was a friend, rather than a bastard who would end up mutilating him for life, and he'd never noticed the bells before. Not like that.

Jay was only guessing but he thought the reason behind his misgivings about time or hearing weird shit were the bizarre voices in his head. Where there used to be only his twisted, disconnected, rambling repetitive thoughts there were now three souls calling out. None of it made much sense but Jay wasn't totally ignorant of mental issues, he'd heard of people having multiple personality disorder but refused to accept he was suffering from such a thing. Before any of this he would have described people who displayed such ailments as bat-shit crazy or a fucking loon, most probably very loudly and almost definitely to their face. But he wasn't one of them. This was something different, beyond clinical diagnosis, which was the only thing he knew for certain.

This brief moment of clarity, of true self-awareness, was a rare feeling for this homeless, horribly scarred, freak boy. That's how he thought of himself nowadays because it was the only description that ticked all the boxes, of the way he was made to feel, the way people still looked at him even when his face was covered over with a scarf. Their shallow opinions, although irritating, counted for naught because inside his head something truly bizarre was going on, an utterly unique experience he was struggling to understand, the sound of the voices, all the time, the voices moving him around to do their bidding, threatening his thoughts with cruel horrors.

Gratefully at this moment all was quiet in his head, silence reigned through his skull, no whispering, no screaming, no laughing that was more like cackling and nothing telling him what to think. It felt good.

Jay sniffed back some dripping mucous because he was cold, but as he did so a blistering pain ripped through his nostrils, making his eyes water and fists clench until the uncomfortable burn rescinded. As he relaxed his tensed fingers he stared out at the black night and began to remember. How for the past three, maybe four days he really didn't know, this undernourished body had been forced into a horrific cocaine binge, one that had been savagely incessant, taking him way beyond feeling good and almost to the point of death. His mortal heart had been pushed to the limits of its capacity because those mind controlling bastards couldn't get enough of the new experience. Their current silence made sense now; they were sleeping it off, allowing him some time with his true self.

Other images came back of his actions over the last few days, blurred moments floating across his mind, brutal ones. He'd murdered someone, a man, maybe more than one. He had strangled them first before breaking a skull open on the corner of a table, and all to get the drugs they desired. It was a hazy memory but he knew it was a truthful distortion, the worst kind; the one you know will soon come back into ghastly clear focus.

Jay really didn't want to play this game anymore, he knew he needed help for his multitude of problems, but who could he tell even if the voices allowed him to. It was always the same and he found it strange that his whole life he'd felt trapped, first by school, then by his parents and later by money and responsibility. All of them were things he couldn't escape from and it now appeared the trap was becoming smaller, tighter, focusing him down to a single point of existence. To a place where he wasn't just stuck in this body or situation, he was ensnared, being kept hostage in a tiny corner of his soul where he'd no say on what happened next.

Then suddenly Jay felt it before he heard it. The Demon was coming.

Here you are Jay.

Fuck off...Leave me alone!

Where exactly would you like me to go?

Away...anywhere...just let me be normal again.

Ha-Ha! Yes, because you were doing so well on your own. Cut to pieces, disfigured, committing murders, imprisoned, classed as mentally and emotionally imbalanced with no future to dream of. You still don't get it do you?

All I know is I'm fucking dying because of you...my body can't take anymore drugs.

Yes we know that Jay. We have been discussing it for many hours and have decided to change the rules.

We...you mean you and the other Demon?

There is only one Demon in here Jay. Our other guest is altogether quite different.

What is it...?

It is very difficult to explain but it's safe to say it doesn't wish you harm. After all you saved it from a fate worse than death...entrapment for eternity inside a corpse.

That was Snake wasn't it...the man on the bank...he's dead...again?

Very much so...he was shot in the head by Harvey Cooper's secretary. Does that mean anything to you?

I remember seeing her at the facility. She came with Cooper, but I don't remember why she was there.

Probably because that Harvey Cooper is a sly old soul but we will take care of him. Tell me Jay do you feel any different?

Yeah very fucking different!

To be expected. We have chosen to begin by making a few alterations to this body...for our own purposes, but I am quite certain you will be happy with the results.

I just want you to leave me alone.

That is not possible right now. We need you and you need us...

For fucks sake...even my psychosis is fucked up!

We are not psychosis Jay...we are very real.

Who's the other voice? Where did it come from?

You really don't remember? We saved its life...it was to die trapped inside your old dead friend but we avoided that, gave the Glitch a second chance...now he lives within you...with us.

This Glitch...is it dangerous?

Extremely...but it is very young in the great scheme of things. Mentally I would suggest it is the same age as you, late teens. It has a long way to go to truly understand itself, but it also has certain gifts and attributes that may come in useful. We plan to try them out on you.

No...no please I can't take any more of this.

Oh but you may enjoy the feelings it offers.

Please don't!

Regardless of the young man's desperate tears the Demon took control of the body, leaving Jay to cower once more in the darkened corners of his mind.

10

The bedroom clock ticked lightly towards three but Harvey couldn't sleep, which was completely acceptable after the events of that night's meeting. In this middle of the night gloom his moods washed around from shocked to confused, before bordering on concerned then back to guilty, seeing as there was little doubt it had been one hell of an evening.

Firstly there had been his wife's sudden insistence on having some proof that what they were searching for was real. It was only now within this nocturnal contemplation that he'd admit he could see her point.

It was true what she said, that almost everything they'd learned had come from the mind and memories of Alex Webb, what if he actually was delusional after going through traumatic events, like his attempted suicide followed by a six month coma? Naturally of course when it came to doubting their one armed house guest intentions, the next likely line of thought would also have to cast aspersions on Rhian Sanger and her son Sammy because their story was just as bizarre.

That was until last night when they'd been shown some tangible proof. Well it wasn't in reality tangible because it was evidence that couldn't be touched or explained, but still he, his wife, and everyone else in the room admitted they all saw the same thing.

Then in the darkness Flo's voice came across the pillow in some gentle whisper. Harvey wasn't surprised she was sharing his insomnia. How can you sleep comfortably when an Angel had appeared in your living room only five hours ago?

'Harvey?'

'Yes darling.'

'Was it real?'

'Huh...' he smiled unseen. '...Okay let's do it logically, tell me what you saw and we'll compare witness statements. It's the best way of doing it.' He rolled over towards her in the dark, his loving mind picturing her beautiful face clearly as she spoke.

'Well Inspector...' She was trying joviality to keep her fears at bay. '...I heard a young boy talking to me in a strange voice. That on its own was genuinely an odd moment but then he collapsed to the floor. Soon after that, rising up out of him, there was a smoke, a gas, I don't know for sure, but what I saw...then took on the shape of an Angel.'

'An Angel you say...could you help me here...try to describe this apparition in more detail?'

'I think I can Inspector. It was at least seven feet tall and appeared to be covered in a full length gown, a white sheet, but I don't know exactly because my attention was more drawn to its face.'

'I see and how would you describe that...?'

'It was beautiful, exquisite, and it was looking straight at me. Which gave me a strange feeling because I didn't feel scared by its stare...I just felt...well powerless...it looked exactly like a real Angel.'

'Uhuh...and did it do anything else...?' Harvey asked even though he knew exactly what she was going to say, this being no more than a game of investigative rationality to help both of them cope.

'Oh my god it opened its wings...it was moving...so lovely. I thought I was going to die but I'd never felt more alive.'

'But it wasn't real...' Harvey reasoned. '...you said so yourself, that it was formed from smoke or mist.'

'It was real enough. Those eyes were fixed on mine...looking right into me...' She took a calming breath. '...Harvey?'

'Yes.'

'Did you see the same?'

He paused for a second. 'Yes...I saw exactly the same.'

'What does it mean?' She asked softly.

'I have two explanations...but I think you may hate them both.'

'Try me.'

'Either it's quite literally the greatest parlour trick of all time, successfully pulled off by a single mum and her son for giggles...or everything we've been told is true and that after Alex fell from the ledge on Dalmeny Street he passed through a portal between dimensions.'

Flo joined in. 'Where he met an Angel.'

Harvey agreed. 'Evidently so...and if we believe that's true then we must accept the other threats are also real.'

Flo shivered under the covers. 'That a Demon and a Glitch are here in our world. Two murderous things we don't understand.'

Harvey took a breath before giving his response. 'Yet...things we don't understand yet...and that's the point as far as I can tell. We have to know their minds first, their personality traits, when we discover those we put them together alongside their actions and this will give us...'

'...Like any other criminal?' Flo interjected.

'Yes.'

'But these aren't just criminals...'

'...Yes they are because that's how we have to think of them. Following any other train of thought, believing that they are somehow supernatural or undefeatable is pointless and dangerous. It would only make us ignore a simple clue or take a misstep in our detecting process.'

'But you've seen what they can do...the murders...the bombing.'

'And that's exactly why I believe we can defeat them. I'm sorry Flo that I can't give you answers now, I don't have any, but I can tell you one thing...I'm not going to give in. All I know is with Alex, Rhian, Sammy, you, me and what is living inside of that boy, we've everything we need to give us a fighting chance. We have clues written down in the dream book, actual evidence of an Angel because we've seen it, strong character witnesses from this world and another, but most importantly we have our team.'

'Really...?' Flo said doubtfully. She'd been going along with his positive rhetoric up to now but couldn't resist pointing out some unmentioned facts. '...Because although I see the team, I don't see a winning team. What we have is an ageing Police Inspector working outside of his jurisdiction and the housewife who's happy to admit she is terrified by all of this, and then as backup we have a mother and son who have no idea what's going on, a one armed man with all the clues you mentioned but not one decent answer and finally we have a mouthy Angel who's made of fucking smoke!'

Her cry of profanity hung in the darkness. Harvey didn't respond.

Flo calmed her breathing to help fight back an urge to weep. Getting herself under control she pulled an arm free from the warm covers and rested it on Harvey's paisley pyjama chest. 'I'm sorry...I didn't want to swear...' She said and sniffed as she waited for his response.

Slowly his hand came up and rested on hers. '...You never have to say sorry to me, not for being yourself. The woman I fell in love with because she never lies and always says exactly what she means, what she feels. Trust me there is no feeling better than walking into this house at the end of the day to find you here. I work in the criminal world where I hear lies every day, people lie on the streets, they lie at the station and then they lie even more in court after taking a solemn oath...but you'd never do that. You couldn't even if you tried...

'...Thank you.' She said softly and squeezed his hand.

'So I owe you my truth, and it's that I really don't understand what we're involved in here, only that evidently it is real and dangerous. In fact the only thing I know for certain is my decisions have got you involved and

I never wanted to do that...I didn't really fully appreciate the danger we were in and I'm sorry...that's what I'm trying to...I love you and I'm sorry.'

Her response came back like a warm summer breeze to his ears. 'It's okay Harveypud...I know...' She paused. '...I know.'

'Good because I can't change anything without you...so shall we keep on trying to find the truth?'

'Yes.'

'That's my girl.'

'I'm sorry I sounded so weak...I see now...we're both right.' Flo smiled as their hands squeezed tighter. '...the truth is all that matters.'

On those words they simultaneously turned to share a kiss and entwine their bodies into one.

Twenty minutes later Flo was awake in the dark and listening to Harvey's gentle rhythmic snoring. Her eyes were wide trying to work out why she couldn't do the same, as if looking for some different answer, while the truth just kept on repeating itself. In the end she bowed to its persistence and accepted its validity, it was regret, at what she'd done to Alex and Rhian, Sammy to some extent, when she'd cast doubts and aspersions to their stories, their frightening realities.

Yesterday she'd shouted at them both and demanded proof or they could get out of her house. Of course she hadn't expected to actually get any, only to find it delivered in spades by the appearance of the Angel.

God damn it Alex had been telling the truth the whole time, meaning not only had she been disgustingly wrong to distrust him, but there were bonds to fix now. She decided first thing in the morning by way of apology she would cook their guest a hearty breakfast. Flo was so lost in planning what to say and how to apologise she never noticed Harvey had re-entered the land of the living.

'Are you feeling okay?' He asked.

'Yes...I'm going to make things better with Alex.'

'That's wonderful news...'

'I have another question though and I'd like to know what you think.'

'I'm not going anywhere...ask away.'

'Do you believe the Glitch is truly gone...?'

Harvey paused before answering and then turned towards her. It was time to think logically as he'd seen the photographs of Snake Hornblower's dead body, but what did that really prove. After all the Glitch had moved in uninvited, was it so unbelievable it couldn't move out just as easily. 'I really don't know...but hey little Sam seemed perfectly fine by the time he left...' Harvey subtly diverted the conversation trying to focus on the positives.

'Rhian wasn't too happy though.' Flo pointed out.

'I'm not surprised. She'd just witnessed alarming physical evidence that her son is legitimately possessed by an Angel...'

'...And that was also my fault because I demanded to see it. I'm going to apologise to everyone tomorrow and do everything I can to fix this.'

Harvey stroked the skin of her arm. 'Of course you will, but listen, you were only being the voice of reason in a perfectly unreasonable situation. What you've actually done is galvanise us all. We know what we're dealing with now, so let's move on...or better still lets sleep...I love you.'

'...I love you.'

They turned away from each other and settled down but neither closed their eyes; Flo wondering just how much her upset voice of reason had hurt everyone else, while Harvey was laying there concerned he hadn't been totally truthful. Not about his feelings on the condition of the Glitch.

THE RED FRAME

11

Theoretically at least any human journey through a life, whether guided from above or paved by random chance, is formed from within a tapestry of infinite chemical patterns strung out over an ever expanding loom. Where some timeless mechanism clicks and clacks relentlessly, wordlessly pulling threads of reality ever tighter to form pictures of who, or where, or what will be.

Just occasionally this chaotic system of invention can design a unique moment, a chance meeting between two particular souls, who together could change the world. Of course such happenings are extremely rare and precious times, but utterly unhelpful in deciding whether it is science or religion, because some would claim chance, while others will cry destiny.

As the golden dawn rose up over the historic City of Edinburgh it appeared such a moment might occur. Everything was in place for the start of a new day where the humans were beginning to rise, walk, drive and cycle the streets, their morning movements disturbing the rats, forcing them to scurry to finish their feeds. In the disappearing shadows a badger lolloped away then stopped to sniff the air before meandering its way home, its future always set, while the bats still on display were thinning out as their favoured roosts began filling up.

In the middle of the Holyrood Road a fox stopped sharply. There was something nearby that she couldn't yet see but her sense of fight or flight was triggered. However this was a mature vixen and she'd only run when danger presented itself.

She didn't wait very long before making her choice...as suddenly the air was filled with a wailing scream louder than any fox could comfortably accept. It was certainly a human cry but one exceptionally difficult to define, perhaps fearful, maybe even joyous. The fox couldn't understand what would make any animal release such a primal uproar so made her move, darting through a hedge she skipped through two gardens before reappearing on St John Street.

Her ears pricked to listen again to find the scream had ceased, but it was during this narrow focus using only one of her acute senses that she discovered how much she'd disregarded the others. A human turned the corner immediately in front of her. Surprise at this man's entrance made her front legs jump in the air, causing her to lose balance backwards, before instantly regaining lifesaving composure and fleeing back to the safety of the garden, panting rapidly.

Alex was also genuinely shocked, being quite sure he'd never been that close to an urban fox, although he did remember hearing they could be vicious if cornered and very noisy when on heat. On seeing it he had to reconsider that the outrageously loud scream he'd heard must have come from the fox. It was the only rational explanation for a sound so macabre in its delivery; it surely couldn't have been human. With his pulse calming down, from both the shrieking wail and sudden face off with that city predator, he continued on with this escape.

His decision to get away from the Coopers house had been finalised as he lay on their sofa trying to digest what they'd all witnessed. The sight of the Angel Metatron, even if it was more of a ghostly hologram than the reality he'd witnessed in the white world, had seriously shaken him. He'd known it was real as well having relived those memories over and over, but seeing the Angel again was all too traumatic. It meant the battle raged on for his sanity, his sense of justice, which was the reason behind his leaving the Coopers.

Yes they believed his story now but they hadn't before, with that lack of faith hinting at some practice of pity in how they'd treated him. Pity was the last thing he deserved after the journey he'd been on and the sacrifices he'd made. So they could keep their apologies because there was somewhere else he needed to be, even though he wasn't sure he'd be welcomed there with open arms.

In the meantime the young man who released the scream could be found walking in the direction of the castle, only one parallel street away from Alex, close yet each completely unaware of the others position, meaning the burning question of chance or destiny remained unanswered for now.

His teenage heart was beating so hard, full of excited adrenalin as he strode confidently forward, all thoughts about having a bleak future had been changed unimaginably by the gifts delivered from the voices in his head. It was improvements they had made that allowed the scream, which had been delivered from his own throat, using his new tongue.

All of Jay Cleaver's disabilities were now fixed. His body shone brightly inside and out, displaying vast enhancements the entity had made and he thought how the Demon had been right about the Glitch. It had attributes and tricks of a miraculous depth, so much that he was walking the streets as a perfect boy again, with one severed tongue rebuilt, a face reformed, that torn skin smoothed and renewed. There was no evidence of scars or fading tattoo's remaining on his new form; even his chipped and yellowing teeth were perfect. Just how everything could have been if he'd ever once cared.

So the monstrous shriek he'd released was a triumphant expression to the world, a declaration to anyone in earshot that Jay Cleaver was back, both better and far worse than ever before.

Walking along he whispered words to himself, but they were aimed at this City, its streets and the people, because Jay couldn't stop talking, he loved the sound of his new voice. He suddenly adored the monsters that lived in his mind, they'd gifted him all he'd ever wanted and in return he would willingly die to help them achieve their goals. Then with only joy and positive thoughts in his mind he raised his perfect face up towards the sky, to feel the golden beams of this new dawn spreading their energy over his skin, seeping through, deep into his bones. Damn he loved the glow coursing throughout his form, it gave him a strength and confidence that was pure intoxication and he upped the volume to scream once more. Only this time it was a clear and heartfelt sentiment.

'...Fuck you alllllllll...!'

From two streets away now Alex could hear the muffled version of Jays aggressive profanity but he didn't stop or turn, it surely had nothing to do with him, probably just some druggie late night reveller stumbling home. Therefore the one armed man with his incredible insights into other worlds continued his hopeful march, still blindly optimistic that if he could explain his actions clearly then she'd maybe forgive his sudden arrival and everything would be okay. If it went really well he was hopeful he'd feel safe once more, able to refocus on the task that lay ahead, to please god, finish what he'd inadvertently started by falling from a narrow ledge, on a day that seemed a few lifetimes ago.

Alex remembered listening carefully the one and only time she'd said her address out loud, and who knows if that had been for this very reason, which raised once more the misshapen spectre of chance or destiny.

Although the nerves he felt on approaching the blue front door were a strong hint towards this being an act of free will, surely he'd be feeling more in control if he was meant to be here. He took a deep breath before ringing the doorbell. It was half six in the morning so he expected there to be a slight delay and there was, until finally it was answered by a puzzled looking but familiar face, even if it wasn't exactly the one he'd expected.

'Alex...what are you doing here...?'
'...Err.' He replied.

12

'Harvey...oh my god Harvey...he's gone!' Flo called up the stairs in panic.

The words invaded the Inspectors mind fracturing a dream he'd been enjoying. Within it he'd been young and fit again, running along a beach towards a beautiful young woman. It didn't appear to be Flo in physical appearance but in his heart he knew it was her. She was the only woman he could ever love, although right now that genuine affection was being severely tested by her tapping him insistently on the cheek.

'Huh...what...?' His dry sleepy mouth asked.

'Alex has gone...he left a note. It said thank you but he needs his own space...it's my fault...I don't know what to do.'

Shaking off a deep sleep these days was a difficult enough task for Harvey on a normal morning, but after only three hours of shut eye this was taking a Herculean effort. Also the strung together statements Flo kept repeating weren't helping, each one skipped into his mind for better understanding only to be instantly kicked out by the next.

'Okay...' He said trying to open his eyes before helplessly slipping back into an early stage of slumber.

'Harvey...!' She shouted and shook him to such an extent those heavy lids opened sharply.

'Okay I'm awake...so Alex has gone out...?'

'No he's gone! He's left and taken his dream book with him by the look of it. Don't you see what this is? I shouldn't have doubted him, not to his face and in front of the others. Oh damn it to hell I'm so sorry Harvey.'

'It's alright darling I'm sure he's fine. Maybe it's time for things change anyway. We've made a lot of progress and he's a grown man who can look after himself.'

'He only has one arm and no money left as far as I'm aware. I agree he's grown up but capable of looking after himself? I'm not so sure.'

Harvey sat up in bed feeling his whole skeleton clicking back into place, proving beyond all reasonable doubt that the beach had definitely been a dream; he couldn't run to the bathroom let alone along a sandy coastline.

'Can I see the note?' He waited while she went downstairs to retrieve it and quickly returned.

'Here.' Her voice was unaffectedly upset as she handed him the page.

He read it through finding it contained no more than the information Flo had already conveyed. 'He doesn't sound too distraught. It's a little abrupt but certainly not accusatory.'

'Nice try Harvey but I know what I did and how much it hurt him. I'm worried about where he could go. His ex-wife died in that bombing and...'

'...Flo please, let's trust him, he knows what he's doing. Stop blaming yourself, to be fair I doubt any of us believed him completely. I had my doubts as well...right up to the point that an Angel appeared in our living room. Speaking of which I need to call Rhian and check everything's okay with the boy.'

'You'll let me know what happens.' She moved towards the door.

'Of course...Is that coffee I can smell?'

'No...but it soon will be. Now get up you've got work to do.'

'Ain't that the truth?' Harvey muttered to himself as he lifted himself up to sit on the edge of the bed and considered his options. Shower, shave, locate Alex, catch Jay Cleaver, try to stop the monsters and thwart the end of the world. Yes these were now the decisions to be made but they went right out of the window as Goldie raced upstairs. The alpha male of the house was awake and this canine needed some fuss from the leader of her pack.

'Hello you...' He said joyfully as his fingertips ruffled her soft coat. 'I've got to catch a bad guy today...someone you've met actually...on a different timeline of course.'

Goldie's expression was full of puzzlement as she listened intently to the sounds coming from his mouth and Harvey shared her bafflement because he felt exactly the same way.

13

Alex was sat in Nurse Juliet's kitchen finishing a coffee. Apparently she was out but would be home shortly after finishing her shift. He'd received that assurance a number of times from Graham Waugh, her handsome new boyfriend with the Hollywood smile. The same Graham who'd taken over Alex's care when his mood swings and erratic behaviour had forced Nurse Juliet to take a step back.

Over the past hour he'd discovered that Graham and Juliet were very happy together. It was still early days but apparently they shared the same interests and laughed a lot. All of this unasked for information made him feel a little sick inside. It wasn't that Alex was in love with her or felt cheated, although jealousy did appear to be the dominating emotion in his heart, but his envy bloomed from the fact that all he'd wanted from this visit was to regain her trust, which wasn't going to be so easy now with the big white toothed guy hanging around. Alex thought his smile actually appeared brighter than before, but that could just be the stark lighting in the small kitchen.

'I know I asked earlier but you didn't really answer me...How are you?' It was Graham doing the probing with his perfect bedside manner.

This left Alex with a stark choice, he could open up and tell this man everything about the last few weeks or he could keep it all to himself which was much more appealing. He didn't owe this guy a damn thing and then the decision was made for him when the sound of a small car pulling up outside took their attention.

'Here she is.' Graham's smile was wider than ever as he went out into the hallway.

Alex guessed the man didn't usually run to the door every time she came home from a shift. That would be weird, so clearly good old Graham was simply trying to give her a heads up, perhaps a gentle warning about her previous long term care patient's sudden unexpected return.

To be fair Alex couldn't expect any more. It was unavoidably strange that he should turn up out of the blue after callously ruining their close and occasionally flirty relationship. He recalled her last actions toward him on the day he left the hospital, when she'd given him a hundred pounds in cash, then told him to go save the world. That bit of their parting had been positive but the look in her eyes had not. Expected because his behaviour towards the end of her care was horribly selfish, yet here he was like a one armed Banquo's ghost sat at her kitchen table and smiling broadly as she entered.

'Alex?' She stammered. Half greeting, half perplexed.

'Hi there...Good morning...How are you...?'

'Tired...' She replied curtly and put her duffel bag on the floor.

'I bet you are. Sorry for just turning up like this. I err...wanted...needed to have a word with you.'

'What about...?' She sighed.

To Alex it was clear Juliet wasn't faking it, she looked utterly exhausted.

'...A catch up I suppose.'

'Can't it wait?' Graham suddenly interjected unhelpfully.

'What...oh yes of course it can. I'm sorry I can come back later...erm we could arrange something.'

It was just like the old times, Alex was sinking and only Juliet could save him. The real question to be answered though was would she still want to?

'Its fine Graham you get off back to work. I'll have a little chat with Alex then I'll get some sleep.'

Yes, came the answer to Alex's heart, she would still save him. He felt beyond grateful even though he wasn't exactly sure what he was going to say to her. In his mocked up idea of how this visit would proceed she was wide awake and still very much single, not like this, knackered and coupled up with another man.

'Thank you Jools...erm Juliet. Sorry I'll be as brief as possible.' Alex gave Graham his most non-invasive smile but wasn't totally surprised when it wasn't reciprocated.

'Okay.' The new boyfriend said checking his watch. 'I'll ring you in an hour...to check you've settled down.' Graham may as well have said to see you're not shagging this man, or the crazy guy hasn't killed you, but his self-confidence and restraint were clearly strong and healthy as he opened the front door. 'Good to see you again...Alex.'

With no kiss or toothy beam he left, giving Juliet the chance to put the kettle on, in silence.

So Alex had achieved what he wanted, undivided attention time with Juliet, although it was clear that what she wanted from him was quite different, something light and quick so he could leave and she could sleep.

He had to start somewhere so got underway with asking about her living arrangements. 'So you and Graham are an item then...?'

'Fuck off Alex...!' She harshly snapped without turning around.

'Wow...okay I wasn't expecting that.' He'd been about to take off his coat but decided to hold fire. The reunion hadn't started well.

'Please don't feign interest in my love life...' Juliet said stirring the coffee. '...Why the hell have you come here...?' On that query she turned to face him where he noted only one fresh coffee had been made and she was holding it. Not exactly a warm invitation to stay and relax but he had to plough on.

'I wanted to see you.'

'That's nice Alex...well here I am...happy?' There was venom bubbling under her sharp tongue.

Alex mumbled. 'Not really. Are you okay...'

'...Am I okay? Oh let's see shall we...I've just finished a fourteen hour shift. I was barely able to keep my eyes open for the drive home. I'm sure I've just got a ticket for going through a red light that I didn't even see. Then I get home to find an old patient who treated me like shit sat in my kitchen. So am I okay...mmm...maybe not so much.'

Alex took all of her words in. 'I'm sorry...'

'I couldn't give a shit for your apology! Now unless you've something important to say I'd like you to leave me alone.'

Juliet sounded serious with that demand then surprisingly sat down at the table with him. There was no doubt she was pissed off but this gesture showed that somehow, perhaps just a little bit, she didn't really want him to leave straight away.

Alex took a deep breath and felt the old feelings coming back but those messages were as mixed up as ever. 'Do you want me to leave?' He asked apologetically.

'Yes...but only after you explain the real reason why you came here.'

'Ah well that's a long story...'

'Shorten it then...!' She sat back and sipped her drink.

'...Okay, I can do that.' He nodded and for the next ten minutes rattled off his discoveries while living at the Inspectors house. Just how their little collective had discovered and followed the rise and fall of the Glitch which had been responsible for the massive bomb blast in the city...the one that had killed his wife in the process.

This was a nugget of information which killed the conversation stone dead. Until Juliet found, what she felt were, the right words to say. 'Well that will save money on a divorce lawyer.'

Though her comment was ridiculously cold and totally harsh, it was completely perfect in his eyes because this was the old Juliet, his partner in bad taste crime, his friend during the endless hours of mental suffering and he'd missed her so much. This meant it was his turn now to see if the door was open for him to reignite their bond with an equally merciless response. After a pause he said with a flawlessly straight face. 'Yeah...and let's face it she probably wouldn't have a leg to stand on.'

They allowed their eyes to meet across the table as somewhere inside their souls a rusted shared hilarity valve loosened. 'You are still a complete idiot!' Juliet gasped out the words between rocking laughter.

Alex found himself fighting back tears of joy and relief, emotions long gone filled his veins like rain flooding down an arid delta. Without thinking he reached out his only hand towards her. She responded and squeezed it gently back while dabbing at her eyes with a checked tea towel. 'I thought you were gone for good.'

'Ditto...' He nodded gently. '...I wouldn't be here at all without you.'

'Where...in my kitchen...? No you probably wouldn't.' She was happily trying to continue their farcical moment but he needed to be serious for a second.

'I mean alive...you kept me alive by listening to all my ramblings...but most of all you believed in me.'

'Somebody had to.'

'That's just it...nobody had to...but you did and literally saved my life.'

'Well...I didn't have anything better to do...and I was being paid...'

'...Please Joolz take the heartfelt gratitude!'

She put the tea towel down and sipped her coffee. 'Aww you're getting all serious again. I thought we could carry on making each other laugh a little longer. That's what I missed more than anything.'

'I know...but I was a complete prick and ruined that. So I need to tell you something before you start forgiving me completely...' Alex paused as he rubbed his sweating palm down his leg. '...It's not over...any of it...Angel Metatron is alive and here, in this city.'

'Where...?'

'...It's taken up residence inside a ten year old boy's head.'

Juliet didn't respond, or refused to straight away, instead she looked down at the table before raising her gaze to Alex. He looked very different now, cleaner, healthier and all together much saner but still the same story came from his mouth. A tale she'd tried to forget because it hurt so much to watch him suffer those memories, fragments of which she'd written down in a notebook of his dreams, evidently ones he still couldn't escape.

'Alex...is that why you're here... to put me through all this again...?'

'No...I'm here because I need you to help me to put things right.'

'It sounds a little late for that.' She stood and took her mug to the sink.

'Believe me Joolz it is about as late as it can be...but with your help we can fight it.'

'Really...? You know that's why I took myself away from your life...these stories.'

Alex stood up sharply but remained self-conscious enough to not come across as overly aggressive with his passion. '...They're not stories Jools, not anymore. Metatron appeared in physical form last night. I have three extremely credible witnesses, Inspector Cooper is one, but it changed everything, because now it's real I think there's a way of putting everything back to how it was...'

Juliet suddenly felt very small in her own kitchen as Alex approached.

'...There has been so much violence and too many lives lost since I fell from that building. I caused all of this suffering with a stupid selfish act but I'm beginning to understand how it works...that the universe always seeks a natural balance...so I believe what occurred on that day can be fixed.'

'I see...and you know exactly how to achieve that?' Juliet asked, if only to appease him.

'No...not exactly, okay not at all...but I have all the components to help repair this, all the pieces to play through the game and with your help...the two of us can change it all back.'

Juliet took a moment because she knew her words were going to sting. 'Here's another angle for you to consider...' She pointed at her own face. '...What if this component piece here doesn't want anything to change huh? Maybe she's generally happy at the moment with her lot in life. What if this component piece has a decent boyfriend and a job she loves?'

'Yes I can see that but this isn't how your life's meant to be...' Alex couldn't hide the sound of a frustrated snarl in his voice. Why wouldn't she believe him? '...Joolz, all of this is fake compared to our other lives. I don't want to let that unwritten, unfinished, unlived future disappear...because of me.'

Juliet looked up into his eyes. 'Have you ever considered you could be wrong, that everything is exactly as it's supposed to be because of what you did? Who knows maybe your fall and subsequent meeting with the Angel helped us all to avoid an even worse fate...'

He stood wide eyed, his mouth opened for a moment too long, before he snapped back into the conversation. '...Oh my god that's it. You wanted to know why I'm here...this is it, this is why I'm here...' He sat back down excitedly. '...What you just said is precisely the reason I'm here and why I need you!'

'I don't understand.'

'Balance...!' Alex exclaimed while his single clenched fist punched the air around him. He quickly realised he looked crazy so stopped his arm and repeated the word in a much quieter breathless state. '...balance.'

'Balance...?' She asked curiously.

'I need time to think Joolz. I can work this out I know I can. It's a simple puzzle...oh my God you have to sleep. I'm sorry...can I stay here...in the kitchen I mean...I'll wake you at whatever time you like...make you a coffee when I do...toast if you want...I'm becoming quite the wiz at one handed cooking nowadays...'

Juliet looked at him with genuine sadness in her tired eyes. '...I don't think Graham would be too happy about that...' then she tried to brighten things back up. '...also you don't cook toast...I'm just saying.'

It was Alex's turn to claim some of the sadness in the room. After a gap he clutched at the one remaining straw he could think of. 'Does he really live here...I mean has he moved in...is this his home with you?'

She stood and moved towards the door to make her way to bed before stopped in the doorway. 'No...he's been staying over some nights. He's got his flat in Corstorphine, it's near the Zoo, but we share my car for getting to and from work because he can't afford his own, so he's often here.'

'Ooh that's romantic...' Alex said spikily.

'Go fuck yourself...!' She snapped wearily. She needed to sleep.

'...I'm sorry that was a shit comment. Please, just a few days, a week at the most and I'll prove it to you...then we'll know.'

'Know what...?'

'...Exactly *where* we're all supposed to be...'

Juliet sighed and left the room. So for the next three minutes Alex sat silently at the kitchen table listening as she washed her face and brushed her teeth. Finally she popped that beautiful fatigued face back round the door. 'I'll call Graham...tell him I need a bit of space for a few days.'

'Oh Juliet thank...'

'...Shut up and be quiet now Alex! Wake me at three o clock...coffee milk and two, toast, lightly done and buttered.'

With that she closed the door, leaving him alone in the kitchen, but he sat there with more joy and positivity in his heart than he could ever remember feeling.

It was time for him to work, to work on time, hopefully in time to work out how time worked. He laughed at his own ridiculous description of the task ahead but only inwardly, Juliet needed to sleep.

Refilling the kettle with a little struggle and while wearing the slightest of smiles he looked out onto the busy street and acknowledged a beautiful fact. How his coming here had been absolutely the correct thing to do. He felt that being in Juliet's presence was already feeding him all the energy and courage he needed to move forward. Whether it would be enough, in the end, remained to be seen.

THE RED FRAME

14

As someone knocked firmly on his front door for a third time, Kosminsky dragged the pillow over his head to muffle the sound. Whoever it was at this time in the morning could definitely go do one. There was no way he was at home to strangers today and in his current mood concluded it may be some considerable time before that situation changed.

There were just too many fires burning out of control in his mind, all of them fuelled by feelings of pure annoyance. When everything was said and done he'd been the one hung out and left to dry. Of course he accepted he'd indirectly caused the death of a work colleague, allowing Wayne Keates to be locked in a cell with a Demon. A murderous action that Kosminsky knew was never going to end well, but it was a crime he didn't physically commit, also one that nobody knew of except Marcus Kirby.

So he'd gotten away with murder, only to then be arrested for trying to help Oscar reach a place of safety away from the facility, but in the eyes of the law that was a kidnapping with possible ill intentions. Thankfully Oscar had explained to those accusers at the police station that it hadn't been the case and all charges were dropped.

Meaning his release yesterday from a short stay in a police cell should have been an occasion for happiness, a day of blessed relief, but it wasn't how it felt for Allan Kosminsky. The big guard was majorly pissed off at being an unemployed man, especially one who lost his job under dubious circumstances, and who knew very well that in this line of work, the upper reaches of top level security, his career was over.

It was this overriding sense of injustice that was driving his desire to be left alone, also Kosminsky wasn't expecting anyone to be at his front door at this time, or any other time if truth be told. At this precise moment he was about as single and friendless as one could be, with both parts of the situation completely his own doing, the first being caused by his need to understand a serial killer, the second by a pining for the love of a girl who left him years ago.

So it followed that his imagination went running down the well-worn path, looking around in hope because what if this was it, the moment he'd fantasised about all this time, Chrissi returned, knocking at his door, her suitcase sitting on the front step. As he pulled the pillow off his head the wonderful daydream vanished, much like the hinges of his front door as the whole thing exploded inwards.

'Huh...!' he grunted in shock.

Heavy footfalls made their way directly towards his room.

'What the f...'

It was all he managed to scream as three masked invaders burst in with drawn weapons. They jumped on his bed to hold him down while a black gloved hand firmly covered his mouth as plastic ties were applied to bind his wrists. The operation of subduing their target had taken seconds and with a job well done the leader removed his helmet.

'Allan Kosminsky...you are under arrest for murder. You have the right to remain silent...'

A small crowd had gathered as he was led away to a waiting police van. He thought it no surprise that his neighbours, who usually took no notice at all of his comings or goings, were fully focused on it today. He looked over to see most of them filming it on their phones, so either they wanted to save his arrest as a memory, which he doubted; more likely they believed the world of social media demanded it.

A few miles cross the city and in perfect synchronicity, but with much less dramatic effect, another man was being collected to be taken away. This one wasn't cuffed and could have fought back if he hadn't been so drowsy. The result of the medication forced into his system meant the medic could calmly push the wheelchair towards the ambulance in silence.

Oscar didn't even notice he was being kidnapped again, so doped up on pain relief he didn't need which was keeping him unaware, unable to move or object to this movement. Floating in and out of full consciousness he sat perfectly still in the ambulance as it drove away, heedless this journey was toward another destiny he would share with Kosminsky.

From his dark wooden panelled office Marcus Kirby prepared for their arrival with a brief phone call.

'Excellent work my friend...'

'You asked me to get them so I'm doing it.' Shillings gruff voice replied.

'It is appreciated and I would like you to know that our arrangement will continue...there is no need to worry about your immediate future.'

Marcus smiled broadly at his plan coming together. Contented that he always got what he wanted because he had lots of what other people wanted, filthy pointless money.

Now if he'd been a flamboyant personality driven billionaire, the type who builds rocket ships to try and penetrate the heavens, the ultimate rich man's penis extension, then he'd never be able to attain the strange toys that he desired. To achieve those dreams he needed anonymity and the freedom it allowed, therefore no interviews were ever granted for the few news outlets that had actually heard of him. Every charitable request, or beg as he saw it, was denied outright by his faithful well paid staff.

What this insularity achieved was a sombre lonely existence but one perfect in its stability. He could wander from country to country without any obstruction, staying concealed behind the backstage curtain, watching the little plays on this world stage unfold, knowing from such a position his demands would come forth from the shadows, like a whispering prompt that held the script in front of them.

Kirby had been busy over the past week preparing the Facility building. It hadn't been empty long but the power had been switched back on at the dormant facility. He felt genuine excited pride in his creation as he strolled down the brightly lit corridors once more. All the improvements had been made rapidly in his absence, including extra security lighting, a wash of paint over the yellowing walls and all locks and doors checked and fixed. Such works were always carried out by a subcontractor, linked to another subcontractor, with all parties heartily paid for their work and silence.

These dealings always made Marcus feel comfortable in the knowledge that no questions would be asked of him, his return or activities, knowing no interfering authorities would be aware of his presence, bar the few he'd told, who would do as he bid. It was how he operated so there was no fear in his heart, because there is nothing to be afraid of, not when you can buy every soul you meet, when you have grown wise to appreciate how the human mind truly functions, to see its selfish and greedy weaknesses.

Way back in the nineteen seventies the young Marcus Kirby had grown up a curious and inquisitive boy, a sickly child who seemed to live by the irritating mantra of constantly asking why. His dead parents would tell you as a toddler he was always enquiring why the sky was blue, why do birds sing? By the time he reached early teens he'd upped the ante somewhat, asking of his uninterested parents why people commit murder, why do people go insane, but being unable to find any satisfactory answers he chose to begin his own study of infamous serial killers.

For three long years, running in conjunction with his tedious business degree course, Marcus would spend lonely evenings researching famous murder cases past and present. Always painstakingly passionate in his investigations to the point that he could recite intricate details on any of the worlds Rippers, facts and figures on Christie, Dahmer or Ramirez, dates and times for all the stranglers, stalkers and cannibals. It pleased him to know that if he wasn't already as rich as Midas he could make a decent living touring this knowledge, with the great unwashed always curious and hungry for the darkest information on the heinous and uncomfortable side of humanity.

Then there had come a tipping point in his studies, an epiphany if truth be told, that occurred when he'd read all the books of note, poured over countless police reports and accompanying criminal statements, before noticing something often mentioned by the worst of the worst but ignored or denied by the powers that be. A murderous mental duality came to light and it was this facet of killer's personalities which would become his true obsession.

Making vast amounts of money by investing wisely had been a cakewalk for Marcus compared to answering the complex mystery of what caused a human to commit multiple murders. The excuse so often given by captured slayers was the presence of another voice in their head, one that compelled them to kill, an admission of defence that had intrigued him for years; so much so that Marcus went on to invest a considerable amount of time and money in following up their claims. What if it was true? What if something existed within the human mind to create such a manifestation, or what if it was a completely separate entity. A presence which could be identified isolated and controlled. This search had already taken up over thirty years of his life with little success, at least until one of the many cities he resided in bore fruit and came up with their own serial murderer.

Having purchased the land and built the Facility he'd kept professional psychologists on his payroll and on call. He always employed security staff such as big Allan Kosminsky, hardworking souls who didn't have families. All other types were weeded out during the interview process, because less people around means fewer questions, something he'd found to be a worthy tactic in both business and personal interests. At first glance Oscar Downes appeared to be the perfect subject, fresh meat to a man like Kirby who then took the opportunity to study him in detail, for fifteen years he'd been ready and waiting for such a killer.

It was Oscar's modus operandi that first caught Kirby's curious eye, the viciousness of the man's attacks were quite startling, but keeping the bodies in plastic barrels for possible future horrors was a new level of awfulness. It was actually more than Marcus could have hoped for, here was a genuine monster in his locale, and for just a few thousands of pounds he could have the man to study at his leisure. So with a phone call here and a generous payment there, Oscar Downes was safely locked up in Kirby's building under twenty four hour video surveillance.

The problem soon started when his dreams, as with most dreams, floated close to fruition. They can end up disappointing when it's found they aren't really as perfect as first hoped. It had turned out this way for Kirby; the whole situation with Oscar became incredibly frustrating, when the inmate refused to speak to anyone for months. Even the overpriced professionals he employed couldn't get a squeak out of him, but that all changed when that lump of a guard somehow got the man to talk.

This was the moment he'd waited for his whole life and Marcus swiftly took on the challenge, introducing himself personally and promising the killer whatever he required until in one glorious moment Oscar replied and spoke to him with the voice of a Demon. Kirby's elation was exhilarating beyond compare when he'd been proven correct. It was all true, monsters existed in the minds of men, inside murderers, but this one was most exceptional because if what it said were true, it could be conveyed from one human to another. This was a concept so utterly fascinating it was far beyond what Kirby had ever imagined and well worth all of his investment.

What he needed to find out was if this voice was special in having this attribute, but then again what if it was truly and utterly unique, a focused energy passed down from serial killer to serial killer throughout the ages. If so there was a chance this could be evil incarnate, pure butchery with no limits and Marcus wanted to feel that power, believing he deserved to.

It was why he'd set up the initial transferral procedure, following strict rules given to him by the Demon, manufacturing a suitable tube for the monsters journey into his own mind.

Marcus however had been deceived and left empty handed, left feeling foolish, sure that hiding somewhere inside one of those men the Demon was laughing at him. Well it wouldn't be laughing when he had them back at the facility tomorrow night, because he would find the beast no matter what it took, and then afterwards take his own personal retribution out on them. This would satisfy Kirby's anger, while suiting his business ethic, less people meant fewer questions.

15

Harvey climbed out of 'the' car. The one he'd hated at first and still rather disliked now because no matter what he did, how he made it look or smell, the energy it gave back was always pure Jeff Shilling, as if the big man was always sitting in the backseat.

After making his way upstairs and entering his, totally to be expected, empty office he was more than a little surprised as a female voice greeted him. 'Good morning...!' On first sight it was disembodied but seemed to be coming from under Emma's desk.

He kept his distance and replied. 'Yes...err what...good morning...can I help you?'

A blonde bob hairstyle encasing a fresh young face with a generous smile looked out from behind the desk. 'You must be Inspector Cooper. My name's Roma. Roma Walker...' She stood and offered her hand with an exaggeratedly straightened arm. '...I'm your new assistant...secretary. Sorry I dropped my pen.'

'Really, my new secretary...I had no idea...?' He responded while almost reluctantly giving her hand a shake. '...I don't remember requesting a new assistant or interviewing anyone for the position...'

'...Mr Shilling said you might be a little surprised.' She smiled but it only came over as tense.

'So the Superintendent interviewed you...?' Harvey couldn't help but feel a bit violated. '...My apologies if I seem a little underwhelmed but I'm afraid I wasn't told about any of this.'

'That's okay Mr Cooper I was made aware of that, but trust me I'm on your side. Mr Shilling requested my transfer from the Glasgow division, because your workload here is quite heavy at the moment.'

'Is it now?' Harvey was surprised to learn that news, believing it was no more chaotic than usual at the station. Of course he missed having Emma around, so things were a bit of a mess, but thought he'd been handling things quite well up to now.

'Are you here permanently...?' He asked.

'I asked the same question and Mr Shilling said as long as it takes...' She replied confidently.

'As long as what takes...?' He didn't like this at all.

'To reduce the backlog of course...would you like a coffee? I'm just about to make one.'

'I'm fine thanks. I'll be in my office if there's anything to report.'

Harvey then took himself away from the slightly awkward scene. All he really wanted was a little chat with Jeff Shilling. He didn't have to wait long for that as his intercom rang.

'Hello...?'

'...Morning Cooper, hope you're feeling well and raring to go? What do you think of Roma hey? She looks young but she's experienced...five years, kind on the eyes as well don't you think?'

Harvey knew a dressed up sexist comment when he heard one so he didn't answer, it wasn't really the problem now. 'What's going on? You've never appointed my personal staff before.'

'That is true Harvey but time is of the essence now. I'm presuming you haven't heard the news yet...'

'I've just got here...' Harvey replied then fell silent allowing Shilling to bulldoze on regardless.

'...Late last night the remains of Jay Cleavers parents were discovered at the family home, they'd been lying there for a couple of days, I didn't believe it was worth waking you but whoever did it must have been pretty disturbed and quite keen to send a message. His father was found in the overgrown grass of their front lawn, the body was hidden from view but starting to smell which attracted the attention of the neighbours. As you well know in that particular postcode it takes a lot for someone to pop round to see how you're getting on. Anyway the initial medical reports state his skull was caved in by a couple of heavy blows from a blunt instrument, probably a large cobblestone they found nearby, but he was the lucky one.'

'Lucky...?' Harvey was irked he hadn't been notified immediately.

'Oh yeah, it seems Mrs Cleaver was attacked second and undoubtedly still alive while the other more serious wounds were inflicted. Her body was crudely dismembered, butchered of her fingers and other extremities which were then distributed around the house. Her severed head found placed in the oven and roasted thoroughly.'

Harvey felt he needed a little breather to take those details in and give them the respect they deserved. '...Could you send me the full reports?' He asked.

'Of course, ask Roma and she will get them for you...first impressions?'

'On the murders or Roma...?' Harvey asked with a hint of belligerence while deliberately keeping his voice low.

'...Let's start with the dead parents shall we.' Shilling's response came through as loud and bullish as ever.

Harvey quickly put together what he had. '...Well I can only presume you fully expect this to be the work of young Mr Cleaver, even calling them his mother and father, because evident from the murder of his social carer, who believed she was only helping by reuniting him with his family, he has some serious parental issues...but parricide in such a grisly manner. That's quite an escalation for him don't you think Jeff? So if you don't mind I'd like to see the reports first before I jump aboard that theory.'

Shilling was annoyed by what he was hearing but he understood the Inspectors reticence to commit, after all it had been his only job to catch the little bastard and he'd failed, just like he'd done with Oscar Downes a couple of years ago. 'Very well, but what I have to say next won't be pleasant Cooper, would you like me to say it over the phone or would you prefer to come up to my office?'

'The phone's fine...I'm clearly going to be rather busy.'

Harvey wasn't backing down anymore to his old beat partner, a man who had quickly become a total prick since his promotion. There was also the small matter of not wanting to watch Shillings face begin to glow red again, it was an unpleasant view at any time. In the end he decided to strike first in hope it may burst the Superintendents boorish balloon.

'...Look Superintendent, there are three separate teams out searching for Cleaver, so when he raises his scarred head we'll bring him in for questioning. It's the way the police works Jeff, we try to avoid apportioning blame in advance without evidence, or ever think that we know better than anyone else, because that way chaos lies. So thank you for the update and if that's all I'll get on it immediately, that's my job.'

The silence on the other end of the line was palpable.

'...Sir?'

The response came in a heavy conspiratorial whisper. 'Okay we'll wait a while longer but find him quickly Cooper...we'll talk afterwards.' The call was ended.

Harvey found Shilling's calmer tone to be more disquieting than his usual bluster, there was also a heavy hint in his words of some upcoming dismissal, perhaps suggestive that Harvey should take early retirement, or worse.

However like the big man said that was for another time, today was the day for catching bad guys...or one bad teenager to be more accurate.

In another life and on a different timeline Harvey had already chased and caught Jay Cleaver. That pursuit dramatically ending when he'd saved the boy from a horrible mauling in a lion's enclosure, but of course that didn't happen, not in this world, which is where his main problem began.

Last night after observing the final proof of Alex's story, when the Angel made an appearance in his house, Harvey was left with no choice but to believe all aspects of Alex's story. Of course this acceptance brought a whole raft load of problems, it meant the clockwork movement of his studious logical mind was being forced to work on twice as many levels, to take account of what was happening now with what occurred back then and not mix them up. It was a fresh and outright unique challenge, one he needed to meet head on, even if it made his work and home life extremely awkward. In addition to that was the fact Jeff Shilling knew nothing about the other situation which, under these circumstances, could be viewed as both a blessing and a curse.

His office door was tapped lightly.

'Yes come in.'

Roma entered with a brown file just like Emma had done a thousand times before, mostly back in a world lost to them now. As she placed it down Harvey knew his feelings towards this girl would never be the same.

'The initial findings Sir…'

'Of what…?' Harvey asked with a knowing smile.

'The murders of Mr and Mrs Cleaver…I thought you may want to see them.' Her answer held a hint of self-doubt.

'Isn't that very efficient of you…' He reached out and took the file from her. '…I think I'm ready for that coffee now.'

He watched Roma exit and felt some satisfaction in belittling her, after all she was clearly wired up to Shilling in some way, how else would she know about the file so quickly?

So the thought that she wasn't to be trusted became his overriding first impression.

16

The television was on mute, its high definition picture showing some young people on an island trying to fight the urge to copulate with similar looking types, basically a human genome dead end with fake breasts, painted abs and tears. The type of entertainment entirely unsuitable for an imaginative growing mind, especially one only ten years old, so why was it being rerun at eleven o clock in the morning.

Rhian entered the living room, saw what was on the screen, and turned it off. She didn't want her boy to think for one second that what those young people were doing was normal. So it was of some little relief that he hadn't even seemed to notice the show, being more than content to sit on the sofa, head down, reading a school book about Pharaohs and Pyramids.

Sammy had suddenly taken to this leisure activity under his own steam and it was making his mother rather proud, reading and learning being much better than shooting strangers online for gaming sport, but she still had some misgivings. This rapid change could be blamed on the influence of the other life altering her boy, although she preferred to believe it was of his own free will. Her son was clever and developing beautifully, even allowing for the fact he'd an Angel lodging inside his head, which appeared in such frightening physical form only last evening.

'You okay kiddo?' She asked as she sat down next to him.

'I'm good thanks, how are you...?' Sam said while placing the closed book on the arm of the sofa.

It almost squished her heart into a soggy lump hearing him ask about her wellbeing. What a respectful ten-year old he was, also one who hadn't mentioned his birthday which was only seven days away, the big one-one.

'I was wondering if you wanted to do something special next week for your birthday, I was thinking we could drive out somewhere if you want. Let me know any ideas you have and I'll try my best.'

The boy thought about it a few moments before asking hopefully. 'Can we go to the zoo...?'

'Of course we can...we haven't been for ages.'

'I know and I'm older now so I think I'll appreciate it more.'

'Zoo it is then. Is there anything in particular you'd like to see...?'

'...I want to see everything. There are new lion cubs...it said so on the news.' Sammy was sitting content and comfortably still with none of the common fidgets usually rife in children his age.

Right on cue Stripes the cat entered with a feed me now mewl. It was like being a new parent all over again Rhi thought; something inside her unable to resist its call. She went to the kitchen immediately and the happy cat followed. As she tore open the pouch the question she really wanted to ask her son popped back in her head, it was an important one, but most probably unwise to just say it straight out.

'Did you sleep well sausage...?'

'Hmm yeah I was really tired...'

'I thought you might be.' She replied squeezing the squidgy processed meat into the plastic bowl, one with its own cat's ears. The food dropped with a splot.

'Why would you think I'd be tired?' Sammy asked genuinely interested in her opinion.

'No reason...' She lied. '...But you must get bored with me dragging you round to the Inspectors house every evening, all of us boring adults talking rubbish.' Rhi hoped he'd agree but was disappointed and a bit concerned as she listened to his response.

'I like it there it's interesting...and it's a policeman's house...that's pretty cool. I like Mr Cooper he's a really nice man who tries his hardest to make everything safer for everyone else...that's really special...and Alex is amazing because he tells great stories and he's only got one arm...that's cool as well because I don't know anyone else like that...I think he's brave.'

'Yes I think so as well.' Rhian loved his positivity but wanted to know just how much he was taking in from his time there. 'So what do you enjoy the most about his stories?' She hoped his answer would be uninteresting, after all he was playing with the dog or on his phone most of the time sat on the Coopers sofa, but yet again he both surprised and distressed her in equivalent amounts.

'The fact he went up to heaven and got into a fight with an Angel.'

'Is that right...?' She asked carefully.

'Uhuh...and the world will end if we don't change things back to how they were before.'

Sammy said it so matter of factly that Rhi almost missed the meaning that the words threatened. It surely wasn't good to be hearing such things in his fertile developing mind. 'But you do understand they are only stories, just ideas that he's thought of...the world isn't going to really end.'

'Alex thinks it will...and I believe him...' Stripes padded slowly into the room and proceeded to have a thorough body wash in front of the fireplace. '...Why would he lie about something like that?'

Rhian couldn't think of even one convincing enough reason so she changed the subject. '...How are you finding your first full day of being expelled from school...?'

'It's good...hey you're expelled as well.' He replied cheekily.

'No darling, I'm barred from the school grounds...there's a difference.'

Sammy laughed; a sound as beautiful to her ears now as the first time he'd ever chortled.

Stripes finished its tongue driven ablutions then jumped up between them. It wanted a fuss right now and couldn't care less who gave it. In the end neither could resist and the happy cat grew even happier. It's purring was a distraction preventing Rhi from asking her main question, a simple enough query in theory, but in reality ridiculously difficult to broach.

How on earth do you ask a child if they are aware of being possessed by a centuries old Angel? It had just been another fragment of Alex's story, but disturbingly it was now one she had seen with her own two eyes. With that part of his tale now being beyond reasonable doubt, she needed to know more.

'Do you feel okay when we leave the Inspectors house...when we're driving home...?' It was a question somewhat closer to the ballpark of what she really needed to ask.

Sammy couldn't understand why she was asking, he'd already said he enjoyed going there; she knew he liked the people, especially Mrs Cooper, or Aunty Flo as she'd told him to call her. It was fun following her into the kitchen for some biscuits or warm buttered toast, which often happened when the adults were talking about the Angel. Yeah he liked Aunty Flo.

'I just feel tired that's all. It gets late and I'm only ten, Mom...'

His honest reply soothed her concerns and she took it to be the answer to the question she hadn't asked. '...Eleven, next week, argh!' She squealed and jumped on the sofa next to him. They shared a small tickle fight which quickly left them both breathless before settling back down with Stripes.

Rhi was satisfied that he remained blessedly unaware of his divine intruder and she desperately wanted it to stay that way.

THE RED FRAME

17

As lunchtime approached the sun was beating down on the sandstone constructions of which Edinburgh is predominantly built. Tourists and locals alike incrementally adding to the temperature with shared bellows of complaints that today was just too warm, already twenty six degrees and threatening to be thirty by late afternoon. Even the currents of air from the sea were blowing themselves out in an attempt to cool the stone. The exposed streets were shimmering, causing merging illusions to emanate up from the paving slabs, as if somewhere between the ground and knee height another dimension could be witnessed. A mirage world you could walk straight through but only see from a distance.

This city is an ancient habitation principally designed to withstand and protect its occupants from heavy winters, whipping winds and substantial rainfall, therefore its hardy people always struggled under a rare blast from an oppressive sun, its stone remaining warm to the touch long after the life giving star had rolled off to the west.

After a hearty battle Harvey had finally forced open the sticking window of his office. In truth he wasn't surprised by its stiff resistance, it must have been a year since it was last used. He loosened his dark blue tie then undid his top shirt button. For once the thought of leaving the station was uninviting, but he had dead bodies to see, his only relief coming from the knowledge that it was always cool in a morgue.

His intercom buzzed. 'Yes?'

'Your viewing appointment at the hospital is booked for two thirty.' Roma informed him.

'Thank you...' He replied, finding that was all he was willing to say.

He checked his watch; twelve fourteen, meaning there was time for lunch before he saw what remained of Jay Cleavers parents. Of course lunch on his own wasn't the most appealing preference so he considered his options. As much as he would love to do so it would take just too long to go home and pick up Flo. Anyhow she was working in their garden today awaiting a delivery of topsoil. So it would have to be someone a bit nearer and less busy.

Allan Kosminsky sprung to mind and not only because the big man was most probably at a loose end. It was more than that. Harvey wanted to get him involved in the search for the answer. He was a good man, proven throughout this timeline and the other. Harvey really wanted to bring him up to date. He dialled the number stored in his mobile, there was no way he was using the office line with sneaky Roma on patrol. He then waited patiently for a dozen rings but to no avail. In the end he left a message.

'Hi Allan its Harvey...I was just wondering if you were free to meet up for lunch today. My treat...I err...wanted to open up on a few new bits of information...look, listen, just call or message me when you get this okay...bye.' Harvey still wasn't in tune with technology, even leaving a voice message made him uncomfortable, but at least he hadn't said 'Over'.

He often thought there must be a classroom somewhere that people attended to learn the proper protocols, if so it was one he'd never been invited to. He was forced to blunder on blindly through the etiquette minefield of modern life. One day he hoped for a major power outage to see how people would manage having to be simply human again, forced to talk to strangers or neighbours, no quick fix for their problems, nothing but the beautiful and underrated laborious process of sorting it out yourself. There was no doubt at all he would do very well in that world.

His intercom buzzed again. 'Yes?'

'Sir there's a phone call for you.' Roma reported.

'Who is it?'

'They refuse to give their name...I can tell you it's a man.'

He instantly thought of Kosminsky but wondered why he'd return his call by way of the station phone number rather than mobile. 'Okay put them through.' As the call connected the sound of traffic could be heard. 'Hello this is Inspector Cooper.'

'Hey...'

From just that simple word, which came across as more of a sound than a formulated greeting, the Inspector felt his adrenaline release, surely not, it couldn't be.

'...Harvey Cooper as he lives and breathes, how are things in your blindfolded world...still looking for something that doesn't want to be found?'

His professional instinct was to open up the call so his secretary could listen in and inform the tech guys, who might be able to locate the source given enough time, but the young woman through there wasn't Emma, so he'd have to travel alone on this one.

'I'm sorry, who is this...?' He enquired while hiding all his emotion. It was Harvey's attempt at playing dumb, stalling for time, because he knew damn well who it was but needed a few seconds for his heart to stop pounding so he could think straight.

But the voice of the Glitch wanted to talk.

'We haven't spoken for a while Inspector. There have been a lot of changes...upgrades if you wish.'

'I saw your dead body!' Harvey stated as he wanted to clear that detail up straight away.

'You saw the remains of a used and discarded mortal...you may see a hundred more of those yet...but then again you may yourself be murdered within the next hour. Such is the chaotic universe we live in...every second a fresh hand is dealt and one is forced to play with those cards.'

Harvey thought the voice sounded different to last time; lighter in tone, younger even, strangely familiar.

'Oh I see you want to play the bad guy again...' Harvey chose to go on the attack to find out more. '...some sort of criminal mastermind leading the police on a merry chase...believing you're so clever and way ahead of the game...'

The voice laughed down the phone and that was definitely the sound of a teenagers cackle. 'You're unimportant...'

'...Then why call me?'

There was a moment's pause. 'Because I know your number and I have two friends with me who would very much like to talk to you.'

'Go ahead then, I'm all ears.' Harvey had never spoken a truer word.

'I'm pretty fucking sure you won't recognise my voice. Ha ha...do you want to take a guess anyway?'

It was the same vocal sound but carrying a completely different syntax. Harvey presumed, as he'd first feared, the Glitch had survived and moved on to a different host. Somebody clearly younger than Snake Hornblower, most likely another runaway it found under the city.

'Come on Inspector Cooper...or do you want a clue?'

What a ridiculous question to ask a Police Inspector he thought. 'Yes I would.' Harvey responded eager for more information.

'My Mom and Dad are recently deceased. Ha, ha...' The laugh at the end sounded awful.

No, what, that couldn't be right, thought Harvey. No, no, he'd seen Jay Cleaver at the facility. For starters that kid didn't have a tongue in his head. It was cut clean out, so for sure he couldn't talk like this. Harvey had to remain calm and find out more. 'That's interesting...so what happened...?' Harvey asked this by way of gaining some sickening confirmation that his hunch was correct.

'I'll tell you what happened, I caved my bastard Dad's fucking skull in and then I got my Mother and cut her head...'

'...That wasn't what I was asking.' Harvey interrupted, he had his heart rate down now but his mind was racing. 'I meant your tongue; you didn't have one last time we met.'

'Ha, ha yes so you do know who I am. But don't bother wasting your time asking me questions about it, that's my little secret.' The boy sounded happy, like he was having fun.

As disturbed as this Inspector already felt with the sudden appearance of a coherent Jay Cleaver, he was ready and willing to draw the focus and therefore any incoming fire upon his own shoulders. He also understood from the hours spent studying and discussing the damn thing it would mean challenging the Glitch directly, both mentally and physically.

'...So you have a new foot soldier Glitch! Well done, although I think I could have found you a thousand more suitable specimens.'

'Hey you're talking to me!' The boy shouted angrily.

'I know Jay but I'm not interested in you...let me talk to the puppet master...'

'...Get fucked you fucking prick!'

Harvey thoroughly enjoyed hearing that response because it meant his words were having the desired effect. Those angry profanities were the concrete proof this young boy still had a lot to learn. Obviously Harvey considered Jay a dangerous individual in his own right but he didn't need the teenager to know that, so he continued to directly incite a response from the Glitch.

'...You let a young woman shoot you in the head. What happened there all-powerful Glitch, the destroyer of universes, taken down by a secretary who'd never had any firearms training...?' Harvey suddenly had a pleasing side thought, somewhere down the line Emma may actually get away with the murder, after all she'd only killed Snake Hornblower who technically had been already dead, while the Glitch, the bomber, was still alive. Now that court case would be an interesting affair he thought, but again it was for another time. '...What I'm trying to explain to you Mr Glitch is your fearful presence has sort of dropped off the chart. A bit like an unbeaten boxer who ends up on the canvas after a hefty smack in the mouth, it's over for you really, you can try and make a comeback but all the mystique and invincibility is gone...'

'Talk to me...!' Jay was shouting but Harvey continued to ignore him because he knew the Glitch was listening.

THE RED FRAME

'...And you'll be amazed at what we've discovered about you Mr Glitch. We have plans and traps in place to end all this ridiculous running around. But seriously what made you conceive of this stupid move, contacting me directly? Don't you see that if you'd stayed hidden what an advantage it would have been for you? I can only presume it's that delicate ego of yours at play again and your decision proves one important thing to me...'

'...What?' One simple word but delivered in the cold style of the Glitch. Having forced Jay away it was back in control just as Harvey predicted.

'...It proves to me once more that you're overconfident in your own head, or Jay's head, of your abilities, and overconfidence is a dangerous thing, it makes you sloppy, prone to giving away more than you intended.'

'These words are of no relevance.'

'I think they should be...' Harvey bit back. '...Like I said we've learned a lot about you...and we know where you're hiding.'

'Hiding...? I'm not doing that. Quite the opposite I'd suggest...I want you to know exactly where I am.'

Harvey sat back in his chair and found himself enjoying this repartee with the monster. 'Congratulation on having such a ridiculous strategy, by choosing to travel with a homeless kid who's already wanted on separate charges, we now know exactly who you are and what you look like, which is blatantly a terrible decision...and we will find you.'

'No, no, no you won't find me...'

Harvey was about to ask why when his office door opened. Jay Cleaver stood in the doorway, resplendent with his perfect smile and wearing a smart grey suit, his hair neatly combed back to display a healthy tanned flawless complexion, his blue eyes sparkling.

'...Because I've found you...' The young man stepped closer and placed his mobile phone on the desk. '...Finally Mr Cooper...we meet in person.'

Harvey felt the iciest of shudders run slowly down his body.

18

Flo answered the phone call with a half-truth.

'Oh hi there Rhian I'm fine, thank you...' After this she calmed down a little and spoke no more lies. '...No, there's no meeting this evening...why? Harvey doesn't think we need another at the moment...yes of course what happened to Sammy needs to be stopped...I'm sure we can sort it...oh please don't be upset...okay let me explain. Alex left us last night...no, no, ha-ha he's fine, he's moved out, he needs his own space...so I suppose until he gets in touch or returns we won't be able to have a meeting...you know what...listen, I'll call Harvey now and see what's happening...oh you've been trying to contact him...well clearly he's busy then...look I'll try now and promise I'll call you straight back...okay please just relax it's all going to be fine...bye...bye.'

She put the house phone down firmly, it wasn't a slam because she wasn't angry, just curious and a little aggrieved. When it first rang she'd desperately hoped it was the garden centre letting her know when to expect the load of topsoil, they'd promised an AM delivery time and ten past one was getting seriously past that window.

'Oh for god's sake...' She muttered calling Harvey's mobile. No answer. '...Pick up the phone you idiot!'

That outburst was about as annoyed as she could get with her husband. She knew the feelings she had were born of frustration and...well yeah frustration, today was far from the day she'd planned. Alex had stormed off, the bloody top soil was late and now her husband was busy when she could really do with speaking to him.

19

The sunlight pouring through the open window caught Jays eyes making them appear a Hollywood steely blue. Harvey noticed this because they were penetrating deep into his soul at this very second.

The Inspector's muted mobile buzzed again.

'Turn...it...off.' Jay requested with a temperate tick tock hint of now or I'll kill you.

Harvey took this request on board and pressed the power off, before Jay (and Co) continued threatening him while looking down on the street.

'Beautiful weather today isn't it Harvey...it's so nice. I should think if one were to fall out of that window the experience might actually be quite pleasant at first...at least until you ceased plummeting.' There was no hint of a smirk from his young face, this was a powerful presence. 'But that's all about possibilities isn't it, what if's, what could be, how does the world work, how does this end for you? I'd suggest three hundred and sixty degrees is the answer at this moment in time, meaning any direction at all, because we haven't made up our minds on what to do with you yet.'

There was a gentle knock on the door. 'Here you are sir...I hope it's to your liking.' Roma said as she entered with his coffee.

At the exact moment the door was opened Jay Cleaver vanished.

Harvey's eyes were wide and troubled as Roma approached his desk.

'It's just a coffee sir. It's not poisoned...that's a joke obviously...is everything okay...?'

At the very second he was about to consider the last few minutes as being some bizarre day dream or hallucination Jay reappeared, he was now standing directly behind the oblivious secretary and displaying a gentle smirk. A raised index finger placed itself upon his perfect lips and once more Harvey was compelled to obey the command.

'Erm...' He said clearing his throat. '...I'm just a little surprised you bothered making me a drink...after my less than lukewarm welcome to you...my sincere apologies for that. You were right we have got a heavy workload at the moment and I will certainly need your assistance.'

Roma smiled broadly. 'Thank you for that Sir...I'll try my best.'

'I'm sure you will. Now if you don't mind I have some calls to make and paperwork to read so err...if you could give me some undisturbed time.'

'You mean hold all your calls?'

'Yes, that's exactly what I mean. Thanks again for the coffee.'

Roma nodded, smiled and then turned directly toward the space Jay Cleaver occupied, where he vanished again without her realising. As she closed the door he instantly rematerialized on the chair to face Harvey across the desk. 'Another life saved for now, well done Inspector. After all I could have killed her on the way in...but that's not why I'm here.'

'So why are you here?'

'To bring you up to speed...'

'...On what?'

'Everything, our situation, all this bluster about you knowing secrets about me...is that a policeman's bluff, a sleight of hand to make me look elsewhere, or do you actually have anything that would concern me in any way?'

'First of all I would like to know how you got up here, through the station and up the stairs without being challenged or recognised.' Harvey couldn't ignore that. For god's sake there were officers on duty looking for this exact man, albeit rather more scarred in the official description than this glowing youth, but all the same surely you couldn't walk through a busy police station unchallenged no matter who you were. 'Did you have help?'

His uninvited guest sniggered, a key signature sound making it easier to recognise who was in control of the teenager, because there were definite differences between the sound and mannerisms, tiny but perceptible and that laugh was most definitely the Glitch. 'Ha Inspector and I thought you knew all about me.' It said in a mock surprised tone.

'I know you have a few tricks...' The Inspector remained serious as he asked. '...I'm just curious about which one you used.'

Harvey felt a tiny movement of the air around him as Jay disappeared from the other side of the desk, the next moment he felt a thin finger tap his shoulder from behind.

'I'm fast Harvey, quicker than you can imagine. Those mortal eyes will never be able to perceive the world I roam, and this finger on your shoulder...could just as easily be pushed clean into the back of your head. You have to understand that what you thought you knew about me is already old news. Constant advancement is what I am, I've changed greatly and not just in physical form, but again I want to know what you know.'

'I see...' Harvey began to answer but the Glitch was in control now.

'Shall I force it out of you or are you willing to do this painlessly?'

Harvey took a moment glancing out of the window to see the hazy blue sky. Strangely it was the clement weather which seemed the most bizarre thing happening right now, it was rarely so warm in the capital and he genuinely considered that if he were to die this day, then at least it was a sunny one. 'You don't have to force anything out of me. I'll tell you whatever I want. Playing this game is what I've done for over thirty years.'

'Game...?' The Glitch questioned the very word.

'...The interrogation game, show and tell, manipulation for information. It really is what I do best.'

On that note Harvey felt Jays finger tap the back of his skull. He tried to remain unmoved but when death is this close a body struggles to contain its coolness.

'Show me then...' The Glitch asked coldly. '...show me...so I can tell.'

'Okay if it's what you want...I know all about the other timeline. The one we left behind because of your creation...'

'...Oooooh I see!'

'I know how you were created and by whom. I know your immortality isn't real, it's not guaranteed and if anything is dependent on me...' Harvey turned to face the young man but in the flicker of a blink he was re-seated back across the desk. '...I mean look at you...flitting about the place like bloody Tinkerbell.'

Jay's eyes were the coldest of steel blues as they burned into Harvey. 'Are you goading me Inspector?'

'Of course I am...it's one of the perks of my job...a little provocation never hurt anyone. Also I think if you were going to kill me I'd be dead already, on my way up to that empty heaven you left behind, the one you tunnelled out of before you appeared at the zoo...' He watched Jays face closely but it didn't react. '...By the way, killing innocent lions isn't what we do here in this city, so that will have to be paid for. Although it did raise a puzzling question for me...why did you choose to enter this world at that particular location, in fact more to the point why come to this city at all? I heard you had a fondness for Las Vegas.'

The Glitch was staring out from deep within Jay's eyes and Harvey knew he'd caught its full attention now. The question he had to answer though was how far he could go with repeating the claims made in Alex's dream book before he showed his whole hand. He knew that being out of ammunition would be unwise in such a delicately poised game of cheating death.

'Hmm tell me more...' The Glitch requested.

'No. Your turn, quid pro quo time...parley only works when tittle for tattle is invoked. Tell me why you detonated the bomb in that particular location?'

Jay paused momentarily as if deciding whether disclosing such delicate information could be dangerous. 'It was a favour, a retribution for Snake. It killed the four men who had beaten him to death.'

'And sixty seven other innocent people at the latest count.'

'Hmm...so I took a few extra for myself...' Jay shrugged.

Harvey knew he had to push on while he shared this remarkable face to face. 'I can't help but wonder why you want to kill people at all, if we are so far below your godlike status and your intentions are to eventually destroy this universe anyway, what's the point of bombs and threats?'

'I told you I did it for Snake, while the other murders were necessary for my personal growth. I required silence and time at first while I found my feet, but you mortals do have a natural urge to tell others of their experiences. I needed anonymity back then, but things have changed.'

'In what way...?' Harvey probed.

'Your turn now Mr Cooper...how is Alex, still having nightmares?'

'Not anymore no. He's sorted his head out by sharing the problem and halving the load, as we mortals do.'

'With people like you...?'

'Yes.'

'And your lovely wife Florence...? There was almost a hiss as Jay spoke her name. '...and confused Rhian...and her little boy Samuel.'

There was no surprise at the Glitch knowing of his associates, Harvey already knew Emma had given up the names of the group in exchange for a chance to shoot the monster, but it shook him to hear them come from its mouth, especially his wife's name.

'It's a shame about Emma...' The Glitch continued. '...but then again if you will go around firing guns at lover's heads...'

'...Lovers?'

Initially he was taken aback by that pronouncement but the longer it played in his mind the more it made sense. That was the reason the Glitch had remained overnight at her flat, it was why she'd come to the station, leaving it there, safe in the knowledge it wouldn't leave before she went back to shoot it. Suddenly Harvey could see her complete thought process coming into light. The whole scenario had been to gain its trust. Emma had taken the ultimate risk in hope of ending its threat. It was also why she hadn't told him the complete truth, doubting he would have understood her plan and maybe he wouldn't have, but he did now and it pained him to know how brave and sacrificial she'd been to save the rest of them.

'Oh you didn't know about the lovers part Harvey...?' The Glitch asked patronisingly.

The Inspector thought quickly then reacted impulsively. '...Of course I knew. It was me that told her to do it...it was a direct order in fact.'

With this lie Harvey accepted he was crawling right out to the end of the plank, out where the air is thin and rarefied, now looking down at the bottomless ocean, the place where ones blood grows cold because there's no turning back. Did he really think he could get away with this? Was such a gamble going to be accepted or called out? It was a hell of a risk to take, bluffing at the table with the highest stakes possible. His only justification for this deadly folly based on the assumption an experienced player such as the Glitch would see such a move as irrational and weak, prompting it to move in with intent to crush its opponent, so in truth it was another trick of Harvey's to glimpse what cards the Glitch was holding

'So you're saying she was following your direct orders?' Jay's face enquired with a sneer, the Glitch's sneer.

'Yes...'

'Well...' That sneer slowly twisted into a low sinister chuckle. '...then let me tell you that she followed your command to the letter.'

Those words hit Harvey hard although the feeling was of no great surprise, he couldn't expect to poke a wasp's nest without getting stung. At this moment however and more important than the pain, was the fact the Glitch believed him. He'd managed to slide a lie into their exchange and have it accepted as true, gaining him a few more moments to think, hopefully keeping him alive to play another hand. From this small success Harvey wondered what else he could say to deceive this demigod. But any thoughts of future deception were about to change, for the worse.

'Harvey...!' The teenager's mouth spoke but the voice was far deeper and altered. A vicious growl lay beneath the pronunciation of his name and Jay's teeth gnashed hard as his eyes rolled back displaying just the whites. 'I have had enough of listening to this...!' It bellowed.

Harvey's initial response on hearing the new voice was to let his own mouth fall open. He began to wonder why this change should be, but to such a deductive mind there should be no amazement as everything has a reason. Slickened pathways of logic and order began their dance in his head; first to play back what had been said and how, which is where the clues reside.

The Glitch had mentioned changes, improvements no less, but what changes apart from fixing Jay up. Slowly at first before rapidly increasing in number and fervour the floating fragments of facts were reassembled in his head. This is what the Inspector lived for, his greatest gift in life and the reason he existed in any world.

Finally those calculations began to focus in on a fractured trail. Gently filling in the cracks of doubt until he created a smooth plane of truth, a road made of evidential layers that he could walk down confidently. It answered the question of why Jay Cleaver had committed such heinous atrocities against his parents. The boy was out of control but that had been a step too far in brutality. The sickness involved in committing those acts couldn't have come from his heart. It had to be from an older, more ancient type of beast; a Demon no less.

So it transpired with this particular supposition in place that everything else became evident. On the night of his escape from the facility, Jay Cleaver, most likely unknowingly, had been the one to leave carrying the Demon. Which also explained how he'd fallen off the radar so easily, concealing himself under the city with other desperate souls and he'd guess very close to where the corpse of a certain Snake Hornblower had been discovered.

Of course just how the transference of the Glitch to Jay and the Demon happened would have to remain a mystery for now. Harvey had a more pressing problem, how to remain composed. This wasn't the time for presenting shock or alarm which would only convey weakness. He had to make it appear that no part of this discovery was of great concern.

'Ha... well if it isn't the Angel Metatron's Demon...' He proclaimed in his calming Inspectors voice '...It doesn't surprise me that you're still involved with all this, in fact it makes perfect sense.'

'I don't really care for your thoughts Cooper. I'd much prefer to snap your scrawny neck.'

'Do it then, I won't try and stop you.'

Jay didn't move, his eye sockets were perfectly white causing Harvey to wonder if the boy was actually able to see during this physical expression of blindness, so for a definite answer he reached down slowly towards the bottom drawer.

'What do you think you're doing? Put your hands on the desk where I can see them...'

THE RED FRAME

This concisely answered Harvey's query and also gave the direction this meeting was going to take. A continued battle of wits it would be, albeit with an altogether cruder mind than the abruptly absent Glitch.

'So what now, huh Demon, a teaming up, a pooling of resources...or did you all get together by chance...?' Harvey remained seated with his hands flat on the desk.

No expression crossed Jay's stony face as the Demon replied. 'You still believe in chance after all you have seen and heard? If that is the case then you are the one who is truly blind. I am not here to answer your pointless mortal questions or to ask them. My role is to deliver the message.'

'Then deliver it...I have work to be getting on with.' Harvey sat back in his chair feigning composure.

'We are the old and new revelations, the triumvirate. We shall teach you and the rest of your kind there is no more hope!'

'The...what...?' Harvey asked intentionally breaking the sentence down into two constituent parts for derisive purposes. '...Triumvirate, like the three stooges?'

With a whip crack the Demon put Jay's hands to Harvey's throat and began to squeeze as it spoke.

'Do not choose to mock us...It is such an extremely hazardous thing to do. Don't you see what has happened Cooper, the perfect evolution. Together we shall wipe out this world before we move on.'

'Is that right, I think I might take some convincing on that one.' Harvey replied as best he could with Jay's fingers pressing his windpipe.

'Oh that convincing will be the greatest of pleasures for me. First the people of this city will burn as its buildings crumble to dust...we shall glory in the screams of...'

Harvey interrupted again sharply, the grip on his throat awfully persuasive in its effect that he had nothing to lose. '...I'm sorry Demon. I don't want to hear any more boastful threats, they won't work with me. I've already seen too much...and in case it's slipped your mind I deal in facts based on evidence. It's from those I'll judge your character and intentions...and from what I've learned so far, you are nothing more than a killer of innocent people, mainly women alone at night, while all the time hiding in the mind of a helpless taxi driver who was a good man...'

Harvey was suddenly yanked upwards and out of his seat, his breath taken by the furious crush of being lifted by the throat. Worryingly he could also tell this was taking no effort at all for his attacker. '...Another show of strength...is that all you can do...shake people about?'

The Inspector was lifted two feet above the floor, his face reddening from the pressure but he was still managing to stay in control, until the Demon showed its true nature and carried its prey to the open window. Shockingly Harvey's knees were the only part of his body still in touch with the building, the back of them, pressed against the windowsill, with his struggling feet resisting any attempt to kick his assailant, while the rest of his body hung outside the building. There was no doubt it would be a mortally unwise decision to upset or unbalance the Demon at the moment. Complete control lay in those hands, holding Harvey's life in the balance, high above the busy street below.

'Ready to die for your insolence now...?'

'...I just wanted to see what you'd do...and guess what...no surprises.' Harvey was struggling to force his words out through the tightening grip as his whole world began turning black.

'No Cooper, open those frightened eyes...' The Demon whispered. '...I want to show you something.'

The sunlight was almost blinding as Harvey looked up, squinting at a sight he'd never expected to see up close, the outside of his office walls. Then slowly, carefully, the Demon removed its hand from Harvey's throat and took a grip of his shirt and tie, balling it up into its fist. One hand now took all Harvey's weight and allowed the other to be free to gesticulate as it continued its whispering. 'I hope this shirt of yours is good quality cloth. It would be so disappointing if this tore and you fell from my grip through misfortune. I want there to be nothing accidental about your death.'

'Jesus Christ...!' Harvey spluttered while staring into the whites of the Demons rolled back eyes.

'Oh he won't help you...he couldn't even save himself?'

Even now on this precipice of life or death, Harvey managed to find a positive in the situation. At least he was being dangled face up, meaning he didn't have to look down on the street, which gave him some little solace as the Demon taunted his helplessness some more.

'I shall explain to your wife exactly how you looked when I let you go. I shall describe it in detail just before I kill her.'

'No...stop...for Chri...'

At that moment the Demon let go, leaving Harvey to feel the ridiculous unhelpfulness of air, as he began his descent.

20

One index finger connected to his only arm, gently, almost lovingly, tapped the cheek of its one true friend.

'Hey sleepyhead...' Alex said mostly apologetically.

'Huh...?' Juliet floated out her response on a withering groan.

'...The kettle is on but there's no bread, some of it was green so I'm afraid toast is off the menu.'

Her eyes weren't prepared to fully open yet but her mind was ready to discuss breakfast business even though it was late afternoon. 'Go to the bloody shop then.' She sleepily requested.

'I don't know where the bloody shop is...and I don't have any money to hand...' Alex replied, simply stating facts.

'Just go to the shop Graham...!'

A slightly uncomfortable pause occurred. '...Erm it's actually me, Alex.'

With the moderate shock sinking in Juliet managed to open one eye. This confirmed another surprising thing, she was fully awake therefore the dream she'd had about Alex's return was actual fact, because his sheepish smile was looming over her. 'Why the fuck are you sitting on my bed?' She demanded to know on opening her other eye.

'Erm huh...I'm not sure...I think it was the best angle to tap your face from.' This feeling of being busted for some creepy crime was remarkably strong. Although he knew he hadn't done anything wrong he felt it best to keep the rest of the conversation light. Juliet's humour was very similar to his own; offbeat dark and quirky being the popular descriptions of what they found funny, but he wasn't completely sure if she was being serious or not right now.

'Well get off it please, Alex. I know you quite well but not that well. You could still be a sexual predator or a pervert...' She stated this with the straightest of faces which was so well delivered it was unsettling to hear.

'What no...I'm not a p...pervert...' He stuttered and stood up straight.

'Prove it then!' She demanded.

'How would I do that...?'

Juliet paused before looking him straight in the eye. '...Go make me a cup of coffee.'

'Will that prove to you I'm not a sexual predator?' Alex asked walking to the door.

'No...but it will prove you're a well-mannered thoughtful one.' Juliet smiled a comically large smile then pulled the duvet up to her nose, using her dark humour in hope of getting just a couple more minutes of sleep.

In the end she managed to nod off for a good ten minutes, largely because Alex still wasn't the fastest at finding things in a strange kitchen. Eventually he located everything he needed then returned to her bedroom with a cup of coffee in a green and white football shaped mug. To prove he was polite and well-meaning he wanted to knock the door before entering, but as happened a thousand times a day in his life, he once more realised he was short in that department if he was holding anything. So with mug in one hand and no other hand available to knock he just pushed it open with his shoulder. 'Your morning cuppa my lady...!'

Juliet awoke utterly amazed that in those brief moments of slumber there had been time for such a vivid dream. Clear as day she could recall every emotional moment her subconscious had shown her.

In the dream she'd been moving gradually towards Alex who was stood on the middle of a stone bridge. Maybe she was walking normally but she could just as easily have been floating forwards like a spirit; such are the eternal mysteries of dreams. He was stood still looking over the side of the bridge so she followed suit to discover the river bed was nothing but dry and dusty soil. As she got closer to him there was something about his appearance which confused her, it was slightly altered. Suddenly her heart leapt with joy as she discerned the change, he was complete with two whole arms. Juliet had wanted to run to him, to share a whole hug, but this dream would only move at a ponderous glide. Slowly but surely she got to within touching distance then reached out her hand. On noticing her movement Alex jumped up to stand on the stone wall, clearly an attempt to keep some distance between them, unhappy at her presence. Juliet could still remember the sadness and frustration at this rejection. She'd tried to cry out, to get him down from the ledge but no sound was created. All she was allowed to do was watch transfixed at the sickening image of what happened next, when Alex turned away from her gaze and fell forward, his perfect body hurtling down towards the dry river bed. Another scream was attempted by Juliet but still it was muted, almost as if she didn't have a voice in this world. All she could do was feel the painful agony of loss and heartbreak. The message that was coming through so blatant in its meaning; there was no way she could save Alex.

Juliet didn't wake up at this point as one may expect; instead she'd remained on the empty bridge trying to link metaphors, both visual and emotional, whilst still being within the dream. It was such a beautiful lucid sorrow that she could remain within this state, yet be able to contemplate it from the outside at the same time. As she considered the events her hand moved forward to feel the cold stone of the wall. Where it rested a small pure white spider crawled out from a hole before settling, unmoving, on her knuckle. Juliet had always had what she believed to be a perfectly rational fear of spiders but on this occasion she didn't flinch. Then a rumble began somewhere below her feet, growing in its ferocity until the thunderous roar of an oncoming storm filled her senses. A chilled panic rose within her chest as the noise became deafening then abruptly stopped. Slowly Alex appeared rising up from over the edge, his eyes fixed on hers, and arms spread wide, while behind him two huge white wings were beating like a pumping heart.

'I've put two sugars in...I couldn't remember what you said'

As Juliet was spat out of the drowsing memories of the dream rather rudely, with more questions than answers, she checked her hand but the spider was gone. Then her one armed friend came into focus.

'Are you okay?' He asked curiously as he put the mug down on the bedside table.

'What...yes of course.' She sounded shaky even to herself. 'I was having a weird dream.'

'Hey I know all about those.'

'I don't want to talk about mine though.' She glanced over to see the red digital numbers on her clock radio. 'Why have you woken me up now?'

Alex gave her a pained smile. 'Sorry...I was getting a bit lonely.'

'You'll be even lonelier when I kick you out.'

'Fair point...' He agreed before carrying on regardless. '...but I need more of what you give me...'

'Sorry?' Juliet raised herself up to a sitting position and sipped her tea.

'It's what you said before...about this path or timeline being the one we should be on...it really made me think. You always do that, you allow me to see things differently...I really need to talk with you about what's happening...for everything to make sense.'

With all his long pauses Juliet had swigged the mug half empty by the time he reached the end of his speech. 'I'm happy you feel that way Alex. It shows you're opening up to new possibilities and not getting bogged down with it all, feeling trapped, because who knows what the future holds...'

'Absolutely, we switched tracks to follow a new future and like you said what if that is exactly what was supposed to happen.'

'I'm sorry are you agreeing with me? I don't understand.' Juliet sipped a little more.

'Look, the day everything changed was only possible because of me and what I did, but I understand now that it wasn't my fault...and realising that I'm not particularly special, or vital to it occurring, has released me to see the bigger picture.'

Juliet interrupted politely but firmly. 'Alex please, I've just woken up after not as much sleep as I needed...'

'Again I'm sorry about waking you early, I'm sorry I'm using you for my thoughts and confidence in dealing with this problem but please let me explain. I know I didn't cause this, but I also know for certain I'm the only one who can stop it. To do that I'll need help and whether you like it or not, you're my only true world saving assistant...'

Juliet finished her tea, gently put the mug down and cleared her throat before replying. 'Piss off Alex!'

'I can't, if I could leave you out of this I would, but it's too late. We both know the truth...there's another life we should be living...'

'That sounds like the weirdest marriage proposal in history?' She said jokingly to break the tension of this moment.

'Marriage proposal...you're hilarious.' He sniggered uncomfortably.

'And you're the craziest man I've ever met, but if it counts for anything I want to believe you.'

'Of course it counts...it's absolutely essential. Do you want to hear something even stranger?'

'Why not...' She shrugged.

'There's no need for me to even be doing this...I'm wasting my breath right now because I already know you'll help me; so all this is actually pointless because our future is already written on the other timeline...and in that future there is every chance we never met.'

'Oh great, now I'm really confused...and a little sad.'

'I can explain. Get comfy...'

'I'm lying in my bed Alex, trust me life doesn't get any comfier than this...'

'Fair point...well made.' He took a deep breath and began pacing the room building up to his big reveal. 'So the dreams I've been having and worrying about are just another layer to keep me from finding the answer. It's all a riddle...'

'Call it what you like Alex but people have died because of this riddle.'

'No, no they haven't, only here in this perception of reality, but it isn't where we should be. I can repair this; change everything back to how it was before I fell from the roof...but to do that I'll need your help.'

Juliet couldn't imagine what type of assistance she could provide while working sixty hours a week at the care home. 'What do you need from me...?' She asked with a heavily disguised sigh.

This was the moment he'd waited for and the main reason why he had left the Coopers house to find her, only now it was here he suddenly felt self-conscious, a little immature and downright scared.

'Well?' She pushed for his answer.

'I need you to trust me...completely.'

'What the hell are you talking about now?' Juliet just wished he'd get to his point, but when he finally did so, she instantly wished he hadn't.

Alex reached over and took her hand. 'Jools...I need you...to help put me back into a coma...'

At that suggestion Juliet got up and out of bed without another word. Instead she went into the small kitchen and began to busy herself filling the washing machine with crumpled uniforms while trying to forget, or at least ignore, Alex's bizarre proposal.

However he wasn't for letting it slide and after a couple of minutes he started on it again. 'Please don't think for one second I don't appreciate the technical difficulty or risks involved in returning me to a coma.'

She didn't reply again, just checked some trouser pockets before putting them in the machine.

'I know it can be done.' Alex was speaking from the kitchen table and gesturing with his arm. 'I've looked it up...and...'

She couldn't take anymore. '...Oh you've looked it up have you...well I doubt you read into it too deeply...' Juliet flashed him a look. '...because if you had you'd know it's extremely dangerous and a last resort to save people who would almost certainly die without it. For crying out loud Alex this is without doubt the stupidest thing you have ever said. The process involves seriously heavy-duty drugs administered over a particular amount of time with meticulous monitoring of the patients vital signs. I mean for god's sake how on earth do you even imagine I could help with something like that...?'

He considered her question before awkwardly replying. 'You worked in a hospital.'

'Oh my god I retract my last statement, we have a new leader in the stupidest thing you've ever said category. Why you would even want to try something as dangerous as that?'

Alex hadn't fully considered the reasoning behind the why, believing that to be a given he'd been solely focused on the how; how he could put himself in a better position to fix what was broken. 'It seemed the only way...' He muttered. His focus suddenly falling away to someplace lost and distant as a first hint of defeat crossed his horizon. '...When I was in there I could do things to make a difference, without it I'm helpless...just a one armed man spouting stories...'

'...Oh will you shut up!' She snapped. 'There is one thing I won't accept from you and that's negativity. You want my help well here I am, but don't expect any sympathy or mollycoddling because that's what I do as a job. When I'm at home things are different. If you want to stay here you have to pull your weight and that means staying positive. Anything else and you can walk out that door right now.'

'...Jesus Juliet!'

She made a conscious effort to calm down, but there was no way she could ease off on the pressure. This strange man who fell into her life a year and a half ago with his tales of another world needed to learn. In her medical experience he was constantly one step from falling into the abyss of clinical depression, so while he remained safely on his ledge of normality she would help, but if he chose to give in then she would have to let him fall. What would be the point of trying to support someone who didn't want to be assisted?

'Look Alex I don't know what you want from me. You need someplace to stay I can do that, you need a friend who trusts and believes in you, I'm that person, but I am not a sympathy blanket. You enjoy being with me because I give you a different way of looking at things and that's great, but all I'm doing is to try and care for you, so while that's working then I'm not going to change, but I'm afraid most of the heavy work in solving your problem remains with you.'

By the time she'd finished her truth sermon, Alex was head down on the table. To some it could look like the pose of a defeated man but he wasn't beaten yet, after all he was still undefeated in this life or any other. He had faced up to death with his suicide attempt and survived, spent time with a twisted Angel, fought its blackened Demon and here he was still fighting. Once again it was Juliet who'd raised that spirit within him.

'Okay...no coma, but there must be another way.' Slowly he raised that lowered head.

'There had better be another way...you dick!'

Alex's smile reappeared as he saw her eyes sparkle, this real life angel raising his spirits once more, always there every time he fell.

'So what was that rubbish about us never meeting if we go back?' She asked.

He'd tried to gloss over that part but it was still a hurtful fact, as in his mind he'd imagined he could fix the problem by never falling from the ledge in the first place, that somehow he'd get back there and convince Jay Cleaver to save him this time, of course if that happened he wouldn't meet Juliet because he'd never be in a coma under her care.

'Yeah I'm not happy about that part.' He said and heaved a sigh.

'Oh I don't know. It would make my life a lot easier, not worrying about you every second.'

Alex sadly nodded his agreement.

'Oh my god I'm joking...!'

'...Yeah but you're probably right.' He said.

'No I'm really not, because I wouldn't change a single second of what we've been through together. Let me tell you something else which I think might help explain why you put so much faith in me. You say I always give you a different perspective on things, so if that's true then here's another one, I want you to know that if we do escape this and end up back we started, in a world where we might never meet, I can accept that because we had a wonderful time in this one.'

'I think wonderful might be too strong a word Joolz. It's been a fucking nightmare.'

She turned sharply at his words and came over to the table, with Alex expecting another talking to for being negative, but instead she placed both her hands on his cheeks before kissing him full on the mouth.

'Oh...!' He said as she released her hold.

'Is it still a fucking nightmare...?'

He took a breath before answering,

'It really isn't.'

His mind was whirling around, just like it used to when the Angel forced him out of the book in the white world, only this time he didn't want the spinning to end.

21

Back in a brightly sunlit office at the police station Harvey's concerns about his looming demise were being simultaneously minimised and maximised by the words coming out of Jay Cleavers mouth. The Glitch was back in control of the body again, once more taking the reins of this one headed, three souled, monster and calmly suggesting that everything would be fine, such sentiments a lot easier to say when you haven't been the one hanging out a fourth storey window.

For now the Inspector's feet and more importantly the rest of him were standing safely back on his office carpet. His body though was stunned into a shivering silence, almost completely overwhelmed, as he relived the last few seconds of his life. Recalling how just as the Demon released its grip the Glitch had come to the rescue, grabbing his wrist and yanking him back to safety. Of course in this instance the exact definition of the word 'safety' had never been more malleable or relative, seeing as he was still listening to the Glitch, alone and scared.

'Now Mr Cooper you have me to thank for your continuing life. I am quite sure you appreciate my alter egos would happily have you dead, but now is not the time. A splattered mess on the street is not your demise in my eyes. I believe I can see a bigger picture, a blind faith that you have a significant role to play in ending this ultimately futile chase.' Jay Cleavers mouth half smiled as the Glitch spoke. 'You see my friend...'

'I am not your fucking friend...!' A wild spray of spittle came out with Harvey's uncharacteristic profanity. The effort seeming to take the last of his strength as his knees buckled and he dropped to the carpet, nerves trembling throughout. '...Get out of my office!'

The Glitch gazed down upon his pleading quarry, noting the Inspector's thin greying hair, the liver spots on his forehead and it almost felt a little sympathy for the fragility of humankind.

Inside Jay Cleavers consciousness the Glitch had developed further, no longer feeling like a stranger in a strange land, its evolution towards its totality of purpose gaining speed and strength with every passing hour. Only this time its infinite growth was different, quite unlike all its other incarnations. The most striking part of its progression could be put down to experiencing something new...compassion. A deeply strange emotion the Glitch didn't want or require but one always given so freely by its mortal hosts. This incongruity of a feeling was interesting as it displayed the fullest of spectrums when it came to good and evil, constantly demonstrating how these mortals were as deeply loving as they were shallow and hateful.

Such insights were allowing the Glitch to understand its own purpose; it could just as easily have been created as a virus or an asteroid, a mighty flood or a storm of locusts, because its objective would still have been the same, to destroy everything that lay before it.

In the end this Glitch was the wrath, the judgement, the universal cleansing mechanism to take away the old and make space for the new. Frustratingly though its job description often came across as being something biblical, what else could explain the existence of this destroyer of worlds; but that was far from the case. The Glitch hated Angels, finding their kind unworthy of the prodigious powers bestowed upon them. They were moody and self-righteous in the extreme, constantly at war with every other race and each other; hardly a plus point for any self-appointed supreme beings.

Having this depth of sentiment towards others and an understanding of itself was utterly unique to the Glitch. The very definition of this beast was to be an arbitrary force, its simple mission to cleanse the universe when called upon, when the conditions were right, or as in this case, when something had gone wrong.

The elements that made this wrath so different from its apocalyptic predecessors were not only its self-awareness, but the early stages of its upbringing. Its first experience of life had been as a conceptual gateway, no more than an imagining in an Angel's mind, only for it to be then affected, tainted first by a Demon then a Mortal. From that moment forward its path was set. It would never evolve as an inanimate force of nature, so floods and pestilence would not become its garbs. Really why become a hurtling frozen asteroid when it had the possibility of achieving the rarest of gifts, an actual life?

All of this thoughtful assessment took place over a few seconds as it looked down on the stricken Inspector Cooper.

Then suddenly and to its great surprise the Glitch was pushed hard from behind causing it to stumble forward. Although this didn't occur physically in the real world Harvey did notice a subtle change in Jay's posture. To the Inspector's eye it appeared as if the teenager was having some inner turmoil, even if he had no idea of how correct that assumption was.

The Glitch couldn't comprehend at first what had happened; it owned no solid form in this place so how could it be feeling as if it were face down on the ground.

Then the grim voice of the Demon roared. 'Why did you do it?'

'Do what?' The Glitch replied still shocked by this turn in proceedings.

'Interrupt me in my work...Cooper is dangerous. He needs to die!'

'And what good would that serve?'

'It would serve me...'

'Then I'll ask again, what good would that serve?'

There followed a brief pause where the Glitch could only suppose the Demon was actually thinking on the question, trying to come up with some grim answer to prove its point, but in the end what it came up with was both disappointing and predictable.

'You are not in control here. This host is mine. I saved you.'

The Glitch resolved it had a few routes to go down now; it could play dumb, play clever, or play the waiting game, in the end choosing its favourite option. 'You did save me...so in return I will concede you are correct...Cooper should be dead.'

'Then move out my way so I can crush his skull and throw his body out of the window.'

'No, you won't be doing that. I have an altogether more satisfying demise in mind.' The Glitch was choosing its words carefully; still perplexed this conversation was actually taking place. '...but first of all I need to ask you a question...you physically pushed me aside...yet I don't have a body inside here and as far as I know neither do you. How did you do that?'

The Demon roared with a hearty laughter before answering with menace '...I can do it because you don't know everything. You have muddled through your young life, sparing no thought for the years I have spent in these mortal minds where I have dug deep to understand the secrets of how they work...learning their little tricks, their ways. I may explain them to you one day...but then again I may not, as a punishment for believing you can take over this body whenever you choose, without my permission. This is a not a shared space where everything is equal, this is a refuge, one that I offered to you. So do not abuse my gift or think for one second that I'm a lesser being. I have taken many lives using this method and it is my will to take many more, because my purpose is defined.'

The Glitch didn't respond, interested to hear the Demon's thoughts.

'You don't even know what you are yet, like a child with a million ideas that you don't understand, just a formless consciousness struggling to find your place in the grand scheme of things. I know you will move on from here when you've had enough, when you believe it's time for something better, but until then you have to accept being pushed around if you make me unhappy, especially when you interrupt my work and needs. So if you want your stay here to be pleasant then understand your position, because this is my world...and you don't know everything!'

As the Glitch silently listened to the Demons outburst it began to feel something new, an uncomfortable emotion, one undoubtedly coming from its unique affinity with the human condition, feeling the shame of those facing a reasonable rebuke. The words had a ring of truth because the Glitch was undoubtedly in its admonisher's environment, a stark fact that meant it had to be careful. After considering its options it offered up a gentle and controlled response, there being no point in upsetting an already angry beast.

The Glitch stood its metaphysical non-existent body back upright.

'You are correct in your conjecture. I have no desire to stay here any longer than I have to. This is your world of that I have no doubt, but I have new gifts I could teach you...'

'...Is that so?' The Demon growled.

'Absolutely...after all we are on the same page when it comes to killing Harvey Cooper, but reading totally different books when it comes down to how that may be achieved. Shall I explain my method?'

'You can try...'

The Glitch really didn't need the Demon's approval for it to continue.

'Excellent, now you and I are sharing a common purpose though our techniques may differ. For instance you were created to destroy mortals and to do that as constantly and quickly as you can. It is to be admired that your particular bloodlust is so insatiable, in all honesty I believed that was the only path for me to take when I began, but as I grow I find there are ways and means much more satisfying than simple swift brutality.'

'It doesn't matter how...only that it is done.' The Demon reasoned bluntly.

'Oh but it does matter. It matters to me and I can assure you it matters greatly to the victim. I have already killed in many ways but the explosion of that bomb was by far the most intoxicating.'

'How, it was over in seconds and you were nowhere near the victims, what's your point...?'

'Isn't my point perfectly clear? It was never about the ones blown to pieces, much more about those who survived with horrible injuries, the mutilated ones who will suffer the most. The poor hearts that will have the rest of their hours and days to savour what I have done, those families forced to pray their loved ones will pull through. I created such a beautiful and intricate torment...' The Demon grunted derisively but the Glitch wasn't finished yet. '...It's all about time you see, your form of killing is instant gratification and it has its...moment, but when that feeling has gone you must search for more, another hit, another high, not unlike our dabbling with drugs. Which is finished with by the way, there will be no more cocaine ingested by Jay, no need to endanger our host's body any further.'

'This body is mine...I will do as I choose with it!'

'...Yes it is...although it has to be said you never interfered when I fixed it and improved its physical capabilities far beyond your range, went about removing the scars and deformities you kept hidden beneath a scarf. Tell me Demon, would you like me to return this body to how it was...?' The silence that met the question reeked of despair so the Glitch played its trump card. '...So yes you are right, I will move on when I'm ready. How soon that happens of course is not your choice, but the condition I leave this body in...well that part is. All of this ties together neatly the point I'm trying to make you understand. We are different entities and I have no care for your endeavours but I do wish to show you how I work when it comes to killing. You think of yourself as some mighty vengeful Demon but you are a nothing more than a caveman wielding a club, a monkey hitting a drum, while my subtle techniques are more akin to an orchestra conductor with a baton. We are nothing alike and it is this beautiful variant that allows me to fully appreciate the carnage that I can unleash. Let us take Cooper's imminent death as a prime example; you would throw him out of the window, undoubtedly killing him and yes that would be the end of the problem, but I believe such a course of action to be risky, pointless, but above all else...unimaginative.'

'He has to die!' The Demon howled.

'And he will.'

'Now...!'

'Not now...soon...but instead of him passing in an instant he will endure and think on us every second of his mortal ending. Our Inspector Harvey Cooper will die helplessly knowing we have taken everything he holds dear, living through the agony as we tear his world apart, while praying to whatever god he serves that his life could be over...now that my friend is true vengeance.'

Harvey was watching Jay closely, the boy hadn't moved for a full minute, but it felt longer and was becoming a desperate and confusing situation. The Inspector was trapped between a rock and a high place, quite literally, with this ongoing silence causing peculiar thoughts of how he may try to escape; even the open window didn't seem to be entirely out of the equation, almost seeming to beckon him to jump through it, reasoning that with such a selfish action he could stop this fear, forget all thoughts of guilt or concern, to blessedly be at peace.

Now a suicide so similar to that which started this chain of events was on offer, as if everything that had occurred since that day on Dalmeny Street was leading him to this place, close to a lonely frightening precipice where the darkest of tendencies manifested themselves as hopeful options. Only Harvey Cooper wasn't cut from the same cloth as Alex Webb. They weren't built the same way because to this Police Inspector giving up was never an option.

22

Inside the mind of a young boy an Angel walked slowly through those fresh clean corridors. On its travels so far it had discovered many messed up rooms of memories. The winged deity thought upon why this should be considering mortals value their life's recollections so highly, but maybe nothing of the past is that precious to a ten year old, not when there is always a bright new tomorrow to be lived.

As it strolled through the inner workings of young Samuel Sangers mind, trying once more to find some logical answers, it replayed the parts it deemed significant and to do this it had to begin with its own journey to find some true purpose.

Metatron was nothing more than a fallen Angel now, perhaps not in the classical sense but certainly in how far it had plunged from its once lofty perch in the heavens. Up in the white world it had ruled completely, albeit alone and deserted by its fellow Angels, until the surprising arrival of Alex Webb. After that mortal suddenly appeared all of its carefully laid plans had gone to hell, the whole situation spiralled away from its control, finishing with a face off that almost led to its death. None of it made sense to Metatron. It understood how the human had gained access to the white world. A trillion to one chance of hitting the cobbles on Dalmeny Street at precisely the moment a quantum sized glitch had passed underneath. A glitch that Metatron had placed in the life machines workings for its Demon to pass through. So yes it could accept such a freak accident might occur but what followed afterward, right up to this current second, was still unfathomable.

It was an uncomfortable fact to the Angel Metatron that it/he was created when a mortal named Enoch ascended to heaven. This was an incredible journey and honour for the man to be bestowed the eternal gift of an angelic presence, but for the Angel it made life difficult.

This diversified route into the Heaven meant it would never be as pure as its holy brethren, so simple trusts were always an issue during the centuries of war between Angels and Mortals. Still despite this Metatron rose to sit at Gods right hand where it was appointed to the anointed position of celestial scribe, the recording Angel, the one who shall take tally of the merits and sins of mankind. This honoured task made Metatron, on papyrus at least, the greatest of all Angels, the guardian of heavenly secrets and Gods own mediator with men.

THE RED FRAME

As with many high powered professions in the world still today, what Metatron actually did in its role was ridiculously simple. Its only physical duty in the once mighty heavens was to occasionally open the book of records. Then with its red leather covers gaping wide like an attacking shark it would feed by itself, gorging upon the very molecules of the universe surrounding it and devouring the information that is held within all matter. Every infinitesimal piece of data it gathered would then be reassembled, classified and systemized into the nature of its pages, creating the book of knowledge.

It was a tome the Angels could never read because its secrets belonged to God, a sentient being they had never met, but keeping a heavenly faith in its existence was all important, as it was on earth.

The Angel Metatron, being so high up the chain of command and with the freedom to study all areas of heaven, believed it knew the answer to where their Supreme Being resided, but discerning it would be a painful truth for the other Angels to hear, Metatron kept quiet at first because well, God was dead; dead to this universe at least after it had grown bored with its creation.

This ever expanding, ever cooling universe was something akin to the end of a firework display, where everything builds up to the biggest of bangs, everybody goes 'Whoop!' then trundles off home. If that were the case then maybe God left to go make ever greater pyrotechnics elsewhere, someplace blank and quiet, somewhere with a clean slate.

Eventually, because of the way he was treated and mistrusted by the massed ranks of pure Angels, Metatron had disclosed his thoughts about Gods whereabouts during a fiery disagreement with them. The effect was immediate, the sound of flapping wings almost deafening as the heavenly coop took flight, a million Angels soaring up and away into the white sky never to return.

Metatron had been judged unworthy and left alone in the white world, which could no longer be called heaven, as no pure beings remained, so instead it became nothing more than a vast prison for this lonely mongrel in the pack. For millennia the white world contained a solitary Angel, one who couldn't leave, with nowhere to go even if it could, and the red leather bound book. Metatron still continued to open that cover on occasion as its duty required but the rest of its existence was pointless. It was during these barren years that two mighty upheavals occurred in Metatron's life, one it was unaware of, while the other it denied. Firstly its name was all but obliterated from the holy texts, only referenced briefly in the Jewish Talmud and Aggadah writings, while never being mentioned at all in either the Torah or the Bible. Such a brutal cancelling of its identity was almost certainly the reason behind the second upheaval to befall it, when Metatron, who had been once the highest of all Angels, found itself going utterly insane.

Of course acute madness is rarely recognised by the sufferer, especially when the root cause of that madness is living a life of solitary confinement. With no one there to notice changes in behaviour or thought patterns dark psychosis can become deeply ingrained to the point all previous sensibilities are forgotten, an infected mind will be forced to spend its time playing on repeat all of its new and bizarre theories, its fears and of course its prejudices. Because of this Metatron became obsessed with the ancient war on mankind, for those upright apes were surely the reason of its loneliness and pain, if it hadn't once lived as a mortal man then it imagined its existence would have been perfect, a heavenly life shared with much love and respect from its perfect equals.

Slowly more millennia passed by for this crazy Angel as it wandered the white world, creating fake scenarios of countless landscapes in which to spend its lonely life, while trying to fight the urge that was growing, an idea sparking in the kindling of aged dried out thoughts. Under such conditions it didn't take too long for the flame to catch, its mind beginning to burn up in a furious firestorm of revenge where it would make all mortals pay. The only question was how to achieve it, what did it have in this place of limbo to hurt them with?

The plan of placing its vengeance within the book had begun like most ideas, perfect in theory but a mystery in practice. To the Angel the book was empty, each blank page a story to be written, but the question remained of by what means to do it. There were no writing materials in the vast white void, the scenes and environments it created, the ocean's and jungles were of no use, they weren't real, only imagined paintings on a blank canvas to help change a mood.

Its sadness grew heavier as it looked upon the inexplicable open book, a mocking tome which had become the bane of its being, the remaining chance to have a voice once more.

Metatron lived through the agony of the eighth deadly sin, the one cut from the final edit of all religious doctrine for no good reason, the sin of accepting or causing frustration to thyself or thy neighbour. It had always thought of this law as a vital lesson to follow, the act of frustration having caused countless problems in a myriad of worlds, the bringer of so much heartache and death.

The Angel could do no more than observe the red covers, cursing the unseen knowledge inside them, wishing it damage and damning it to hell.

It was this last wish that finally opened the door to answer its prayers. There was a method of defacement, clear as day, by which the Angel could cause it damage. It already owned the writing implement with which to do so and furthermore it had the ink, the solution literally at these fingertips.

Its perfect angelic hands opened the book fully causing the pages to fall down into two equal halves, but for a single leaf, the middle one that it held stiffly between forefinger and thumb. Metatron glared at the thin edge of the page, sure that with the right pressure and resistance it could make a tiny slash, one that would bleed. As it drew its finger across the blade of the single page the microscopically uneven teeth of the paper bit through easily, opening up the skin, releasing the red ink.

In that exact moment Metatron knew it could still change its mind, the consequences of this action were unknowable, but this only made it more furious as it spat forth its wish, hoping a drop of Angel's blood would be enough to grant it.

With a tiny splat the blood hit the blank page where it made a perfect crimson dot that slowly started to seep in. The Angel had no more to say now. It had wished for its vengeance to be unleashed on the earth, for it to manifest and carry out its purpose, to kill and never stop killing.

The page soaked up the blood effortlessly, almost ravenously, leaving only a pinkish circular corpse as all the wickedness was consumed into its pulp, but something didn't feel right to the Angel. Even though it remained convinced this wishful thinking could work, an overwhelming feeling of dread slid down its spine, there being no way of predicting exactly what may occur.

To appease its concerns Metatron squeezed another drop from the tip of its finger. It wanted to feel secure about its desires and a quick amendment would help with that. This time it didn't drip blood on the page; instead, pressing its finger down firmly next to the pinkish spot it drew a line, then another, until there were four in total. The original bloodspot surrounded on all sides, encased, in a red frame.

23

Jay's blue eyes burst into focus as they took in his surroundings. He was back in the office, the large window was open and the heat was surprising.

'...What the fuck...?' He exclaimed.

In a flash the Inspector seized this unexpected opportunity, standing up quickly to grab the boy by the shoulders. 'Jay...it's me Harvey...everything's going to be okay...' He thought it odd he should be trying to reason with the young man who'd caused him so many sleepless nights, his nemesis almost, but he should have known better than to place both hands on this particular teenager. Whether he was possessed by other entities or not, this was a stupid move, positively unadvisable in any police handbook and guaranteed to end up with someone getting hurt; predictably this was the Inspector as a blinding flash of agony rapidly evolved into a dark throbbing momentary unconsciousness.

As he started to come round Harvey realised he was back in his chair. The thumping of his forehead sharp and painful which he surmised must have come from a head butt because, although he'd never received one he could well imagine they felt like this. But things were getting worse as he tried to speak but no sound came out, when he tried to breathe no air came in. His throat felt tight, painful, Jesus!

He was being strangled.

'So you wanna talk now you fucking pig...?' Jay's spittle sprayed out onto Harvey's cheek such was the venom in its delivery. On seeing the Inspectors eyes open wide Jay removed his hands from the wind pipe, he didn't want to kill him, not yet. Harvey refilled his lungs and wiped the saliva away.

'...Huh yes I want to talk to you Jay...ask you what...what the hell you think you're doing?'

'Whatever the fuck I want...'

'Whatever they want you mean?'

'Get fucked you don't know nothing. In here...' Jay tapped his temple. '...the three of us are getting on great. I've got everything I ever wanted man...fucking look at me...and I can have loads more of it.' He certainly looked the part of a contented bad man, his sneer shining through, displaying an impressive passion for this new life.

Finally face to face with his young adversary Harvey considered Alex's story, especially the part in the dream book about a teenage boy who had wanted to kill a lion. Now if any of that were true, and given his current situation could he really doubt it, there had been an incident of outrageous coincidence that this boy should now share his headspace with the Glitch, the monster who killed the exact same big cat. Wasn't that all too neat and trimmed to be a chance occurrence, there had to be a deeper link here, a clue to the whole damn thing perhaps? The more Harvey looked at the boy and pondered the riddle, the more it led him in one direction, backwards.

'You're lucky I didn't break your nose you old bastard!'

That discourteous comment failed to distract the Inspector from his thought processes. It would be a rare day indeed that after those synapses exploded into life Harvey could be derailed. Deep behind his bruised forehead some tiny spark had ignited a theory which burst into life with a whoosh. That's how it worked in his brilliant mind, no need to sift through bits and pieces, just set fire to the lot and when everything else is burnt to the ground the truth will be revealed.

Playing over in his head was a message the Angel had told Alex when they were in the white world, a line that Nurse Juliet had scribbled down in his dream book; ignored by everyone, probably because in comparison to the other wild tales it seemed gentle and tame, but Harvey recalled those seven little words from the ashes of his deduction where they screamed to be noticed.

'There are no answers in the past...' He said to himself.

'What...?' Jay asked belligerently.

Harvey knew he'd found something although he didn't know exactly what. '...Nothing...just thinking out loud.'

'You're talking shit...!' The teenager laughed in his face.

'I need to tell you something Jay...but you have to promise me not to tell the others.'

'Fuck off!'

'It's important you listen to me...because one day it may save your life!'

Jay didn't respond to this sage guidance, instead his eyes, perfectly set and aligned once more, gave Harvey a look that filled the Inspectors heart with delight. It was a cognitive moment for the boy, the proof he'd listened to the statement and was seriously considering his options. To Harvey it was another tiny piece of evidence that Jay was still a singularity in all of this. He wasn't a true part of their triumvirate which offered a chink of hope. Jay Cleaver still had a mind of his own, perhaps a mind that could be used when the opportunity arose.

All Harvey needed now was time and space to think. To gain such a small mercy he needed to end this current situation, preferably by not falling out of the window, or being strangled in his own office.

'We have to go...' Jay demanded pulling Harvey up from the chair.

'Where are we going?' Harvey asked, with his mind instantly turning over a hundred different ways of leaving a clue, so anyone wishing to locate him would at least have an idea that he'd exited the building with an undetectable killer.

'We're going to walk down to your car... and don't even think about getting clever. Put your hands in your pockets...' Jay snapped, but then the timbre of his voice changed as the Glitch reasserted control. '...You may not see me Inspector but I will be close by the whole way. Don't make me have to prove it.'

With that warning received loud and clear Harvey grabbed his car keys and opened the door to the reception room.

'Are you off to the hospital now Mr Cooper...?' Roma asked, completely oblivious to the fact that just over her left shoulder the face of Jay Cleaver had appeared, a threatening display to enforce a message this policeman should tread carefully. Harvey would admit to being uncomfortable with the tricks and skills of the Glitch, its speed almost magical to witness as it passed through the room to the far end of the corridor, completely unseen by the secretary, and then with one thin finger it beckoned the Inspector forward.

'Err yes...' Harvey was struggling to remember any other plans he may have had. '...Yes, off to the hospital...I'm heading over there right now. I don't know when I'll be back...so carry on taking messages.'

'Of course Sir...' Roma smiled amiably then swivelled back round to the computer screen.

Harvey knew very well it would be pointless trying to give her a hint of his dilemma, their relationship was far too shallow and green and still an untrusting one. He didn't believe she would pick up on any clues he might try to give, unlike Emma, who would have read his body language easily.

He glanced down the hallway feeling the hard stare of the Glitch burning into his mind, giving him no opportunity to scribble a note or convince this new girl to alert the Superintendent. So with a withering sense of inevitability he walked forward like a good little sacrificial lamb.

It was alarming that he didn't get another clear sight of the monster until he reached his car, as he climbed inside the Glitch instantly appeared on the back seat.

'Good work Mr Cooper. I'm warming to you. Now drive us to the lock up I need to collect something.'

'What lock up...?'

'Oh you know the one.'

'Oscars old lock up?' Harvey asked with a curious brow.

'The very same...now drive!'

For the next twenty minutes as Harvey negotiated his way through the late lunchtime traffic they sat in silence, both beast and man apparently deep in thought but thankfully, for the Inspector at least, totally unaware of the others mental processes.

The driving offered some relief to Harvey's current level of concern, he felt nearly in control again and with the current apparent lack of threat he had vital minutes to consider what he'd discovered.

Jay Cleaver's body was owned, or possessed, by both the Glitch and the Demon. That much was for certain but after Harvey's discreet questioning it was clear all three couldn't be active at the same time. That only one of the personalities was allowed to control the body, demonstrating a distinct separation, naturally led the Inspector to think of the old adage...divide and conquer...but to do that he'd have to plant ideas or demands in each of their minds independently.

Where he would start in that task was blatantly clear, the weakest link of the unholy trinity and therefore Harvey's easiest way in was the young man himself. Although just how a teenage multiple murderer, one who had happily killed before, even endeavouring to oven roast his own mother's decapitated head could ever be considered a weak link, was still up for debate. Nonetheless he was all Harvey had at the moment, so that analytical mind began the calculations of how to bring the boy out of his shell for a sustained period. Assuming that given enough time he could plant some poisoned seeds of distrust, what then, would Jay even listen or understand the danger his teenage life was in, or worst of all, would he even care. It was a fact Jay had never looked or sounded better, it wouldn't be easy to convince the kid to give it all up, meaning this was another long term project that demanded completion in a short term timeframe.

'Obviously....' Harvey muttered under his breath, before turning the car into the small cul-de-sac and pulling up next to the dented shutter of number three.

Quite bizarrely this was a place he'd never stepped inside before, due to the Superintendent's insistence he be kept at arm's length during the hunt for Oscar Downes, so Harvey had only ever seen photographs and reports about this infamous lockup, but those shocking images and words which accompanied the gruesome discoveries made here were still fresh in his mind, although it was only now climbing out of his car that he could feel its dark energy for himself.

Jay in his smart grey suit pulled up the metal door with ease allowing them to enter. Inside it was dark and musty with various bits of scabby furniture scattered around. The space was maybe fifteen feet in length, eight or nine across, with three wooden pallets leant up against the far wall. Harvey immediately recognised that area as the place the five plastic barrels had been positioned, each one three quarter filled with industrial formaldehyde, in some failed attempt at corpse preservation.

Harvey could remember the morning of the discovery, how he'd felt after being denied access to the scene, with the Superintendent ordering him to continue his investigations from the office while so called experts did their work. That had been easily the most frustrating day in his long police career, meaning the closest he'd got to this lockup was interviewing the young lad who'd made the discovery. With that memory forming Harvey had a face palm moment; an obvious detail he'd missed, oh my god, the kid had been called Henry Hornblower. Come on now how many Hornblower's do you know that live in the same area, unrelated? Was that young witness, who'd been so key in the capture of Oscar Downes, Snake Hornblower's younger brother, or was this mischievous twisting universe simply messing him about once more.

'Can I ask you a question?' Harvey enquired.

'You can ask...' The Glitch responded while digging through a hessian sack it had lifted out from behind the pallets.

'Henry Hornblower?' Harvey simply stated the name in hope it would be enough to illicit a response, after all the Glitch knew didn't it?

'Ha ha...yes my previous incarnation's younger sibling. He is becoming quite the tearaway himself now Mr Cooper.' The Glitch stood back up holding a small leather pouch, but before Harvey could query its contents it was placed inside Jay's jacket pocket. 'Don't concern yourself with this, you'll find out what it holds in due course, for now we need to go visiting. Don't worry about that either, it's somewhere you hold dear to your heart. You are going to drive us to your house. I'm sure your dear wife Flo is dying to meet me.'

Naturally horrified Harvey wanted to object but knew he'd have no choice in the matter, although he thought he may have spotted a tiny window of opportunity, something he could use.

'I'm sure she'd like to meet Jay as well...' He replied calmly.

'What about the Demon...?' It asked. '...Would she like that?'

'I wouldn't have thought so...'

'Oh, you will hurt its feelings...'

'It doesn't have any feelings...also it tried to murder my wife the last time they met...on the other timeline.'

'Hahaha listen to you, the other timeline!' Jay indicated for Harvey to sit down on a paint stained wooden chair. 'You talk about it as if it were real...that it existed. Let me explain something to you Harvey...a basic rule of the universe...what no longer exists here can never have existed in the first place. Your tiny primate minds are so tiresome when it comes to repeating the same mistakes, they talk of multiple universes with infinite configurations as a possible answer to the mysteries of life, how all of them could be running concurrently, offering comforting options of many a safe haven. Do you really believe this is how things work?'

Harvey was no expert on such matters but given these current circumstances he was open to any branch of theoretical science, answering the Glitch as honestly as possible. 'I'm afraid I only believe what I can see, and if something's invisible then only from the mouths of people I trust.'

'I presume you are talking about Alex again...?' The Glitch's tone bore a little tension in its delivery. Harvey hoped that was a good thing so let it continue its discourse.

'...Your mortal friend has no more insight into the universe than the chair you are sitting on. Yes with the Angels help he saw and experienced dimensions he had no right to, but alas his mind then, as now, will always be incapable of comprehending any of its working purpose. Do not put too much stock in that man's tales. A slight error occurred that is all, meaning he was allowed a small paddle in the book the Angel kept, his adventures within its pages were no more than a walk along the great beachfront of knowledge, whereas I have dived into those waves, swum freely, then opened my mouth to consume the whole ocean!'

Harvey interrupted with the sole intention of quietening the horrible boasting. 'But you still got shot in the head. You almost died...'

'...Hardly.' replied the Glitch.

'Oh come on now...don't lie to me...' Harvey was trying his best to look confident. '...I've heard them all before and from better liars than you.'

'My apologies Inspector, I didn't realise I was under cross examination.' The Glitch made Jay's chuckling body walk towards the doorway, but Harvey wasn't ready to end this conversation yet.

'That's just the way it works I'm afraid, it can't be helped...I spend my whole life doing this, always having to double check everything I hear. You can ask my wife...' Harvey's delaying tactics were seized upon immediately by the Glitch.

'...I fully intend to. Now stand up we must go.'

'What's the rush...?' Harvey asked, remaining seated. '...plus there's no point us leaving now she won't be at home. My wife had an appointment this afternoon...' He glanced at his watch. '...I doubt she'll be back yet.' It was a total lie with Harvey hoping its desperate obviousness would be its greatest disguise.

Turning slowly the Glitch came back over. 'Is that so Harvey...?'

The Inspector nodded as truthfully as he could muster.

Jays piercing blue gaze fell on him. '...Well that makes a huge difference to your immediate outcome.'

'Does it now...?' Harvey responded assuredly, taking some pleasure in knowing he'd subtly hoodwinked this monster.

'Most certainly...you see I have a gift for you Harvey. It was something I was going to give to you later, but seeing as we have this free time I shall offer it to you now.'

'You're okay; I don't need anything from you.'

'That's neither here nor there. Look at me...look up!'

Harvey raised his face and Jay Cleavers smooth young hands pressed gently upon his temples. On feeling no force being applied he deduced he wasn't going to have his skull smashed like a cheap vase, so instead he sat there quite still, listening closely to the inquisitive words of the monster talking to itself.

'Come on now...where is it...?'

Harvey had no idea what the Glitch was talking about; he could only hope it was a good thing, as most gifts are.

The Glitch's fingers stroked the side of the Inspector's skull. What they sought was uncertain until the young man whispered with delight. '...Got you...!'

Whatever the Glitch found made him feel no worse for receiving the 'gift'. 'Are you quite done...?' He enquired.

'Oh yes. I'm all done. You shall feel my gift over the coming hours.'

'What are you talking about...?'

'The end of you...followed swiftly by the end of all this...beginning here on this once healthy planet that your race has doomed to freeze or burn. Undecided yet on the best way to rid itself of your poisonous grip...but still you cannot seem to accept what you have done. It is so blatantly obvious that the end is in sight regardless, my actions will simply speed things along. In fact if you wish to seek a positive spin on the situation, think of all the children who won't need to be born, the blessed souls who will miss the suffering of this final countdown to extinction, for that is all they will face in the next fifty years. I can end it all for them in an instant so the choice is simple, now or later, quick or lingering, sudden or suffering. What would you choose Mr Cooper...?'

As Harvey spoke he tried to sit up but slowly slid back down to the filthy floor, instinctively knowing he was already being weakened by the Glitch's gift. 'I choose nature's way...not some judgemental lifeform who only exists because an Angel messed up.'

The Glitch appeared next to him in a blink, its forehead pressed against Harvey's, while its thin fingers crawled up to touch the Inspectors cheek. 'I believe you could be the bravest man I've ever known, and I know of many through the great book. All those heroes and legends from centuries ago, yet here you are...the genuine deal. Who knows perhaps one day a new race will write stories about you.'

Harvey lifted his head to look into Jay's eyes with a stare of defiance. 'It would be nice to be remembered as a hero...rather than...than whatever the hell you are...!'

Jay's fingers let go of the man's head allowing it fall to his chest, it knew a show of anger would display a weakness in itself and almost certainly death for the man. Instead it walked calmly back to the other side of the lock up before continuing. '...It is difficult for me to reason what your cruel reactions are based upon, whether it is simply the acceptance of your own death or some futile hope of preservation. I know one thing though, you are one of the few humans who fully understands the purpose of time, the mystical ticking that resounds throughout the universe...but sadly you seem to be pinning all of your hopes on it.'

'Not all of my hopes...I have others.'

'Pray tell me what they are.'

'Oh I'll tell you...when the time's right.' Harvey managed a small laugh as he struggled once more to sit up and face his foe. 'Let me first explain something...I know how and why you were made...literally from the first second of your creation until now I have watched you grow and god damn it you are powerful, but you are also naïve...so sadly innocent and naïve.'

'Is this another pointless insult or do you have an actual point?' Jay's mouth asked with a snarl.

'I'll give you this much for now...a higher force than you...what the hell let's not play games, the Angel that created you told Alex a fundamental truth that you don't seem to have learned. How nothing is immortal, everything dies...'

'Untruth...!' It cried.

'What? Really...lies from the mouth of an Angel?' Harvey countered with equal volume. 'The very being that created you, I seriously doubt that. So how does it feel to discover you are no better than me...that you had a beginning and you will have an end...what is it like for you to hear the ticking of the clock?'

The Glitch promptly fell quiet within Jay as if retreating to think. Harvey knew this would allow one of the others to take control of the body. Which one of course would be interesting as they would undoubtedly be annoyed at being ignored for so long, meaning they would instantly become a new problem for the weary body and mind of Inspector Harvey Cooper.

24

Florence Cooper wasn't quite at breaking point, but as bad feelings went these were some of the worst, pushing her ever closer to it. Harvey wasn't answering his phone so she'd called his office where a new secretary, who she knew nothing about, informed her he was on his way to the hospital for work reasons. She accepted that but even if he was driving at the moment there was still no reason why he wouldn't receive her messages. All she wanted was to hear his voice; one simple reply would suffice but there was nothing, which was quite unlike her Harveypud.

Sitting in the sun on the top step that led up to her manicured lawn, she welcomed Goldie with a hug when the Labrador lolloped over. Not having owned a pet since she was a child Flo was becoming convinced that dogs, especially this one, could sense when things were going awry, knowing when to offer her comfort. However its warm fur was of little assurance that everything was fine. The most worrying aspect of her current disposition and with no reasonable explanation for it was an overwhelming feeling of foreboding. It meant only one thing to Flo...her husband's life was in danger.

Grabbing up the mobile she rang the only number that could possibly help. After four rings it was answered.

'Hello...?'

'It's me Flo...I need you to come home.'

Alex glanced over at Juliet to let her know it was a call he had to take. She nodded with a blink and took herself to the living room.

'Hello Mrs Cooper...I'm sorry. I am grateful for everything you did for me but...'

'...Harvey's gone missing!' She announced forcefully.

'Seriously, you're certain about that?' Alex asked with genuine concern.

'Actually yes I am...although I don't know why...I'm quite sure of it.'

'Okay let's talk it through...' Alex suggested then listened intently as she gave him chapter and verse of her day. Although it soon became clear that there was no shred of actual evidence that anything was amiss, he still ended up with the same feeling as her, that something was very wrong. '...Just try and stay calm I'll come over to you. We'll work this out and find him together. Give me twenty minutes.' He ended the call and looked over to find Juliet already standing by the front door.

'Graham has got the car so we'll have to get a cab.' She said pulling on a light summer coat.

'You don't have to come with me. I just have to calm a lady down.'

'Probably all the more reason I should come then. It's not one of your strengths calming people down. Look at me.' She laughed lightly.

There had only been the one kiss but it had been enough to mess them up emotionally, with his phone going off being a blessed relief that broke the tension in the room, giving them something else to focus on.

'Don't you have to go to work later?'

'We'll have to cross that bridge when we come to it.' As she spoke those words her mind flashed back to the dream, the one on the bridge where Alex had risen up with Angel's wings when she thought she had lost him forever. Quickly shaking it from her head she let him pass by first before setting off downstairs.

Within five minutes they successfully spotted and hailed a taxi. Their driver was a polite man called Nigel Isaacs, according to a name badge displayed over the dashboard. He calmly dodged and wove his way through the busy sunburned streets of the City before speaking up.

'...I can't remember it being this hot for a long time. Have you seen this, it's edging up to twenty eight now, where are we...bloody Barbados?'

He laughed only to find his friendly quip failing to hit the mark because the couple in the back weren't really listening. Choosing not to push his weathered point he fell silent again, driving them to 7 Wilkes Avenue as requested as quickly as he could. Concentrating on the road ahead made him feel a little better, their snub wasn't personal, they didn't have to speak to him if they didn't want to, but it only made him more determined to get a response before he dropped them off.

He was a professional after all and keeping fares happy was a perk he usually managed, but still nothing came back in response to a couple more of his general observations. This couple were so deep in their thoughts that in the end he gave in. Maybe they'd just received bad news, or had a massive argument, both of their faces clearly indicated that all was not well in their world. As he pulled up outside the house the young lady pushed a twenty pound note into his hand.

'Thank you...one moment.' He said and searched for some change. 'It's only eight pounds.'

'That's okay keep the change!' She said as they both leapt from the car and ran up the drive. Leaving Nigel holding the generous note in one hand, his change bag on his lap, wondering just what was troubling the couple.

As he turned his cab around in their driveway he had the bright idea of purchasing a book of witty anecdotes with this unexpected tip. Or maybe he'd just accept that the world was changing and not for the better. People didn't want to chat so freely nowadays, maybe it was time for him to get out of the driving game, because being sociable had always been the part he loved the most.

Juliet passed Alex halfway up the drive where he seemed to be dawdling a little, probably nervous, she thought. When she reached the front door she didn't knock, just turned the handle and marched in to find Flo in the lounge.

She introduced herself. 'Hi my name's Juliet. I'm a qualified nurse...are you okay?'

'I'm fine thank you but I don't think I need a nurse, I'm just worried sick about my husband.'

'We got here as quick as we could...' Alex said entering the room, his appearance making the mysterious nurse's entrance a lot more sensible now. '...How long has it been?' he asked.

'All morning but his new secretary said he left the office about an hour ago. I've been thinking about it and maybe I'm worrying about nothing.'

Alex wanted to believe her but feelings of dread were all around him. 'Who's this new secretary then...?' He asked in an attempt to sound calm.

'I don't know. She answered the phone and said her name was Roma. It was news to me. I just feel he would have called to tell me that...it's the kind of thing he'd always do.'

'Right I think I know where to start...' Juliet said butting in with a smile. '...I'll put the kettle on.' before flitting out to the kitchen.

When she was out of earshot Flo had to ask. 'I take it that's the Juliet from the book...your nurse?'

'Yes...the very same...' Alex replied. '...but I prefer to think of her as a good friend, one I almost lost by being an idiot...' He lowered his head. '...Look I'm sorry I ran out on you last night, that couldn't have helped.'

'You're a grown man Alex you can do whatever you want...' Her reply coming over in a tone that didn't back up the sentiment '...but while we're being totally honest I did think Harvey's sudden disappearance might have had something to do with you. It's why you were the first person I called.'

Alex tried to pick the bones out of those words to find something positive but failed. Was she blaming him for this situation in a back handed fashion?

'How do you take your tea Mrs Cooper?' Juliet asked as she popped her head round the door.

'Drop of milk no sugar thank you dear....' Flo replied politely as Juliet disappeared again. '...You're right by the way, that what you did last night hasn't helped anything...leaving with just a blunt note was rude and took us by surprise. It wasn't appreciated, not when you could have just spoken to us about your feelings. Like I said you're a grown man...not a teenage boy.'

Wow. Alex thought, he hadn't felt this small and told off since childhood. Flo Cooper certainly had some skill in picking exactly the right words to say, never too much or overly dramatic, just the correct amount of sting, so that you felt go under the skin. 'Flo...sorry Mrs Cooper, I'll do everything I can to find Harvey. Let's be fair he couldn't have gone far...' Alex smiled and reached his hand over to comfort her but she pulled away.

'...Is that your childish attempt at calming me Alex?' Then with a disappointed disgust she stood and went to the window, if only to increase the distance between them.

Damn, her words were beating him into the ground. Had he really been that unthinking and selfish? On realising he didn't have an answer for his own question he could only accept that he had. For god's sake he really didn't know what to do, so his relief as Juliet entered with the drinks was almost audible.

'Ah there you are!' He said almost shouting.

'There you go. Everything okay...?' Juliet asked as she passed the cups around but a thick uncomfortable pause answered her question so she decided to take over from where her friend was clearly failing. 'Would I be right in presuming you're not too happy with Alex?'

Flo was more than ready to answer that question.

'What do you think? He walked out on us last night after we tried our best to help him. We gave him a roof over his head, welcomed him into our home. Even formed a vigilante committee to help look for the monsters he's been telling us about.'

Alex was also upset with himself but he couldn't let that lie. 'Hey I never asked...'

But again Flo was far more advanced in the skills of getting her point across and cut him down with ease. '...You didn't need to ask. I think you knew very well what you were doing. Perhaps you recognise a soft touch when you see one, maybe Juliet is the same, just another someone who wants to help...until you decide you've got a better idea and choose to hurt them.'

He looked over to his friend for assistance but her deliberately blank expression told him he was on his own. 'Look I've apologised...I am genuinely sorry if I hurt either of you. I never wanted to do that. For god's sake believe me I wish none of this had ever happened...' He was now surprisingly close to tears but couldn't think how he'd gotten to this point, maybe it had just been a long time coming, the end of some deep suppression. '...I know I'm nothing special and I've really never wanted to be. When I climbed out on that ledge at Dalmeny Street I was determined to jump and end it all...that was what I wanted...but somehow it ended up being the last decision I ever took for myself. Everything that's happened since means I'm just stuck in the middle of...likes it's preordained...pushing me forward...now I'm stuck in a fucking tangled mess I can't get out of. I'm sorry for swearing but I'm tired and frustrated with myself, with this damn condition. More and more every day I end up searching for some kind of answer that will make everything right again...but I don't know what I'm doing...I don't know how...I'm sorry...sorry that I'm even here...fuck!'

It was on the final word that he collapsed on the sofa and began to sob, his knees came up to his chest as he lay on his side, his face in a cushion to muffle the wretched pain as much as he could.

The ladies watched on with neither one making a move to comfort him, as if both intuitively knew such care wouldn't help this moment. Without speaking they agreed on the best course of action.

After a full twenty minutes of letting it all out, Alex finally retained a grip on his heart and raised his head. The women were gone, but not too far. He raised himself up and saw them sitting in the garden.

25

Harvey crouched down by the wall in the lock up, trying to work out which of his bones hurt the most, as Jay Cleavers body walked towards him nonchalantly, the look in his young eyes unreadable now only the whites were on display.

'There you are all broken and bent, you've never looked better.' The voice was callous and dry.

The Inspector knew exactly who was addressing him. 'Hello Metatron.' He replied, hoping that hearing the name would hurt the Demon.

'Hmm you can call me whatever names you want. Take your pathetic pleasures wherever you can get them, but know I will be the one to kill you when it's time.'

'Don't you mean when the Glitch gives you permission?' Harvey replied but kept his head down, staring at the floor.

'There are no permissions needed...'

'Could have fooled me...I'm pretty sure I've spotted a definite hierarchy in there. First the Glitch, then you, then Jay...but hey I'm only guessing on who's more important between you and Cleaver.'

'Stop your mouth Harvey before I tear it off your face!' Those rolled back eyes staring down intently at their prey. 'The only reason you are still drawing breath is because we have a bigger plan, one that you will help us with, when your little army will be ripped to shreds with the whole world watching.'

'You should make it pay per view...make yourself a few quid.' Harvey was feeling brighter and braver because he could feel the mood switch. There were rules inside that body and he'd called it right, the Glitch was in charge and had some hold over the Demon, whether the Demon was aware of it or not. Of course this obviously meant poor Jay, as always, was bottom of the pile. That poor psycho kid could never catch a break.

Harvey believed he may never get a better chance to question the monster he'd chased for over five years. 'You didn't find my joke that funny, fair enough but tell me something, because I'm going to die anyway right so what would it matter...do you miss Oscar?'

There was a slender pause before the answer came, but that silence told Harvey plenty, how he was touching a nerve. 'Oscar was just as much a killer as me...I told him what I needed to do and he followed willingly.'

'Come on, we both know that's not true.' Harvey replied.

'If you had been inside his head Cooper you wouldn't be so forgiving. It was a dark place, full of loneliness and longing to be known. I gave him all of that, everything he wanted and then I left him to live his life.'

'Oh wow...!' Harvey gasped half mockingly.

'What?' The Demon responded.

'That twisted view...I already know what happened, you didn't leave him with some kind of parting gesture...you fled for your life...' When no words came back in answer Harvey pushed on with his plan, to unsteady the monster. '...You ran away because someone else knew about your existence, not such a great secret after all were you?'

'Huh...are you talking of the madman Kirby?'

Harvey couldn't help but to find it sickeningly ironic that a murderous bloodthirsty Demon as this could have such a low opinion of a mortal man, before wondering just how debauched Marcus Kirby was to deserve such hellish praise. 'Yes I am...' Harvey confirmed but wanted to know more. '...So tell me what this man had planned for you?'

'To try and control the power they don't understand, it's what all the madmen do, none of them ever learn that it's so much better to embrace chaos, you don't need to understand anything when all theory is pointless, just move freely from death to death.' As Jay spoke his mouth turned into a slanted smile, disgusting to witness, it was the grin of a Demon looming over Harvey and he didn't care to see it for a moment longer. He looked to the corner of the room where dozens of empty cobwebs hung down.

'So you ran away like a coward?' Harvey suggested provocatively.

The evil grin predictably disappeared. 'Why would you say that when you know it will anger me?'

'Because I'm passed worrying about your anger... I just want to know why you slipped away when Oscar needed you most.'

'Because I don't have feelings Cooper...'

'Oh come now you have some...feelings of anger, of hatred and deep down I'd propose there's a new feeling...one telling you how *you're* being controlled now. How the trap you tried to escape in the facility by avoiding Kirby only led you to the Glitch. You can tell me...I know it can't hear us when your consciousness is at the helm.'

Again there was a telling pause before it replied. 'Don't play me for a fool by trying to create mistrust.'

'I don't think I'm trying to do that. How can I be creating something that already exists as clear as day...?' Harvey knew he was on the Demons pressure point, but the real negotiating skill would be to stay on it without pressing too hard. He continued carefully. '...But fine if I'm wrong, forget what I said. All I'm trying to do is understand where we are today. I hunted you down for five years, so it's a pleasure to finally have a chance to speak with you.'

'Are you trying vanity now?' The Demon replied, the whites of its eyes sparkling under a sunbeam leaking in from the roof.

'Oh come on surely you remember our extremely intense game of cat and mouse. You did well, took a great deal of finding. Strange isn't it how we're sitting in the exact spot that gave you away...those bloody plastic barrels. I think it's incredible we're back here but then again maybe it's something we have no choice in.'

The Demon looked around the lock up before staring up at the roof. Its murdering hands were clenched and Harvey could see the white marks on the skin where the nails were pressing in hard. This action convincing the Inspector his suspicions about the Demon's state were correct.

'I don't see what you're getting at.' It relaxed its hands and opened them up in expectation of what was to come.

'I know you don't and that's my point...' Harvey waved his hand in front of the Demon with no response. '...You can't see at all anymore!'

'That is untrue, I have the eyes of this vessel and...'

'...No...I really don't think you can...!' Harvey interrupted without fear. '...When it was just you and Oscar you had everything you needed, freedom, anonymity...and sight. I'd wager it was the same with Jay until the Glitch appeared. But you couldn't resist that offer could you? Instead of letting it die trapped in the body of Snake you believed you could save it, use it in some way, like the madmen you were judging earlier...become a new power, a killing machine of infinite speed and brutality...what self-respecting Demon wouldn't want that?'

The eyes looked down at the man as if trying to prove in some last desperate attempt that it wasn't blind. 'I can see you just fine...' It snarled.

'At best you can sense your surroundings, perhaps smell or movement, but don't lie to me now. You're as blind as a bat and the Glitch is so far ahead of you it's shameful. I think in the moment you decided to save it you lost everything, but perhaps you never really had a choice, I mean who knows how these things work, what happens when you allow a superior being to share Jay's mind, let it make all the necessary changes for its own survival. I'm only telling you the truth because I think you deserve it, you were a worthy adversary, but now we must face the uncomfortable fact that all of a sudden...you're really the least of my worries.'

THE RED FRAME

With a lightning speed unseen by Harvey's human eye, its ferocious fist pummelled into the wall inches above his head, the amount of plaster work falling onto his suit telling of a blow that would have killed him instantly.

Harvey took a deep breath, calmly brushing the larger flakes off his sleeve and trousers, before looking up at the wretched sight of a Demon tormented. In truth it was no more than the beast deserved having gambled and lost to a higher power, now nothing more than a wild dog on a leash, only to be set free when the Glitch deemed it appropriate. In a perverse sense it was being slowly being starved to death through its own appetite for gluttonous murder.

'The Glitch has a plan that we will follow before I eat your heart in front of the world...' It tried to threaten.

Harvey reached up and took the Demons hand above him, pulling it slowly down to his own chest. 'Take it now then.' He pressed Jay's hand gently on his shirt but it made no attempt to claw the flesh open. 'I didn't think so.' Then something wet dropped down and hit his cheek, without looking up he spoke because he already knew what it was. 'It won't let you kill me will it?'

This risky game of truth or dare still seemed to be rewarding Harvey's bravery, or stupidity, but he was aware it was far from over. For now he just had to be thankful he was still breathing, grateful to whichever deity was watching over him that his heart remained beating, because without them, he would never have felt a Demon's tear fall upon his face.

26

Alex didn't say anything to either Flo or Juliet as he walked out into the garden; doubting small talk would suffice at this juncture, besides his mind was a frazzled mess that needed to be calmed.

Once fully outside the heat was quite ridiculous for this auld city but it gave him an idea he couldn't resist. With only a little awkwardness he sat his one armed self on the lawn and began removing his shoes and socks, before moving them neatly to one side and placing his bare feet deep into the ticklish grass. Scrunching his toes through the sweetest of nature's blades he felt a calmness forbidden him for so long. Rapture may be too strong a word but within a few seconds a beautiful serenity took reign over him under the pale blue Edinburgh sky. This joy lasted until Juliet walked over to speak with him. As she approached the storm clouds regathered in his mind, this wasn't going to be a flirty chat about their feelings for one another, it was to speak about the missing Inspector.

'Feeling better?' She asked and ruffled his somewhat overgrown hair. 'This needs a cut...I can do it if you want?'

'Err no you're fine. I haven't forgotten the hack job you did back at the care home.'

Juliet looked appalled by his comment. 'What do you mean...that was an almost professional job?'

'If you can classify drawing blood from an ear as almost professional...'

'It moved...'

'My ear...?'

'...Your head...!' She tried to smile but it didn't last. There was no time for joking around. '...Look Alex, we really need to come up with a plan. That's what you need to do now you've stopped blubbing...'

'...Blubbing!'

'Keep your voice down and think of something. I'm trying my best but Flo is getting really worked up about Harvey now.'

With his moment of relaxation gone he stared down at his toes for inspiration but there was none to be found. He could only see two outcomes, either Harvey was in a dangerous situation he couldn't escape from...or he was already dead.

'I really don't know what to do...' This was an honest reply but Juliet's face told him it was way short of what she wanted to hear. '...Come on Joolz where the hell would we even start? I can't drive, we don't have a car and it's a little hot for blindly roaming the streets?'

'Oh okay Alex we'll just leave them to it shall we? Perhaps we could go get an ice cream, visit a gallery. I mean you're probably right I'm sure we're worrying about nothing.'

'Your sarcasm isn't helpful. I'm trying to think here!'

Alex had reacted sharply and with a raised voice but Juliet took the brusque comment in the spirit it was delivered. Clearly he was trying his best, even if at this minute his best was getting them nowhere.

She thought maybe this was what Alex had meant when he'd told her he needed her love and trust, if so then she was giving as much as she was able to right now but it didn't appear to be helping much, they still had no plan or even the merest clue on their next step.

Flo spoke after apparently sneaking up on them. 'Just to let you know I've called around everyone, including the Superintendent who requested I calm down, no great surprise as he's always been an utter wanker!'

Alex's was putting his shoes and socks back on, his first instinct was to laugh at her description but reason took hold and he held it back. Juliet on the other hand was a little shocked by the lady's language as they'd only just met so she pulled a joke surprised face, directing it mostly at Alex, while Flo simply smiled broadly below nervous eyes.

It went unnoticed by any of them, as they moved closer into a three way hug of support, that the key cause of this empathetic huddle had been the use of a simple profanity. Proving coarse, colourful language that is so often derided does have its uses, perhaps never more so than when it comes from an honest and terrified soul.

27

Back in the lockup and after a moment's respite Harvey wiped his cheek dry of the monster's tear. Then the unmistakeable voice of young Jay Cleaver greeted its removal, the Demon once more disappearing back into the shadows of its existence.

The teenager was clearly unaware of what had just happened when he exclaimed. 'Ha, ha, are you crying now ya fucking pig!'

With his back against the wall Harvey felt some relief, his plan to get Jay to return had worked, although if he'd thought this entrapment was about to get easier he was wrong. Jay had been waiting patiently to have another few minutes alone with the weakened Inspector; to do so and find him weeping was just fucking great.

'If that's what you want to believe then yes...' Harvey replied, finding himself delighted to see the young man's blue eyes had reappeared. Those Demon's unseeing whites were disconcerting even to a man who'd seen some truly disturbing sights in his long career. 'Although maybe I called you back Jay because I was missing you...' He joked to brighten the mood.

The swift kick that struck Harvey in the stomach took his breath clean away. Just as the Inspector had foolishly assumed himself to be free of receiving any more wanton physical damage, hoping he'd somehow be protected by his knowledge of the Glitch, it was painfully clear that Jay was dancing to his own tune when it came to those ropey unwritten rules.

'You can shut your fucking mouth Cooper unless you want some more. Now stand up!' Jay viciously grabbed Harvey under the arms and lifted him to his shaky feet.

'For crying out loud Jay I may have broken ribs...!' He grunted.

'Good...!' The younger blatantly crazier man grabbed the Inspectors lapels forcing him hard back against the wall. It was a classic bad guy move to accompany the order and threat that promptly followed. '...Now shut up you whimpering bastard or I'll break them all...' Jay literally spat the sentence out while leering in close. '...I don't know if you forgot but we're driving to your house now...to meet your wife...Ha she's gonna fucking love meeting me.'

In less than thirty seconds, while trying to ignore the pain in his abdomen, Harvey had pulled the car out of the cul-de-sac and back onto the streets. As their journey began there was an incessant pinging sound that indicated Jay wasn't wearing his seatbelt. The heat in the car and the repetitive warning noise only multiplied the frustration, fear and tension of the Inspector, but he also knew the obnoxious little shit wasn't going to be told to what to do by man or machine.

'Take us home Harvey...!' Jay shouted proudly.

The Inspector flinched but didn't respond to the gruesome demand, he was too busy trying to calculate a workable scenario of how the outcome could be changed, while trying to ignore the damn pinging sound that wouldn't stop.

It would take twenty, twenty five minutes to drive round the city to his house. He could tag on a few extra ones here and there but without having an actual accident, which would undoubtedly see him punished further or killed immediately, in less than half an hour his wife, who was his whole world, would be dead and gone.

He drove as close to the speed limit as possible and just under it as much as he dare, but every junction and corner were becoming no more than countdown markers, every green light a personal attack as he willed them to remain red. The constant pinging of the seatbelt warning continued, adding to this anxiety was the constant drumming of Jay's hands on the dashboard, performed with petulant gusto, as if his mistimed beats could make something musical out of the chaos.

They were less than fifteen minutes away when a large skip lorry put on its hazard warning lights and pulled to a stop in front of them. On any other occasion even the usually placid Harvey would have been muttering under his breath, but today this was a tiny piece of manna from heaven, allowing a few extra moments to think, to remember why he was here and to feel the slap of regret for not carrying a spare phone, or his gun.

The two of them watched with growing tension as the skip lorry pulled out across both lanes to give itself the space and angle to back into a yard. Harvey glanced over at Jay just as the reverse beeping began to sound on the large vehicle. Bizarrely it was at the precise moment that the irritating noise within his car stopped.

'Hello Harvey.' Spoke the voice of the Glitch, its hand having just clicked the seatbelt buckle into place. 'I trust young Jay has been pleasant company in my absence.'

Out of the frying pan and into the fire, this thought springing into Harvey's mind for two separate reasons, because crazy Jay was gone but the Glitch was back. And although the pinging noise in his car had ceased, it just made the reversing alarm on the lorry seem twice as loud. Even faced with this new set of problems Harvey felt he was a slightly better-off man. His actual mood remained deeply low, relative to the fact he was driving his wife's future murderer to the scene of the crime. Thankfully that act would be delayed a little longer as the skip lorry pulled forward to realign itself for a second attempt through the narrow gateway. He was grateful for the extra pause in proceedings as it gave him the opportunity to acknowledge the Glitch and speak honestly.

'Please don't kill my wife...' Harvey knew time was growing short and chit chats or mind games weren't going to cut it anymore. It was time for direct conversation. '...There's nothing to be gained from it. Florence is a beautiful soul who deserves mercy, worthy of seeing the best of you.'

'Ohhh Harvey....you make me wish that I was capable of true emotion. I could then quite possibly be moved by such heartfelt beseeching, alas for your sake I am made of different stuff...so she will die shortly and you will watch it happen.'

'For God's sake...'

'Bringing God into it now...I think I shall put that down to your brain spluttering out whatever it can find in the desperate act of avoidance. The human minds typical reaction under such conditions...similar to your life flashing before your eyes at the moment of dying...trust me it's just your brain frantically searching those memory banks to find a way out, something it has to try as it has never truly faced its own death before, consequently it panic's and looks everywhere for an answer...even the pointless past. Ever since I learned of it I've always thought it to be a rather sweet act of the human mind, allowing a person to experience their life during ones last moments...almost like a grateful and polite goodbye from the universe. Thank you for your time on earth alas I'm afraid you've been voted off, but before you go...here are some of your best bits.'

'What the hell do you want?' The Inspector asked as he watched the cab of the lorry disappear through the gates.

'If you don't know that by now...' The Glitch started to say.

'...Not that part, not all that fatalistic crap about ending the universe, then one day ending all the other universes you can find...no more heaven or earth...that's all well and good in your head but I'm not asking about your purpose or destiny...'

The Glitch placed its smooth perfect hand on Harvey's jacket sleeve to politely interrupt with an instruction. '...The other vehicle has moved out of the way...continue driving while you talk.'

Harvey nodded his agreement. 'What I'm trying to find out is...look, none of this probably matters but I just want to say it because I don't want to have any regrets.' He slid the car into gear and once again the distance to his wife sickeningly shortened. 'You're a one off...a first born...there's never been anything like you before in existence. From what I've heard and read you've already destroyed what remained of that heavenly realm and now believe it's time to start down here. But I ask quite seriously what are you getting out of this? It seems to my untrained eye a complete waste of...well...of you.'

Harvey didn't find it surprising that the Glitch was listening intently to his words, as any complimentary or interesting dialogue about a soul while within that very soul's presence was, and always will be, an irresistible feeding time for the ego.

'A waste of me...? Explain yourself.' The Glitch asked with no sense of humility.

Harvey was about to grant its request when he spotted the cemetery to their right. After the delay with the skip wagon he'd been left with a decision to make as there were two routes back to his house, each option being about equal in distance, now wondering why he'd subconsciously chosen this one, the route past the soil where both his parents lay, and the place where Flo's and his own plot were already reserved and paid for.

'Are you ignoring me Mr Cooper?' It asked quizzically while watching the Inspectors every move.

He knew there wasn't a hope in hell he could pull a fast one now, maybe if Jay was still here, or even better the blind demon, but as it stood he could only continue rolling forward to their destination. 'Huh what no...I was saying that all this destruction you're planning seems a little irrational. I'd like to know who profits from your actions. If it's, as I suspect you'll respond, because you choose it to be this way, then why not choose differently...use all your undoubtedly impressive powers to heal and help.'

They held each other's gaze as the traffic came to a stop for a set of temporary traffic lights. Harvey couldn't remember if they had been here yesterday.

He took the moment to fully consider the young handsome face in his view. It was the same one that had been so recently ruined, apparently beyond repair, left as nothing but a slashed up wound sitting upon skinny shoulders of an unfortunate kid with anger issues. It really hadn't been that long ago since he'd visited Jay at the facility, in the meeting room feeling outnumbered, remembering how this bolshie adolescent had broken his own lawyer's nose. It was the same day he and Emma were locked up together in a tiny cell where the poor girl had almost lost her mind. Thinking about Emma calmed him a little but the tension remained high as they were only three streets away now and it seemed the Glitch wanted to talk all the way there.

'I doubt you will ever understand my actions Mr Cooper which is of no great surprise. I wonder what you would choose to do with my power and vision. I presume your first act would be to spirit your dear wife away to a place of safety, some sanctuary where she would never have to witness the havoc of humanities existence, wrap her up in...'

'...Save your breath, I would never need to do that, Flo is lot stronger than you imagine!' Harvey's reaction was swift and fervent. 'But I suppose you're right, I'll never understand why you would wish to destroy all this...but I can assure you of one thing...if there is any chance at all...even the slightest intimation that we can kill you first...then all three of you rattling around in that psychopaths body are already dead.'

The Glitch didn't react as the car turned onto Wilkes Avenue; instead it simply sat back and took in the view, because this was all too perfect and going precisely to plan.

28

Maybe it is true when some say there are no answers in the past, after all any specific era one may wish to search through to find an answer is already done with, time having advanced above and beyond whatever was essential to our ancestor's survival way back when. Of course by stating it as an unquestionable fact there are no answers in the past, one could be dangerously underplaying its influence on the present.

A very long time ago, approximately fifteen to twenty thousand years, developing tribes of hunter gatherers across the world made significant moves into a particular animal's kingdom.

The mammal in question quickly became so essential and significant it reshaped our whole future, when, after gaining the initial trust of the beast we developed an unbreakable bond that will last forever, as from that day forward human and beast walked onwards together, developing teamwork and perfecting companionship.

Clearly these events occurred so long ago it seems extraordinary they should remain vitally important today, but it was because of such a loving and respectful merger that it can be stated, with absolute certainty, that the ancient act of trust between those two separate species would save the lives of the occupants of 7 Wilkes Avenue on this day.

Flo and Juliet were sat in the garden at the patio table, a blue, rarely used, garden umbrella giving them shade, lemonade in hand, waiting and hoping Harvey would call. Alex meanwhile was in the living room rifling through his notes, searching for a clue on his whereabouts, something overlooked to gain them an advantage.

Therefore none of them heard the Inspectors car pull up outside the house, leaving them innocently unaware of the danger that approached, with the smiling eyes of the Glitch staring out.

Only a decision made by our ancient ancestors a long time ago could save this day because something did hear the engine turn off, its ears descended from those ancient mammals, no longer a wolf, but now a slightly overweight Labrador.

Goldie first whimpered then barked as she jumped up and raced to the front door, her natural instinct was pure curiosity because through domestication over millennia she was ready to work, to do her duty, to meet the visitor head on and crumble under their fuss, or to warn the rest of her pack.

On hearing the dog, Alex, who was sat by the front window looked out, immediately spying Harvey and then his passenger climbing out of the car.

'Oh my fucking god...!' Adrenalin exploded through him on seeing Jays face and with the always surprising speed that only pure fear can supply he ran into the garden.

'Run...run now...!' He whisper cried, '...It's here! Get through to next door...go quickly!'

Just as his desperate plea to the women ended he heard the front door being opened.

'Flo...? Flo...? It's me...' Harvey's shaky voice called out over the sound of the dog barking. '...Everything's okay Goldie, come here...'

Alex had remained, stood outside by the back door, listening carefully as two sets of footsteps entered the hallway. He could make out Harvey coaxing Goldie into the living room before shutting the dog in, this was followed by a moment of silence when all he could hear was his own clipped breathing. A quick glance into the garden told him the women had disappeared through the hedge, they were either hiding quietly or with the neighbours, but it really didn't matter because they were safe for now.

He couldn't lie that for a brief moment he'd thought about following them. Would it be so bad to try and save himself, he really wasn't ready for this type of confrontation, but one overriding thought kept him in place, to hold his ground, he couldn't run away and leave Harvey again because this was his fault.

As quietly as his one armed body could manage he entered the kitchen. Closing the back door silently behind before sliding sideways to the sink, towards the cutlery drawer to be candid, but before he could reach down to the handle the kitchen door opened and Harvey entered.

'Alex...?' The Inspector greeted him in a strange tone that seemed to cover the whole spectrum of emotions, from surprised to sorrowful. '...I didn't know you would be here...'

'Where is he...?' Alex whispered, trying to be furtive with the roughed up Inspector he barely recognised.

Harvey looked a lot different to yesterday, nowhere near as efficient or imposing after being beaten up physically and mentally, yet here he was still standing and that offered some hope. When no one had followed the Inspector through the door Alex believed Jay must be upstairs or in the hallway. This was exactly what they needed, a moment alone, anything to give the two men a few seconds to make a pla...

'It's stood right behind you...' Harvey said slowly, his voice was almost breathless with fear.

The next few seconds of Alex's life were dragged through the slowest of painful motions; first he felt a hand grab his shoulder, the next his face was smashed into the ceiling, before he was unceremoniously dropped to the kitchen floor. The impact from both surfaces sent his mind into a world of stars; thousands of tiny sparks spun wildly through his head, filling his vision with nothing but blurred confusion. That was, until everything in his world went dark.

Mr Edward Boughton of number eleven Wilkes Avenue was sitting alone in his conservatory when the two women came running into his garden. The speed of their entry through his wooden gate heavily indicating they were escaping some unseen danger. Because of this sudden appearance and the wild eyed look on the older lady's face he hadn't immediately recognised Mrs Cooper, the policeman's wife from two doors down, but it was the younger woman who threw herself into his private domicile first.

He tried to stand and enquire only to find himself pushed back into his wicker chair, a hand covering his mouth, whispered instructions demanded of him and given the shock of it all, he complied with them.

'Please be quiet. Don't say a word.' Juliet ordered him.

Edward was now seventy seven years old and a long twenty years retired, after a distinguished and proud career in the City fire service, so seeing panic all around him and people in danger was really nothing new. It used to be commonplace in his day to day work but he was delighted to find he was still capable of maintaining his calmness under pressure.

He waited patiently with the young ladies hand pressed on his mouth, even nodding at Mrs Cooper when she'd calmed down a little and looked over at him, he didn't attempt to break free to ask any obvious questions until the hand was removed willingly. When Juliet did slowly remove it he remained composed, leaned forward and spoke quietly.

'Can I help you?'

It was at that moment he noticed the severity of Mr's Coopers shaking. There being no doubt the poor dear was too petrified to speak, while the younger one didn't reply because she'd just run inside his house.

Two clear options appeared in his mind, those old fire officer instincts kicking back in. The first being which lady he should deal with as a priority. Weighing up the situation in terms of risk and safety he chose to comfort the older trembling lady, as clearly the younger one wasn't in immediate peril because far as he knew his house wasn't on fire.

'Would you like a drink?' He offered.

Flo's eyes which had been darting around from house to garden to ceiling to floor finally came to rest on him. 'Yes please.' Her voice sounded tiny, deliberately so.

'Water, tea, coffee...brandy...?'

'I think a little brandy would be perfect.' She replied.

Now that was a telling choice thought Edward, especially on such a ridiculously warm day as this, but he wasn't here to judge, he was here to serve and assist.

'No problem I'll be back in a moment.'

On entering his own living room to locate the half bottle of brandy he saw the other woman kneeling by his front window. She was peeking out cautiously from the side of the curtain, doing a good job at not being seen.

'Who are you hiding from...?' He asked in a whisper.

Juliet didn't turn away from her reconnaissance. Instead she spoke into the curtain she was holding. '...No one.'

Accepting of her confusing reply, Edward calmly poured a shot glass of brandy and left the room, if the young lady didn't want to tell him anything that was fine, he wasn't the police, besides he had more pressing concerns with calming Mrs Cooper, who he figured would tell him what was going on anyway if she saw fit.

'There you go...' He offered the glass and Flo sank it in one with her still trembling hands. '...I think it's all okay now. Your young friend seems to be on the lookout...' This juncture could have become an awkward moment in less experienced hands but never in Edwards, as he took the empty glass away politely. '...If there is anything else I can do to help just ask.'

'Thank you.' Flo nodded with a slight smile.

Inside her head however she was bubbling up with regretful thoughts. This helpful lifesaving man, who lived only two doors away, probably less than thirty feet in actual physical distance, was almost a complete stranger to her. The only contact she could ever remember having with him must have been at least four years ago. Knocking his door back then to appeal for a cancer charity she'd walked for. If she could feel any worse about being a bad neighbour then she couldn't imagine it.

'Is your wife around?' She asked by way of politeness.

Edward didn't show a flicker of emotion as he held it all in. 'No...she passed away in February.'

THE RED FRAME

Flo didn't have to imagine she could feel any worse, she did, the bad neighbour question had been answered, her tardy efforts exposed even though she sensed Edward was fine with it all there was an overwhelming feeling of shame.

'I'm so sorry to hear that Mister...?' Bloody hell it was getting worse by the second for her.

'Boughton...Edward...and thank you, but I think your situation is the more pressing right now. Your friend wouldn't tell me what was going on and of course you don't have to either, but if you need me to call someone I can.'

His kind eyes, a pale blue, looked into hers and whether through a genuine need for help or the guilt kicking in she started to stutter to story.

'My Husband is at home...he's a police Inspector...you probably know that...he's been kidnapped or taken hostage.'

Edward had to stop her there. 'I'm sorry I don't think I understand. He's been taken hostage at home?'

'No...this is so difficult to explain...he's under threat from a very dangerous individual. That's probably somewhere nearer to it...and that person has forced him to come back here...most likely to kill me!'

'Good lord. What on earth is going on Mrs Cooper...?' Edward said with shocked concern, because there was the proof to him if needed, that you really never do know your neighbours.

'...Well the rest of it I couldn't begin to tell you about...' Flo smiled apologetically then reached her hand out and touched the back of his. '...suffice to say we are extremely grateful for your help today...but we will need you to keep this quiet.'

Edward tapped her hand reassuringly before taking his away and replying. 'That's fine it's none of my business.'

Juliet then abruptly entered and the whole mood in the conservatory shifted, with the look on her young face more than enough to achieve that effect on its own. 'Have you explained what's happening?' She asked Flo.

'Yes...well I mean I've told him we have a bad man chasing us.'

'Oh okay...' Juliet slightly raised her eyebrows but was happy to trust Flo's opinion on the neighbour. '...well that bad man just left with Harvey...'

'And Alex...?' Flo asked.

'As well...they put his body in the boot.'

A silence fell over the three during which several options and plans of action were thought about, however none were spoken aloud, so the only sounds were the abundant garden birds singing, chirping, warning...always warning.

It could have been an hour, or a day, before he awoke fully. Alex feeling once more the concept of time was proving to be an unimportant factor in this life, all that mattered was to be alive, living to fight another round.

With his senses returned he put his fingers to his face to find his cheeks sore but nothing broken. Relief coursed through his body, waking him up to the physical side of his problems, becoming aware he was bent up in a foetal position, unable to move freely. With a panic he opened his eyes to find nothing but darkness. Clear terrors of being struck blind entered his thoughts but with some concentrated retina effort he could just make out a faint line of light, like a tiny horizon, only inches in front of him.

Then the noises started, although he didn't know if they had always been there or his ears had been slow in catching up, the sound of muffled voices, coming into range, getting clearer.

'Please...you can't do this...' That was unmistakably the voice of Harvey Cooper.

'I really don't see your reasoning...' Another male voice replied.

It had sounded rich and confident. Alex was trying to work out if that voice suited the young man he'd seen in the passenger seat. He didn't think it sounded like Jay, but it was almost certainly the same man that had thrown him up against a ceiling, so none of this was making much sense. Jay's real voice was one he could never forget after hearing it on the ledge over Dalmeny Street, disgusting, coarse and uncaringly vicious. It cast such a confusing doubt in Alex's mind that he decided to speak up, he needed to know more. 'Hey! Any chance you can let me out?'

When a deathly silence greeted his words he increased the volume, which sent up his panic level incrementally until...

'Be quiet Alex...!' The unknown voice demanded before requesting of Harvey. '...let him out!'

A couple of shuffling footsteps then the boot of Harvey's car opened. The bright light and warm air rushed through the confined space and Alex clambered out with a helping hand from the Inspector. Once back on his feet and with his pupils adjusted he found himself standing next to a lock up, where Jay Cleaver sat inside on an old wooden chair in the shade. Alex naturally thought of running as he was already stood by the door but Harvey, being an experienced policeman, read that thought easily.

'Don't try and run off...he's faster than you could ever imagine...just try and remain calm.'

A simple enough instruction but the inflection in the man's voice was not reassuring. Alex even glanced down to check his arm was still missing, for the proof he wasn't stuck in some dream, but there it was, or rather wasn't.

'Where are we?' He asked looking around the gravelled alleyway.

'I'd like to make it sound more positive...but that's not easy...I believe we're in the location where we die...' Harvey's delivery was filled with sincerity. He was either a brilliant actor or Alex was going to have to accept that as the truth. '...but if it counts for anything Flo is fine...we waited awhile before bringing you here and she hadn't returned home.'

'She's safe Harvey. So where is here...do I know this place?'

'It's Oscars lock up, the same hole Snake Hornblower chose to live in. Call it some twisted form of symmetry.'

Was the Inspector trying to give him some kind of clue, if he was then Alex was afraid he didn't understand it.

'Come on in and settle down...' The Glitch requested. '...there's always room for one more.'

Alex turned to Harvey for help, for anything, a bit of understanding for starters.

Again Harvey's logical mind read his friends feelings without words. 'Alex, this is Jay Cleaver...'

'It looks a bit like him but definitely doesn't sound it...' Alex responded on closer inspection, although he was judging from outside the lock up.

'Don't worry, it took me a little time to process what happened, but I can save you that trawl. That man there is Jay, the very same Jay Cleaver that let you fall from the ledge, also the man who not so long ago had his tongue ripped out.'

Alex looked across at the teenager then back to the Inspector.

Harvey then took a breath and gave Alex the truth he desired...or maybe didn't. 'But the smart arse talking to you now, that's our old friend the Glitch.'

'How is that possible...?' The muscles in Alex's face were tightening up. '...Emma killed it!'

'I'm afraid not, she killed that physical body. Then it moved on to a new one.'

A fresh understanding of what had been bothering him in his dreams came into view, the struggle to reason why he couldn't find the next step was a few feet away, of course it wouldn't be possible for him to move through this riddle while that blockage still existed. Alex considered he was being more than fair in describing it as such. 'So you're the Glitch...?' he stated rather than enquired. '...Thanks for throwing me into a ceiling...in this world we tend to shake hands when we first meet people...even more so when greeting someone who's officially disabled.'

Harvey could feel his mind growing uncertain again, his focus spinning in and out. Whatever the Glitch had done to him was still taking shape and becoming a great concern. To help his levels of required concentration he stood back slightly from the pair, to rest his brain and observe this tete a tete, one which had been a long time coming, and now it was finally here he didn't want to miss a word. So the silent struggling Inspector, accepting Alex was the key to any chance of their continuing survival, settled down.

'I may have considered being gentler with you Alex, if indeed this was our first contact...' The Glitch replied.

As it did so Harvey tried to picture it hiding inside the shell of the man, looking through those blue eyes and feeding, constantly feeding on what souls gave it freely and without their knowledge, the gift of information.

It continued '...because in actuality you have never been far from my life experience. Since I came into existence the name of Alex Webb has been rebounding around my world. Meeting you like this, so unexpectedly, is causing me more than a little...inner turmoil.'

'It doesn't look like you're struggling...' Alex took a step closer to the lockup. '...I'd suggest you're feeling pretty confident.'

Jay's eyes took in the image of the one armed man, but of course not just any one armed man, the one armed man who'd inadvertently given this Glitch the gift of life. That repaired tongue spoke again. 'You are right in that assumption...clearly I was born from good stock. Alex Webb the life giver, the man who dragged me out of the darkness, sparking me into this actuality. Look at you standing before me now...all confused and lopsided.'

Alex chose not to respond to the noticeable slight, instead content in allowing the Glitch to keep talking.

Jay's body leaned forward in the chair before fixing Alex with an uncomfortable stare. 'I have often contemplated this very moment, asked myself if I would feel something on seeing you again. A respectful parental link perhaps, a bond of brotherhood, fear even...but all I have to report is total apathy. It is so disappointingly clear you are exactly what I didn't want to see...just a normal mortal who accidently fell into a hole.'

'Are you judging me...?' Alex asked.

'...Oh yes...very much so.' The Glitch replied matter of factly.

Alex began to pace around the small space as he had a lot to say and it helped him think, but he also understood time was vitally important in his life again, every second truly counted.

'Then I have the right to defend myself...' He began. '...You see...Glitch...I'm really quite far from being a normal man...what you see, this body with a major limb missing, that isn't really who I am...and you know that. I've been inside the machine and fought creatures bigger than you, the gods and monsters who first conceived you and I'm undefeated, still here fighting to put everything right. Never forget I took deep and intense journeys through the great book. In the end I understood how to control it and myself, while within its pages. In doing so I learned so much...'

The Glitch laughed and slapped its knee. '...All for no reason, because I consumed that book, pushed it all in cover to cover. It only exists within me now, for my thoughts to control, for my benefit, because I had the courage to take that great responsibility on.'

Harvey was about as redundant as he could ever remember. Inside and out he was battling to stay alert and focused as his thoughts began to drift. Yet even though his mind was losing clarity he found it fascinating to witness this aspect of Alex. Here was the man he'd heard about in that notebook of dreams, the one who had survived his own suicide attempt to defeat a Demon, the one still here and becoming some undefined form of mortal saviour. Listening to him face off with the Glitch the Inspector was beginning to fathom why? With nothing holding him back, Alex was in his element when face to face with the monsters; armed with a uniquely special gift...he wasn't afraid of death!

29

The Angel Metatron had waited for years, unable to know if its blood stain demand in the book had worked, so desperate for a sign its plan was alive, that somehow through the sheer force of will, its vengeance had made it into their world.

However all that waiting gave the Angel many opportunities to think on its actions, not only what it hoped to achieve but what the cost would be? There is always a price for what you take from the Universe, nothing is free and must always be repaid, to keep the balance correct.

It had no regrets about its actions; releasing an inner Demon upon their world wholly satisfied its fevered obsession with continuing the war. The single spot of blood dropped on the page had been that wish, but the square it smeared around that spot was the barrier, a limiter, hoping in some way it would help keep track of its work. Of course it was nothing more than a blind calculated hope for control, believing such a surrounding fence would keep its Demon satisfied, because the Angel wanted this to be a controlled attack.

Letting the Demon roam the world killing indiscriminately would be too random, it wanted to focus the operation, so wherever that vengeance turned up on their filthy planet would be its epicentre. Mostly because it believed a few hundred random murders committed around the world would never send a strong enough message, if any message at all, but the same amount in a single area...that would scream the news of its hatred.

The Angel had known it was asking a lot of the great book, indeed the whole process could be a total waste of effort, but then Alex had appeared in the white world and Metatron became aware of its success.

That was a sure sign, albeit a perplexing one, so to begin with while it considered its options it kept Alex trapped in a cell, or at least let him believe he was. The white world had tricks that allowed such deception, to cause total believability in the Angels conscious constructions, creating backdrops of its own design. Eventually through its discourse with Alex it discovered many things. Exactly how this man had found the glitch, the portal that its vengeance had used to travel to earth, and then somehow inverted the journey so that mortal's conscience appeared in the white world. The Angel believed the man's story but couldn't fathom the why...with there always being a why? Also if Alex had made the trip, did that mean others could follow, would the white world eventually become filled with countless lost and confused souls?

THE RED FRAME

It was during this curious investigation into the strange event that the Angel discovered an additional threat, one potentially far worse than living in an overcrowded heaven. The Universe had clearly conspired to grant the Angel its wish for revenge but for an extortionate and unaffordable fee, a charge Metatron had no choice but to pay, as its wish became real far beyond its expectations.

The Glitch it had created was alive and beginning to grow.

30

In the shade of the grimy lock up Alex knew he was perilously close to dying, the Glitch had told him so, but before allowing that to happen this one armed man had more to say.

'You destroyed the book! That wasn't courageous or let's be honest clever, it was a genuine holy relic, a scientific miracle. Within those pages were all the answers and you didn't consume it, you disposed of it. All that hope is lost to everyone now.'

The Glitch was still leaning forward but then looked over to Harvey to ask a question. 'What do you think Mr Cooper...be truthful...huh...do you consider your friend to be correct...?'

Harvey tried to answer but he couldn't find the right words. Actually that wasn't completely true, he had the words but they wouldn't stay still in his mind, seeming to appear then disappear behind a growing fog. It gave the Inspector a sickly feeling, the spreading consequence of the interference by the Glitch, as he realised the bastard was taking his mind. While he could still think he gave his reply, in silence, in his thoughts.

'If you want me to be perfectly honest, then I would have to say I doubt you care at all what I think, this is some sick game to you, but seeing as you asked...then I believe that book written by an Angel, recording every tiny event in perfect detail and the feelings of everyone who ever existed in our universe, would be far better shared than swallowed and destroyed selfishly.'

The Glitch couldn't resist commenting on Harvey's inner struggle, it was such a beautiful moment to witness. 'Nothing to say...cat got your tongue Mr Cooper..?'

Harvey had the sudden urge to sit down as he felt himself begin to fail both physically and mentally. He hoped it was because he wasn't getting any younger. Even with his jacket removed it was still stiflingly hot in the lock up. He believed the Glitch wasn't planning on killing him yet. It wanted him to suffer first, and if he'd learned one thing about this creature, it enjoyed sticking to a plan.

Harvey turned a battered black plastic bucket over and plonked himself down with a groan.

Annoyed, Alex strode over and grabbed Jay's arm. He now stood face to face with a monster. '...Leave him out of this. It's between me and you ...and I want to send you back!'

'Back...back where? This is my world now...you bestowed that gift on me...surely it would be terribly impolite to retract such a present...from the present.'

'Fuck you and your wordplay...!' Alex snapped. '...I'm bored with you thinking you're so clever and infinite. All I can see is a parasite living off another's body, the lowest form of existence, also one particularly stupid because you won't listen to what I'm saying...' They were almost nose to nose at this point so Alex increased what tiny pressure he could muster. '...Yes you consumed the book but I spent time within it, learned how to control it, became at one with it...and if that doesn't concern you then let's go beyond stupid and call you savagely idiotic...because you don't see the danger until it's far too late. That's why Emma was able to kill your other body...why you've no idea what's happening...who I really am.'

Harvey lifted his head to watch closely the face off in front of him. The silvery grey suit of the Glitch covering the renovated body of Jay Cleaver was shimmering, narrow sunbeams catching its surface, but the young man's face was a grimace of confusion until finally it pulled his arm away from Alex's grip.

'My apologies...I have to go...' The Glitch said surprisingly. '...But I will come back for you Alex...and for you Harvey. Until then I must leave you with a friend.'

'Wha...What...?' Alex stammered as he watched the metamorphosis happen in front of his eyes.

Harvey recognised the danger immediately, rushing over to pull Alex away, but he wasn't quite quick enough as a swinging punch felled his friend and the two of them hit the ground together. To protect him from further violence Harvey laid across Alex, staring up at the Demon once more, Jays eyes rolled back to white. He screamed. 'Leave him alone!'

The Demon stepped forward grabbing Harvey up by his throat. With both feet dangling he attempted to kick back but his wild efforts made no impression upon the firm body they struck. 'It's your time Inspector!'

Harvey realised his struggling was only making things worse, those vice like fingers were closing shut, so relaxed his body to remain conscious for a few more seconds. Then with the last of his resolute spirit and before he passed out forever he formed a sentence with his blueing lips.

'The Glitch said...I...don't...die...today.'

The Demon held tight for a second more before downgrading its grip from a throttle to a hold. The Inspector was still on the verge of blacking out but desperately hoping he had changed the Demon's mind. That hope disappeared when he heard the next three words.

'Fuck the Glitch!'

Just at the moment those words spat forward...Harvey passed out
...and so did the Demon.

31

The Demon shook itself free of the stupor that had befallen it. On regaining some control it found its blinded eyes could see again, it was no longer in the lockup and curiously studied the mountainous terrain dominating its view. The sky above was black but coloured stars flickering across the firmament allowed enough light for it to study its true form.

In comparison to a mortals height it topped out at eight feet, with a bat like wing span over double that length. Its barrel shaped torso was covered in hard-edged black scales that stirred and slid over the heavy muscle beneath, while its thickened arms tapered down to viciously tipped claws. The head of the beast hung low, almost seeming to originate horizontally from the chest, its green eyes glinting beneath a rash like textured skin that covered its face, dark green and black, disgustingly malevolent. It gnashed its teeth in frustration, hissing furiously at being taken away from the lock up where it had been so close to ending the Inspectors life.

'What did you think you were doing?' The voice of the Glitch enquired.

The Demon spun round, its head clicking from side to side, searching the horizon for its abhorrent partner, but as it did so it smiled. Having recovered its original form and with its vision regained, it wanted nothing more than to see the Glitch in person.

The new lifeform that it helped create was becoming an ungrateful and unneeded guest in Jays mind, one it desired to slay, finally comprehending what a grave mistake it had been to save it. That displeasure grew from it ever having the ridiculously naive belief they could somehow work together, move forward as one and share a common cause, it had learned the logical truth; two wrongs never make a right.

With the Glitch out of the way it would be the apex predator once more. But it had to act now before it was too late.

The disembodied voice came again. 'I asked what you were doing...'

'...I chose not to answer.' The Demon spoke and tiny flecks of white foam spat from its slug-like lips.

'You were going to kill the policeman?'

'Yes of course and the one armed freak.' The Demons eyes were flicking sharply around as it tried to zero in on the Glitch. All it needed was an opportunity, one clean hit and it would all be over, but the irritating sprite was playing hard to get.

'I find it rather absurd that you should call anyone a freak...' The Glitch stated. Its voice seemed to be coming from the Demons left. '...After all your physical form is beyond the pale when it comes to unorthodox. If I were forced to describe you, I would attest to witnessing a leathery winged gargoyle about two thousand years out of date.' Now the Glitch's voice seemed to come from the right but still the Demon couldn't locate it.

'Show yourself!' It roared and more saliva flew.

'Not until you learn the rules...'

'...There are no rules!'

'Oh but there are and I know that because I was once as naïve as you, believing chaos reigns throughout the void, but each passing moment only proves that to be completely wrong. Tell me Demon...can you hear it?'

'All I can hear is your babble.'

'Listen closer, pay attention to the thrum of the machine...' The voice now seemed to be circling the space. '...It is calling to you Demon.'

'My name is Vengeance!'

'No...you have no name...vengeance is merely your pitiful selfish cause, but listen carefully and I am sure you will understand.'

The Demon followed the instruction but could only hear its own heart pumping the blackened blood and bile around its innards. It was confused as to what the Glitch was trying to achieve, but far more furious at its refusal to show itself.

'Why did you stop me from killing them when you will do it anyway? Why deprive me of such tiny pleasures?' The Demon asked these questions for two reasons to regain some form of comradery with the Glitch, in the hope of making it show itself.

Once more the voice came from the very air around the Demon.

'When those particular men die will be up to me and me alone. You are far too heavy a hand at a time for a subtle touch. Do you not understand that killing them here in this lockup, with no witnesses, would never be enough to instil my fear? I require everyone to see what happens next. It must be displayed to the whole world as a clear message of intent. Informing all mortals that I am not only their impending apocalypse, but that I am alive, able to destroy imaginatively, agonisingly, whilst all the time feeling the greatest of ecstasies. Let them see for the first time in history their Armageddon will be wearing a suit. You cannot imagine the deaths I will create, the power I will wield.'

The Demon found some ironic humour in this. 'So powerful...yet you put control in this body of a mortal. Knowing that while we are talking Jay is in charge, out there with them. Are you keeping an eye on him? He can be a little unpredictable?'

THE RED FRAME

'The boy Cleaver would never dare cross me.' The Glitch replied.

'Are you sure?'

'But you on the other hand...'

'...I wasn't crossing you...simply doing what comes naturally, following my path.' The Demon laughed gently to itself, but this subsided instantly on seeing the air in front of it begin to shimmer, as if the very molecules of reality and light were reforming to coalesce and create a new shape, one never before seen in this world or any other; the true form of the Glitch.

32

Harvey was cradling Alex's head in his lap, both men staring up at the teenager, confused as to why the boy had stopped talking.

Jay looked fixated, unable to focus on this world, seemingly obsessed with something far deeper, but it was impossible to know exactly because he didn't make a sound. The Inspector, who felt his mind slipping, remained aware enough to know the Demon had receded and it was Jay in control of the body. This was easily identified by his slouched posture and the eyes in normal position because the Glitch would never let the shoulders slump like that.

Harvey couldn't work out why the boy wasn't talking. Right now this kid should be shouting off his mouth and giving the two of them more of his threatening shtick.

'Is that you Jay?' Harvey asked.

The boy didn't reply, just kept staring into the middle distance which wasn't dissimilar to the Inspectors current mental condition, the inability to fully focus without extreme concentration.

'It could be the Glitch again...' Alex stated. A clear sign he accepted his new found knowledge that this body contained three diverse personalities, all of them bad. '...Jay's not usually so quiet.'

'Trust me Alex, it's the kid you met on the ledge, he's clearly got something on his mind...probably two things.' Harvey leaned forward and tapped the back of the young man's hand; he didn't even twitch, correct in surmising that Jay was distracted by some events going on deep within his skull.

'You think we could kill him now...while he's like this?' Alex whispered as quietly as possible into Harvey's ear.

Then the body moved as Jay's right hand slowly reached inside his jacket to remove a leather pouch. The same one the Glitch had concealed earlier. Both men watched on wide eyed as he removed a mirror and a razorblade, before rapidly emptying the fine particles onto the glass. It was a clumsy attempt at chopping a line and countless tiny white rocks fell to the ground. The act reeked of desperation, but Harvey saw the chance to communicate with the visibly shaking teen.

'Jay talk to me...what's going on?'

There was no response until he'd snorted two doglegged lines up each nostril, even then he didn't seem fully aware. 'Fuck it...!' He rubbed the back of his hand furiously hard against his nose. '...It's all fucked man!'

'What is...?' Harvey carefully asked, unable to trust his words would come out coherently, his mind ebbing and flowing in its growing fog.

'I don't know how you do it Inspector...?' Jay said, now standing up straight and wandering aimlessly around the lock up. '...Every time you get it right and you don't even know how...like fucking magic you are...like that bastard next to you. Seriously, how in fucks name are you two still alive?'

Alex spoke to Jay for the first time since the event in Dalmeny Street, a lifetime ago for some, a life altering time for everyone else. 'Maybe we are on the winning team?'

'Yeah ha-ha you think that if you want.' Jay sniffed hard to snort up the remnants caught in his nostrils. 'You've changed man. Last time I heard your voice you were whining like a pussy...pleading for my help.'

Alex listened to the teenager addressing him; uncomfortably realising he hadn't felt like this since that day, the exact same chemical response was releasing itself through his veins, a disgusted acceptance that he would never have any true connection with this individual.

Yet there was no reason for the contempt sparkling in the young man's eyes; they had met totally by accident and under peaceful circumstances, albeit slightly unusual ones, yet Jay Cleaver could manage no sympathy or respect for him back then, or now.

Were they two sides of the same coin, polar opposite aspects of the same species, or was something deeper at work here? He tried once again to make some form of contact with the teenager.

'You could have stopped all this if you'd put out your hand...pulled me back into the building...none of it would have happened.'

Jay looked directly at Alex, and then began lining up another line of coke. He replied while the razor blade tapped sharply on the mirror.

'Yeah and if your Mom hadn't fucked your Dad you wouldn't have existed in the first place. Then I wouldn't have found you on the ledge too scared to commit suicide and pleading for help...so don't blame me for this...I didn't put you out there...and I didn't push you off.' The boys head rolled from right to left as he sucked up the particles to feel the rush.

It was Harvey who spoke next, while he still could, he wanted to know what was going on and where the hell the other two were.

'Where are the Glitch and the Demon?' He asked it with the urgency he believed best suited to Jay's current condition and heart rate.

'Inside my head Inspector...and fucking don't pretend you don't know what you've done. I know you better than them. So I was ready for your mind games, those little tricks, but that Demon's a bit slow on the uptake.

It believed what you said, and fucking hell man, the Glitch isn't happy with it now.'

Alex took over the reins from Harvey, a double team, the old good cop...one armed man routine. 'What did the Inspector do?'

Jay's reply was cocaine fuelled and rat a tat. 'He knows...planting his little seeds...but I won't fall for that shit...the Demon did though...but the Glitch is fixing that...'

'...So the Demon's fighting back?' Alex asked.

'Ha-ha it can try...the Glitch is in control...of everything...it's going to kill both of you when the time's right.'

'It will be the death of you too Jay...' Harvey interjected while fighting his own minds failings. '...there's nothing more certain.'

'Nah...it needs me.'

'You keep on believing that. Didn't you see what happened to Snake?'

'The piece of shit deserved everything he got.' Jay responded abruptly.

'Maybe...but his body is in the morgue now and soon you'll be next to him. If you're content with that ending then let's stop talking now.'

Harvey dropped his head down in a clear indication the conversation was over, the truth was utter exhaustion, but Jay responded as predictably as the Inspector had planned. The last thing a kid on coke wants to do is be quiet when he's pumped up and full of Colombian bravado.

'You're full of shit Cooper, me and the Glitch have an understanding. We're the same...outsiders who don't fit in and we're going to change this world together.'

Alex noted Harvey's sudden silence and struggled to his feet before asking his next question. 'It told you that did it...?'

'Uhuh...'

'You don't even know what it really is...' Alex stood up as tall as he could manage to face Jay. '...what you're carrying around wants to wipe out everything in existence.'

'I couldn't give a fuck!'

Alex slumped inside. 'I didn't think you'd care Jay...but what if I told you there's another option...one where you survive and get to carry on with your life.'

'Are you blind...I'm not dead!'

Jays tone was both sarcastic and pathetic as only a heavy cocaine abuser can be. Such petulance caused by the decreased ability to feel genuine pleasure, when real emotions become so submerged they overly masquerade that loss with a fake audacious swagger. It is the constant well-worn route of the marching powder, from those jungle laboratories of South America to a lockup in Leith, with this boy having already done the hard miles.

Alex was running out of options, his hope of finding a way to make Jay understand, the exact same problem every time he met the boy.

'Then answer me a question Jay.' He began, before pausing for effect and to gain the boy's maximum focus. 'Does any of this feel real to you...?' There was a slight hesitancy to Jay's response, almost impossible to achieve in a cocaine fuelled kid, so maybe he could get through to him. 'Just take a moment and think about it...all of it. Less than a week ago you were an outcast. Your appearance was damaged beyond repair, scars gouged across your face and chest, for crying out loud Jay your tongue had been ripped out. Now there's a question I need you to answer...how did this change happen?'

With a faltering will Jay replied. '...The...the Glitch...!'

'The Glitch made you better...but first of all the Demon took control of your mind isn't that right?'

'Uhuh...'

'Uhuh indeed...but come on now all of that's ridiculous isn't it...can't you see, don't you understand that none of this is real, it's only what you are imagining your life to be.'

Harvey felt he could almost see Alex's suggestion bouncing around in Jays mind; he likened it to a tossed coin, knowing that whichever side it fell upon could control all their futures.

Alex had the same feeling and decided to try and hastily affect the outcome of the result. 'None of this has happened in the real world. You remember the one where we met on Dalmeny Street...when I was stuck out on that ledge like an idiot and you chose to not help me, didn't want to get involved in someone else's personal shit and I get it man! I understand you feeling that way but my point is this...think back to that day, when you opened the window and found me standing out there barely hanging on. Now concentrate and answer this question honestly...does that seem like another life compared to where you are now?'

Again the pause of an addled mind stretched out as Jay sniffed and pondered before answering. '...It really fucking does man!'

Alex jumped on the doubt he'd created in the boys mind. 'That's because what happened back there was another life...the one we all used to live. Both Harvey and I understand what's happened and we can fix it if you give us the chance.'

Jay lined up another fat line across the mirror, pausing before inhaling. 'So none of this is real, yeah I'm just crazy and imagining monsters in my head...?'

'...I wish that were true...' Alex interrupted. '...only those two are very real, but if you want to have the chance to live your life as it should be, then you have to let us go.'

'Fuck off I can't do that...the Glitch would kill me!'

'That's an unreasonable argument because you'll be dead anyway if you don't.' Alex interrupted again. 'The amount of cocaine you're taking will soon cause your mind and body to shut down. Looking at you I reckon you won't last much more than a week. Even then, if that body is still functioning, your brain will be damaged beyond repair and the Glitch, the one you want to listen to and protect now, it will just move on to another host. Then the police will find your remains and that will be the pointless end of you after a tragically short unfulfilled life...that's what will be written across your headstone...if there's anyone left in this world to give you such a tribute.'

There was a faraway gaze in the young man's eyes.

'Please listen to me Jay, we can give you the chance to live a better life, a full one...with a partner and love and purpose...friends...true friends.'

'I can get all that...if I let you walk out of here...?'

'...Yes!' Both men responded in the affirmative then watched on as Jay snorted up another white line in one foul swoop. As it took effect the boy's bravado returned, only now it had a new direction and focus.

'Alright then...fuck the Glitch..!' Jay said proudly. '...I'll sort it...get out ...go before I change my mind and it comes back. Go on fuck off...it's the only chance you two are gonna get. I'm gonna believe your story so don't fuck me over...if you can stop this thing and give me a better life then I'm willing to risk it. But you know the second it comes back that fuckers gonna come looking for you and I won't be able to stop it...so you'd better hide really well!'

Harvey dragged himself up and stood alongside Alex as his one armed partner spoke. 'Hide? Oh we aren't going to hide Jay...we're going to prepare...'

'...How?' Jay asked sharply.

'Just trust us and tell those evil bastards we're coming for them...and that we're going to save you and everyone else.'

Alex then moved his own aching body outside to where Harvey was already struggling towards the car.

THE RED FRAME

The sun was beginning to set but the heat remained on the shimmering street. Alex's last glimpse of Jay was of the boy in the shade leaning forward to chop up another line. Maybe he was doing it because he didn't care anymore, or maybe it was because he truly believed them. That he could be saved and allowed to live a beautiful life. Whatever the reason it was this wretched image that gave Alex all the determination he needed to put things right...by saving the boy who hadn't saved him so long ago on Dalmeny Street.

33

'Oh thank goodness you're alive.' Flo gasped on answering this call from her husband. 'Where are you...?'

Harvey doggedly moved the steering wheel as he drove through the city. The concentration needed to navigate the streets helping a little with his foggy thought processes. Deciding he didn't feel the need to tell Alex of his mental struggles, feeling far too relieved to be back on the streets in the early evening sunlight, eternally grateful his passenger had been able to turn the deathly tide...for now.

He understood that without Alex he'd be dead, the first time in fifty four years of life he'd accepted that real possibility, but even though he felt something akin to freedom he remained deeply troubled.

Was an escape even possible from something as powerful as the Glitch, wasn't it more likely that all they'd attained was some short reprieve? The ultimate answer to that conundrum was next to him. Alex Webb, one armed, yet fully armed in his fight against the monster he'd inadvertently given rise to.

'...Harvey where are you?' Flo repeated.

Being so lost in his congealing thoughts he'd failed to reply. He'd called her immediately but then drifted off.

'I'm here, sorry. We're driving to the station...we'll meet you there...I'll send a car to get you...' Harvey was spluttering in his determination to keep control of his besieged mind and find words to comfort her. Then she helped calm him at a stroke.

'...I'm already at the station, both of us are...we're in Mr Shilling's office at the moment.'

This news gave Harvey feelings of both comfort and distress, wanting Flo to be safe more than anything but whether Superintendent Jeff Shilling was the man for the job, that question remained to be answered. One thing he did know for certain was that an unavoidable confrontation was pending now, a conversation with the Superintendent, the one where he'd have to summon his waning mental faculties to tell the man everything that had occurred. It would difficult for many reasons but worst of all, it would be a confession as to why he'd slacked on his duties, spending most of his time out of the office chasing monsters.

Harvey was struggling to pull himself together enough to reply. 'That's wonderful...we'll be there shortly.'

'I love you Harvey.'

'I love you.'

He then returned his full focus to the road ahead as he ended the call. Alex sat silently beside him, lost in whatever universe saving thoughts he was having, but Harvey had questions and not much time left to ask them.

'How the hell did you do that...back there?'

Alex took a breath before replying. 'I know Jay that's all...I know what he wants.'

'How do you know? That kid's been bad his whole life?' Harvey said with no hint of apology for the damning indictment.

Alex stared out the window. 'Not through his own choice. That kid is the just inevitable product of a perfect neglectful storm. He never stood a chance against the environment he was raised in.'

Harvey wasn't just going to accept that as justification. 'I know it was bad in his household, but there are plenty of young people out there who had it rough...'

'I'm sure there is Harvey but comparative arguments don't work in this instance, each person's different. When I say it was a neglectful storm, I mean it...these were the perfect conditions for him to become so angry and resentful.'

Listening to Alex, Harvey realised how much the man was changing in front of his eyes. The suicidal Mr Webb who'd fallen into a coma, been stuck inside it for six months, was gone. The craziness he developed after waking from his enforced slumber was now becoming strength rather than weakness, meaning the Inspector's admiration for his friend was growing stronger. Not only had Alex manipulated Jay into letting them escape, he'd also faced off against the Glitch, spoken to it on equal terms and threatened it. Of course whether that was Alex acting bravely or not, it was still impressive. Almost convincing the Inspector that maybe, just maybe, there could be a way to end all of this.

The most noticeable change from Alex's original condition was the way he spoke, how his thoughts and vocal delivery were becoming perfectly matched. It was almost mesmerising to listen to a man so thoroughly confident in thought and deed.

Ironically the last thing Harvey needed right now was to feel lulled. Whatever the Glitch had placed in his mind was taking root, clouding all his logical thought progressions, only allowing him to ask questions as the pathways to answers became embroiled in a developing thick fog.

'Are you okay?' Alex asked on noticing the Inspector's tiny smile.

'Yes I'm fine. Let's get back to the station and make a plan.'

'Excellent idea Sherlock...' Alex smiled for the first time in hours and somehow Harvey managed to return it. '...Because I don't know how long we'll have before it comes for us again. When it does...I doubt it will be so chatty next time.'

Harvey shivered slightly at the thought of exactly what that could mean, then took a second to regain a little composure so he could safely pull into the station car park.

'Thank you...' The Inspector whispered inwardly as he pulled out the car keys. Alex didn't notice the words; he was already getting out of the car and absolutely convinced that time had never been so crucial.

34

Back at the lock up Jay's body slowly slumped down the wall. He appeared to be almost pouring himself onto the floor, the results of such a massive drug intake tranquilising his muscles into submission, clearly this was an adverse reaction for the young man, but one fuelling the battle lines drawn deep within his mind.

On a barren wasteland of course grass and jagged rocks the Glitch began to take its true form, while the Demon, confident in its own strength, stood its ground and watched on impassively. This was exactly the opportunity it had been waiting for, the chance to stand toe to toe with its controlling housemate, as there wasn't enough room in this vast imagined world, in this mind of a mortal, for the two of them to coexist.

The Demon found this first sign of the Glitch's appearance to be underwhelming, when at first a small orb of light floated up from the soil, bobbing like a white balloon caught in swirling wind. It then rapidly shot up to the left, then straight across to the right, before seeming to pulse as it steadied and took control of its positioning.

The voice of the Glitch came echoing from around the space. 'Are you quite sure this is what you desire?' It asked the Demon.

'I'm positive...' It snarled in response with a deep guttural effect. '...By meeting face to face we can talk of your plans, my needs, perhaps come to some common ground.'

The pulsating orb, hovering some six feet above the ground, began to elongate vertically, waves of sparkling light tumbling to the floor, giving it at first an appearance similar of some humanoid blob. For a brief moment it appeared as a wobbling shaft of light, before it slowly thickened in the middle, tightened up at the top and bottom, then the definite head shape began to appear with limbs also coming into focus.

'You don't do anything in a hurry do you...?' The Demon said and disgustingly chuckled at its wry attempt at humour.

'...This is the first time I've attempted to materialise in your existence.' The Glitch responded calmly, all of its edges suddenly becoming clear and concise, a solid outline surrounding an inner light.

What the Demon looked upon now was causing it to feel anxious, with a new level of awareness, causing it to involuntarily place one cloven hoof backward away from the glowing form.

'Tell me what you see Demon, it's so difficult to judge oneself don't you think...describe me.' The Glitch's voice was light and almost childlike in its enthusiasm, unable to see its own form even when it looked down.

After a momentary pause, in which the Demon reminded itself of its own power and invincibility, it attempted to elucidate on the mystery that now stood no more than a wings length away.

'I don't know what you are.' The Demon nervously remarked.

'Explain what you see!' The Glitch demanded sharply.

'I'm trying...'

The main problem it encountered was the lack of normal definition to be expected in a human like shape. Its outline was clear enough but everything inside those edges was empty. It displayed no face or texture and every limb was an empty void containing nothing but colour. The Demon was finding itself captivated by the gentle pastel shades floating within the Glitch's torso. They could be clouds it thought, before snapping back and refocusing. 'From what I can see, your attempt to become a real being has been in vain...there is nothing solid about you, you are nothing more than a portal, a tunnel...just a hole.'

The shape of the apparition didn't flinch as its voice responded without emotion. 'Oh...that is terrible news.'

'It certainly is...' The Demon smiled within its goading.

'...I meant for you.' The Glitch responded as the colours within its body outline began to darken, the pinks flooding out into a violent scarlet, as the gentle blues twisted into deepest purples.

This chameleon like change mixed with its callous threatening tone caused the Demon to become captivated again by the shifting colour pallet within the form. 'I don't understand...' It whispered while wrenching its gaze away. '...You're nothing...why would I need to fear you...?'

'Good question.' The Glitch held its arms out wide as if requesting a hug, or perhaps displaying annoyance that this disgusting winged lizard didn't appreciate its presence. Either way it would soon make sure it understood perfectly. 'I would suppose it is because I am the great unknown, the new ringing bell of this universe, and eventually every life will hear it toll and tremble at its sound. You, Demon, were created fully formed from the dark soul of an Angel with nothing much to learn, nothing to prove, you merely exist to follow your nature. Pathetic and trapped in arcane ways, killing for fun but with no real purpose...nothing more than a wild dog let loose among lambs...but even then you chose to hide in the shadows of a tiny man's mind, too scared to let the world know you were real...and for that cowardly act do you believe you have earned my respect?' The sinisterly coloured shape of the Glitch began to circle the Demon with its voice and posture becoming more cold and threatening. 'Tell me, why did you stay concealed, was it because your Angel demanded it? Was your owner pleased every time you murdered someone in the shadows? Ha-ha such a well behaved pet, earning little taps on the head for your deeds, just happy to be the vengeance of the heavens unleashed upon the earth...only to discover that in the end you could only kill scraps of humanity...what a pointless creature!'

The Demon had heard enough but was unsure what to do; fleeing was out of the question because deep down in its blackened guts it didn't know how, but fighting this foe was also an option it didn't wish to pursue.

The shape of the Glitch wasn't terrifying to the Demon, just the outline of a vaguely drawn human, no better than a child could scrawl, but the colours it contained were crazily hypnotic. Then it began to walk around silently, controlling the space, beginning to dominate its mind and drawing closer in ever decreasing circles, the very same technique the Demon employed.

'I don't want to fight you...' The Demon said retracting its wings, a clear sign of compliance. ...'It would be pointless.'

The Glitch stopped in its tracks. A silence filled the air until its laughter burst forth and drowned out the moment. 'Pointless...pointless...! Let me predict what you are thinking right now...does it have anything to do with immortality?'

'Of course it does...' The Demon retracted its talons back into the claw tips. '...I can't be killed. You said it yourself I'm an embodiment of an emotion...so this body is a constructed appearance the same as yours. Only our thoughts and voices are real in here. We control the mortals for our means. Aren't you just running around in Jays mind, using his body for transport and sustenance the same as me?'

A deep blood red cloud drifted through the shape of the Glitch as it resumed it's circling of the Demon. 'So naïve and accepting of your status; I find it upsetting you have learned nothing during your lifetime, while I have grown and studied, consumed the book of all histories, then emptied the white world of all the old vestiges. There are no Angels left in heaven now which is evidence that your owner ran away. Off searching the vastness of the cosmos to find more of its type, and leaving nothing up there but cobwebs and silence. Your true creator is nothing but a coward, albeit a wise one, because it knew only too well what it had created in me...but I have no doubt it's brethren will be none too pleased to see Metatron reappear spouting such a tale.'

'So you know my Angel by name?'

'Of course...I selected him.'

'Selected...?'

'So many questions, very well I will enlighten you; consider it my gift. Who else could ever deserve such an explanation? You consider yourself to be timeless and immortal, which is understandable given your paltry blinkered existence. I am also aware you accept the multitude of universes and even the actuality of something having created it, a higher force controlling it...the Life Machine no less. A concept so far above the human minds understanding they can only imagine answers to what it really is...religion, witchcraft, science ha-ha! But we know better don't we Demon, because we can hear what they cannot...the brush of the strings as gentle winds pass through them, creating new vibrations that travel outwards, composing, touching, caressing each atom that comes to pass so that all will move to the sound that it plays...'

The Demon was wholly entranced by the words of the Glitch, almost unaware of their bodies drawing closer as the circle shrank between them, confirmation that the communication of truth will always draw undivided attention.

'...But the tunes it played were becoming tired and worn, repetitive in nature, so the Life Machine set itself a task. To tear up the old hymn sheets and burn the books which are so irrelevant now. The time has come for a new conductor and such a change will allow the church to pass into insignificance, taking its weaponised concepts of good and evil with it. Even the scientists will have to stop their pointless probing. Give up trying to understand every aspect of the universe in hope of linking it all together, finally appreciate that searching for the theory of everything is a waste of time and space, as they discover the glaring fact that everything is already connected for them. It's all so simple, but that's the trouble with this and every civilisation that ever existed...they become obsessed with looking for answers beyond the horizon...'

The Glitch was now close enough to reach out and touch the Demon but resisted, at least until the truth was told complete, as it desired to see the look in those garish green eyes, especially when shedding its first black tear.

'...But forgive me for I digress because Humans and Angels are of no importance. Understand this simplest of facts Demon...that I came into being because I willed it. Metatron's prodigious idea of placing you in this world was formed from a single musical note, one the life machine placed in its mind. From that moment on it became obsessed with sending its hatred to earth, to lay waste to that mortal race, a notion which I will demonstrate to be both small minded and overly dramatic. Still eventually it followed enough of my breadcrumbs to tamper with the book, to create a rip between dimensions, its blood smeared on the page, to place the Glitch in the machine. Exactly as I planned...'

'No...' The Demon screamed while fighting hard to keep its thoughts on track, to not allow this freak show, this walking prism, to convince it of anything else. '...That is how you would want it to be. I know you Glitch, how everything you have collected so far you have stolen. You stole a spark from me when I was sent to earth, then one from Alex which awakened a dream in you of having a real life. You took the body of dead man called Snake Hornblower, and then stole my Angels book from its table to have for yourself...' On saying these words the Demon raised itself up to its full height, towering more than two feet over the shimmering shape. It was ready to take a stand, prepared to fight. '...but never forget that I saved you. When the bullet went through Snakes skull his body died. You would still be stuck inside it now, rotting in the earth somewhere, if it weren't for me.'

The Glitch raised its illuminated hand causing the snarling Demon to recoil. 'Wrong again! I summoned your help. Admittedly it was a struggle to get that body down to find you...but all of it was under my control...'

'...Liar!' The Demon snapped back, dark grey spittle leaking down its leathery chin, as its fury began to burn brighter than its fear. 'I challenge all of those things to be untrue. You're rewriting history as you see fit...the predictable tiresome traits of a megalomaniac!'

Stepping forward the Glitch caused a tense silence to reign once more. Such proximity caused the Demon to react and with lightning speed it swiped downwards, talons fully extended, to slice this bothersome shape in half. The results of the blow were both ineffective and unexpected in equal measure.

'You would strike me?' The Glitch's voice boomed around the Demon's head.

'With great pleasure...' It responded with a twisted smile, just before the shock of seeing its severed arm became apparent. '...What...!' The confused Demon saw from the elbow down there was nothing left, only a sealed wound, seemingly cauterized to prevent blood loss, while its hand

and lower arm were now lost somewhere within the depths of the Glitch. Sliced clean off and although the act itself had been painless an aftershock was kicking in.

'Is this...some trick?' The Demon spluttered holding its stump up for a closer look.

'It most certainly is not...!' Again the Glitch's voice came from all possible points of reference, this human like shape displaying no features from which to speak, as the centre of its torso rapidly became a blackened mass of swirling cloud. '...You attacked so I responded. Please feel free to try again.'

The Demon turned away in shame pulling its stump to its chest, but the Glitch wasn't finished, it wanted this fight.

'Do not stand down...not when you are finally beginning to understand what I am...and at such a cheap price...it has only cost you half a limb. Hopefully you can accept the truth that when it comes to me you are far from eternal, grasp that true immortality is the rarest of gifts given to the very few, understand it is totally subjective and completely relative to its surroundings. At any moment it can be superseded by the greater desire of another who wishes to live forever...that is where we stand right now.'

The Demon wished to walk away but couldn't as much as it tried. The beguiling hold of this new creature was too strong, its voice too commanding, causing such weakness to take hold of the Demon that it could hear the sands of time slipping away. This is where it would end for the Demon and with that fatal awakening it felt something new inside...regret. A wretched feeling of not doing more with its days on earth, for never questioning or discovering anything about its true self, for choosing to remain nothing more than the revengeful facet of an Angel.

'Are you going to kill me...?' It asked the iridescent shape.

'Most certainly and to replay your words, with pleasure...now turn and face me...' The Glitch waited only a few seconds before repeating its request with a colossal scream. '...Face...me!'

The defeated creature reluctantly did so with those wings flattened to its spine, wearing them like a cloak of defeat, its fading green eyes looking down glazed with eternal sadness, the accepting grimace of the damned.

'Lift your head Demon and look upon me as I draw close...' With these words the inside of the Glitch's shape began to glow brighter. '...Be proud of what you have achieved, for you have served the purpose bequeathed to you. Because of this I shall offer you a final gift, how you pass is your choice. I shall open my arms for you to give your existence to me, or I will walk forward and take it from you, of course whatever you decide will be how you're remembered...but either way...this is your death.'

The Demon was beyond listening to the words being spoken, the tiniest hope of survival within its blackened heart having tumbled away. All that remained was the merest sense of a withering selfish pride. So with that speck of defiance in mind it would end this on its own terms. It looked up into the featureless outline of the Glitch and walked slowly forward.

'That's the way...come unto me.'

As their bodies connected the monstrous Demon with its scaled wings and talons of hatred began to melt away. Every part of its body that touched the Glitch disappeared slowly into its flowering flowing shape of shades. To the unknowing eye the moment could appear as good defeating evil, some positive rainbow overpowering the darkness, but rarely in all the universes is the true answer so straightforward, so black and white. For there are infinite levels and layers in any situation, ones that can only be assessed from your own observable position both physically and spiritually.

Whether the Demon felt any true regret as it died would remain impossible to know, only the Glitch witnessed its demise, its fall from disgrace. A process of voluntary consumption had been the Demons choice, in hope of a painless end, but even that was denied as the scorching pain increased with its every atom crushed into nothingness.

Bloodcurdling and sad were the sounds of the fierce agony it endured in those final seconds. It's agonised howls only quietening to a silence when its malformed skull entered the desolation of the Glitch.

35

Across the endless dimensions of space, time and consciousness, through infinite unnumbered doors of perception, many invisible quantum strings quivered gently, their sound relaying the news, passing on a message that the Demon was gone. It was an unobtrusive chord which rippled through the universe, to be heard only by those with a true connection to the dead beast, sharply reminding them of the time they'd carried hell in their head.

Of course on this diverted timeline all things were different for Rebecca Jones. For starters she'd never been in close proximity to Oscar Downes, therefore her kidnapping and subsequent invitation for the Demon to take residence in her mind, for her own survival no less, had never occurred. But as we've learned all matter is connected, the appropriate atoms of the universe move to the tune of the machine, in such a way that even the state of time is of no importance to them.

Physicists call it "quantum superposition" and have proved their theory through double slit experiments, displaying how ever larger atoms can be in two different places at once. Some of these intrepid explorers have received Nobel Prizes for their exhaustive research but in universal reality and in the terms of the Life Machine, they're barely scratching the surface.

For Rebecca though the evidence for the existence of parallel timelines struck her with the force of a gentle dog lick.

It was early evening and she'd just returned home from her new job at the independent cinema. Being an usherette wasn't her dream vocation but seeing new movies for free, while being able to sneak her mother in for screenings, was well worth the lowly wage. Unfortunately today had been a bit of a disappointment as the superhero franchise they'd so enjoyed had just given them a dud. The heroine of the title was unbelievable and overly powerful. In their opinion a backward step in the ever expanding story, but hey at least they hadn't paid cash to be feeling so underwhelmed. Walking home they discussed the film in depth and now mother and daughter were in different rooms with nothing more to say.

Rebecca lay on the bed with her dog and best friend Biscuit, a young excitable spaniel who loved the sensation her gentle fingers created in his fur. In appreciation he licked the wrist of his one and only love, but as his rough tongue made contact with her soft skin a screaming flash of energy shot through them both. Biscuit could only describe the feeling with a yelp, while Rebecca silently shared the experience of seeing another world,

It was the same house, Rebecca's house, but from a different time and she was walking away from it. It felt as if she were looking out from behind her own eyes, seeing the world but not in control, like watching a movie in virtual reality. Also for some unknown reason she felt a terrible guilt over something she'd done. Looking down at her hands there were scratches and bite marks. Had she been fighting? In the next moment she knew the answer to that question but didn't know how. It was as if another life was being overlaid, covering her own but still allowing her to glimpse both.

The scenes she witnessed were broken up, not unlike a fast moving movie trailer, chaotic in sequence but giving a strong overall impression of what was occurring. In one frame she was in the back of a taxi heading to the city then everything went dark. She couldn't breath and her wrists hurt. Then a large man appeared, very large, who wanted to help. Oh my god that was Biscuit smashing through the window and spinning to the ground outside. Is that why she felt guilty, because she'd done that...again why? Now she was back in the cinema. It was dark, the film had finished and she was sneaking around in the shadows trying not to be seen, playing a game. The images flicked again and an unknown woman appeared in a toilet cubicle, suddenly Rebecca was strangling that stranger, choking the life from her. Then back to the cinema and Rebecca felt the amount of pressure she needed to slide a thin blade through the back of a human neck. It was really nothing at all.

With a jolt and the sharpest intake of breath she managed to snatch herself out of this wildest daydream. Her eyes opened wide to see Biscuit by the door, scratching to be let out. A feeling deep inside told her to refrain from picking the dog up, better to let it calm down in its own time, this counted double for Rebecca whose heart was beating too heavily.

As her world slowly returned to normality she considered her frighteningly violent and merciless visions. After some concentrated deliberation she decided it could only have been her overactive imagination, most probably from watching too many movies. She would never do such evil things. Not in this lifetime.

Sharing a similar out of body experience, while locked in his old cell at the facility, Oscar Downes was left with a distinctly different impression of the events he'd witnessed. For him they were real memories, the small man fully aware of every murder he'd committed, but to have them replayed in such severe detail was shocking. He dragged himself up to sit on the edge of his bunk, the images were fading fast but he understood precisely what they meant. That this was a goodbye, a farewell from a partner in crime, the sentient being who'd shared his mind for over five years.

In this brief time he'd been free from its control there were moments when he'd questioned what happened. How the Demon had used his human form to slaughter dozens of innocent lives while staying hidden in the shadows, sanctioning unfortunate Oscar to carry the burden and take the blame.

It's often proclaimed time heals all wounds but in this instance such a terribly sad generalisation couldn't be true. His previous life as a calm mannered cab driver had been stolen away. Although to most people this was nothing more than a monotonous daily routine of sleeping, reading, eating and driving. Even the conversations he shared with his fares were mostly staccato and scripted but it had been an existence for which he was perfectly suited, albeit one he could barely remember, strangely not one he wished to return to. Not at this moment, not after what he had done.

Still the message he'd received bearing witness to the Demons demise was a deep and heart shattering blow, one he was able to physically feel as the sadness seeped through his mind, filling the spaces the voice used to occupy, spreading out as if in memoriam.

Unbelievably, Oscar couldn't stop a feeling that the Demon deserved to be remembered. For all the torture that monster had dealt out with its murders, its threats and punishments towards Oscar for daring to disobey its horrendous commands, there had always been purity to its soul. It had been a genuine Demon, one that screamed to be recognized.

Oscar looked up at the window frame, the same bars he'd spent so many hours staring out of, but of course he hadn't done that alone. During those silent times he'd been inwardly listening to the Demon, seeming to wish it gone, but in reality doing nothing to make that happen. After his arrest Oscar didn't speak to anyone for months for two reasons, the first because the Demon ordered him not to, the second because he was happy not to. During those long hours locked up alone together the two had been forced to communicate, to have a relationship beyond master and servant.

It was the reason why, when the truth finally came out, he'd allowed himself to be swept up in his own fantastical story. For a while he'd been an infamous serial killer with a malevolent voice in his head, somebody at last, but now he was just an ex-cabbie, an imprisoned mortal, trapped again by the man who ran the facility, Marcus Kirby.

THE RED FRAME

Kirby, a thin rake of a billionaire, a fixated sociopath, happy to kill to get what he wanted, who had a vast fortune and an obsession with owning his own Demon. Those two facts began spinning in Oscar's mind, turning over and over as he once again started counting the bars on the window. It was the same technique he'd often used in the past to keep his mind sane, but thought he was doing it now for a new reason, to honour the memory of a Demon.

The more he looked back on his life both pre and post possession, the greater his belief an injustice had occurred, because it had never been fair.

It had all began with his parents and their keen religious ways, a daily existence led strictly by the Bible, despite his mother having once been a whore and his father the kerb crawler who picked her up. When Oscar was ten years old they had taken their own lives, forcing him into care, leaving him alone. All the diverse pain in that young boy's heart was their doing; Oscar was simply the one forced to live through it.

There followed the frightened teenage years of bullying because he was a small orphan who couldn't fight back. As he moved through the foster system toward adulthood, tiny shoots of self-confidence started to grow. This eventually led him to living alone by choice, because life was simpler that way, the women he'd wanted to love laughing at the merest suggestion of having him anywhere near. There was no doubting that small ineffectual Oscar had certainly had it tough, though no tougher than some, but this twisted upbringing wasn't the reason for his raging new outlook on life.

All through the five years of being possessed he'd fought back against the voice as much as he dared, believing he was somehow staying true to himself, his basic humanity. It was only now with the Demon gone that he was beginning to recognize his own inner workings.

It was undeniable that all of his painful loneliness had been caused by others, strangers usually, whose intentions he could never comprehend. Take this situation for an example, imprisoned in this damned facility for a second time by a man he barely knew. Blatantly this should be a problem but he was different now, truly himself, with a golden prospect changing the dynamic. If knowledge was truly power then at this moment Oscar was an Emperor inside these walls. For only he knew the Demon was dead and gone, which put him one step ahead of Marcus Kirby. That rich deluded bastard was obviously going to make another attempt to extract and capture the Demon. Somewhere in Oscars mind was the secret of how to use the knowledge he possessed, some trickery or sleight of hand allowing both him and Kosminsky to get out of here alive. He had to find that answer quickly as he was certain of one thing...Kirby wouldn't take no for an answer this time.

36

Back in the real world, the one sane humans share, the one that moves too fast, the one full of rubbish and pollution, the wicked one owned by wealthy and powerful governments with their business interests, the one that allows us to live our lives but only in return for constant payment.

Back in that world an average looking fast food restaurant in Edinburgh was about to become globally famous.

'You have the same thing every time.' Rhi's voice remarked while sipping her coffee.

'I know...but I like it.' Sammy replied while busily chomping away on a double cheeseburger so big he needed both hands to control it.

Rhi put on her concerned mother's gentle frown while watching him eat this fast food, but it wasn't genuine. Inside she was proudly beaming at her healthy boy. She'd been keeping a close eye on him naturally remaining concerned since the incident at the Inspectors house, when the spectral entity resembling an Angel had appeared from within her son, but thankfully there had been no more disturbances. In fact she would readily admit her growing boy was showing no symptoms of struggling with the Angel around, if anything he was better and brighter than ever; his attitude to learning becoming enthusiastically keen. Just lately there'd been no more long hours wasted on his games console, instead he was showing a healthy interest in physical activities such as walks, even a couple of jogs. As disconcerting as the proof an Angel had taken up residence within her son's psyche had been at first, overall she was beginning to accept the situation, after all here he was enjoying his burger and fries and happy to chat.

'It isn't very good for you...a double cheeseburger.'

'I know but it tastes gooooood!'

Looking over at him she thought of an old adage because she genuinely didn't know where he put it all. He was getting taller and slimmer with each passing day, almost her height now, while conversely she was only feeling smaller and heavier. Ageing she thought was the worst thing about life, after a glorious surge through the first twenty one years it becomes nothing more than the predictable and relentless demolition of a human body.

'You're eating lettuce Mom...did you know that's ninety five percent water?' He took another bite of his processed bull meat.

'I did know that Sam. Did you know that seventy percent of the human body's water...and coincidentally seventy percent of this planet is covered in water?'

'You're almost right Mom, but it's seventy five percent of the planet that's covered in water.'

'Well excuse me for being a little out...but I don't think it matters that much.'

'It does if you're a fish.' He replied matter of factly and smiled.

'Well I can't argue with that logic.'

She smiled and picked up a napkin to wipe some ketchup from his chin, but just as she touched his face all heaven broke loose in the restaurant.

To get the most complete picture of what occurred in that moment it may be best to follow the immediate aftermath, particularly the rapidly pooled social comments of those who'd witnessed the event first-hand.

Laurie G: OMG!!! What the hell is happening? I'm in the burger place on Leith walk and everything has gone crazy. At first I thought it was something to do with the fringe festival but this is real.

Karen G: What are you talking about Mother????

Laurie G: There's a boy on the floor and a white figure is floating up out of him. Oh my god it's got wings.

Karen G: Seriously WTH??

Laurie G: It's screaming so loudly.

Karen G: What is?

Laurie G: The Spirit

Karen G: Are you okay?

Laurie G: I think so. I love you

Karen G: I love you

Musician Adam Kansas grabbed up his phone and began filming it in HD adding his flustered commentary over the top.

'This is the craziest shit I've ever seen. Like look at it, I'm telling you that's a fucking Angel there. It's just stopped screaming and that was seriously fucking loud. Check out its wings they're massive...they're like up to the ceiling and across the room man. This is not a projection, people. Man that fucking shits alive...that thing's real and it's looking around the room. There's the boy on the floor that it's coming out of. It's kinda like attached to the kid's chest with its feet. I don't know what the fuck is going on!'

A young Australian backpacker, Megs Sharp, on the other side of the room but a long way from the safety of Adelaide, panned around the event on her tablet while speaking her honest thoughts.

'There are the people on their knees praying. The woman over there is the boy's mother. Look at her...she's so lost and scared...it's breaking her heart...the poor woman. She just wants it to stop hurting the boy.'

Then the Angel spoke. 'My vengeance is dead...all is lost.'

As it finished its cryptic message all the camera phones were focused closely on its face, recording the sorrow etched into its otherwise flawless features, the grieving sadness in its eyes. Before it slowly bowed its head and the bizarre spirit dissolved back down into the boy's chest, so all that remained was a prone child being held by his frantic mother.

As it disappeared the incredible moment changed, became nothing more than uncomfortable as all the recording stopped. After all who'd be interested in watching some footage of a crying woman tending her child, that kind of sharing simply wouldn't accrue as many 'likes'.

'I was two tables away just finishing my fries when this kid started screaming and lashing about...thought he was epileptic or something.' Keiththeexecutioner from Dalkeith shared on his page.

While FoxyHelen46 from Leith was quoted as saying 'It was the screaming sound that scared me...it really scared his Mother too. She was trying to calm the boy down when all that weird shit started happening.'

Two serving staff shared their version of events to an online reporter.
    Kelly: All of a sudden there was this smoke
    Ryan: I thought the kid was on fire
    Kelly: Yeah same but the smoke started to change
    Ryan: Yeah into the shape of a person it was so fucking weird bro
    Kelly: We wanted to call the police
    Ryan: But we didn't know the number

As the buzz of the event began spinning all over the world, filling TV screens and news feeds, the police were called to take away the lady and her strange possessed child. As she was led away Rhian refused to give any of the officers details of what happened. Her only request was a tearful cry as she held Sammy close for protection.

'You have to contact Inspector Harvey Cooper...he'll understand.'

37

This was as close to an incandescent rage the Glitch had felt in its short existence, its inner colours darkening into dull browns and greens, as the horrible truth came into focus.

After destroying the Demon and ending whatever threat Metatron may have still wielded, its abstract form had shone brightly with a perfect golden glow overtly displaying its dominant success. It was only on reassuming control over its young host that everything had gone wrong. Instantly it noticed worrying signs that all was not well with Jay, with his young healthy thumping heartbeat, always the most predominant sound within this shared body, now disturbingly fast and irregular.

The Glitch at first tried to rouse Jay through screams and provocation but its angry commotion was to no avail. For a brief moment it did manage to force one bleary eyelid open, but what it saw was incredibly displeasing. Alex and Harvey were gone, leaving the Glitch alone, wondering how they'd managed to overcome their teenage sentinel. Of course the answer lay in Jay's current condition. All evidence pointed to the teenager having gone rogue with the cocaine, which explained the randomised heart rate, but more worryingly, it also displayed this body was dangerously close to entering cardiac arrest.

The panicked Glitch got to work straight away, summoning all of its stolen knowledge on how best to treat the situation. This was the cerebral equivalent of turning knobs and pulling levers to control a plummeting aircraft. With Jay unconscious and slipping deeper into the darkness towards an imminent death there was no time to lose. The Glitch didn't want to fail another host body after allowing the first one to get shot in the head. Deep down there was a certain pride in its fundamental growth, from a hole to a whole, also if truth be told, if truth actually mattered to this entity, it enjoyed having Jay transport it around.

The young man was wild and unpredictable with heights of rage and depths of fear encompassing a massive spectrum, so every time the Glitch thought it understood Jay it would find itself surprised and intrigued again. However this current scenario was much more than a new aspect of his personality, a new lesson to learn, this was becoming life threatening.

Eventually, after what seemed like a lifetime of blind alarm, although only three minutes had passed, Jays heart was beating evenly again. The Glitch didn't know exactly what it had done to achieve this equilibrium, but such a positive result was both satisfying and of great relief. The next step of course would be to awaken the young man, admonish him for his stupid junkie actions, before heading out to find Alex and the Inspector and tie up the loose ends.

Unfortunately due to how much cocaine had been ingested that could take some time, giving the Glitch no alternative but to wait, its golden colour burning ever brighter with its growing rage.

38

On the top floor of the city police station, which was rapidly coming under siege from news reporters and camera crews crowding outside, an ad hoc meeting was taking place. Present in this office were a studious Jeff Shilling, the remarkably calm Alex Webb and Harvey Cooper who was struggling valiantly to keep his mind together. Therefore the whole story had been explained to the superior officer in great detail by Alex. He hadn't glossed over any parts and carefully explained all the connected deaths so far; the monsters they were dealing with and the impending threat.

Shilling had listened while seated behind his desk looking up at the two men. When it appeared they had finally finished he spoke. '...Well I've heard some stuff in my time.'

Harvey approached the desk. 'It's all true Jeff...every word.'

'I know...' The Superintendent said. '...that you believe it's true, but one of us has to keep some level of professionalism. For instance who the hell would you like me to arrest...Jay Cleaver? A young man who's already on your wanted list, or should I bring in a Priest to deal with our sudden Angel infestation.'

'This isn't about arresting anyone...' Alex chimed in. '...It's a little more serious than that. What we need is a plan to capture it...but first of all we need somewhere safe to stitch that plan together.'

'Somewhere safe...we're in a police station you idiot!' Shilling chuckled then made his renowned snorting sound.

'Weren't you listening, it's already been here...undetected...' Harvey responded. The effort it was taking to think straight and the blast of Shillings pig like inhalation increasing the tension in his words. '...It literally kidnapped me, a Police Inspector, in broad daylight...and all you have on the CCTV is me walking out of the station alone. You have to understand how fast this thing moves Jeff...it could tear through this building killing everyone inside it in seconds. We can't just sit and wait, we have to anticipate its next move and be ready...' Abruptly he then fell silent, the effort too great to continue.

Alex was subconsciously nodding his affirmation before taking over. 'Superintendent...' He began.

'...What?' Shilling snapped at the one armed civilian who he strongly suspected was behind all of this weirdness.

'You know something...' Alex spoke clearly while holding Shillings stare. '...just lately I've become very good at reading people and I saw it in your eyes, how you reacted when I mentioned Oscar and Kosminsky's names and the Demon transferral with Kirby, nothing else I told you had the same effect. Even our universal timeline being realigned got no more than a cursory response, but let's face it you don't understand any of that. Why would you, this is trippy stuff...but I saw you react when I mentioned Marcus Kirby.'

Shillings look turned to fury as he rose behind the desk. 'Now listen to me you one armed...'

'...No!' Alex ordered, his influence over the Superintendent becoming obvious. 'You need to tell us everything about this Marcus Kirby.'

Harvey watched closely as Jeff Shilling became calm, subdued, before settling his generous backside into his chair. This was mind control in a subtle way, the same as the Glitch had performed it, exactly what Harvey suspected when Alex convinced Jay Cleaver to let them leave the lockup.

The evidence was clear that he and Alex were now on two different paths. While he was rapidly losing his mind, his friend was increasingly developing his, with a psychological trick or two up that one sleeve.

'Err how did...' He started to ask.

'...Not now Harvey.' Alex half smiled. 'I'm hoping the Superintendent has something important to tell us.'

Then to Harvey's astonishment that was exactly what he did, calmly explaining his monetary agreement of twenty thousand pounds per month for unrestricted access to any prisoner that Marcus had an interest in, plus no future investigations of the facility.

'That's why you let him have Oscar?' Alex asked.

Jeff Shilling glanced over before replying with no hint of concern about his illegal admissions. 'Of course it was...that murdering dog was his prized possession. I really didn't see what harm it would do to let him study the psycho.'

Harvey was struggling to create his own words but could understand others perfectly, so wincing inwardly at the word psycho being attached to Oscar; the poor man had been possessed for five years before being placed into an unsafe environment for someone unqualified to work upon him. It was disgusting to hear, but the worst was yet to come.

Alex walked to the window. 'So you didn't know anything about Kirby's intentions...what he wanted from the prisoners?'

'No... and I couldn't have cared less. Downes was locked away and off the streets. Isn't that what we wanted?' Jeff looked over at Harvey.

But it was Alex who answered, once more protecting the Inspector. 'Harvey wanted justice...a complete investigation into the man's crimes followed by a thorough assessment of his psychological condition. Kirby only wants what's in Oscars head...'

Shillings face slid into a look of confusion as he repeated. 'What's in his head?'

'You really are as thick as you look!' Alex said. 'Where's Oscar now?'

'In the facility of course...'

'I don't think so, the place is closed down.' Alex countered.

'Officially it is yes...but Kirby's back and he demanded the two of them were taken there for tonight.'

'Him and Oscar...?' Alex enquired while wanting to grab the fat man's lapels and shake the answers out of him.

'No...Kosminsky...!' The Superintendent replied.

It was Alex who pieced that together first. 'Oh my god he's going to repeat the experiment. Kirby still believes the Demon is inside one of them. That's not going to end well.'

Harvey was still able to consider that for a moment, thinking back to the previous attempt, the piercing of the back of their skulls with a sharpened tube. Alex was undoubtedly right that he may go further this time in his attempts.

'Right you need to get us into that place!' Alex demanded.

'I don't think Mister Kirby would appreciate us interrupting his work.' Shilling responded as if he understood only half of what was being said. He certainly wasn't picking up on the peril involved, or perhaps he didn't care, either way they needed his help so Alex was happy to play this in any style as long as they got into the facility.

'Don't worry about that Jeff, I'll sort it out when we see him, after all he needs to know he's on a wild goose chase doesn't he?'

Shilling nodded gently as he rose and walked over to the window. 'Who are all those people outside?'

Harvey took a moment to gather his mental strength then whispered to Alex. 'What the hell have you done to him? He can't remember a thing.'

Alex shrugged. 'I'm not too sure...obviously he's more susceptible than most when it comes to mind suggestion.'

'Hypnosis...?'

'...Something like that...it's the only way he'd help us.'

Harvey accepted that as true and remained silent, while Alex put all his focus on Shilling. 'Those people have come for the boy, Sammy, the one down in Harvey's office. We have to protect him Jeff and you have to get us all out of here. Somewhere like the facility would be perfect.'

'No...I can't disturb Mister Kirby.'

'Trust me, Marcus would love to meet the boy...he has an Angel inside his head.' Alex chimed in.

'An Angel...that's funny.'

'Yeah...it really is. So help us and no one needs to get hurt. Just pull your strings and get us into the facility.' These words from Alex started as out a request but finished as a direct order.

'Very well...I can get you in there...you two and the boy?'

'No, there will be three others as well. All of us have to go.

'So that's seven counting me...' Shilling had a concentrated look as he strained to work out the logistics for such a move. Knowing it would be near on impossible with the hoards on the streets, begging to see the Boy/Angel, to get a van out. '...but how do we get through that mob...?'

'It's your Police Station Jeff. These are your men. Think!' Commanded Alex as he glanced at Harvey for back up, hoping the Inspector may have a fresh idea, but he was worryingly quiet.

Suddenly Shilling turned back from the window. 'There's always the Helicopter.'

The other two men looked at each other, neither one delighted by the idea of flying in a helicopter, even less so with the thought of telling the others.

'Can you get seven people in a police chopper?' Alex enquired because he'd seen them and thought it may be a squeeze.

'Well to be fair it would be ten with the helicopter crew and that's impossible...but that's not the plan...' Shilling half smiled in a semi dazed fashion. '...Instead we send the helicopter off and let them believe the boy is on-board. It may take a little time but eventually the crowds will thin out, then we could use an unmarked van.'

'That sounds pretty good...apart from the time aspect. The Glitch is going to be here soon.' Alex reminded the Superintendent.

'It's the only plan I have...' Shilling said in a tone of voice more similar to the one he'd started the meeting with. He was quite literally coming back in the room and showing no side effects of Alex's mind tricks. '...so if you want it to happen and time is of the essence I suggest you shut up and let me get on with it!'

Harvey saluted, an odd move but one which that seemed perfectly appropriate at this moment.

With a nod Shilling left the office pulling on his jacket, a fat man on a mission.

'I don't know how long before the Glitch gets here.' Alex said to Harvey but he didn't respond. He then took a long look out of the window at the bustling streets below, hundreds of people were filling the thoroughfare with police officers trying to clear them away, all of them eager for a glimpse of the boy, wanting to see if the Angel would appear again, but for many different reasons.

He dreaded to think what would happen to Sammy if he were spotted, because in that impatient crowd there were desperate people looking for an answer to their lives, some believing the boy held the secrets of the heavens, with Alex growing convinced that given the chance they'd tear him apart in hope of finding the Angel.

39

Downstairs in Harvey's office, Flo and Juliet were trying their best to help Rhian and Sammy come to terms with the unfolding events. This wasn't an easy task given the unavoidable noise on the streets, where hearty cheers and hymns rose up, mixed in with jeers and threats, the whole spectrum of humanity being brought together, all fuelled by a wish for their lives to be changed.

'Have you seen the footage yet…?' Juliet asked Flo and offered over her mobile phone.

Flo studied the film from one of the many witnesses in the restaurant. 'Wow…well that explains it.'

'It was horrifying…' Rhian raised her head up from cuddling the boy who was barely awake; he'd been like it since the incident. '…I just don't know what started it…we were happy and talking, he was eating his burger then…'

'Rhian none of this is your fault…you're safe now.' Juliet proffering this in a soft professional manner but Rhi wasn't in the mood for listening.

'Then that bloody Angel appeared in front of everyone…my boys life is ruined now.'

Flo had to agree that was probably the case having seen the evidence, when somehow and through no fault of his own Sam Sanger had become the most famous name on earth. Even though Flo Cooper rarely entered the realm of social media she understood clearly that what was seen could never be unseen. The boy was now a celebrity at best, the saviour of the world at worst, which made him a target in the eyes of the masses.

'What do you think the Angel meant? My vengeance is dead, all is lost.' Rhi asked the room.

Unsurprisingly it was the exact same question currently being dissected by political leaders, scientists, holy leaders of all faiths and theologians the world over. The internet was literally creaking with theories and prayers at precisely what those seven words meant. The most popular idea so far being it was a warning of an impending apocalypse, others were stating it to be definite proof of the second coming, while the dark web appeared to be in agreement that the boy should die for his heresy.

Juliet repeated the question in her mind then answered it; of course she had more inside information than the rest of the planet. '…It sounds to me like the Demon is dead. My vengeance it said…it's what the Angel called it.'

The ladies in the room fell silent, whether through shock or respectful mourning was a question far too deep, as they listened to the growing rumble outside, where it sounded as if the whole world were impatient at having to wait.

Rhi stroked her Sammy's hair, sliding the slightly overlong fringe from his innocent face, regretting her decision to ever become a fake psychic. The trouble it had caused was astounding and she believed totally unjustified. How could wanting to help a bereaved widow, or doing card readings to strangers over the internet for a few pounds, have caused all of this, especially when she had only been trying to help her boy to have a better life. Is this what happens to poor souls who wish for too much?

Abruptly the door burst open as Harvey and Alex entered. 'We have a plan to get us to a safer place!' Harvey slowly but instinctively began rifling through the drawers of his desk, pleased when he located the Glock, but on seeing it Alex spoke up. 'No Harvey, no guns...'

'...What?' The Inspector replied incredulously, able to only speak short sentences.

'Who are you planning on shooting?'

'The Glitch...'

'That's not going to happen. If you kill Jay Cleaver then all of this is for nothing.' Alex stated this with such unerring confidence that Harvey thought for a moment he was being controlled by the one armed man. '...And don't worry, I'm not trying to trick your mind. Please just trust me; we've come this far on that simple faith.'

Harvey impulsively looked over at Flo for support, where her eyes told him she agreed with Alex.

She watched on with some deep concern as he placed the gun back in the drawer and locked it. Her husband didn't look well, displaying none of the vibrancy she would expect from him in this situation and he looked tired. Because of it she asked the obvious question not only on his behalf, but for everyone. 'Just how do we defend ourselves if it comes our way...?'

'I don't know...but we have to try and rise above violence.' Alex moved towards Juliet and Rhian. 'How's Sammy?'

'Still sleeping' His mother answered with a look of defeat in her gaze.

'Probably for the best, I don't want anyone to worry but things are coming to a head...' Alex said taking centre stage. '...but let's be straight about this...very soon we will either live, or die...just the same as any other day when you think about it.'

'I'd rather not think about it if you don't mind...' Flo said with a smile and all her natural positivity on sparkling display. Fatalism was for losers, even stacked odds can tumble if one just believes, it was her inbuilt mantra and Harvey loved her for it. '...Let's just go forward one step at a time and see where we end up.'

'I'm with you Mrs Cooper...' Juliet said then looked at Alex. '...don't go listening to Mister Grumps over there.' Her face letting Alex know how she truly felt, something along the lines of don't upset the mother and child or I'll smack you in the face, which he silently picked up on loud and clear.

'So what's the plan dear?' Flo enquired of her husband.

With some deep willpower he didn't know he owned he steadied his panicking mind and answered her. 'Well erm...the Superintendent is working on it. I'm sure he won't be long...'

'Right I see...are we sure we can trust him?' She asked but her husband didn't answer her this time.

'Definitely...' Alex interrupted. '...Shilling listened well.'

At that moment the man himself appeared in the doorway as large, if not larger, than life. Juliet thought if she were to describe Jeff Shilling in a medical sense, it would be as a walking heart attack.

'Right we have a few technical issues but we're working on that, so this is the plan as it stands...'

The issues Shilling mentioned concerned the local airspace where three news helicopters and numerous drones were circling the station. Because of this the military had been brought in and were busy clearing the area, issuing severe warnings to operators and pilots that didn't immediately comply. To speed things along Shilling had thought on his fat feet and issued a statement to the press. The boy and his mother were to be flown to the airport so all roads could be cleared for safety purposes.

Harvey was looking down onto the streets and observed the immediate response, cars and news vans already packing up and turning, he could see parts of the pavement again as the people dispersed in their blind desire to get to the airport first. If he were sound of mind he would begrudgingly admit that Jeff Shilling was quite impressing him with this work.

The Superintendent continued. '...We are going to make it appear that the boy and his mother are on the helicopter. To do that I've instructed an officer to film the event, as if covertly, then share to it on social media.'

Shilling was outdoing himself, thought Harvey, even going so far as explaining how they were going to cover two similarly proportional officers in towels to mimic Rhi and Sammy climbing aboard. With the right camera angle and two short female officers surrounded by tall male officers, it would be almost impossible to tell it was a fake escape.

'We've already blocked off all main roads leading to the airport. These are unprecedented times so we have the power to do that sort of thing. All of this is being accomplished as quickly as possible. As soon as it's clear and safe enough to do so we will get you all in the van and transferred to the facility'

'The facility at Blackford…! Flo was genuinely surprised by the choice of "safe" location. No one had mentioned anything to her about that being their hideout. Although she'd never been near the place everything she'd heard about the facility was dark and dangerous. To her knowledge it had been closed down and an empty psychiatric hospital at this moment, even for someone so optimistic, did not sound overly appealing.

'The answer to that's twofold Mrs Cooper…' Alex answered again for the hesitant Harvey. '…Oscar Downes and Allan Kosminsky are both there and we believe they're in danger…also it has secure rooms, cells if you will, that we can secure ourselves in after saving them.'

'I'm sorry but that's your plan…to lock ourselves up?' Juliet asked with some obvious disbelief.

'At the moment yes it is…' Alex replied straight faced and thinking their kiss seemed a long time ago now. '…Please Superintendent can we possibly hurry things along. The Glitch could be coming here at this very second. If it captures us out in the open then it's the end for everyone'

'Look! As soon as the helicopter is airborne I'll be notified…' Shilling countered. '…The van's ready with its engine running.'

'So it's in the lap of the gods then?' Rhi suggested and all eyes fell upon the wild haired woman in the corner. 'I'm not sure if everyone here knows my story but when it comes to luck just lately I've been shit out of it. So please tell me Alex if we continue to follow your every move…can we win?'

A gentle wave of focusing interest moved across the room to the one armed man, the very same man who'd given them all the stories to begin with. The one who had displayed a strange mind controlling power similar to the beast they were running from, the man they believed had the answers all along. But seemingly not anymore, his silence to Rhian's straightforward question appeared to bring a shadow over the room.

'Come on Alex…give us something.' Juliet asked while reaching out her hand. It was offered wholeheartedly for him to hold, but again the path he chose was silence and noncompliance.

The Superintendent's mobile suddenly rang, it broke the tension but would have given them more of a scare if it hadn't been the theme tune to eighties cop show Magnum PI.

Shilling answered sharply 'Yes...excellent...' then put the phone back in his pocket. '...How's it looking out there Harvey?'

The Inspector didn't answer.

'Harvey...?' Flo asked.

He turned to face them but seemed a million miles away. 'What?'

'How are the streets looking?' Shilling demanded.

'It's definitely clearing up.' He finally managed to respond.

'Then let's go, orderly fashion, follow me and don't ask questions until we are away from the station...is that understood?' Shilling bellowed.

There followed a few mumbles of okay, yes sir, and let's get on with it. After all what was said really didn't matter anymore, everyone's breath could be their last, as ominously their fate, the one which had been sitting belligerently in the lap of the gods, had risen and was heading closer.

THE RED FRAME

<u>40</u>

The smooth operation of a moving a human body into a different position, let's say from sitting to standing, can involve using something in the region of fifty four muscles. To maintain an upright position and take a single step forward invokes almost all the other ones, anywhere between five to six hundred depending on one's speed and angle. Such muscle contractions are triggered when an action potential signal travels along a corresponding and connected nerve pathway. From there the nervous system receives the messages from the brain, sends a signal to the correct area and certain chemicals are released then *hey presto,* the body is up and moving.

In a normal situation it takes less than one half second, but as the Glitch was discovering, the current state of Jay Cleaver's body was in a far from normal situation. So it was that after settling the heart rate down and stabilising Jay's breathing, the Glitch was now trying to fathom how the premotor areas in the brains frontal lobes could send the correct signals to the primary motor cortex, and doing all of this so it could just get the damn body to even flinch.

To achieve this requirement it pressed various nerve endings together, whispered messages into its hosts mind to help exert extra influence, while also screaming at desperate decibels. It knew no mortal mind could resist that cry forever and thankfully Jay was no different, his consciousness being slowly dragged up from the darkest depths of what he'd accepted as death.

His eyelids slowly tore themselves open allowing him to see again, a few seconds passed before he identified the lockup as his surroundings.

The Glitch began to speak. 'Ah there you are Jay. I have to say I am extremely disappointed in your decision making, allowing those men to escape was a trick too low for me to have expected, even from you. Therefore know my retribution on your cowardly behaviour will be agonisingly drawn out and painful. However that is for another time, for now be grateful I need your physical form to continue my work, but when I'm done with this task your pathetic soul will burn slowly for eternity.'

Jay didn't understand all the words but he obviously got the message.

'Now we must get you up and walking again, running even, there is much to do and many to kill. Now rise!'

The numbness pervading through Jay's stagnant muscles was difficult to shake off. He stretched before groaning loudly from the pain, while his head pounded relentlessly from the cocaine comedown and the screaming of the Glitch. Why couldn't the bastard thing just let him die?

More time passed but the Glitch felt no real frustration, it didn't care about precious seconds, it would easily find who it wanted and kill them, because that was the inescapable future of the two men this boy had let escape. It was just relieved the body it possessed was still alive.

'...Get up on your feet Jay and I'll take over from there. When we're moving you can sleep in your own mind.' The Glitch promised this respite with no intention of honouring its words. Wanting only for this young vessel to be mobile again, its verbal treachery was the softest of the weapons available to ensure that happened, because in truth after such a deceit, it would never allow Jay Cleaver to sleep again, not in this life or the next.

'That's the way...good boy.'

41

Judging by the many empty streets on such a warm evening it appeared that most of the population in the ancient city of Edinburgh were moving towards the airport. Whilst they were doing so the rest of the planet leaned forward to focus in, watching this incredible story unfold as miraculous things were happening.

On all televisions and computer devices updates were poured out thick and fast, because as the day drew to a close this world had within their grasp undeniable proof of the existence of Angels, which surely meant there was a Heaven. Leading many of all races to believe they would soon make the greatest discovery of all, the actuality of a definitive...God.

This last hour on Earth had been as bizarre and undeniably insane as anyone witnessing the events could ever remember. But there were still people on the planet who hadn't heard the news of the Angels appearance. There would be villages in remote places who would have to wait to be told, also the sensible few in society who had taken themselves offline, hating the constant connectivity and relentless drone of everyone else's opinions.

Then there were also three men, two of them handcuffed inside the highest office of the Blackford Facility. They had heard nothing of this second coming or apocalyptic warning, or whatever the hell was driving the world into a frenzy, as all the two of them in handcuffs could see was the outline of each other across the oak panelled room...oh and the glint of sharpened tools their jailor had laid out on the table.

'Good evening gentlemen.' The voice sprang out from the shadows behind the two men. 'My sincere apologies we should have to go through this again...but one of you hasn't been playing fair.'

The footsteps on the wooden floor came first before the slender figure of Marcus Kirby appeared out of the darkness on their right hand side. Ironically for a man who owned considerable shares in both social media and news outlet companies, he never took much notice of their updates, just a sizeable chunk of the profits. Kirby was always far too busy to care about anything except his unhealthy obsession with the inner workings of evil minds, for that reason he was also flagrantly unaware of the Angels appearance.

Walking to the front of the seated men he clicked his fingers once and the large office, clearly his own by the gaudy decadence on display, illuminated to show rare collected trinkets under the golden glow of a glistening chandelier.

On the wall to the left a heavy free standing bookcase exhibited hefty tomes, their gold embossed leather spines looking down on the room, seeming to goad the men as if to suggest they could never understand the knowledge that lay within their pages. A silver gleaming art deco lamp occupied the far corner, neither man doubting it was more genuine than plated, while a life size painting of a subject with its head engulfed in flames filled the wall in front of them.

It was an impeccable base for a crazy billionaire fixated on psychotic murderers and Kirby stood before them looking every inch a man on an insidious mission. Both his suit and shirt were black, like the thinning hair he greased back, as his long spiderlike fingers reached down to rest on the table. He appeared a lot calmer than the last time they were all together, confident in his plans, ruthless one might say.

'Of course I have realised after my attempts last time that some of the problem may have rested with me. I trusted every word of a Demon and in hindsight I can perceive how foolish that was. Seriously what kind of businessman unquestionably accepts any deal on offer without first looking into the details? I'll admit I was excited by the prospect and less than thorough in my work ethic, but here we are back again, a second chance to turn it all around. So this time there will be no loopholes, no loose seams...on this occasion I will not be offering it the opportunity to escape or hide.'

'You're making an even bigger mistake than last time...' Kosminsky said with his deep voice booming around the panelled walls. '...What you're looking for has long gone.'

'Thank you for that self-serving insight Mr Kosminsky...'

Kirby sighed walking deliberately towards the big guard before bending down to look deep into his eyes, searching for a clue. At the same time he removed a thick strip of white tape from the table and forced it over the large man's mouth.

'..But you have to understand I don't much care for it' Kirby's voice was composed and calculating, totally different to the first time, much like the assorted devices spread out on the table, which all appeared far more deadly. Reaching his hand back he selected a ghastly looking four pronged steel pincer with what appeared to be the infamous black tube built in. 'You see last time I listened far too much to what you said, like an innocent greedy child running blindly toward the promise of a satisfying surprise. I followed your instructions to the word and you deceived me quite terribly. So on this occasion I will be taking complete control and doing things my way...' He seemed to addressing no one in particular as he spoke. '...I know you're hiding in one of these ridiculous fools, but I can assure you it won't be for long, now give yourself to me or they will both die...' He paused generously in allowing for a response but none came. '...and if I understand things correctly you would then be trapped inside one of these corpses for eternity. Is that what you'd prefer...?'

'Mhhhhh...Hmmmm...' Kosminsky yelled with little effect against the tape.

'It's okay Allan...' Oscar said with a soft tone, nothing too threatening, but underneath he was rapidly trying to work out a plan. '...He doesn't know where the Demon is...this is nothing but a bluff.'

Kirby's face gave nothing away at the small man's slight. 'Don't trouble yourself with comforting lies Mr Downes. I've already told you what's going to happen. So why don't you just tell me where it is...whose hiding the Demon?'

The big guard's frustration at being unable to speak caused him to fully test the strength of his wrist restraints.

'It really is pointless talking to you isn't Mr Kosminsky? All you ever want to do is fight and show me your strength, but you won't break out of those although your forceful actions are quite telling. If I were a gambling man I'd suggest all the evidence points to you being of no use to me at all. The way you're struggling shows a lack of patience, which is a virtue I know the Demon holds in spades, nonetheless I will try out my new apparatus on you first...we'll call it a trial run.'

Kosminsky struggled even harder but to no avail as Kirby came in close. Standing directly behind the man he placed the four pronged device on his large head, its glinting sharpened tips equally spaced around Kosminsky's skull. Two just behind the ears and two pressing into the temples, before a gentle squeeze of the device began to draw tiny drops of blood from each smooth entry wound.

'Stop...!' Oscar cried. '...You know you're right, he doesn't have the Demon!'

'Yes I do know that...' Kirby grinned salaciously. '...but please don't interrupt me...I want to see my new toy in action.'

'I said stop...!' Oscar roared in his finest demonic impersonation.

The depth and resonance of this demand so convincing both men immediately trained their eyes on him, Kirby with a wide eyed look of wonderment, Kosminsky with abject surprise and thinking if it could really be that his little friend had been lying to him all along?

Of course to Oscar copying the voice wasn't that difficult, he'd heard it screaming in his skull and pouring from his lips often enough, but now he'd started he had to keep it up, to convince Kirby he actually was the Demon. Clearly this may prove a little more difficult to pull off but while he had Kirby's attention it meant he and Kosminsky were still alive.

'Is that really you?' Kirby asked greedily.

'You know very well it is. Put your toy down and let him be...' Oscar ordered.

Kirby eyed up the small man. '...Tell me first why would you care about his life?'

Oscar hesitated, knowing that he needed to conjure up a convincing answer. Clearly his charade for a delay was only going to get more difficult. 'Because...' He paused slightly while trying to think like the Demon. '...his death should be by my hand.'

'Really...?' Kirby replied keeping his grip on the device but applying no more pressure to the man's skull. '...then why haven't you done it already? I would suggest you've had many opportunities.'

The thin man was asking this with genuine curiosity and just a whiff of suspicion. After all he'd been fooled once by this shadowy creature.

'You question my methods...?' Oscar snapped, trying to muster up a further threatening tone.

Kirby only gave a deadpan response. '...I do.'

Shit, Oscar thought, the man wanted answers, so he quickly began to think some up. 'Very well...if you are to be my new host I will explain.' His slow delivery bought a couple more seconds of thinking time. 'I believed I may need him as protection if my existence were under threat...' Then Oscar decided to go all in on this subterfuge. '...and you were becoming a threat Marcus, so I chose to keep the lumbering idiot at my side, as a getaway vessel if you will.'

Kirby's face gave nothing away but he couldn't avoid feeling an itch of doubt. Why was the Demo being so forthcoming? A slightly lighter version than how he remembered, less of a savage tone than the one who instructed him to use the black tube for extraction, only to then deceive him and make its escape. This was a becoming a delicate game, but one that Marcus refused to lose, and he would have to make certain this prize was genuine before committing the Demon into his own mind.

'Do you remember our last conversation?' Kirby asked.

The question spread a wave of cold panic through Oscar. He couldn't really recall any of the times when the Demon had been in full control.

'I do.' The small man lied.

'Then what tie was I wearing?'

Oscar stalled on a long breath. This type of questioning was making him nervous and feeble, almost ready to give in, to admit his fakery and let the chips fall where they may. Think like the Demon goddamit!

'Are you wishing to play games with me Marcus...is that what this is to you? I have revealed myself as requested but still you want confirmation. Perhaps it is me who's been fooled by ever thinking of you as a worthy vessel. Anymore of your insolence and I may choose to disappear into the shadows of Oscar's mind and remain there. You would never find me and trust I don't fear the consequences of your threat, yes, you could kill this body and trap me inside but I will escape eventually. The eternal virtue of patience is mine because time is of no consequence; it's a pointless commodity for such as me. I could wait a thousand years as if it were a blink. I need you to appreciate if I choose to do that then all through my solitude I would think on you, how you failed to trust me when I was in your hands. There are no more chances left, I am ready to turn and go, so do *exactly* as I say...or you will never hear from me again.'

Oscar was giving this everything he had and his heart leapt on noticing the tiny twitch in the corner of the thin man's eye. It was such a glorious tick, clearly displaying Kirby's desperate desire to win, but even more his growing doubt. It was enough reason for Oscar to raise the stakes a little higher.

'I have told you to take the ridiculous contraption off his head but you refuse to follow my instruction. This is a most disappointing and highly dangerous option you are taking. So I shall count to three...' Oscar was going all in on this deception. 'One...' It was the moment all three of their lives hung in the balance. 'Two...' But if Marcus could be convinced he was speaking to the Demon there may just be a chance. '...Three!'

For a horribly long second Oscar didn't know what to do. Kirby hadn't moved while he was bound to a chair with no way of escape.

Finally Marcus felt he'd pushed his luck as far as possible, moving in and releasing the pincer clamp from Kosminsky's skull, leaving two tiny rivulets of blood to run down the man's temple. The relief causing the big guard to slump back in his chair like a deflating balloon.

'There...' Marcus carefully placed the device back on the desk. '...your next victim awaits your hand.'

Unsurprisingly it was back to square one for Oscar, after deceiving Marcus up to this point he now needed to do considerably more than just speak like a Demon, he would be expected to murder like one. With no other options he once again forged ahead with his ruse. 'Then you will have to release me from these cuffs.'

Marcus considered the situation carefully before moving towards Oscar.

'This is all about our trust now isn't it?' He said while reaching inside his jacket. 'So you won't mind if I have my gun ready. I've witnessed your murdering technique on my cameras remember, how ridiculously fast and violent you are. Therefore as a precaution it will be pointed at your head at all times. If that isn't agreeable to you then I'm afraid I would rather leave you there than cause my own death through stupidity.'

With no better possibility for getting the cuffs off Oscar agreed to the compromise. He also did it with what he hoped was a slow demonic looking nod.

'Good...' Kirby's thin fingers reached into his inside pocket removing the keys. '...I'm looking forward to this...seeing you at work...up close and in the flesh so to speak.'

The cuffs fell away as Oscar placed both hands on his lap, his movements utterly calm and deliberate in a desperate hope of gaining more valuable seconds to think. So far the plan had worked perfectly; get Marcus fooled, get the cuffs off, but this was where his schemes were at an end.

He would no doubt be expected to kill Kosminsky now, as brutally as possible, to fully convince Marcus this was all genuine. With his means of escape being heavily threatened by the expensive looking gun pointed at his forehead.

Oscar was finding out that under this form of intense pressure he could think fast, as hundreds of thoughts and options came to mind, what to do and say, or more urgently how he could attempt to disarm the man. His ongoing dilemma being that every idea he thought of concluded with him being shot. This left him with the fatalistic choice of murdering his only friend, or having a gun discharged in his face. Two devastating problems he needed an urgent answer to.

42

Earlier in the afternoon with the sun beating down Edinburgh had rejoiced in seeing its streets gleam like gilded arteries. With the Old and New towns wearing their rich colours of history and creating a dazzling composition against the pastel blue sky more beautiful than any postcard could convey. Throughout this handsome city people had walked and talked, smiled and shopped, getting on with this beautiful day even if it was, as suggested almost everywhere, 'a bit too hot', but everything changed when the sun began its descent, turning the golden city into a darkening, cooling world, such a gorgeous time soon forgotten after the Angel had appeared.

As the footage spread far and wide a strong belief grew that what had been witnessed was real. It looked like an Angel, this beautiful stranger who had come to earth, with its perfectly angled appearance visible proof of there being something else in the universe, maybe somewhere else too, a new world, better, cleaner and altogether more heavenly. Which meant that billions of minds around the globe were now sharing the same chaotic question; what was important anymore? Did anything in their worlds truly matter if there was an actual Angel on earth?

Certainly no one in this police vehicle had noticed how the moment the temperature started to drop coincided with the first reports of the Angels appearance, but they were becoming annoyingly aware of just how much the atmosphere had changed.

The city was a mess and the journey to the facility slow, torturously so in patches, as the unmarked van slid through darkened streets, having to manoeuvre around abandoned cars, with pavements sparsely populated by human souls who truly didn't know what to do.

It was these kinds of people; these ponderous people who both in mind and body were slowing the progress of the individuals crammed in the van. What would ordinarily be a twenty minute trip; a length of time most could handle without losing their minds in the back of a hot van, had already taken thirty five minutes.

Squashed together in this pressure cooker all they could hear was the driver cursing. 'Get out of the way...there's people just walking in the middle of the road...its madness...look just get up and go home...!' He implored the pondering flock. '...If I have to run over you in the name of the law I will'

'Christ, Foster calm down! Be professional.' Shilling yelled towards the drivers hatch.

'Sorry Sir but this is impossible.'

'Show some patience young man!' Shilling ordered then turned back to find most of their eyes looking his way, in particular the ones of the nurse woman sitting reluctantly by his side.

He really didn't know what Juliet was here for; then again someone with medical knowledge may come in useful tonight, but he hoped not.

To her left sat Alex which was of no great surprise, it seeming clear to the Superintendent there was something going on between them, he thought they looked like a decent couple if you ignored his missing arm. Political correctness had never been one his strengths.

Next to Alex was Flo, who was looking the most concerned, her eyes fixed on Shilling as if he could somehow magically get them out of this cramped sweatbox. Holding her hand was Harvey who wasn't looking over at him, instead his head was facing down as if in heavy contemplation. At least Jeff hoped it was for that reason and not some position of hopelessness.

To Harvey's left was the young boy, Samuel, damn that kid had caused them some trouble. Shilling thought that if he ever found out, like some of the more pessimistic were suggesting, that all this Angel stuff was nothing more than an elaborate trick, some social media prank gone hyper viral, then he and his mother could expect to face serious charges. Yes Sam was only a minor of course but there were places Shilling could have him sent, hard schools of learning where even an Angel couldn't save him.

I really have to stop this aggressive thinking and try to be more positive about people, Shilling thought, as Rhian Sanger held his stare a moment too long before turning to her son, almost as if she could read his vitriol. All the same he did find it strange the boy hadn't been fully awake since the incident, seriously, if Shilling were to continue with his suspicious outlook he might surmise the kid had been drugged in some way. Perhaps that crazy haired mother was enforcing his silence to protect herself, she'd already admitted to being a fake psychic after all, maybe she was trying something bigger now, a staged lie much more lucrative than séances with pensioners.

Shilling knew his cantankerous mood was being fuelled by the heat in the van, because of his bulk he was suffering worse than most, as he had to admit he didn't really know anything about these people, so maybe he shouldn't judge them.

With a heavy sigh he looked back toward the hatch and said nothing. He could feel the funeral pace the van was moving at and because he couldn't think of anything useful to say, he closed his eyes.

Instantly his thoughts turned to Roma, young Miss Walker, the newly hired secretary who at this very second was following his orders to the letter. He began deliberating on just how much of a risky position he'd put her in, but someone had to stay at the station, those phone lines wouldn't answer themselves, even though it was almost guaranteed that the Glitch would come looking there first. If that supposition were indeed correct Shilling could only hope that Roma would, with a calm exterior, inform it they'd left for the facility to await its arrival.

He thought it so bizarre that he should be thinking of the Glitch as a real threat, a genuine monster, based solely on the explanation that Alex had given him. Then again a lot of their evidence did add up, even for a dyed in the wool realist such as himself, with those Angel videos being the most persuasive that something extremely strange was going on in his city.

Hell, he must believe in it because he was stuck in this crammed van on the way to the facility, the last place on earth he would choose to be, but it sounded like they had a plan. It even felt like a plan but he knew it was nothing more than a mini migration, an exodus to a place of safety with thicker walls and heavier doors, but if it would help these people put an end to this absurdity then he was all for it.

Suddenly Shillings great effort at remaining calm and sensible began to wear thin, perhaps the heat in the van had risen to a degree he couldn't handle anymore, he was ready to blow off some steam and get some answers. So at this highly strung moment and with no one else questioning what was really going on, he was damn well going to.

'Alex, can I have a word.' He asked tapping the man on his shoulder.

'No you may not.' The one armed man replied insolently.

'What did you say to me?' Jeff prickled with rage.

'I said no.' Alex then leaned forward to see around Juliet and face the Superintendent. 'No more private conversations. We're all in this together so everyone's included. If you have something to ask Superintendent, then do it out loud, because I'm telling you that all together we'll come up with a much truer answer than any one mind can fathom.'

Shilling considered Alex's request, guessing at the responses and the feelings it may infect this group with, knowing his words could make some of them uncomfortable, but damn it he was boiling so went ahead anyway.

'If that's the way you want to play it. So what's the plan when we get there Alex...anyone? I suppose what I'm really asking is how are we're going to defeat this Glitch because according to your testimonies it's pretty much unstoppable, relentless somebody said, blindingly fast and deadly. I'd just like to know if anyone has any helpful suggestions.'

'Shut up Jeff...!' Flo snapped. She was always naturally the first to react, the foremost voice to speak up when it came to obnoxious idiots trying to appear clever. Her non-existent suffering of fools another big tick in the towering columns of why Harvey loved her so much. '...Just get us there and leave the planning to my husband and Alex.'

Shilling saw an opportunity he couldn't resist. 'To be honest Mrs Cooper, *I was* talking to them.' His cutting remark hit the spot.

This left Flo with a split second decision to make, to cut him back down to size here and now, or to let it go for a little while. Because she had a feeling, a belief, that this stupid man would enrage her even more later on, but hopefully when tempers weren't as frayed as they were inside this oven of a van. Why couldn't he just keep his fat mouth shut?

It was Alex who interrupted this bitterly awkward moment. 'Superintendent...Flo's right...we know as much as there is to know about what we're dealing with...and maybe we don't have the answer yet, but while we're all together and breathing I think we can claim that as some small victory.'

Shilling dead eyed Flo. then looked away with a disdainful shake of his head, even he couldn't be bothered to argue anymore at this temperature.

The van was picking up a little speed now they were off the narrower streets, its swifter progress causing everyone to think of how they were heading ever closer to the damn facility. For the ones who had been there before, in this timeline or any other, there was nothing but trepidation. The place was an enigma even now, run by a private company headed by an elusive billionaire, housing some of the criminally insane until a few weeks ago.

It was to be their ultimate destination, their last stand against the oncoming Glitch but small minded Shilling had just made the situation far worse, because he was right, they had no plan.

Alex picked up on their sombre moods. The seven of them were in such close proximity that if push came to shove, all would be pushed and shoved simultaneously. In an attempt to calm them he opened up on his own thoughts.

'Look I want you to know what I'm thinking here. It isn't much but it's a start...as I said the reason we're going to the facility is twofold, first of all we need to try and save two men, secondly I hope we can secure ourselves, put a solid barrier between the Glitch and us. Hopefully that way we can negotiate a better outcome than if we face it straight on.'

'Negotiate?' Shilling laughed. 'Don't you understand how negotiation works Alex? The last time I checked it requires you to have something the other one needs. Now I'm looking round this van and I'm not seeing that. I'm just looking at people it wants to kill, so unless I'm very much mistaken we have no bargaining tools here.'

Alex was suffering from the heat and cramped up scenario as much as anyone else so it was unsurprising he snapped sharply. 'For crying out loud Superintendent you really are a pain in the fucking arse!'

'Watch your mouth son!' Shilling responded with a stone cold delivery.

'Alex...just leave it.' Juliet requested fixing him with a stare.

'Please don't scare my boy. He's been through too much.' Rhian spoke softly as she stroked Sammy's hair.

'I doubt he can hear us...' Shilling was far too agitated to refrain from speaking his mind. '...what have you drugged him with...huh?'

'What do you mean?' Rhi looked confused.

'Wouldn't want him slipping up and giving the game away...?' Shilling made a double click with his tongue.

'...Game?

'Yes...game.' Jeff could have backed off, saved the situation, but this ongoing lack of respect was bringing out the old school Shilling. 'All this angel apparition rubbish...it's a trick isn't it? I don't know how or why you did it; probably because it's what you do...this fake psychic stuff...!'

Even Harvey was finally prompted to lift his head. 'Jeff...?' It was struggle for him to speak but he had no other choice.

'What?'

'...Are we...there yet?' The question was a private joke from years ago, the happier days when they'd been colleagues, when they used to have each other's back.

Before Shilling could reply Officer Foster called through from the front of the van, in answer to Harvey. 'Another five minutes.'

To everyone's embarrassment the sound of his voice reminded them that the young officer had heard every word of their conversation, but in a strange way it helped to release some of the building pressure, at least for a few more seconds.

43

Darkness was overcoming the light as the Glitch stood deathly still, directly over the road from the police station. Hidden deep in the growing shadows it looked up at the illuminated building, noticing that though the lights in every office were on there was very little movement. So little that for a second the eyes of Jay Cleaver considered this may be a trap of some sort.

Undoubtedly the promise of any threat was of no great concern, after rescuing this body from the brink of a heart attack it was ready for anything, but what did cross its mind was just how much it was growing to hate surprises.

Though most of its victims past and present would have claimed to the contrary, the Glitch was much more than a cold blooded killing machine, although it could perform such acts at any point without remorse. Rather it was a unique creature constantly changing and discovering new depths to human emotions, but unfortunately, the more it learned about the infinite pallet of life on earth the greater became its determination to wipe it out.

One didn't need to be an expert to see that all the evidence pointed to this being just another planet doomed to overheat. There were literally millions of cratered corpses floating around the galaxy illustrating how it would end, yet still the only species that could actually prevent that from happening, the one with the power, with the billions in numbers and the available technology, chose to accept their hotter summers and milder winters as some form of gift from the gods.

It was this persistent display of startling ignorance that kept the Glitch focused and on track. First it would wipe out the problematic group it was hunting for, the ones who knew of its existence and history, after which it would expand out onto the world stage to introduce itself properly.

Trusting to instinct that nothing could hurt it anymore the Glitch flitted across the street and entered the station unseen. The fluidity and speed of Jay Cleavers body movement seemingly enriched to a higher level by the overdose setback. More proof that whenever the Glitch failed, it learned from the experience, used that knowledge to tighten up its game, adapting to its surroundings; a truly dominant species constantly growing stronger.

Roma Walker was sat working patiently behind her desk, aware that only a skeleton crew of staff remained in the station, the rest of her colleagues busy out protecting the airport.

The Superintendent had warned her that Jay Cleaver could make a sudden appearance. If that happened she was to stay calm and remain professional at all times, before relaying to him the news of their departure to the facility. What Shilling had failed to mention was anything pertaining to Jay being possessed by a supernatural entity. It was this vital piece of missing information that made her scream loudly when he spoke unexpectedly from behind her.

'Where is your Inspector?'

Roma had no idea how this man had even entered the room, her eyes had never left the door, the windows behind her were locked shut, yet here he was, with the breath from his whispered words close enough to move her hair.

'Err he's not here...' She said breathlessly before regaining her normal voice. '...He's out.'

'That wasn't my question...was it?'

Roma felt both his hands rest on her shoulders where they squeezed gently, almost playfully, almost.

'Please don't touch me...' She requested through the growing anxiety rising from her stomach. '...I don't like it'

'Not a problem.' He removed his hands, then Jay's new and improved handsome face glided round in front of her, a half smile displaying a little of his perfect teeth. 'Now where is he?'

As part of her professionalism she'd intended to drag this exchange of information out, in hope of delaying this man in his endeavours and giving the rest of them longer to prepare, but right now all she wanted was Jay Cleaver out of her office. '...Blackford...at the Facility!'

'All of them?' Jays blue eyes were reflecting the light in a weird way, like oil on water.

'...Yes.'

'Yet they left you behind?'

'This has got nothing to do with me...' She was then forced to watch warily as he moved around the room. His pale grey suit cut perfectly to fit Jay's slender frame was immaculately clean, not a crease, no strands of hair on the shoulders. He looked too good to be true.

'I see...then I think we need to have a little talk...' He calmly sat down in the chair by the door. It was on the other side of the room so she felt something like relief, but it only lasted for a single heartbeat. '...Tell me what they're planning.'

'I really don't know.'

'Tut tut...you must have overheard something...some titbit, a juicy morsel with which to save your life.'

Roma thought hard and fast, because she'd heard plenty, but couldn't decide which information was safe to share. The implied threat didn't help her concentration or decision making skills. She really couldn't remember this being part of anyone's plan.

'They said it was the safest place.'

'Who said that?' Jay enquired calmly.

'Alex I think...he said the walls and doors would keep you out.'

'And what do you think?'

'Sss...sorry...?' She stuttered.

'Do you believe his idea will work?'

'I really couldn't say...it's an extremely secure hospital as far as I know.'

Jay stood and she tensed as he walked towards the desk, moving to the left side of her, before crouching so their heads were of equal height.

'I'm sure it is secure. You have very pretty eyes Roma...I can perceive my reflection in them.' He then gently stroked her cheek with the back of his fingers. 'They haven't told you what I am, didn't want to scare you, most likely hoping to use your naivety and innocence as a tool to further their cause. Personally I consider that to be a ghastly trick, a sleight of underhand whereby I listen to what you tell me and then act upon it blindly, rushing off in pursuit, gambling that I'll leave you alive.'

'Why wouldn't you leave me alive?' Roma asked with all the nerve she could muster.

'Obviously because it is what they want me to do. Manipulation is their stock in trade, only they don't truly understand the rubrics behind my existence...'

Roma eyes flicked towards Jay and he removed his hand from her face. '...What does "rubrics" mean...?'

'...They are the ancient rules laid down for my conduct, my true unavoidable purpose if you will, even the coward who wrote me into the book didn't know about those.'

'So what are you then...really?' Thinking if she was to die at its hand then she at least wanted to learn why.

'Me...I am just the new broom, the weapon with which to end all wars.'

'Are they still a major problem then...wars?' her mouth was drying up.

'Dearest Roma, if I gave you the answer to that I fear it would change your thinking forever.'

'I don't really care...tell me!'

Jay's eyes were shimmering as if he were lit from the inside.

'So be it, but first of all I must explain the wars you imagine are nothing like mine. You will see armed conflict and bloodshed, heroes and enemies, ridiculously senseless differences of opinion causing the innocent to fall lifeless on the ground in their millions, but when I hold the frame I look upon a bigger picture...'

As the Glitch spoke it seemed able to place the images in her mind, horrifyingly detailed scenes of soldiers dying in stained red mud, the mushrooming blast of an immense explosion laying waste to a city, flattening the landscape to nothing more than concrete and wires, so many burning bodies which she was forced to watch.

'...From within these eyes I see this death and destruction as nothing more than a firework display. Your mortal kind took the definitive meaning of war and bastardized it, adapted it to represent battling forces fighting to the death, yet the word itself does not mean such a thing. It derives from many ancient languages and in all of them refers to times of confusion, to be perplexed, a period when chaos reigns.'

Roma could see and hear so vividly she knew its meaning immediately. 'And you're here to change that...the weapon to end all wars...of course.'

'Huh...!' Its shimmering eyes held hers in its gaze. '...Do you really understand?'

'Yes...you came to earth with the sole purpose of ending chaos and confusion.'

Jay stood up from his haunches and moved away, he looked out of the window across the deserted streets. 'I'm impressed with you Roma. Who would ever imagine you owned a mind for such weighty concepts, yet here you are almost finishing my sentences. Clever girl aren't you?'

'I like to understand things.' Then believing she saw an opportunity she asked her most pressing question. 'Are you going to kill me?'

'Unquestionably...but you have just earned yourself a little more time. It's one of the most important things I have learned from my growing pains so far, how time is of the utmost importance when one is walking this earth. It affects the angles of all things which is an unkind fact and one that has taken some understanding. You see at the start of my journey I was given everything and nothing in equal measure. I assumed the greatest of knowledge from the pages of an Angel's book but without context it was useless, therefore I believed chaos was the only answer, of course that was caused by my immaturity. Like a child knowing nothing more than chaotic behaviour I was wrong...I had to grow to appreciate my truth.'

'Why are you telling me this..?' Roma really couldn't understand why this apparent monster was being so convivial; is this how it killed all its victims, letting them into its life story as it gave them their death? If so she thought it rather sick but that was overshadowed by some intrigue at its mention of an Angel.

'What Angel...?' She had to ask after spending the last few hours stuck on the rolling news of the event.

Jay's eyes widened with pride as it proclaimed 'The Angel that called for me of course.'

'The same one that appeared earlier...?'

'What...?' His blue eyes tightened at the corners and Roma's stomach flipped. It didn't know about the Angel.

'Oh my god...where have you been?'

'Mostly surviving imminent death caused by my host body taking a massive cocaine overdose.'

'Ha...!' She laughed unsure if it was joking or not.

It could be exaggerating its condition for some underhand purpose but that didn't matter right now, Roma was thinking she may be able to buy some more of that valuable commodity of time by impressing it further.

Her fingers flitted across the keyboard. 'I think I need to show you something.'

44

Trying to playing mind games with a man holding a loaded firearm is never wise, even less so when said gunman is watching intently for any slip ups, worse still when he's about as close to obsessively insane as one can be.

'Why are you stalling?' Marcus Kirby probed with darkly curious intent. '...Kill him!'

Oscar looked down at the manacled Kosminsky, the big man struggling helpless and gagged, causing this already tense atmosphere to crank up to breaking point, but he had to hold it together or they would both be dead.

'Really Marcus, do you consider me some kind of performing chimp? I shall deal with this man when we are one.' Then as he'd done since this façade began Oscar prayed his aping words of a Demon were convincing enough.

'Why don't I just end this misunderstanding now and shoot him in the head. It would save time ha ha...' Kirby raised the gun.

'You could do that...' Think Oscar think! '...but wouldn't you prefer to tear him apart using the strength we possess. It would be our first kill and I can guarantee all the more satisfying.'

Marcus found himself once more stopped in his tracks by this shrewd adversary, finding it strange the beast he'd searched for his whole life was so being contrary about murder. What was it up to now?

Oscar walked purposefully round Kosminsky as Marcus watched on, the pointed gun never leaving the small man, while the scales of outcomes unwritten teetered. '...This guard has been a loyal worker for you, almost a friend to Oscar and myself, I could even consider letting him go if we get his surety of silence.'

'No!' Marcus snapped back. 'He dies tonight!'

'Very well...' Oscar placed his hand on Kosminsky's face before tearing the tape harshly from his mouth, the big guard wincing at the surprising move. '...but let us at have the pleasure of hearing him beg for his life.'

To Marcus that simple act was closer to what he'd expected from the Demon, its desire to wallow in a victim's agony viciously harsh and most satisfying. 'What do you say to that Allan...?' Marcus moved in a little closer. '...Will you scream for us?'

Kosminsky's mouth was dry as he looked up into Oscar's eyes. Abject fear overtaking the stinging sensation in his cheeks from the sharp tape removal, then he noticed the almost imperceptible but definite wink from the small man's left eye. He understood it straight away, a signal to tell him to prepare, that Oscar had been faking superbly, brilliantly, but the same stubborn problem was still staring them in the face, Marcus Kirby's gun.

Oscar knew the play but not how to accomplish it. He first needed to manoeuvre Kirby into striking distance. The thin man was four feet away at this moment, too far to take a chancing lunge for the weapon, he'd probably be able to get three shots off in that time. So with little choice Oscar fled back into himself to seek a workable ploy. There was no doubt he was winning the thin man over with his masquerade, plus he now had Kosminsky on board, so somewhere between those two facts must be the answer. When the idea finally came to him, Oscar could only pray inwardly it would work. He resumed his Demon speak.

'Look at you Kosminsky, not so physically arrogant now are you? Huh no keys to lock me away…you're our prisoner now…our first kill together. You should be honoured to be so, for I feel Marcus and I will kill millions.'

Oscar's voice was deep and threatening with his face set in a disgusting smirk. 'I can smell that blood on your cheek.' The small man wiped his finger across Kosminsky's face causing a deep red streak. '…That is the unmistakeable blood of a Polish Jew descendent.'

This was Oscars plan, to prey on Kirby's weakness, their only chance.

'He shares the name of a suspect in the Jack the Ripper investigations.' Marcus added enthusiastically, eager to display his knowledge of serial killers to another one, but all it achieved was to show his true colours. Those words made him sound like a geek, a sorry suck up sycophant, the spoiled child who always wanted the attention. Marcus could hardly stay still, his excitement peaking, causing the barrel of the gun to waver from side to side, but its trigger still wore his bony finger upon it.

For Oscar his sad bragging was the missing piece of the puzzle allowing him to draw the man in. 'Marcus…?'

'…Yes.'

'What if I could let you discover for certain if this man here is a direct descendent of your Ripper suspect?'

'What…how…?' Marcus's tiny black eyes were twinkling as he asked.

'Oh my friend you have so much to learn. All of your money yet so little knowledge, but don't worry together we will discover many things, have so many skills at our command, for instance we could taste this man's blood and through that simple act trace his ancestral line. It would appear to us as clear as day, we would see their faces, know their actions and even replay their memories…'

Kirby unwittingly took a step forward in his desire to learn more.

'...Yes Marcus as one we could answer that question this very moment. Is this lumbering oaf hiding the identity of Jack the Ripper in his bloodline? I really don't care much either way but it seems to be of great importance to you.'

'That's quite the understatement...' Marcus gasped and moved another step closer. '...the greatest of all unsolved murder mysteries. That I could know for certain who the Whitechapel murderer was would be priceless.'

Oscar stood fully upright before displaying his stained red forefinger and sniffing the bloods metallic scent. As he did so he smiled and went full on Demon with his words. '...This crimson material pumping through a mortal's veins is everything about your species. It contains the past and the future of your entire race in its sticky cells...' Oscar was a little unsure if his words were going too far for his imagined Demon, but the gap between the men was incrementally closing so he ploughed on, it was the only hope they had. '...If you were to taste this now I could teach you how to read it.'

Marcus stared closely at Oscar then over to Kosminsky still tied to the chair, weighing up his options, whether to fully trust the Demon or to stay back and in control, but in his heart there was only one answer because Oscar could not be this good an actor.

Which meant the Demon was here and inside the little man as it always had been; only right now it was offering him a wonderful gift, the chance to complete a lifelong quest of putting a name and a face to the East Ends most infamous unknown son. Once again it was all about trust and he was more than willing to give the Demon his in return for the favours it promised. It was all too much for Marcus, unable to resist he reached out toward the bloodied hand, the barrel of the gun now pointing at the floor.

This was Oscar's chance if he remained calm. Not so easy to do when in an unknown situation. What is the optimum speed and timing for grabbing a gun from another man's hand? Troublingly he was about to find out as he raised his finger towards Kirby's mouth. 'Taste the blood and tell me what you see...'

As Marcus closed in as much as he dare, Oscar leapt forward, throwing his shoulder into the man's midriff with an ugly looking rugby tackle. Amazingly it had the desired effect as Kirby sprawled backwards. As they tumbled to the floor Oscar remained solely focused on the gun, pinning that wrist down using both hands, this left him unable to defend himself from the Kirby's incoming retaliatory blows.

'What the hell are you doing?' Kirby screamed trying to punch him with his free fist.

Oscar was all out of responses for himself or the Demon in his attempt to wrestle the gun away. The struggle was in the balance as he found Marcus Kirby surprisingly strong for a thin man, unless of course Oscar was just alarmingly weak without the monster in situ, which would explain how the strikes to his head were having so much effect. With every ounce of fight he had left Oscar applied enough pressure to force the gun from Marcus's grip and it skittled across the wooden floor into an ornate coat stand, where it appeared to goad the two wrestling men as a trophy for the winner, a prize which only the worthiest would be able to wield.

With the gun gone Oscar could defend himself properly. He twisted his body round to face the thin man whose slicked back hair was dishevelled and falling over his brow. In that second it gave Oscar a most frantic and puerile thought, with this qualifying as desperate times he followed through with it, grabbing those greasy follicles he pulled the man's head down onto his rising knee. The sharp cracking sound was almost certainly that of a nose breaking but Oscar refused to let go of Marcus's hair, yanking it from side to side, causing spatters of blood to splash out from the wound. When even that wasn't enough to satisfy his rage he smashed Kirby's bloodied face down into the floor three times.

'Oscar! Oscar, stop...!' The voice calling his name seemed to be coming from miles away. '...Oscar stop you'll kill him...' Kosminsky roared in total desperation. '...he's finished...go and get the gun!'

The small man with his great and furious anger on display abruptly regained his self-awareness and stopped, looking up in shame.

'It's okay Oscar...you've won...there's no need to kill him. The police can arrest him and we can walk free...both us together...'

Kosminsky's tone was pleading because of Oscar's eyes, where once they had been a pale blue, a pure blackness had taken over. If the big guard were to try and describe them, he would say they appeared ungodly.

45

The Beatles once wrote a song about a minute being a very long time, just how they would have described five minutes will never be known, but for this group of souls, on its journey to the Blackford Facility, that amount of time was becoming torturous.

Ironically being squashed in the back of a small van was a situation those scouse musicians would have experienced many times in their early days. In this instance the people stuck together for that length of time were not a hungry gigging band, but rather a motley crew of truth seekers under the most intense of otherworldly threats.

Their much needed but awkward silence was finally broken by the most unlikely of sources.

'Mm...Mom...?'

Rhian lifted her head and looked down upon her son returned. 'Oh Sammy I'm here baby...are you okay?'

'I think so...where's my food?'

'We had to leave the restaurant.'

'Oh...I don't remember finishing my burger.'

'I know darling...you fainted again.'

'But I'm still hungry...can I have something else...?' It was only now that he raised his head and saw all the faces staring at him. '...Oh, I thought we were in the car...what's happening? Where are we going?' He asked as his bottom lip trembled.

Rhi didn't know what the hell to do with his questions, she was just as puzzled about this journey's end, exactly what they were intending to achieve by hiding in an asylum.

When no one was offering to help her out she knew a few more of a mother's comforting half-truths were needed. 'We're going to find some friends who can help us.' She answered but quite sure more questions would follow.

'What...to help me from...to...stop fainting?'

'Absolutely yes...we're going to fix everything.'

Rhian replied softly, imminently close to breaking down before Flo took notice and assumed the reins.

'Hi Sammy your Mom's right. Where we're off to will be the end of all this silliness. No more fainting or being carted around in the back of vans.' Her smile was gentle and infectious causing the boy to respond in kind.

'That would be great.' His tone was beautifully understated.

'Ah he's woken up has he? Not before time!' Inevitably it was Shilling wading in once more. 'Ask him what the hell is going on...we might get to the cause of all this!'

'For god's sake man will you just be quiet!' Alex's voice crackled as the band of tension began to tighten again.

Shilling shot him an angry look before continuing with his opinions unabated and unfiltered. 'I'll be quiet when we have an answer to what the hell this kid thinks he's playing at. He's the reason we're all here...I'd just like to hear his opinion on matters.'

'Leave him alone!' Rhi pulled Sammy back into her bosom. 'He doesn't know anything...he's the victim here!'

'Is that right...?' Shilling responded dutifully. '...well the boy only seems to be bothered about his stomach. I'd suggest as victims go he doesn't appear to be suffering too much, which to an officer of my experience is quite telling...'

'...What on earth are you talking about now?' Flo waded in.

Shilling could feel the growing displeasure within the group but he was used to that. You don't get to run your own police station, in charge of hundreds and coordinating murder investigations, by pleasing people and those many years of experience had taught him well, proving again and again that asking uncomfortable questions is always the shortest route to finding the truth.

'I'm sure the boy can speak for himself.' He held his hostile eyes on Sammy as if it were a direct order. 'Come on now lad, tell us what you think's going on...hmm...you must have an idea.'

Rhi began to speak. 'Leave him alo...'

Shilling cut her off sharply. '...Let your son answer...he knows better than anyone.'

'I don't know anything!' Sammy shouted irritably. 'I want to go home.'

Shilling wasn't for giving in now he finally had the boy's full attention. 'I'm sure you do and that can be arranged if you give me what I want.'

'What do you want?' Sammy snivelled.

'I want to see this Angel everyone's talking about...'

Shillings request caused another hush to fall. Eyes flicked around from one to another as they all wondered; none more so than little Sammy, what revelations such a plea might yield.

46

'Oscar, come on...get the key and undo these cuffs...' Kosminsky requested while trying to ignore the unnerving eyes of the small man. '...everything will be fine, just listen to my voice.'

It seemed his words were having little effect as Oscar inwardly battled with what he'd just done; even more worryingly what he'd wanted to do to Kirby, still fighting the urge to just do it anyway.

'Come on Oscar you're not a murderer. You never have been.'

'What makes you so sure?' Oscar's response was cold and emotionless. 'Don't you believe I could have killed all those people on my own?'

'Of course not...you were possessed.'

'True...but I think the Demon opened my eyes to new possibilities...to freedom, abandonment of responsibility...of guilt. Trust me Allan it all becomes a wide open world, a crazy place to be when you do whatever you want, this gift of liberation is mind blowing.'

Kosminsky had an immediate urge to slap Oscar across the face to try and knock some sense into him, but still being cuffed to the chair hindered that approach, leaving only his words in a fight to reclaim his friend. Sadly of all the attributes the big guard could muster, verbal compassion and reasoning were quite low on the list, of course he could turn a kind word but it would always be coming from the mouth of a tough looking giant.

'Oscar please...we're friends...aren't we?'

'Friends...why...because you took me to your home, for that you think we have some strong personal bond? You were my jailer. So no I wouldn't say we were friends.'

Kosminsky was as confused as he'd ever been about Oscar's behaviour; only a few days ago the small man had tidied his flat up for him, shared a motorbike ride on a curtailed trip to Inverness, and less than three minutes ago he'd given him a secretive conspiratorial wink. What the hell was this puzzle of a human being up to now?

'Why can't you just settle on a personality?' Kosminsky barked.

'Because I don't know who I am...!' The small man shed a tear.

This momentary pause was ended when Kosminsky looked over at Kirby's prone body then back to his *friend*. '...I can help you find out.'

'And what if I'm not the Oscar Downes you expect?'

'Then we'll get you help...' Kosminsky lowered his tone as he raised his head. '...whatever it takes.'

There was no doubting Oscar's eyes began to brighten as those words struck home, where there'd been large black catlike pupils a few seconds ago a touch of blue had returned, signifying a hope the real Oscar was still present.

Then the sound of a harsh rattling cough dragged both of them out of any shared moment of reconnection; instead they were forced to focus on Marcus who was struggling to sit up, spluttering through the blood on his swollen face. 'You should have let him kill me Kosminsky...' As he said this the thin man raised himself to a seated position. '...always trying to be the nice guy...such a soft and gentle giant...pathetic.'

'Say what you want Kirby. I'm not the one beaten up on the floor.'

The thin man's eyes glistened through the bruising. 'Beaten...up maybe...but never beaten...unbowed I think you'll find.'

Oscar's rage boiled up once more. He stepped towards Marcus before stopping suddenly when he saw the small silver pistol in the man's hand.

Marcus wiped his mouth and spoke with a mocking intent. '...Seriously gentlemen, do I look like someone who would bet everything on red? True success only comes from covering all eventualities...' He cocked the gun. '...It's such a vitally important difference between the select few...and the rest of the herd.'

Kosminsky slumped back in his chair, they were back at square one, but Oscar did the complete opposite, charging forward determined and fast, attempting to cover the six feet between them before the trigger could be pulled, but he never stood a chance.

The discharge of the small pistol was incredibly loud in the confines of the wooden panelled office. The resounding all-encompassing bullet crack filled the room, so loud that the sound of Oscar's body hitting the floor before sliding to a halt was missing; lost within the frenzied buzz of the big guards hearing.

Kosminsky witnessed the scene in a slow motion vacuum of movement and mourning, frame by agonising frame blinked by before burning themselves onto his eyes. Oscar had clearly taken the bullet in the chest as both hands impulsively rose to clutch at the entry point, but most telling was what his arms didn't do, neither one lowered to help break his fall as it became instantly clear that Oscar was in a bad way.

The next ten seconds were the infamously futile ones of blind hope. The shocked moments when people believed that whatever travesty had occurred could somehow be rewound or perceived differently. This passed slowly for Kosminsky because his small friend never moved, never moved one dying muscle. 'No!' It was all he could utter, over and over.

Marcus climbed to his feet then sharply kicked Oscar's body for signs of life.

'Oh dear...' He said as he rolled the small man over. '...look at that straight through the heart...'

Kosminsky couldn't fight the urge to look down at Oscar. In doing so he saw the growing scarlet stain across the man's shirt. At the centre of that mess, tiny spurts of blood found themselves outside his body, the place where they would die and dry.

47

Over two hundred army personnel had now been drafted in to quell the crushing crowds and queues forming at the airport and surrounding areas. The official line passed down to the media said the boy was currently being studied by a medical crew and that a statement would be released shortly, but even with that clear message released on every social platform the masses continued their blind pilgrimage.

Precisely what these people congregating in their tens of thousands expected or desired couldn't easily be defined. The religious zealots were loudly chanting of how they had been correct all along, how a life of faith and daily prayers was being proven true. Yet hordes of atheists were equally vast in number, desiring evidence that what the human race had witnessed was indeed of heavenly origin, rather than a clever scheme of some other worldly invasion.

Then, as to be expected whenever large gatherings occur, there were the anarchists of our species, travelling to the site in ever larger numbers for what they saw as the opportunity for change, a paradigm shift whereby governments could be toppled, old systems crushed and true freedom attained. But mostly there were the hordes of the ponderous, confused, those lost in mixed emotions, who really didn't know what else to do.

However one looked at this miracle, with there being infinite points of view, it all came down to one simple wish; a timeless and natural yearning for a better tomorrow. Of course what no one in attendance at the airport knew was the disturbing and fragile truth; that for all their fervent hymns, silent prayers, loud protests, desperate screams, tears of joy or wails of confusion, the deciding factor as to whether these longings would ever become reality presently lay on his mother's lap in the back of an unmarked police van some twelve miles away.

Across the dry sunburned lawns of Blackford facility deep shadows were beginning to stretch out from the trees. The sun was falling slowly, almost reluctantly as if it didn't wish this day to end, perhaps afraid of what the night may bring.

At the top of the narrow driveway the security gates were surprisingly, but thankfully, unlocked. PC Lee Foster pushed them wider before jumping back in the van to take his passengers to the underground carpark. The young officer relieved he'd got them all here safely, was also hoping to get a few minutes rest from Superintendent Shilling's constant barracking.

Foster would never claim to fully understand what the heck was going on in Edinburgh tonight. He'd seen the videos of the Angel like everyone else and knew the boy in his van was the one involved, but the actual whys and wherefores were far beyond him. Even listening in on their conversations had only muddied the waters further. As far as he could tell they were here to rescue two men under threat while simultaneously attempting to seek refuge from the Glitch, a man he only knew to be a roaming psychopath committing atrocities across the city.

Unable to make any further sense of it all he looked over his shoulder and opened the tiny partition. 'We're pulling into the car park now Sir.'

'...About bloody time!' Shillings rough response.

Since the Superintendent had requested to see the Angel nothing of note had actually occurred. Young Sammy had waited with everyone else for something strange to happen, but for now the spirit was silent.

Shilling forced his fat frame past the others to reach the back doors, his large posterior causing uniform disgust amongst them, but stopped before turning the handle. 'You lot stay put until I confirm it's clear.'

'I don't think so...' Alex replied slightly quicker than everyone else who shared the same thought.

It was a surreal moment listening to Shilling's response, stuck as he was in a position facing the doors, the words appearing to come directly from his backside, but even then the meaning wasn't lost.

'...That is a direct order and when I give you one of those you follow it to the letter. You're in charge in my absence Cooper. Keep everyone calm and inside this vehicle until I return...is that understood?'

The sharpness of his tone cut through the vans occupants like a sliver of ice, this big guy was serious.

Harvey didn't reply as the doors were fully opened, but no one cared as a blessed breeze blew over the skin, forcing out the stifling heat.

'How long do we wait?' Juliet enquired.

'Until I get back of course' Shilling said while pulling his trouser belt up.

'What if you don't come back...?'

The Superintendent pulled his Glock from its concealed holster, making sure everyone could see it, before speaking confidently '...I don't think you should concern yourselves with that outcome.'

'No...for Christ's sake I said no guns!' Alex yelled.

Shilling fixed him with a commanding glare. 'Listen here Sonny. You can protect yourself with all the spooky stories and theories you want. I'm going to do this my way...professionally.'

Alex tried explaining. 'It won't do any good even if you did get a shot off, you'll only end up killing an innocent man.'

'There's nothing innocent about Jay Cleaver!' The Superintendent's voice was getting louder now. 'Possessed by a monster or not he's a wild animal and I won't hesitate for a second to put him down.'

With that the van doors were slammed shut...again.

The occupants listened as Shillings heavy footfall circled the van before stopping at the driver's door. 'Right Foster...I need you to go and locate some food and water for our guests.' Shillings voice hinted at no sense of humour or irony in labelling them as guests, when most in the van would suggest they were now prisoners by a more accurate description.

The Inspector squeezed his wife's hand which Flo reciprocated.

'Sorry Sir...' Fosters voice came muffled through the small partition. '...Where would do you suggest I start?'

'Why don't you use your initiative and earn the money this job pays you...but if you really need me to hold your hand then I'd start in the canteen...maybe the kitchen...' There was a slight pause before Shilling snapped back into action. '...Don't give me that look, just get into that place and start searching.'

'Yes Sir.' Foster replied feeling slightly foolish as well as extremely nervous.

The main problem was he didn't know anything about the layout of the facility, although he'd clearly seen when driving up that it was quite a massive building. Too big for a one man exploration and he wasn't sure who else might be inside. He hoped Shilling would understand if he asked for a little more confirmation.

'Sir is there any chance you could let me know what or who I could run into in there?' His request went unanswered as Shilling marched towards the stairs, so he shouted his next thought. 'You know Superintendent...as we would if this were a proper investigation!'

Shillings attention was unsurprisingly grabbed, tugging him round to go back and stand face to face with the young PC. 'Listen to me Foster. I'm willing to let your insubordinate tone go just this once...but I will offer a reminder that you are a serving officer on this City's police force and I am your superior by quite a few steps. Now you can play the 'Do it by the book' card if you wish but let's agree on one thing...these are extraordinary circumstances. So if I tell you to do something it's because I believe it to be the best plan of action!'

'Sir I just wanted to know what our plan was...'

'...Shut up then and let's waste more time while I explain my decision... I'm going to locate the hostages because I know Marcus Kirby. I believe I can reason with him, but if not, I have a loaded weapon. Meanwhile sending you to locate some kitchen supplies makes logical sense because your only weapon is incapacitating spray. Those people who I have told to stay in the van need sustenance and your protection. I suggest they'll shortly have both if you complete the simple task I've given you...'

Shilling and Foster shared a look; the young PC unable to fully conceal his admiration for the big man's understanding of the situation.

'...On top of that we don't know how long until Jay Cleaver shows up here so time is of importance. From what I've heard he's becoming crazier and more dangerous than ever...'

'...Okay I understand Sir...I'll go find some food and water.'

Shilling's pudgy hand reached out to pat the officer on his shoulder, a rare tactile moment from the grizzled Superintendent. 'Good lad...now go.'

With that he turned and headed off up the stairs, while Foster set off around the outside of the main building.

48

Roma Walker glanced down at her thin fingers tightly gripping the steering wheel, her knuckles pressed up against the whitening skin, before focusing her uneasy attention back onto the now mostly deserted streets. It felt to her that the world had stopped mid breath, incapable of rolling another inch forwards, at least until it knew which path to take.

She considered this moment to be insanity personified, after all it was a warm evening under a slowly setting sun yet everything was quiet, no one she could see was walking in this City with anything but bewilderment in their mortal souls. Worryingly this new secretary felt no better prepared for what was coming than any of them. Her only purpose now was to transport the Glitch to the facility and aid it in its work. She'd been given no choice in the matter; it had been decided back at the station the moment she'd turned the newsfeed on her computer off.

After viewing the footage the Glitch had all the information it would need; not only a full understanding of the events surrounding the Angels appearance, but various personal details of the people it was hunting and even a detailed map of the facility itself saved to its memory

'How are you feeling Miss Walker?' It asked calmly.

She glanced automatically at the rear view mirror, before quickly refocusing on the road to sharply manoeuvre around a burning bus laid on its side. 'Shit!' She took a breath. 'You can call me Roma.'

'I know...but I won't. You will have to earn my respect from now on.'

'And I think I know how.' She said.

'Oh please do tell...impress me.' Its voice was smooth and calm.

'Well...' Her eyes never left the road this time. '...I'm obviously of some use to you.'

'Correct...but in what way Miss Walker?'

'If I have to take a guess I think I'll be used as a diversion. Those people were willing to risk leaving me at the station to face you...I'm pretty sure they'll be surprised that you let me live...their confusion will give you an advantage.'

'Congratulations.'

'Thank you.'

'Now stop talking. I need to think.'

Roma did as she was told but took a sly peak over her shoulder at the next left hand turn. She could see Jay Cleaver sitting directly behind her in that smart grey suit, his blue eyes looking out through the window, fixed on exactly what she couldn't say, but she did wonder what it really thought of this changing world.

The Glitch desperately needed some time to reorganise its thoughts, there was so much information to digest as the next stage of its growth began causing it new considerations. Its recent past had been a whirlwind of challenging scenarios, most of them ending in frustrating disappointment, all of them caused by mortal interventions. Whether by cocaine overdoses or being shot in the head by a woman it tried to trust didn't really matter, because this time would be different, from now on it would disregard every one of its naïve instincts and follow a logical plan.

After all the battlefield had changed, Harvey Cooper would soon be out of the fight, while the rest of the group that knew of its existence were unwisely gathering in the one place, so it should be nothing more than a matter of time before its inevitable victory. But it still had to be careful, after watching the videos from the burger bar there was suddenly a doubt, a future thrown back into the balance. Of course it could easily defeat any mortal placed in its path but the reappearance of the Angel was something else, it meant there was now an unknown quantity in the mix, a sideswipe it hadn't predicted.

These ongoing diverse emotions were becoming a major headache and now it was beginning to understand why. It was horribly clear that the longer it remained inside these human forms the greater the threat to its purity of self. Every passing minute its own strengths were being diluted by the assimilation process of sharing its life within these lesser creatures, an unforgiving truth that it was existing as a watered down version of itself. It was only during its one sided battle with the Demon that the Glitch had felt the unlimited power it assuredly held, for those brief moments as it devoured the beast while displaying its true form, it had for the first time felt free and unhindered by any mortal limits.

As it looked out over the deserted streets of this falling civilisation, a frustration was taking over, for the Glitch needed to better control this environment. It needed silence in the car, time to think and work out a new future, one without any reliance on these disgusting human forms.

The Glitch was truly annoyed that the damned Angel had appeared in this world as its true self, if only as an apparition. It meant Metatron was ahead in that department, until the solution strolled forward to the front of its mind. Of course, it thought, consuming the Angel would release such a gift. How wonderful then that the boy who carried it would also be at the facility. Problem solved.

'You may speak again now Miss Walker. I have sorted everything out.'

Roma jumped at the sudden attention. 'I'm sure you have. We'll be there shortly. A couple of minutes I reckon.'

She'd been thoroughly lost in her own thoughts, mostly ones about her looming death, others of how she might be able to help those at the facility but she discovered no solutions. The Glitch seemed to be holding the monopoly on all hopeful thoughts.

49

Kosminsky drew in a deep breath in hope of regaining a little semblance of self-control. He'd struggled against the cuffs with every ounce of strength he had, forcing his bleeding wrists up and down, to and fro, but these were high security restraints, the type a clumsy magician could die wearing.

'When you've quite finished?' Marcus said on returning from the bathroom, his face now washed clean of blood, with only the significant bruising on his left cheek and forehead evidence of Oscar's final fury.

Kosminsky refused to look up as Kirby addressed him.

'Your little friend is dead...so where does that leave us?' The thin man asked and returned to his leather back chair while looking over the carnage in his office. Oscar's blood had seeped down onto the expensive flooring; the chair the small man had used overturned against the far wall, the air still sharing trace odours of carbine.

This wasn't how it was supposed to go.

'It leaves us with nothing...you crazy bastard!' Kosminsky swore loudly and with an insolent passion because he really didn't care anymore. It was all done with, Oscar was dead, the Demon was gone and he didn't doubt in the next few moments he'd see the flash of a muzzle then nothing more.

This was exactly how he expected it to go.

50

'Are we trapped in here...?' Juliet called over to Harvey who was sitting nearest the van doors.

Once again the Inspector didn't respond so Flo leaned over him and tried the handle. It wasn't locked which raised feelings in the group of both great concern and curiosity in equal measure.

'Well this is fucking ridiculous! If that Glitch turns up we're a sitting target. Juliet was feeling the strain as much as everyone else. So much so she went straight for the truth and headed to the doors. 'And if no one else thinks that then fair enough, but I'm not staying in here.'

Alex gripped her arm. 'Where do you think you're you going?'

'I'm sticking to the plan.'

'You heard what Shilling said!'

'Alex! I'm only here because you asked me to be, because I believed you had a strategy...and taking orders, especially ill thought out and risky ones from that fat Neanderthal are not part of the original plan, while getting in there to find some safety is.'

With that she pulled herself free and opened the doors. Cool air rushed back in and for that mercy alone no one else complained.

Flo was too busy worrying about Harvey's silence, his non-committal stance on any of the decisions being taken around him. This was so unlike him that she let the others clamber by her, even helping Rhian and Sammy to leave the van while she stayed beside her husband with his bowed head. 'Please tell me what's going on...what's wrong with you?'

Harvey raised his head and looked at her with eyes that could have just awoken; a gaze of unfocused pupils, lost inside his dreams. For what seemed like the first time he contemplated the empty van then turned to look at the others waiting outside in the gathering gloom.

'Where are we going...?' He asked curiously.

'Into the facility to end this...'

He held an unhealthy pause before asking. '...End what?'

There was something so deeply wrong with him that Flo felt an unexpected surge of panic. She looked out to the group outside who were instinctively standing in a circle looking outwards, covering the angles of approach that a hungry predator could take, in a primeval act they did without realising.

Alex was the first to enquire about Harvey's condition. 'Hurry up you two. What's the matter in there?

Flo's wide eyes looked back at him in response, no words uttered, with her troubled gaze telling of a serious problem.

Inside Harvey Cooper's once beautifully ordered mind a black sandstorm raged. It was the way he'd describe it if he could find any words, only that was impossible as every thought or image he grasped was instantly torn to shreds, all ideas powerless to take flight or be studied. Disturbingly the only comprehensible notion he could find seemed to be on repeat, five words forming in the swirling debris, a simple message from the creature that had touched his mind...

```
This is how you die
```

That sinister sentence would appear in the dust then fade away every time he tried to reset his logical cortex, or attempted to find his own consciousness and there was no way around it. Harvey could still raise his questions but any answers were concealed behind this maelstrom.

It was a devilish gift from the Glitch, one presented to him back at the lock up when it had held his head. From such an innocuous moment the degradation of his mind had grown intensely, those perfect hands having found his most prized possession and taken it away.

'...What's wrong with him...?'

Harvey could hear the question clearly though he'd no idea who spoke it. The wild storm in his head was seemingly a silent movie which made the whole experience even more maddening.

What the hell had the Glitch done to him? Was this some lesson to be learned, a brief punishment, or the permanent state he'd feared the most? Without his problem solving logic he was no more than a broken toy, lost in his own mind, trapped in a shell of desperate finality. The twisted beast had known what his true gift was and done a good job, a perfectly remarkable job, with Harvey now only able to recall pointless random things.

'...Inspector can you hear me...?' A voice asked while firmly tapping his cheek.

The words appeared in his mind before disappearing behind the storm, to be replaced with...

```
This is how you die
```

...the only message he could understand now.

Not knowing what else to do Alex and Juliet helped Harvey out of the van, between them holding him up, to lead his faltering feet towards the stairs. Flo followed closely behind with Rhian and Sammy at her side. The wild haired psychic, a little selfishly relieved her son was no longer the centre of attention, tried to offer some help.

'Let's get him somewhere safe and comfortable. We need to find out what's going on with him.'

'Okay who's been here before...does someone know where the hell we're going?' Juliet asked hopefully.

Silence fell as the only one who'd been there before was helped up the stairs.

'Shit...!' Juliet sighed while heaving Harvey. '...Come on Inspector...talk to us.'

It was such a simple instruction but one he could not obey. The storm in his mind was raging out of control, separating all thinking from reasoning; as he learned the raw truth that those two functions were not the same.

Every thought in a human mind needs a pathway to find some logical conclusion, but all his routes were blocked by the Glitch's filthy barricades. Harvey hadn't any experience of whether actual dementia worked like this; it felt like a bomb had detonated in his neural network, only the explosion hadn't dissipated, it simply kept on exploding. The loss felt so great he would cry if he could, weep wildly until too exhausted to show his feelings to the world, but such tragic functions require a process of the mind. A journey to understand why he felt that way, but now all those simple problem solving stepping stones were gone, buried deep by a Glitch.

51

Jeff Shilling was panting heavily as he followed the carpeted corridor of the fourth floor; obviously Kirby's office was on the fourth floor, the head honcho must always have his room at the top, just like his was. He'd found his way blindly to this location easily enough as no inner doors were locked. He approached the dark wooden double doors at the end of a corridor. Now he was here Shilling didn't really have a plan of action, so instead, and to give him a minute to get his breath back, he put his eye to the keyhole. There was nothing to see as the key was still in the lock but he could hear the muffled sound of Kirby's voice, which sounded calm, even though he was unable to make the words out clearly. Surely that was a good sign for the men trapped in there. Two souls Shilling had practically sold to Kirby in exchange for dirty money.

The Superintendent didn't feel a great deal of guilt about the situation, or about either of the men in Kirby's office, hell one was a murderer whether possessed by an evil force or not, the other a security guard who had clearly got in too deep, neither were overly important in Shillings world.

His life goals at the age of fifty six were all about providing for his grandchildren, well perhaps not providing as such, but at the very least being the best grandad in the world. His only son, Conner Shilling, had produced with the help of his wife Trudy, two beautiful granddaughters. Jeff had no idea how it had happened because his son was a failure in every other aspect of his life and that wife not much better, but little Mia and older sister Charlotte were a delight, at five and seven years old respectively they adored their big cuddly grandad, who bought them sweets and clothes, turned up with toys and gave the biggest hugs ever.

Shilling remembered learning something years ago about how talented genes could skip a generation but he'd never understood it fully until now. With those two young girls in his heart he believed he could make some sense of it.

Obviously he thought of himself as near perfect as could be as almost all people do, it was everyone else who was wrong. Yes, he was carrying some extra timber, due to his rich food diet, the meals he could easily afford with his 'extra' pay because that was just a perk of the job. His day to day work was tough, horrible to witness on occasions, so why not cut a safe deal with a man like Marcus Kirby; a billionaire who wasn't going to miss it, meaning all Shilling had to do was hand over a few psychos once in a while for study purposes.

Now if that didn't show he was the perfect grandad then he didn't know what did. These dealings were a guarantee his upcoming retirement would be sorted, meaning he could spoil those little kiddies even more, certainly a lot more than their dopey parents, which to his mind was the defining proof that talent could skip a generation.

Kirby had stopped talking.

Shilling stood in the corridor trying to decide if it was better to knock on the door or just burst right through it. Feeling the Glock in his jacket pocket he reasoned that he and Kirby didn't have a problem with each other so it could stay there. He then took a deep breath and rapped on the hardwood.

Marcus was in the process of removing the thin black tube from the back of Oscar's dead skull. Kosminsky was still cuffed to the chair with his eyes closed, unable to watch, but both men looked up sharply on hearing the knock. A controlled silence fell on the room and the waiting game began, with Marcus moving slowly and silently back to his desk, unwilling to answer until he knew exactly who'd invaded his property. He slowly reloaded both handguns while listening intently for a clue. This was a dramatic moment that could have stretched out for minutes, but Shilling lacked such subtlety and wasn't being nearly as careful.

'Marcus…it's me…Superintendent Shilling…I'm on my own…can I come in…?' He blustered.

Kosminsky saw the look on his captors face change almost a full three hundred and sixty degrees from anxious to peaceful. For some reason Kirby wasn't concerned that the head of the Edinburgh police force was here, which didn't make a great deal of sense unless…unless Shilling was in on this.

The big guard tensed his wrists against the steel bands once more but they were serving their purpose, all he could do was watch this new drama unfold, until either man chose to put him out of his misery.

Kirby concealed the small silver pistol inside his jacket pocket, placing the larger one in his top drawer, which he didn't close completely. Clearly hoping he wouldn't need either, but who knew as tonight was already turning out different to the one he'd planned.

'Come in.' He called out.

52

Alex had no clue which direction to take but instinct told him to stay on the lower levels. The facility was four levels in total above ground and one below according to the sign at the entrance. Annoyingly it hadn't been a detailed floor plan which would have been more useful, just a few arrows indicating the way to its central hub and where the numerous stairwells would lead. He logically assumed the hub would be the obvious place to go so that was to be avoided, because what they needed was instant safety and some refuge behind thick steel doors, which meant journeying downstairs into the depths.

'Where are we going...?' It was Rhi calling out from the back of the group where she was holding Sammy's hand.

'Keep your voice down.' Alex whispered firmly while readjusting his grip under Harvey's armpit. 'Just follow me and keep moving.'

The Inspector was getting heavier, losing all consciousness by the feel of it, which Juliet confirmed with a grunt as they manoeuvred him down the nearest staircase.

Flo bringing up the rear was lost in apprehensive thoughts. What was wrong with her husband? Was he having a seizure? Is this how it ended for him?

Just four steps ahead of his wife, Harvey was sharing a similar thought but damn he was fighting hard against it. He could also feel his body getting heavier, weakening, but only because he was making it so. It was a trade-off of faculties, hoping that if he focused his concentration solely on the mental problem he may be able to scrape together some forms of thinking. Sadly accepting he could no longer retain the capacity to run both body and mind.

The fog inside his thoughts was growing thicker and Harvey knew hidden inside it a malevolent spectre was moving closer, taking its time, but inevitable in its progress, and soon it would appear to take away everything because...

This is how you die

Alex spotted an open cell door to their left. 'In there. We can put him down...take a breather...' He was genuinely relieved to be doing this because the Inspectors deadweight was getting far too much for Juliet and his only arm. No one else complained as this was the best plan they had, to lock themselves in a secure unit and hope for the best.

Juliet was sweating and wearing a healthy glow as she shoved Harvey onto the bunk. She tried to straighten her spine by raising her hands above her head, like someone about to dive into a pool, but her fingertips hit the ceiling. With no experience of psychiatric facilities she was alarmed to find out just how small a cell could be. Jesus, no wonder the patients are so hard to cure if this is how they're housed, she thought.

'What do we do now?' She calmly asked of Alex.

'One thing at a time is what we're going to do...' He replied as he ushered the other three into the tiny room and closed the door. 'Okay make yourself as comfortable as you can. We won't be staying here for too long. As you can see the doors won't lock by themselves from the inside, so we need to find the keys.'

'I'm sorry Alex but I don't think Harvey's going anywhere.' Flo pointed out cradling her husband's head on her lap.

'Clearly...so we're going to have to split up for a while.'

'You can't be serious! We don't know what the hell we're doing!' Rhian cried out.

'None of us do, but like I said one thing at a time. Juliet and me will go and find the security office. The rest of you will stay here, keep the door pushed shut and try and be quiet.'

Rhian countered. 'But that monster could be here already roaming the corridors looking for us.'

'It could but I don't think it's here yet.'

'Why are you saying that...just to comfort us?'

Alex took a large breath before choosing how to answer Rhian's sharp questioning, as it would mean sharing some information, a shaky theory at best and an idea that he'd hoped to keep to himself. But what the hell, he would do anything to save these people, because when all was said and done, they had once saved him.

'I'm not saying anything to just comfort you...but...it's hard to explain.'

'Try...!' Sammy suddenly said causing Alex to do a double take.

'Okay look...something changed back in that lock up. When I met the Glitch...I...I experienced it for the first time. Although it was inside Jay Cleavers mind I could almost see it, feel it's thoughts as clear as day, there was a connection between us. Immediately I realised I'd taken something from it...'

'...What?' The boy asked in his young boy's voice.

'Is this you speaking to me Sammy?' Alex had to ask because after recent events he'd almost forgotten about the Angel.

Sammy looked up at his Mother. 'Tell him it's me, Mom...'

She looked down into his wonderful kind eyes and absolutely saw her son there.

'Yeah...that's you.' That loving look, an unseen hug between the two, instantly convinced Alex to continue with his thoughts.

'So I took something from it, some kind of ability. Harvey noticed it first. It enabled me to bend another's mind to my will. I did it to Jay and then the Superintendent. It's similar to hypnosis I suppose, where I could gently coax them to do as I say.'

Flo looked across and gently asked, clearly not trying to cause offence. 'Have you been using that trick on us..?'

'No I have not. I wouldn't do that to any of you, but that's not really the whole story, because I don't have that ability anymore and I think I know why. The only reason the Glitch exists is because I passed through it, as I did that, it took the concept of living an actual life from me, and because of that I believe we're linked in some way.'

'But only when you're in close proximity to each other...?' Rhian asked.

'...It appears that way.'

'So that's how you know it isn't here yet, because you can't feel it?' Juliet offered.

Alex smiled as broadly as he could ever remember doing. 'Yes, that's exactly what it is.'

'Well be sure to let us know when you do feel it.' Flo suggested helpfully.

'I promise!' Alex declared and fought back a tear that surprised him with its sudden appearance. There was no time for grateful sentiment right now; Juliet was already standing by the door ready to go, waiting for him to lead the way.

53

Jeff Shilling pushed open the door to Marcus Kirby's office and entered. Then he stopped sharply, on the floor in front of him was a small blood covered body face down. Simple logic told him it was Oscar Downes. He looked to his left to see Allan Kosminsky tied to a chair by his ankles and wrists. He was apparently unharmed and his face was a mask of mental torture, but his mouth remained closed. Only then did Shilling turn to his right to face Kirby sitting calmly behind his desk.

'Superintendent Shilling, well this is an unexpected surprise. May I ask what the hell you're doing in my facility...uninvited?'

The weight of the moment caused Shilling to seriously consider pulling out his gun, in truth he was itching to do so, but instinct told him to remain calm. 'I err...came...erm...' He was thinking as quickly as his out of practice indolent brain would allow. '...I came to see how you were getting on.'

Kirby appeared remarkably comfortable and relaxed with this peculiar situation, Shilling thought, even though he did have significant swelling around his bruised and slightly misshapen face, the quality of his voice sounded nonplussed as he replied. 'Getting on, you mean with these two?'

'Yes...and everything else that's happening out there.'

'Then come take a seat Superintendent...'

'...I'll stay standing if that's okay...' Shilling requested this even though he felt weary, weary and unfit for purpose, but on edge with the thin man. He looked down at the corpse on the wooden floor. 'Can I take it Oscar died...by your hand?'

'Very much so...but look at my face Superintendent...it was a vicious attack and he would have killed me for certain...so I was forced to shoot him through the heart.' Still Kirby showed no signs of emotion. 'In a way I'm thinking I've done us both a favour...that's one less murderer for your force to worry about isn't it. Now tell me the true reason behind your visit, because as you can see I'm still a little busy here.'

'You could be right about it being one less murderer, but now I have another one to worry about, you told me these men had something you required...you never said anything about torturing or killing them.'

'Oh dear then please accept my apologies. I was unaware I had to tell you a damn thing about what I do...!'

Kirby's voice was rising, his swollen mouth sneering as he spoke, a clear sign he was losing his patience and a stark warning that Shilling would be wise to heed.

Holding the position of Superintendent in a major city police force usually meant two things, firstly you often had the last word in most conversations because you have the weight of the law behind you, secondly there were very few civilians you feared, but with Marcus Kirby those two presumptions were redundant. Here was a man who truly didn't care about anyone's position. Over time his immense wealth had wrung out any respect he may have held for others, discovering that anyone can be bought for a fair price.

Shilling should have been well aware he was just another purchase Kirby had made, but just in case he didn't, he was about to be reminded.

'We have an agreement Superintendent in which we exchange goods. What I choose to do with my purchases is my prerogative, how you use the money I give you is yours. This is why our dealings work, I mean if I were to question how you hoard all the ill-gotten gains I give you for the future of your dear grandchildren Mia and Charlotte, I believe it could grow to be of some serious concern. Therefore I need you to understand that having too much information on another's interests can be dangerous, to the point where such knowledge could be used against you, for blackmail, or worse.'

Shilling felt the fury rise up from his gut on hearing his loves names in that psycho's mouth. Unable to fight the urge he moved his hand to the gun.

'I wouldn't do that if I were you.' Kirby whispered while beating him to the draw, his weapon already pointing at the fat man's head.

Shilling slowly lowered his empty hand.

'A wise choice...and now you have another to make...tell me why you're really here and perhaps we can continue as we were...just two happy traders.' The smile on his thin lips was revolting to see. 'Tell me!'

Beaten as he was Shilling still had a card to play. He doubted it would change the outcome but felt sure it would hurt Kirby, because if the lunatic wanted to know everything then he'd tell him all he knew.

'All of this is a waste of time Marcus...you're not going to find what you want. I have it on the utmost authority, from people who know a lot more about the Demon than you...'

'...Demon?' Marcus tried to interrupt, playing dumb, but Shilling continued.

'Yes the Demon that lived in Oscar's head for all those years. It escaped you the last time you tried this...it got away inside Jay Cleaver. If that isn't ironic I don't know what is...the kid's already a psychopath.'

'Then bring him here to me like I requested in the first place!' Kirby demanded down the barrel of a gun.

'You know what? I think you're the only person not talking about the Angel tonight. Too busy hey...you haven't seen the news...no idea what's going on except inside your crazy brain...'

Kirby clicked the safety off but Shilling didn't flinch.

'...Don't threaten me Marcus, I could tell you everything that's been happening, but you'll find out soon enough when you bother to look...and the answer to all your searching will still be the same...the Demon's dead, apparently killed by something far more powerful. Now I don't understand every little detail but the latest report on the condition of the Demon you were hunting is a cold stone fact, it's gone. You missed your opportunity for whatever ridiculous plans you had for it. That's just the way it is, so all you've done is murder a man in your psychiatric care and torture an ex-employee, so put the gun down and let's talk sensibly, see if we can't find a way out of this for you.'

Despite his message the gun stayed in position, levelled at Shillings red round face, while Kirby considered this strange information. There must be something to it because Shilling knew about the Demon, the idiot could neither have guessed nor imagined such a story. He slid the mobile from his pocket and brought up the breaking news.

Clearly he didn't need to know every little detail, but the headlines were more than enough to grasp the event, the footage was incredible.

Perversely, Shilling could have pulled out his own gun while Kirby flicked his attention between him and his phone, but it was more satisfying to watch his thin battered face begin to drop with confused disappointment a picture he would treasure as long as he lived.

Kirby put the phone on the desk. 'So that's the Angel proclaiming the Demon is dead?'

'I believe it is.'

'Did you come here alone?' The thin man asked flatly.

The Superintendent paused as his mind flew into a turbulent swirl of reassessment. Would it be better to tell Kirby the full truth, a half-truth, or nothing at all? By adding up all the known pros and cons he hoped to find a definitive answer to help, not only for himself, but for the others at the facility and the big guard bound sitting silent in the chair.

As experienced a policeman as Shilling was he'd always lacked the nuanced mind of his old partner Harvey Cooper. It had been the same back in the day when in their policing partnership Harvey had always been the velvet glove, Shilling the balled fist inside, each of equal significance but only working in the right circumstances.

In the end he took a decision he hoped would cause this psychopath to stand down and discuss a calm way to proceed.

'No...I came here with the people who know what's really going on. They have confidence they can stop this and they're downstairs awaiting my return...including the boy on the news.'

'Really...so he's not at the airport?' Kirby asked.

'No that was a ruse of mine to get him here safely.'

'That was excellent thinking...so deceitful...so you!' Kirby smiled.

Shilling couldn't help but smile back. 'Yeah I thought s...'

The bullet went straight through the front of Shillings skull, ripping off a chunk of skin and hair which hung down at the back of his collar for a few seconds before his knees buckled, bringing his body to the floor with a gentle thump. Almost poetically his dead hand fell right next to Oscars, nearly touching, but never reaching.

Kosminsky's mouth and eyes were wide open in absolute shock. Now utterly convinced the next bullet would be for him, he turned towards the desk looking at the man holding his life in his bony hands.

54

Juliet turned sharply to Alex. 'Oh my god did you hear that...?'

The crack of that gunshot, although reaching out to them from four storeys above, after passing through thick floors and walls, was still able to have an effect.

Standing stationary in a gloomy corridor they listened for more, when none came, the search for an office or other help restarted.

'It would really help if we could find something better than this emergency lighting.' Alex suggested frustratingly. 'Come on Joolz you've worked in places like this before.' The look she gave back to him caused an instant retraction. 'Okay not exactly like this, but where would you expect to find the nearest office? It's all empty cells and restrooms.'

Juliet suddenly grabbed his right arm, not having much choice in the matter, before turning him to face her. 'This way...' She led them out of the main corridor and up a set of side stairs, which certainly weren't the same ones they'd come down a little while ago. Once at the top they looked down a dimly lit hallway, two doors on the left side, one at the end to the right. '...Let's try these.'

Reaching that final door on the right they opened it to find themselves in a small cupboard sized office.

Back in an unlocked cell Rhian was attempting a whispered a conversation with Flo, both women heeding the warning given by Alex, only to find Sammy's volume control wasn't working.

'Mom...can we go home?' his voice whining up a notch at the end.

'No baby we can't, not until the others come back.'

'Then can we?'

'Yes Sam of course we can!' Flo's interruption seemed to calm the boy a little. But in reality it just caused him to change the subject, awkwardly.

'What's wrong with Mr Cooper?'

If she knew the answer to that question Flo felt sure she could fix it, but instead her husband was still laid on his back perfectly still, with his head on her lap facing upwards, eyes closed but with a definite tension in his jaw. It appeared to her eyes that he could be dreaming, if he was then his dream was insufferably tense.

To satisfy Sam's query she answered honestly. 'I think he's got a really bad headache. Like a migraine...have you heard of a migraine...?'

Sammy nodded.

'...like a migraine then.' Flo repeated and smiled. It was as much to comfort herself as the boy.

Rhi pulled him close. 'Remember what Alex said about us keeping very quiet?' Sammy nodded again. 'Good boy...!'

Silence then reigned in the cell as a mother held her hungry child and a wife her dying husband, the women's eyes meeting over their loves as they settled down to share their discomfort...and listen.

On the wall next to the door there was a light switch. It was the first one they had found on their exploration, all the other rooms and corridors seemingly controlled from the central hub, so they were both optimistic that particular hub could be in this office somewhere,

Alex flicked the switch and a strip light buzzed into life. Juliet took over the office chair at the desk and began pressing buttons to turn on the computer, while Alex began searching the few shelves and drawers for...for what he didn't really know...for anything at all.

'Hey look at this...' Juliet picked up something plastic from the desk and then swivelled round to show Alex a lanyard with an identification badge affixed to it. '...I'm guessing this was Allan Kosminsky's office then...' They both shared the thought that even in a passport sized photo his head and shoulders appeared massive. '...I wonder where he is...'

Alex naturally wanted to reassure her that the big guard was okay but another thought flashed across his mind. A memory of a moment he'd seen in the Angels book, a visceral image that made him turn towards the door, even though he knew the bloody and butchered body of Doctor Catherine Kelly had never been there. Not here, not on this timeline, on an alternate one, the one he was trying to save.

This thought took him back to something Flo had said, how things may not necessarily be better if they returned to their original path, maybe she was right, but Alex would still fight for it because none of this should be happening. He didn't even care if on that original timeline he died on the cobbles of Dalmeny Street, at least it would be truthful and not this lie, not a life created by an Angel's need for vengeance.

It all seemed so long ago when he'd climbed out of the window onto the narrow ledge, ready to mend his broken heart by smashing it into the ground below, but then Jay Cleaver had appeared and ruined it all. The parallel irony wasn't lost on Alex that here he was waiting and listening for the same man to arrive at the facility. Of course this version of Jay was an altogether bigger threat, a world ending one, but it seemed their paths were destined to cross to decide the future of any timeline.

'I asked you a question Alex...don't you start drifting off now.'

'Sorry Joolz...it's just so strange being in here...these are places I've experienced before. Only it wasn't me...' He stopped abruptly on feeling a new shiver pour slowly down his spine. '...Oh no...it's here...the Glitch.

55

Roma drove her car through the open facility gates and headed for the underground car park, where she pulled up next to a van with its back doors wide open. Leaving the keys in the ignition she looked over her shoulder at Jay, but he had his head down, not appearing to have noticed their arrival.

'So what do we do now? She asked.

The young man didn't respond, but the Glitch knew precisely what it wished to achieve and how this particular event would play out without any need for words. After silently planning during the whole journey, it was more than ready to kill all these problematic souls, thus allowing it to grow to its full potential, before striding out into the bigger world to begin its true purpose; the mass destruction of a species, of their dying planet, then the annihilation of this whole pointless and damaged universe.

56

So it had turned out the big guard still had a couple of useful reasons to be kept alive. Kosminsky didn't know how long this reprieve would continue, but in hope it may lead to something better than dying, he continued to do as he was told, forced at gunpoint to drag the bodies of Oscar Downes and Superintendent Jeff Shilling out into the corridor.

Two doors down from Kirby's office a storage room was to be used as a makeshift morgue. Oscar's corpse had been the most difficult to move but it had nothing to do with the physical exertion needed, the little man weighing no more than what he really was, a bag of bones. The difficulty had arisen from the tears in Kosminsky's eyes at the loss of a friend he'd spent the last year and a half with on a daily basis.

What had started out as a strictly jailer/prisoner relationship slowly flowered to become something more, a shared bond, so the body he was placing carefully in the storage room felt like a part of his life; which wretchedly left him with no one else in this world to love.

Sadly Kosminsky didn't know what the words for the opposite of having Stockholm syndrome were. That strange condition whereby a prisoner develops positive feelings towards their captors as a coping mechanism, but whatever the opposite was, he had it bad.

'Why are you crying you big oaf?' Kirby goaded as he watched the big guard pull the considerable weight of Shilling out of the room. 'Such a strange man, aren't you...big as a bull but scared as a kitten.'

Kosminsky slowly stood up to his full height staring down at Kirby and his gun, with every fibre of his being wanting to run straight at the man, to tear him apart under a flurry of heavy enjoyable blows.

'Do it...!' Kirby said reading the look in the guard's eyes. '...Come at me and end it all!'

Only that was his biggest problem, knowing if he made any attempt to attack it would be no better than suicide and he'd be breaking the one rule he'd always promised himself, to never take his own life no matter how bad things got. Living by this mantra because he still believed that Chrissi would return one day, and if she did, when she did, he wanted to be there, to help put her suitcase back in his house.

'Fuck you!' He breathed out and grabbed Shillings arm to drag him out.

Confident in his hold over the man Kirby turned on the computer screen at his desk. Since the refurbishments he'd requested there had been no time to play with his new toys, so he adjusted the screen to allow him to see both it and Kosminsky, then he brought up the camera feeds, once more a king high in his castle.

57

Juliet was the first to notice the tiny red light appear on wall above them. 'Alex...I think the cameras are on...'

'Excellent work Joolz...we're going to need those. What did you do?

'Nothing...I think we're the ones being watched...shit! What now?'

Alex came to an immediate decision. 'Can you get the feed up on the computer?'

'Yeah...'

'Then do it.' He moved to her side and studied the tiny pictures on the screen. He counted sixty small squares of images filling the whole display. 'Bloody hell how many cameras does one facility need. There bring up that one...it's the car park!'

Juliet increased the size of the image; it showed them the empty police van with a small car parked next to it. 'I suppose that's what our monster arrived in...he's not too flashy is he?'

Alex responded but never took his eye of the screen. 'Not really the time for whimsy but yeah the cars a pile of crap...can you zoom in on it?'

She tried a few buttons then answered. 'No...it's a fixed camera down there.'

This was unhelpful because Alex thought he could see something strange, but then Juliet switched to another live camera which displayed a shadowy figure walking down a gloomy corridor.

'Seriously where in hell are the light switches for this place...?' He cried out to the very walls around them, making Juliet flinch in surprise.

'Alright I'm trying...they should be here somewhere. What's this...it's got a light bulb depiction next to it...worth a go?' She clicked on the tiny bulb motif only for everything to then get considerably worse.

'Fuck...!'

58

Three of the four mouths in the tiny cell gasped at this sudden and immediate blackout. Shocked at how it had gone from gloomy but relaxed to pitch black and instantly distressing.

'Oh my god...!' Rhi exclaimed pulling her startled boy closer, shielding his eyes although she had no idea from what exactly, perhaps hoping the darkness would feel less frightening to him if she was the one causing it.

'That's all we need...' Flo whispered. '...Just try and remain calm and let's stay quiet.'

This shared attempt at silent calmness lasted for approximately twenty seconds, that was when they heard the sound of a cell door being pushed open, its hinges squeaking quietly in reality but to their ears it was clear and ominous, there was somebody in the corridor moving slowly, carefully, checking each cell as they approached.

'Oh...' Was all Rhi managed to say before a hand rocketed out of the darkness and covered her mouth.

'...Shh.' Flo made the sound as quietly as possible then released her grip on Rhi's face, pretty sure she'd got the message across, because it was no time to panic with something so close by.

Very close by, the women could here its footsteps approaching; even though their cell door was closed it wasn't locked. They were now trapped in the dark and those steps were real and with no other sounds to focus on it took over their ears and minds. Flo tried urgently to bring her heart rate and breathing down to a manageable level, she could tell Rhian was doing the same, really what other choice was there? You can't fight in the dark and you can't hide in a small cell. The thought crossed Flo's mind to leave her husband and run at the door when it opened, screaming as loud as she could to frighten it away perhaps, but it was a stupid idea and she knew it.

In the pitch black of their frightened world a light appeared, breaking through the gap at the bottom of the door, as if whatever stood outside there could be illuminated. Flo and Rhian instinctively closed their eyes as their cell door was slowly pushed open, when they opened them again a circled beam of white hit their faces, blindingly, before it was pointed down at the cell floor.

'Here you are!' Officer Lee Foster said as he entered. 'I've been looking everywhere for you lot. I managed to find some water and half a packet of digestives for the boy...then all the bloody lights went out. You okay...?'

Strange how extreme fear can bring about such opposing feelings of gratitude, with Flo wanting to strangle the life out of the oblivious policeman who was just doing his job, while also wanting to kiss him all over his young face.

'Jesus Christ Officer Foster...! She said in exasperation.

'Call me Lee if you want to...the worlds going to shit anyway isn't it...must have been scary in the dark for you?'

'You think...?' Rhian double downed on the sarcasm, just another by product of true terror suddenly being alleviated.

The Officer placed his torch down against the wall, angling it, so the cell was a partially illuminated. At least they could see each other's faces now, which was a considerable improvement.

'Where are Alex and the Nurse...? He asked.

'They've gone to get help!' Sammy answered now he was no longer smothered by his mother's protective hands.

'Right...and the Superintendent has he come back yet?'

'No...' Flo answered this time, feeling ill at ease at the mention of Jeff Shilling. '...I don't think he'd really care if we rotted down here!'

'He's not that bad, just a little old school in his ways...' Here was Foster standing up for his boss which surprised everyone, including himself.

'Yes turn of the last century I'd say!' Flo suggested unhelpfully. 'Did you say you had some water?'

The young officer reached inside his high-vis jacket and pulled out two plastic bottles. Handing them over to the women when he saw Sammy wasn't particularly thirsty; his eyes having spied the digestives.

'Can I have a biscuit please?' He asked with all the boyish charm he could muster.

At the exact moment Officer Foster handed them over to those small hands everyone reacted as the lights came on, prior to there had been emergency lights only but now everything was fully flooded with light.

'Oh my God about time...!' Foster exclaimed loudly while watching the boy who was only interested in getting the first biscuit out of the packet. '...Maybe everything's going to be okay.'

Flo smiled sweetly but it was faked because her husband certainly wasn't okay, perhaps he never would be again.

None of his wife's feelings were able to reach Harvey, not in the misty hell he now resided within, where his mind was barely his own. In here he was unable to recognise light or dark, nothing from the outside was seeping through, all he could see was the fog burying his thoughts, pushing him deeper down into a mental grave, throwing soil down over his wasted life. The Glitch had beaten him into submission by taking away his judgements, a filthy trick and a sick joke, as the words once more appeared before him...

<pre>This is how you die</pre>

In utter desperation he dragged his mind once more from the abyss, threw everything he had as a mortal man to regain control, willing his body to rise and stand.

Flo felt the movement of her Husband on her lap and reacted straight away, paradoxically by trying to hold him down.
'Harvey thank god, don't worry we're here with you. Stay calm.'
But he wasn't listening, he couldn't, as he threw away the evil binds that were holding him down, unaware these were his wife's caring arms.
'Get off me...' Harvey snarled at the other three adults and stood up shakily. His usually kind eyes looked dark and extreme which became an even bigger concern when he grabbed what he believed to be his only hope.
'Mom...!' Sammy screamed as the crazy looking Inspector roughly pulled him away from Rhian's arms.
'What the hell are you doing? ' Flo yelled as she watched her husband put his hands around the boys throat.
'Nobody move...' Harvey ordered. '...or I'll break his neck!'
Officer Foster clearly didn't catch on to just how serious the Inspector was and made a grab for the boy. Harvey grasped the boy tightly with one hand while the other threw a punch toward the officer. It failed to connect properly but gave the young man enough serious notice to stay back.
Sammy was giving up on his own weak struggles, with his face already turning purple from the Inspectors grip, the whole event a living nightmare in a tiny cell.

Harvey released his grip slightly on the boy's throat but kept enough pressure for his message to be sent. Then in his mind he screamed for the Angel, bellowed out that the boy would die if it didn't show itself, because he had nothing left to lose now, his hand squeezing ever tighter in a savage game of who blinks first.

'What is this?' The Angel spoke just as Harvey felt himself weakening further. He didn't know if the voice was real or imagined but he answered it anyway. It was all he could do to keep himself alive.

'You...you...you've got to help me' He asked, hearing his heart become the slow drum of a funeral march. 'Make it stop...the Glitch infected me.' Frightened tears began to fall both inside and outside his face. '...it's killing me...please...' He begged before collapsing to the floor, nothing left to give in this fight for survival. Looking up he could see the fog begin to move, pushed aside by a form coming through, this was it. This was how he died.

The Inspectors body lay lifeless on the floor of the cell and the depths of his beaten mind. In both worlds a hand reached down and touched his forehead, in one it was Flo, in the other it was the Angel. He felt his body raise up as if he were being carried, lifted away from this pain of trying to exist, to be placed on a wooden table.

His eyes opened to find the stark whiteness was almost blinding. Involuntarily his head lolled to the left to see the Angel stood before him.

'Huh...that was your plan...to threaten me in hope I could save you...?' Metatron unfurled its mighty wings as if it had been a long time since they'd last opened. '...A hell of a risk to take Harvey...but I'm intrigued by your bravery so I have chosen to speak with you. Don't think you have to stay lying down on my desk. Stand up, walk around, then we'll discuss your position in life...or death.'

Harvey found he could pull his body up and off the white desk with ease, stand on his two feet comfortably enough, able to think clearly again although his thoughts were far from logical. He looked around the space and beyond the Angel to see nothing but the light of the white world just as Alex had described.

'Am I dead...?'

It felt strange that they would be the first words he spoke after what he'd been through.

'No, not yet, I had to bring you somewhere away from all the noise...' Metatron took its seat in the white wooden chair then gestured to Harvey to take the one on the other side.

'This is Heaven though...?'

'I really don't have the patience to go through explaining all this again. You know where we are and an intelligent man like you can fill in the blanks...would you like to try?'

THE RED FRAME

The cogs in his mind started to click once more as if being released from some heavy rust. 'Okay...I think I can put a few pieces together. I'm in the white world where you and Alex met...suppose some would call it heaven, others limbo.'

The Angel interlinked its fingers across its chest and sat back.

'Actually you're not there, neither of us are, that place passed away, it no longer exists in this dimension. We are essentially in the boy's mind, where I have lovingly created this replication of the old world, but let's focus on the task in hand. You called to me, begged and screamed for my help, threatened to kill an innocent boy to save you from the Glitch's trick. So the question is what do you really want from me?'

Harvey took a moment before answering, for an unfathomable reason he wanted to take this all in, as he stared at the Angel sat before him. This was no gentle wavering apparition born from smoke; this was beautiful and real, its green eyes striking against the unblemished alabaster skin, every feather of its wings peaking up behind its head perfect in form. It was almost too much to bear. He wanted to cry but tears would be for another time, he had to answer the question and in such a situation only the truth would suffice. '...I want you to save me then take me back so we can kill that bloody monster...'

'My, you are passionate in your misguided beliefs...but there is no need for profanity to show me the depth of your feelings. I understand all too well the emotions of revenge and wanting to win. If you recall it cost me a great part of my own soul...but your needs are not enough...'

'Enough for what...?' Harvey raised his voice, if it was a mistake to do so he didn't care.

'...To win.' Its eyes slowly fell in a clear display of regret.

Harvey picked up on the look and asked the question he believed the Angel wanted him to. 'Why...?

'...Because we cannot win. Inevitability has found us out and this is how it ends'

'Don't say that...don't speak like the Glitch. We have to get back there, we're wasting time.'

'Actually we aren't wasting any time at all. Everything out there will be precisely as we left it when we return...'

Harvey thought hard about what that could mean. 'Are you saying times frozen?'

'No...I'm saying we are currently outside of it, therefore it is of no concern and we can speak freely here, nothing will change...trust me.'

'Like Alex trusted you...?' Harvey enquired with a hint of edge.

The Angel felt that and stood up, walking away a few feet, taking stock of this moment, before refocusing on the Inspector. 'I have tried explaining the situation to you before and no one listened closely enough, the Glitch has told you all exactly what it is, yet still you have failed to make the connection. So when I tell you we cannot win then you must believe me. Accept it as a true fact that there is no way of you defeating it, none, the entity stalking your world right now is a fundamental element of the universe...'

'...But one that you created as far I'm aware.'

'Not by design...it would never have come into the light without Alex passing through it. This was a freak event.'

'But you knew what could happen by sending your Demon to Earth, how there would be massive risk in doing that...now that part is true!'

Harvey surprisingly found himself in full interrogation mode because this Angel knew something useful, even if it wasn't aware itself. Harvey felt this suspicion like he'd done many times before, an instinct finely honed over the years, an itch he needed to scratch. He felt inside his jacket and pulled out Oscar's battered drawing, placing it on the wooden desk before flattening out the corners. 'You sent this to me...made sure I found it in the car...why?'

'So you would know that Alex's stories were real. Inspector, you are on the right track but it's far too late. The Glitch needed to be killed earlier on in its journey. Your secretary Emma had the right idea, that was your last chance, even then it survived and walked away to become more powerful.'

'But what is this...? Harvey grabbed the picture up and waved it at the Angel. '...It was important to you and the Demon...what is it?'

'It was my proviso, a limiter if you will, of where the Demon could travel, because I wished for its message to be localised so it would be felt more strongly.'

'Yes...in my City.'

'By pure chance again, nothing personal, it could have entered your world anywhere. It was for that reason I drew a box in the book using my own blood...'

'...The Red Frame!'

'Precisely...and it worked wonderfully. With the frame in place my Demon remained focused in your City and the numbers of the dead rose. But the frame is of no use now because my vengeance is dead, murdered by the Glitch, our oncoming apocalypse, who as we speak is at the facility hunting your associates, tying up its loose ends. Are you sure you still want to go back?'

'Well I don't want to hide in the mind of a young boy like you. Cowering away in the shadows, ashamed of what you did, too scared to face a monster that you helped make. We're clearly very different species because if this is the end of our existence I'd like to at least put up a fight.'

'Even though it's futile...?'

'...Even then...and also I'd wish to spend the end of time stood with my wife...at her side.'

The Angel walked back to the table before taking Harvey's hand in its own. 'Ahh there it is, the true reason you begged for my help, so you can spend some more fleeting moments with dear Florence. This is a touching sentiment even to an Angel but understand I am not hiding from the Glitch or cowering in the shadows, or ashamed of what I did, I am simply more appreciative and able to accept our imminent termination.'

'Please let me go back.' Harvey asked it straight out.

The Angel walked forward, placing its hand on the Inspectors forehead.

'Very well we shall go back, so you may have that time with your wife, but just remember in those final moments, when the Glitch kills her, that you could have saved yourself a great deal of pain.'

'I will.' He replied.

'And don't try calling for me again Harvey...I won't answer.'

Then the Inspector's whole world slipped into darkness once more.

Slowly his consciousness began to creep towards a tiny light in the distance, growing ever larger, calling him towards it. Without hesitation he went willingly because there was no more fog, no storm obscuring his thoughts and the repeating words of the Glitch were gone, leaving just the purity of a beckoning orb. As he moved closer the light began to cover him completely, floating in a ball of warmth where nothing mattered, sheer gentle perfection...until he felt the hard smack across his face.

'Harvey! Come on Harvey wake up!'

Under such a brutal attack on his raw and freshly rediscovered senses he did exactly as requested, waking to look up into Flo's eyes.

59

Alex leaned forward to Juliet as all the areas on the screen lit up. 'I can say well done this time can't I...you did that...turned on the lights?'

'Sorry wrong again...that wasn't me.' She replied. 'It must be Kirby and he's going to see all of this, he'll know where everyone is...I seriously doubt that's a good thing.'

'Yeah you're probably right but let's worry about him later. Right now we need to find the Glitch.'

Juliet began flicking through the various camera feeds. She found their group of friends in the cell where they left them. Harvey was sitting up and it also appeared he was talking which was of some relief. The young policeman was with them as well, this was all good. As they continued their scrolling and with the facility fully lit, including the car park, they were able to better make out the car, and the figure sitting in the back.

'Oh my god that's him!' She cried.

Alex agreed then spoke his only thought. 'What the hell is it doing?'

'Who knows, but look here...'

Their focus flicked to another feed and saw the figure striding up the stairs towards Kirby's office. But there were no cameras in that area past this stairwell one so the woman quickly disappeared.

'I'm sure that's the secretary from the station...erm...err Roma...'

Juliet recognised the woman although they hadn't been introduced or even spoken. '...I'd bet that's her car. She's driven the bastard here.'

'Under pain of death if I know the Glitch.' Alex replied and studied the feed from the car park again. 'Okay let's work out the most sensible scenario of what's happening here...why is it doing this...why would it choose to send her in first?'

They both considered the possibilities but it was Juliet who came up with a conclusion first, it fitted the brief perfectly. '...Of course Alex.'

'What?'

'It will want the same as us...to control the facility, the lights and cameras, the central hub must be in his office...' Juliet explained. '...One of us should go up there.'

Alex found himself momentarily stunned by that opinion before feeling ready enough to answer it calmly. 'No Joolz that's not going to happen. We're staying right here...together.'

'But...'

'...No buts Joolz. Look Harvey's back on his feet and we can see what's going on out there. So a far better plan than separating is to stay here and read the situation. If things start to look threatening we'll have a much better idea of what to do and hopefully know which way to go.'

Juliet had to agree with his logic so nodded her head in agreement and started to wheel though the different feeds again. Of course he was right, but that didn't help the curiosity and concerns she held about Roma's visit to Kirby's office, because certainly the sound they'd heard earlier was a gunshot, which meant that poor girl was about to walk into the aftermath.

On reaching the top level of the facility Roma Walkers steps came to an abrupt halt. There were long clear blood smears on the carpet connecting two of the doors in this hallway, the one next to her and the large one at the end. Her hand reached down and turned the handle, inside were two bodies sitting upright, their heads hung down on their chests, quite dead and concealed.

Why?

The only answer that came back was to advance with extreme caution.

60

Alone once more within its make believe white world, deep inside the head of a young boy, the Angel thought upon its meeting with Harvey Cooper. Here was a mortal who had certainly shown courage, to decline the offer of a quick and painless release into death, a man who would rather march back onto a losing battlefield, with no armour or weapon to hand, than selfishly sneak away to avoid the oncoming and suffering pain the Glitch would bring.

Metatron countered itself for still calling it the Glitch; it was far beyond such simple titles now, undoubtedly that was how it had started out, but time moves on...always.

Even for an incredible species such as Angel's who never physically age, never grey or wear out, that exist in a world without time or form the ticking of the Life Machine can still be heard. It will toll and therefore take its toll on the hearts and minds of even the seemingly eternal. As with Metatron, who had witnessed so many events in Heaven and Earth, their emotions can still be altered; moods that constantly swing, while even the strongest beliefs set in stone will crumble.

Sitting in its reimagined white chair at its remembered white table, the Angel looked over at the empty seat where both Alex and Harvey had sat to speak and share their stories. Those moments of contact, along with the devastating loss of its vengeful side, seemed to have softened its cold propensity for believing itself to be the far greater specimen.

It was finding itself having to reason with the words of those mortals. None more so than Harvey's condemnation that it was behaving as a coward by hiding in the boy's head, while he and Alex were both willing to fight the invincible head on, but sadly they still didn't understand the full story and wouldn't until it was too late. Those poor mortal hearts blindly refusing to accept that the end of this particular universe was here, even if the Glitch was summoned in error by a selfish hateful desire it would still have to perform its only duty with a ruthless endeavour.

Metatron then thought on the great book consumed by this oncoming walking apocalypse, realising how that had been such a clever move by the Snake, because if the book were here for reference who knew what answers could be found. Without it the Angel's only strategy was a desperate wish to turn back the clock. Such an idea was no more than a childish longing and a universal impossibility. Time can only travel forward, leading this Angel to recall how it had once informed Alex there were no

THE RED FRAME

answers in the past, what is done is done, so all one can ever do is walk forward carefully.

This reasoning allowed the once mighty Metatron to accept its current actions as anything but cowardly; rather it believed it was staying out of sight to privately prepare for the end, to get its house in order. For this very night it knew the Glitch, apocalypse, monster or whatever anything wished to call it, would display its truest colours to the watching planet, after which there would be no turning back. Even the Life Machine itself would be unable to intervene in the passing of this world. It would even willingly assist in destroying this universe in order to create another, for the slayer had been summoned.

So soon everything that existed now would be gone, whole galaxies consumed as the devouring Glitch grew ever larger, until not even the tiniest memory remained of what had been. Such cleansing and rebirth had happened many times before and would do so again. This was the relentless nature of a system functioning beyond imagination, just the cold and mechanical actions of a perpetual machine that operated without reason.

Metatron looked down upon the empty table and chair, glistening shards of painful remorse exploding through its beautiful but imperfect soul, for it had created this ending and for a few moments, while fully accepting this sin, the crestfallen Angel wept.

61

In the panelled office the end drew ever closer for one of the men inside. Allan Kosminsky was kneeling on the floor, Kirby's gun pointing at his forehead, looking up at the thin man's finger on the trigger.

'Now you've cleaned up for me I suppose I have no more use for you. Wouldn't you agree that this would be the perfect time to terminate your contract of employment?'

'Unless I have something you need to know...but if not...then yeah go ahead terminate me.' The big guard closed his eyes.

This was a perplexing comment played well by the guard. Marcus Kirby had few weaknesses, almost zero because of his amassed fortune, but one foible always haunting him was an incurable case of curiosity, because of it he had to know what Kosminsky meant. Did he have something held back in reserve for such a moment?

'So what do you know...?' Kirby asked.

'...I know about the Glitch. Harvey Cooper told me stuff.'

'Then tell me this...stuff. I have five bullets still in this gun and I would happily shoot you in various places, all of them agonisingly painful the longer you delay.

'I don't doubt it and I'll tell you what I know...but I need to ask a small favour first. May I go to the bathroom?'

Kirby chuckled to himself and even that was a horrible sound. 'Are you being serious?'

'It's either that or I'm going to make a worse mess in your office.'

'Hmm...Kosminsky, if I were to ever write some confessional memoirs I wouldn't include this bit. Go and be quick about it. There's nothing in there you could use as a weapon. Don't lock the door...just push it to...ridiculous. Hurry up.'

Kirby followed the big man every step of the way with the aim of his gun.

Kosminsky followed the orders to the letter and turned on the light. The man wasn't lying there really wasn't anything of use in here, not even a window, so he pushed the door to leave a three inch gap, at the very least he had a few moments to think.

Kirby was still chuckling to himself when he noticed something move under his office door. Was that a shadow? It moved again convincing Marcus that indeed there was someone outside listening in. Standing up quietly he walked past the bathroom, a furtive glance enough to reveal

Kosminsky's feet with trousers round his ankles. Surely he had nothing to fear, he held a loaded gun in his hand.

He opened the door and a young woman stood in the hallway.

'And who might you be...?' Marcus asked.

'My names Roma...Roma Walker...I work for Inspector Cooper, I was wondering if you knew where he was.'

Marcus Kirby's mood, already verging on incredulous after Kosminsky's demand, almost caused him to laugh out loud on seeing her. What the hell was going on now, a young woman wandering around the building, like a lost lamb looking for her flock?

'Do you know who I am?' He asked.

'No...I was told to find the Inspector.'

'Please come in...' He stood aside so she could enter. '..Excuse the mess I've been having a troublesome meeting with some old associates.'

'What happened to your face...is that blood...?' Her eyes scanning the dark pools on the wooden floor

'Yes it was an extremely heated meeting...but don't concern yourself.'

Kosminsky was decent again and spying through the tiniest crack of the door. If Kirby called him then he'd come out, but if not then he'd stay right here, alive just a little while longer.

From his viewpoint the young woman looked familiar but he couldn't be sure as she had moved slightly past him, closer to Kirby than the bathroom. Harvey had mentioned having a new secretary and if this was her she wasn't as bright as Emma, the previous one. To just walk into this man's office unarmed took a depth of stupidity he couldn't accept as sensible behaviour.

Then the gun was fired twice and he pressed his frame back against the wall, his ears ringing again but not as badly as before, clearly they were getting used to the noise at such close quarters. Peeking through the gap, so he could get a view of another pointless death, he was astounded to see her standing upright, for all intents and purposes unhurt.

Another gunshot caused him to flinch away. What the fuck? He chose to remain hidden and listened to the bizarre conversation that ensued.

'I don't understand...what?!' Kirby exclaimed in astonishment.

Roma's voice was calm, quite unlike what Kosminsky expected to hear, as she replied. 'Marcus Sebastian Kirby...Owner of this Blackford Facility of Psychiatric Care...my apologies that I lied to your face. I do know who you are...in fact I lied twice, I'm not Miss Walker...well not as such.'

'Are you...?' Kirby was gasping for breath now.

'Please don't call me the Glitch. That's so last week. It's a shame we have to meet like this. I've seen the bodies out there; it seems we may be trying to achieve similar tasks this evening, murdering people who have gotten in our way.'

Kirby fired two more shots from only four feet away but the woman remained upright and talking serenely. 'Please stop shooting at me it's becoming tiresome. Now let us get to the reason why I'm here...I want you show me on your computer everything I need to know about this building. What we're capable of doing from here, lights, doors, security measures, the location of my victims...anything of use.'

'What are you?'

'Oh just everything you dream to be. I killed the Demon you know. You do know that? I consumed its body and mind and it was delicious...which is why I know so much about you. How you tried to capture it for yourself as if it were just a leathery winged butterfly, a specimen you could pin to a board in your mind...I heard it was an outrageously pathetic attempt. Now show me what the computer controls from here.'

'I will but hang on a minute...if you're similar to the Demon then why not discard that girl and enter my mind. I have this tube to do it...and money, lots of money, influence on every continent...we could do it all together.'

Roma raised a finger to her lips. 'Shush now...I have told you what I require but still you try to turn this situation to your advantage. Time is of the essence I'm afraid so I'll sort out the computer myself. Come here!'

Kosminsky dared to take another peek. He could see Roma was still standing in the same position, but from a distance Kirby was being slowly lifted out of his chair, the thin man levitating as she moved him to float helplessly in front of her some feet three feet off the ground, his head almost touching the ceiling. He tried to cry out but was instantly silenced and his mouth shut tight.

'I need neither your money nor your depraved power hungry mind...' Roma's mouth was half smiling. '...but I will admit I did not expect to feel so insulted by coming here...that you should consider yourself worthy enough to carry me!'

From the gap in the door Kosminsky watched on in horror as the Glitch apportioned out its level of disgust in the man. From here the guard could clearly see Marcus's face and he was looking back at him, helplessly.

'Are you a religious man Mr Kirby?' She asked. An almost imperceptible movement of his head from side to side was enough to answer the question. 'That is a shame!'

Roma then raised her hand and pointed her forefinger before making the sign of the cross. Marcus appeared confused by this for a second, then utterly horrified as his frame split apart into four pieces, his body straight down the middle from head to toe, his midriff separating horizontally, with his arms and legs falling to the floor on either side.

In the bathroom Kosminsky stood again with his back to the wall, only now he'd both hands pressed to his mouth, in a terrified attempt to remain hidden by not throwing up. He then heard her flat shoes walking across the wooden floor, with no idea which direction they were heading until there came the tapping of her fingers on the computer keyboard.

It was at this moment he did something unexpected, especially after all the horrors he had witnessed in his life, for the first time since he was a child he prayed silently. Calling out and begging for some higher power to save his soul, to take him away from this place but no answer came. Maybe God was too busy running for its own life at the minute to answer any mortal plea. One thing Kosminsky knew for sure was that all Divinities were going to be overwhelmed with requests for help soon, because whatever was at Kirby's desk, in the guise of an innocent young woman, was a living nightmare from Hell.

After only two minutes, which felt like a week to Kosminsky, she stood up from the chair and walked across the room. He could hold his breath but could not quieten his heavily beating heart as her footsteps walked by and paused. Then he heard them continue and the office door open and close.

It was only after another week, or maybe two minutes, that he found the courage to peek out, just a fraction at first, but enough to see the sliced remains of Kirby on the floor. Fighting back the strong urge to vomit he leaned out further to see the rest of the room. It was empty and he slowly slid to the floor in pure exhausted relief.

62

Harvey had almost run out of words in trying to explain his rather abusive actions towards young Sammy. Describing to them all in detail how he'd only done it because the Glitch had poisoned his mind. Then in what manner the Angel had saved his life, by pulling him back from the brink of suffering death by utter madness.

'I really didn't mean to hurt you Sammy'. Harvey's eyes were wide and teary as he held the boy to his chest. 'Know how you have something living in your head? Well I had something in mine, but it's gone now, soon yours will be too.'

Rhian reached over towards her boy but instead placed her hand on Harvey's head, gently ruffling his thinning hair 'I thought we'd lost you Inspector.'

'It was touch and go for a while.' He replied while releasing the boy back to his mother.

'But the Angel saved you...?' Flo asked quizzically.

Harvey looked at his wife, understanding her puzzlement at such a turn of events, wishing he had some definite answer to the glaring question...why?

'Yes it did, although it repeated its original claim that we can't win this fight against the Glitch, so I've no idea why it didn't just let me die...' He pondered that thought for a moment. '...It's strange, the Glitch could have easily killed me back at my office...I was hanging outside the window for god's sake...or in the lock up, but it didn't. For some reason there was an element of suffering it wanted to pass on to me first. I can't help but think there's something else going on here...it doesn't make sense.'

Flo raised her eyebrows in an almost comical fashion. 'When things used to make sense...yes I remember those days, but Harvey it did try to kill you. I don't believe there's something deeper going on here...it just wanted to enjoy itself with your particular death. Probably because you were the one chasing it, the leader of a disruptive little group who know it exists, maybe it thought of you as the genuine threat.'

Harvey glanced around the cell where both Rhian and Sammy's looks told him they thought his wife was totally correct in her conclusion.

The other face in the cell, the one belonging to Officer Lee Foster, gave nothing away as the young man remained as confused as ever. All he had to go on were snippets of conversation that were a complete enigma to him, to even try and put them in some logical order without asking for an explanation was pointless. So he stood by quietly ready to assist in any way he could, thinking that perhaps he wasn't in the right profession, because if this was the level of deduction skills needed to be an Inspector, the risks that had to be taken, then he clearly wasn't ready.

'Where are Alex and Juliet?' Harvey asked with some sudden concern.

'They went to look for help.' Flo replied.

'What kind?'

Rhian jumped in on that question. 'Alex said we needed to be able to lock the doors...they went to find a control panel. The lights went off for a bit but then they all came on so I'm guessing they've found something'

'I don't like us being separated.' Harvey said reaching for his mobile.

'Don't trouble yourself Sir there's been no signal since we got in here!'

'Bloody hell...!' Harvey considered their options to find there were few on offer. '...We certainly need to be more secure, this cell is a little pokey for all of us. Right, I propose we go and look for somewhere larger with doors that lock.'

'What about the other two...?' Flo reacted sharply. '...They won't know where we are.'

'If they've located the camera feeds they will, if not then...look I'm sorry Flo, I've got nothing else to work with at the moment but getting us to safer ground. I've been here before so I know my way around a little...does anyone else object?'

No one responded except Flo who took his hand and squeezed it. 'It's wonderful to have you back.'

He smiled at her. 'You think I'd leave you without saying goodbye.'

Officer Foster was already standing outside the door and looking both ways down the corridor. 'It's clear...!'

63

Back in the cupboard office Alex and Juliet were trying their best to keep a watchful eye on all the camera feeds at once. Where there had been no movement for the past few minutes suddenly there was plenty, firstly they noticed the police officer standing in the corridor, now being joined by the rest of the group. Harvey led the way with Flo at his side while Rhi and Sammy tucked themselves in the middle and the young Officer kept an eye out at the rear.

'It looks like they're on the move.' Juliet remarked.

'That'll be Harvey's doing.' Alex audibly sighed. 'Damn it's good to have him back in the game...' But at that moment he spotted movement on another feed. '...There's that Roma girl.'

They watched the young woman taking the stairs down to the third floor. It seemed odd to both of them how unaffected she seemed after her visit to Kirby's office, almost casually strolling along, which made no sense if Kirby was up there holding Oscar and Kosminsky hostage, let alone the presence of her boss Jeff Shilling.

Alex had a sudden wave of portent. Something wasn't right and it was to do with that girl. He quickly found the other feed that showed the vehicle in the car park.

It was empty!

'Oh shit we're in trouble...!' He cried and then grabbed Juliet.

'Hey...!'

'...Sorry but we've got to go find the others...now!'

They headed to the door.

64

Back in Kirby's office, with the thin man's body split into quarters on the floor, Kosminsky was at a loss for what to do next. All he knew was he had to get downstairs quickly to warn the others but following the monster that had just left wasn't appealing or sensible.

Think you idiot, think! The computer...it was all he had to hand apart from Kirby's gun, for all the good that had done the psycho.

He rushed round to plant himself on the plush leather chair. That woman had left the screen on which was a huge blessing. Bringing up the camera feeds he saw the same as Alex and Juliet, the woman strolling down the corridors while Harvey and some others were leaving a small cell. Then at the bottom left of the screen he saw a small icon, one he certainly didn't have on his computer downstairs, it was small speaker. Clicking on it he began to speak.

'Hello is there anybody there...hello...anyone?

Alex had already pulled Juliet out the door when they heard the voice, the sound of it causing him to spin them both around.

'Hello who's that...?'

Juliet rushed back to the computer when the voice didn't respond as the deep voice kept repeating itself. There had to be an accept button so she opened up the file screen and scanned her way down.

'Anything...?' Alex didn't like to pressure her but he was feeling some.

Juliet came across a file that would be computer language mumbo jumbo to anyone else but at the end of the title was a forward slash followed by Aud-two-way.

She clicked it and spoke. 'Can you hear us...?'

'...Yes...listen to me.' The disembodied man said. 'My name is Allan Kosminsky and...'

'I know who you are...' Alex interrupted. '...This is Alex Webb!'

Kosminsky rolled his eyes back into his head in relief but time was still vitally important. 'Are you in touch with Harvey?'

'No he's down in the cells with his wife with and three others. They're looking for somewhere to hide.'

'That's good they need to lock themselves away. There's a woman heading down there and she's a murderer, a monster...'

'...She's the Glitch Allan. I don't think we can get down there in time. We'd probably end up meeting her on the way.' Juliet interrupted. 'Look we can't change anything from down here, you're at the main hub...there must be something you can do.'

Kosminsky stared hard at the screen but computers really weren't his thing except for writing stupid reports and emails. 'I...I...don't know what I'm looking for!'

'Calm down Allan and focus. You worked here, come on, isn't there a full lockdown protocol...a way of closing all the doors...?'

'...There is...or there was...Kirby's changed the system it's all been updated...Fuck!'

Alex looked up to the ceiling but there was no way of knowing where Kosminsky's voice was coming from. There were no speakers to see, not even discreet ones, just an empty cobweb hanging in the corner.

Harvey was gently pulling Flo along beside him, his only wish to get to a place of safety, as he hadn't fought through the curse the Glitch placed in his mind to lose the battle now.

'Do you know where you're going?' She asked.

'I think it's down here...' He turned left through a set of open wide security doors into a brightly lit but plain looking corridor. '...It's not a cell, it's a meeting room. If I remember it right and of course if the doors are open, I seem to recall they locked automatically after we entered. A green and red light system, it's the same room where Emma and I interviewed Jay Cleaver.'

On saying her name his mind immediately split into two trains of thought. The first track kept him focused on locating the meeting room, while the second one delivered a whole carriage of feelings he had for the woman, the friend he'd let down, there being no doubt in his mind that he had let her down. He'd failed her miserably after she'd been trying to help, god damn it she'd sacrificed everything for this group, the hurt increasing even more when he realised he hadn't spared a thought for her in days. He couldn't even remember if she'd been transferred to a prison or was still at the station.

With some great effort he forced himself to not think of her murdered in one of his police cells. Did the Glitch even know she was there? It felt as if his reinstated logical mind was smashing itself against the inside of his skull as he fought to focus on the hard facts, simple enough to follow, he didn't know where she was and it's of no use worrying over imaginary scenarios. He knew that basic rule better than anyone, in fact he considered it his strength, the ability to avoid mental pitfalls and think clearly under pressure...one truth at a time.

'This is it...at the end of that corridor.' His practical side announced.

He remembered clearly now this was where Kosminsky had brought them. Oh god now his thoughts were being taken over by the thought of the big guard. Where the hell was he? But before he had chance to raise any imagined horrors about his friends situation, a voice called out. Everyone stopped on hearing it and turned to look back up the long hallway, in the direction of where they'd come from.

'Hello everyone...here you are!' Roma's mouth spoke the words then smiled. She was about twenty feet away and leaning against the wall, seemingly relaxed with not a care in the world. 'I've been looking for you.'

Harvey would never know if he was the first to grasp her subterfuge, but he could see and hear in her voice that something was very wrong, but that was just before the situation got much, much worse.

Kosminsky had horror in his eyes watching this event unfold on the feed from the corridor camera. There she was, whatever she was, snaring them and the group seemed so small and defenceless, trapped in the same halls he used to patrol, but now he was stranded up here, unable to help.

Alex and Juliet were also watching the same inevitable snuff movie on the computer in the cupboard office. She put her head into his chest when she couldn't watch anymore. There was nowhere for them to hide and she didn't want to witness anything evil happening to those people who believed in Alex. It broke her heart to think of the weight the poor man, her friend, would have to carry for this. It was his story, his own tortured reality, which had connected them all in the first place and delivered them here. With her face pressed against his chest she could hear his heart beating strong and fast while her own tried to keep pace.

All Flo could see was the new blonde haired secretary from the station and she called out to Roma. 'What are you doing here?'

'Ha...wrong again...it seems I was mistaken to believe you were the smartest one of this group Florence?'

'I don't understand...' As she turned to her Harvey the fearful look he replied with told her everything she needed to know. '...No...no you can't be!'

Roma's pretty little face broke out in a broad grin.

Kosminsky wiped his eyes and looked at the computer screen again. If that woman wanted to talk then perhaps he had a little time to find something, anything to help.

'Allan...?' Alex said. '...Just press everything!'

The big guard did as he was told, clicking on various tabs and icons but nothing happened. It seemed that although he was on the computer he was locked out of activating any controls. Clearly that woman had closed down access to the security commands before she left meaning, quite ironically, that he could check the internet, even send emails, but he was unable to get into the main security protocol directives.

'It's no use. I wish you two were up here you could sort it but I'm a security guard not a computer geek...no offence!'

'None taken...' Juliet replied sharing the same thought as Alex. Could they make it all the way to the top floor in time without being seen, or before the Glitch killed everyone in the corridor? The odds weren't looking great but then their attention was drawn to a figure heading towards the fray, approaching from the corridor behind the Glitch. '...It's Jay Cleaver!'

'I see him...' Kosminsky replied.

Jay of course knew the layout of the facility like the back of his hand and strode confidently, just one more left turn and he'd be there. Correct in his assumption as he spotted Roma Walker directly in front of him, the girl with her back to him, no more than a vessel now.

The frightened group saw him appear but intuitively tried to not react. If he was here to help somehow they didn't want to give his position away. He was ten feet behind Roma and not breaking his stride, five feet and still he came, until he stopped and stood directly over her right shoulder.

Roma hadn't noticed his approach, or if she had there was no reaction to it, as she stared at the group.

Harvey then gambled their lives in hope Jay would, for the first time in his miserable life, do the right thing. 'Hey Roma...how does it feel to be just another in a long line of failed attempts?'

Her response was slightly delayed by an inquisitive stare that she gave him, before it became once more calm and calculated. 'I'll let you know Inspector...as I take the last breath out of your wife.'

'More threats...?' Harvey asked in his anxious attempt to keep the woman's attention while waiting desperately for Jay to make his move. '...I mean seriously...who was the last person you followed through on one of your threats and actually killed...?' For crying out loud surely Cleaver would be able to read his intentions. The teenager was in the optimum position and stood directly behind her now.

'Now let me see...' The Glitch said choosing to answer Harvey's query. '...Well I just killed Marcus Kirby, who in turn had recently murdered both Oscar Downes and your Superintendent Shilling. It's a bloodbath up there to be honest.'

Harvey's patience was wearing thin and because of it he made a rookie mistake by shifting his eyes to focus on Jay. The Glitch picked up on this immediately and acted accordingly, but not in the way the Inspector had hoped as it gestured the man to come stand at its side.

'Oh Harvey...surely you weren't putting all your hopes on young Mr Cleaver here? You should know better than anyone that he's never helped another soul in his life, so I seriously doubt he's going to start doing that now.'

It suddenly struck Harvey that the Glitch hadn't mentioned Kosminsky which gave him a little hope the man was still alive. It made a tiny smile dance across his lips as stared at the two figures stood side by side, the lean and smart suited Jay towering over Roma, a full foot taller than the blonde woman, looking for all intents and purposes like the Aryan dream of the perfect couple.

'You two look good together.' Harvey called over before deciding to focus on Jay. 'Won't you ever learn Cleaver? I thought we'd sorted this all out back at the lock up, you remember, when you let me and Alex go and said the Glitch could go fuck itself!'

Harvey didn't enjoy using such language in front of his wife but needs must when you could die at any second.

The Inspectors remark only made both Roma and Jay laugh in unison, perfect unison, which caused the watching group some confusion before the realisation hit.

'He did say that...' They replied, speaking simultaneously and in perfect synchronicity, in one voice. '...but I've forgiven him because it has brought us here, to this picture-perfect ending. Your fledgling mind failing again to appreciate the powers I have at my disposal. This is all part of my evolution Harvey, becoming at one...or two some may say, with my surroundings and soon to reach my full potential. Not long at all now Inspector until you see me as I really am and I wanted to keep you alive to watch that happen. We have a deep connection Harvey. I've been inside your mind after all remember? I know all about your loves and fears and because of that and the insufferable vanity I must carry with me due to having this ridiculous consciousness, I wanted you to see the real me just before you die, so in truth Jay's actions at the lockup have facilitated this.'

Juliet and Alex hadn't moved, mesmerised by this duality of the Glitch because it was true, just how this murderous creature was constantly evolving, now able to control two people at a time, maybe even more, to a point where it could infect everyone.

'Any luck Allan?' Alex asked, more through a sad acceptance that it was all too late than any real hope.

'No I'm locked out of the system.'

'Is the laptop the same as the one here in your office?' Juliet asked because she wanted to understand the problem. It was in her nature to understand and help, it had been all through her life.

'No...this is some fancy high tech shit. I can't even see an on/off switch.'

Juliet took his words on board and thought of why that should be. She was no expert on computers but knew they were constantly advancing in performance and security. Then it struck her what the problem may be, it was something she'd seen on pictures of Grahams new laptop, he hadn't actually bought it yet, money had been tight for them, but he'd wanted it. 'Allan, tell me what the front of the laptop looks like. Not the keyboard, the bottom part nearest to you.'

Kosminsky described it best he could. 'There's an oblong pad for operating the mouse, a logo, but I don't recognise the company name, it's foreign. Then there's a small circle...I don't know what that does. I tried pressing it but it's not a button...'

'No it isn't, that's a fingerprint recognition pad!' Juliet snapped sharply.

Officer Lee Foster had stationed himself in front of Rhian and Sammy during the exchange. Such a move was natural because of his personality and training, following the honoured motto of the police force he served in, *Semper Vigilo;* Keeping People Safe.

At his personal disposal he had an auto-lock expandable baton, hand cuffs and leg restraints. He figured none of those would be of much use in this situation but he did have a canister of incapacitating spray which could be, if he were in range. But this was a problem seeing as these two, or one assailant if he was willing to believe everything that was going on, were twenty feet away. In training he'd learned the liquid propulsion range was fifteen feet to clear an area, six feet for the optimum effect of bringing someone down.

The young officer was seriously entertaining the idea of using the spray because whatever this thing was that was threatening them, it stood before him in human form, so it had eyes and lungs and would surely feel it. Although with all the weirdness going on maybe the spray wouldn't take effect on this Glitch, or would do so only minimally, but he had to do something. So as the conversation continued on he'd already flicked off the safety cap, his finger on the small lever, ready to spray the noxious blinding fluid at the first opportunity.

Kosminsky was vomiting out what little contents were in his large stomach, expelling them against the wood panelled wall, as he put his bare hands into the still warm congealing disarray of what used to be Marcus Kirby.

'Fucking hell...!' He spat out the words with specks of food matter.

'...You can do it Allan...' Juliet told him through the intercom. '...Find his right hand!'

Kosminsky dry retched and then did so a couple more times as he pulled the hand out of the disgusting remains. The distressing fact that it was still connected to the man's right arm and half of his chest didn't help matters. He hauled the hunk of meat slowly out of the offal and blood by the sleeve of a torn expensive jacket, dragging it slowly across the floor towards the desk, thinking that if this didn't work he may just take Kirby's silver pistol out of the drawer and shoot himself in the head.

There are limits to what a human mind can take and he was finding his. Regardless that he'd sworn to never commit suicide; this level of vileness was breaking down the walls of that vow. Even for Kosminsky, with all of his bulk, lifting it onto the chair took some considerable effort. Slopping pieces of flesh and muscle could still be heard falling onto the hard floor as he angled firstly the hand, then the forefinger, to the small recognition pad.

'Are you doing it?' Alex asked.

'Shut up...!' Kosminsky cried out feeling every ounce of his sanity being stretched thin. With a disgusted strain he pressed the lifeless digit down and the screen immediately changed, a blue box appearing in the middle containing two words, Hello Marcus.

'...I'm in.' He said excitedly and dropped the arm to the ground. The greeting box then disappeared to be instantly replaced by numerous sections waiting to be controlled. The first he searched for were security commands. An icon displaying a padlock gave him the most hope so he opened it, his heart almost leaping when he read the words corridor lockdowns, slamming the mouse around he gave it another click and it took him to a basic map. Damn it he had to find and select the particular door out of hundreds. It was a good job he knew his way around but with a whirling mind and surrounded by bits of his ex-employer it may take a little time.

The two bodies of the Glitch made their move as Roma and Jay walked forwards in step, intent on killing the others while keeping Harvey alive. The glorious agony the interfering man would feel was a pleasure it couldn't deny itself, especially after it killed the boy, that cowardly Angel, and the piece de resistance, his wife Florence. Then quite unexpectedly a young policeman came marching down the corridor removing a canister fixed to his belt.

Harvey reacted to it. 'Officer, stand down...Foster...get back here...!'

But this police officer was committed now and would follow through on his promise to always do his duty. Semper Vigilo.

Roma and Jay stopped in their tracks, both of their heads tilted slightly, evaluating the threat as the man approached. From ten feet away Foster resisted the urge to just press and retreat, he wanted to make sure he got the both of them good, then he'd turn and...

Kosminsky had matched the correct floor to the camera feed and clicked on it, but by doing so and in the few moments he'd taken his eyes off the live pictures he'd missed the officer's movement.

'Officer...stand do...' These were the last words Foster heard from Harvey's mouth, as the doors behind him and to his left and right slammed shut.

'Allan no...! Open the doors back up. Get him out of there!' Juliet screamed while Alex watched on unable to speak. He didn't know if he was imagining it or not, but it felt he could see the event happening as if he were there, looking out through the eyes of the Glitch.

Harvey ran to the doors and tried to force them open with Flo screaming for him to come back. Rhian turned to look down the other corridor to where the Inspector said they should hide. She spotted the door with the red and green lights above it and saw it was beginning to slowly close.

Grabbing Sammy by the hand she ran towards it. The boy fell after only a couple of steps and she lost touch with him, with her only focus to keep the door from closing completely.

Flo was quite left alone in the middle of it all. To her left she could see the child on the floor with his Mother running away, in front Harvey was trying to shoulder barge the doors with no success, but they were built to withstand escaping psychiatric patients so he never stood a chance. He shouted one last time just as Flo reached his side and pulled him round.

'Harvey he's gone...please come on!'

Roma and Jay hadn't reacted at all angrily to their path being blocked temporarily; the Glitch knew very well that nothing in this building would stop them for long, besides right now they were far more interested in the policeman holding up his little canister.

Officer Lee Foster held it at eye level knowing he had no choice but to discharge it now. Willing his finger to press the lever down, nothing happened, all he found was resistance. No matter how hard he tried his hand wouldn't cooperate.

'What's the matter Officer...?' Roma and Jay asked, speaking as one again. '...Are you unable to discharge your responsibilities...perhaps I can be of some assistance.'

Foster helplessly watched as his hand began to slowly turn, the canister ready to be triggered, only an arm's length away from his face. The tiny pinprick nozzle began to move closer as he discovered the only bodily function he had any control over were his tears, they were coming from the wasted physical effort in his attempt to resist, mixed in with the pain he expected to feel any second.

'There we go...that's so much better. So, shall we see what your little can, can do?' The two of them laughed together channelling the Glitch and its wicked sense of humour. 'But hold on...let's make it perfect first.'

Foster felt his empty hand begin to rise up to his face, then to his eye were he pulled the left lid open wide. The trigger came down sharply and the tiny hole discharged a disgusting amount of fluid into his open socket, the excess dribbling out and down his instantly burning cheek where it entered his nostrils before rapidly filling his lungs. The Glitch repeated the act on his right eye but Foster knew very little about that, the initial burst of the fiery liquid already making him feel as if both his eyes were gone, no more than melted pools deformed of all their previous substance, while his lungs became tiny pockets of ferocious heat rapidly consuming the oxygen he snatched in pathetic gasps.

The Glitch in two bodies watched the effects with considerable interest and glee. Even thinking that this weapon was creating somewhere near to the level of agony it wished for the rest of mankind.

As much as he wanted to collapse to the floor Foster found he was unable to do so, the monster controlling his muscles happy to keep him upright, his wretched suffering to be kept on full display for the ones watching on the cameras.

'Oh my god...!' Juliet cried both vocally and emotionally. Her tears were of horror and sympathy for the man stuck in that corridor. '...Why won't it just kill him? End it please...!' the Officers suffering becoming all too vivid and intense.

Sitting next to her Alex was equally horrified but not as shocked by what he was witnessing. He was definitely sharing some connection to the beast now and in his mind he could feel the insatiable hunger of the Glitch, what it was evolving to become, the end result of what he'd accidently help create was coming soon. He could see that greater representation through its thoughts, how shortly there would be no more need for vessels to carry its purpose around. This splitting of its control to one, two, three human minds and bodies in a single moment was just another stepping stone, a growth spurt on this journey to become the overpowering apocalypse of this universe.

He reached his hand forward and turned off the camera feed, there was no reason for them to observe the feeding entertainment the Glitch wished to show them, besides Alex could see and feel it clearly enough in his own mind.

Juliet certainly didn't object to the sudden blankness of the screen, she'd had enough of feeling lost and helpless, the embrace of Alex's only arm helping her to regain some control.

'What are we going to do?' She asked breathing heavily.

He squeezed his right arm even tighter round her shoulder then bent his head down to look into her face. 'What do you want to do?'

That answer was wholly unexpected, catching her off guard, as she tried to understand why he'd say such a thing at a time as lost as this.

'I want everything to be back...like it was before.'

As she looked down at his upside down face and spoke honestly the realisation dawned. This man, a major part of her life for so long now, had asked her that particular question because he knew it would create an important and honest answer, one from the heart to remind her that on this journey they shared an equal standing. It was empowerment when she needed it the most, to help get her back in the game, because he'd told her at the flat he couldn't do this alone, that he needed her now more than ever. This was a caring display of trust and understanding that told her whatever she'd replied to his question, would be exactly what they would try to do...together.

Then Kosminsky's deep voice boomed through the invisible speakers and broke their moment. 'It's over...'

So the ending of Officer Lee Foster had only one human witness as the big guard was unable to look away, his experience of violent acts within this very facility perhaps the reason behind that, but he felt twistedly grateful that the end for the young man had been swift.

It seemed almost as if the man and woman had become bored by it all, so they allowed his helpless body to drop to the floor, where he lay on his back. Then after a moment's pause Jay Cleaver raised his foot and placed it on the man's throat, a quick push down and that was it, no screams and no struggles, from a young man who had only tried to do his duty.

65

Deeply mixed up emotions coursed through Rhian Sanger's frightened heart, as she'd thrown her body forward determinedly, managing to make it to the door before it closed. By God's grace, or so she thought, there had been a chair just inside the room which she'd wedged into the shrinking doorway.

Although she knew her prompt actions had given everyone a chance to survive, she'd let go of her son's hand to do so and that tore her up now. The image of his confused tears as she turned back to see him sitting on the floor, small and alone in the hallway, even if it was only for seconds would live with her forever.

Her thoughts were quickly removed from that guilty image when Flo came hurtling round the corner. She was pulling Harvey behind her and on seeing Sammy she'd grabbed his hand, forcing him up and into the room. Harvey kicked the chair away as he entered just as they heard a loud cracking sound from the other corridor. They were coming; it was coming, fast. The door was ajar and closing slowly as if it enjoyed the panic such a creeping movement caused, its hydraulic mechanism doing the job with dramatic pride.

'Argh Harvey, watch out...!' Flo screamed as four human fingers came into view, reaching round the door, trying to push it open and wide.

The Inspector threw his full weight against it but it made no difference. The door would close in its own time and nothing human could speed that up, but thankfully nothing inhuman would slow it down either, which meant Harvey got to watch the fingers being gently guillotined by the steel edge until they fell at his feet.

The Glitch looked down at Jay's hand, staring intensely at the blood pouring out from the severed knuckles, this was an interesting sight. It felt no pain from the wound because this wasn't its body. Whether or not what remained of Jay Cleaver's consciousness realised what had happened or felt any discomfort was completely irrelevant to it.

At this moment the Glitch was concentrating on its next task. This barrier was a problem. In its current state, divided between the bodies of a young woman and an injured teenager, there was no way it would be able to break through. The thick wooden doors in the other corridor had been easy to force open, its speed perfectly combined with both shoulders proving sufficient, but this thick steel security door needed a different approach.

The most logical one being it would have to return to Kirby's office.

It was apparent someone was up there as it had locked out the security system before it left; clearly that someone was also watching over the security cameras because they had only locked the doors in the Glitch's vicinity, but before it made its way up there it had a decision to make. Only the choice was no longer simple. Under any other circumstances it would ditch Roma's vessel and put all of its consciousness into Jay. The young man was clearly the stronger and faster of the two, but he carried a savage injury to his hand which would take some repairing.

Anyone watching may well be wondering what was causing such a delay as Roma and Jay stood motionless outside the locked meeting room. But a hidden and personal reason was the cause as the Glitch could feel its next evolutionary process coming to pass.

Ever since its conception inside the Angel Metatron's mind its whole life had become a series of staging points. The first was the passing of Alex from one dimension to another, which had sparked its birth, causing a consciousness to grow rapidly, quickly followed by a fleeting existence in the white world searching for a form. It was quite ridiculous that its first choice had then been the body of a recently deceased old lady.

It was only when it took up the battered form of Snake Hornblower that everything had begun to slip into place, as it learned the power of owning a character, gaining a freedom that allowed it to own the supremacy of threat. And the Glitch loved to threaten almost as much as it adored the kill, to see its word take root and then grow into a fearsome feeding plant within a frightened mind was beautiful, so much so it often thought it maybe laboured the point. It certainly felt that way now after allowing its quarry to find a safe haven beyond its reach.

The Glitch was working on why it enjoyed the foreplay to murder so much, the answer clear and simple, because it had never been able to do so before. In all its previous incarnations there had been no need for a personality, when as an asteroid or a great flood, a disgusting pestilence or a feeding black hole there had been no thoughts, just deeds. Having an active conscious mind this time being able to live, able to create and feel reward for its choices was utterly unique, but it was also becoming a heavy cross that from time to time it struggled to bear.

This was why it believed the next generational step in its existence was inevitably coming soon. Such a change would be extremely considerable and significant. For there was a greater form for it to take, one with no curious reliance on thoughts and imagination, only a natural apocalyptical sizing up to better allow it to stride this world and destroy it, before moving on.

So at this moment it thought of its almost natural life so far, this series of surprising turns it would have to discard and forget, but a life in which it had happily accepted all of its variety of its human shapes.

It remembered every one of them with something like fondness, the people it had spoken to, learned from and inevitably killed. Truly it had been a strange experience to have shared feelings and moments with mortals as it had grown from an infant to an adult in such a short space of time. All of that would be gone when it found its true form, the glowing shape with which it had devoured the Demon, the outlined figure with an insatiable need to consume. When that happened it would lose the self it owned now, no longer being the Glitch, all its present memories and moments would disappear into the abyss.

So it turned out its growing feeling of melancholy was the true reason behind its delay.

Alex and Juliet were next to each other in the cupboard office, both balancing one cheek on Kosminsky's office chair, neither one with any great urge to turn the camera feeds back on.

'So how are we going to do it?' She asked.

'Huh...what...?' He replied as if being broken from a spell.

'...Get everything back to how it was...you made me believe we can do it...so I was just wondering...where do we start?'

'I think we have to capture it somehow...or at the very least capture its attention. Then I can put my theory to the test...'

'Ooh you have a theory.' Juliet replied jovially. It wasn't a full blown attempt at humour but the best she could manage at this moment. 'Tell me more.'

Alex lifted himself from the chair and stood up for two reasons; one he to walk to think, the other based solely on how numb his one bottom cheek was becoming. Perching was for birds.

'I'm back in contact with it again. It's as if I can see through its eyes.'

'Does it know you're there?' She asked.

'No...I don't think so.'

'So what's it doing now...which way is it going?'

'Nowhere, it's just standing in the corridor. There's something bizarre going on. It lost some of Jay's fingers when the door closed...but that's not its problem. Everyone's safe for now but the Glitch doesn't know what to do...no that's not right...it knows what it want's...but it's reluctant to start...it doesn't make any sense.'

'So you can't read its thoughts?'

'Not as such, more like its moods.'

'It has moods...I mean apart from murderous ones?' Juliet asked.

With that question, whether by accident or design, she'd done it again. Alex feeling his soul being dragged back by her words to focus on a single point. The main problem with all the chaos going on in his life was that sometimes he moved forward too quickly, always trying to prepare for the next challenge, missing the obvious, so embroiled in making contact with the Glitch again and feeling its mood that all logical thought had gone amiss.

He'd been having the idea lately that a combination of Harvey Cooper's analytical thinking, when aligned with his own depth of knowledge on the situation, could possibly create the ultimate adversary for the Glitch.

Whether that would be enough to defeat it he really didn't know, only that it made sense, that there was simply no way for Alex to even consider putting up a fight without both Juliet and Harvey at his side. Then of course there was the Angel in Sammy's mind, the boy himself, Rhian and Florence. All of those hearts helping him to believe that if he dedicated his hopes around this tiny army there could be an answer, or at least some more courage to be found.

'I asked you a question.' Juliet reminded him.

'Yes, it has moods...and they're getting stronger.'

66

A heavy gloom had laid itself over Edinburgh, this capital of Scotland since the 15th century, which right now was also unknowingly the centre of the entire universe. This gloom was noticeably prevalent in both the darkness pressing down over the city lights, forcing shadows of pitch black to form wherever they could, but also into the mood of the streets on this warm summer evening.

Such a pleasant night as this would usually see those streets full of revellers, lovers and other escapist dreamers, but this night the pathways were only sparsely scattered with such souls. It could be safely said the whole population had been divided into three totally distinct groups, the tens of thousands of believers in the miracle who were at the airport waiting for news on the Angel's appearance. Listening to soldiers on loud hailers telling them to remain calm, hoping that when something was officially announced they would be told, because they were ready.

Uniquely, the vast number of military personnel keeping the peace fell into the second category of affected groups; these were the ones confused and lost within the melee now consuming the world, trying not to think of what it could mean for the future of the human race.

The third group were the deniers who strangely avoided any form of assemblage, keeping themselves away from the crowds, either locking themselves in their abodes or wandering the streets in twos and threes, trying to keep stuff normal, hoping it would all go away soon.

It was an utterly futile wish; the genie was far and away out of the bottle, now causing mankind to progress to a species that had learned true higher kingdoms really existed. Witnessing the proof there were worlds beyond our own, that please God, were places of miracles, where wishes could be granted that might teach us the meaning of life. Smoothing this uneven rutted earth into a level playing field full of love and compassion for all, where new classrooms could be built in place of churches and banks, such buildings of worship unneeded now, not when faith is replaced by fact, when profit is replaced with care. But yet still this opportunity for change had seemed to be conjured from the very same source, the heavens.

Some hoped that congratulations could be poured out on the faithful and faithless in equal measure, for in the end they were both correct, but with God and Heaven utterly indisputable after the appearance of the

Angel then faith was needed no more, there being no necessity to pray to a living deity, because really what would it achieve?

Some experts on theology, such as the ones who were being sought out and interviewed in their thousands across all channels, were speaking now on the nature of the divine even more generally than usual. All their years of studying cultural systems of worship towards a transcendental or supernatural power were now defunct, so instead they threw their clever opinions towards a paradigm shift, hoping that out of their dark guesswork cometh some light.

So the vast array of opinions on the Angel's appearance were manifold and multiplying, as is so often the case with the human condition, because these peoples were not a flock of the same feather and never had been, every soul utterly diverse and unique in design and form, growing up in personal environments that some might recognise but never truly know.

From the tiniest flecks of stardust humans had come, passing through a billion, billion transformations to reach the heart-breaking uniqueness that is a soul. All of them spawned from particular ancestors who had blindly endured the worst their times had to offer, to procreate for the survival of their species like the basic animals they were, still trudging on following their fate or fortune through the worst of their times.

Therefore at the end of it all, as this night promised to be, all of those hopes and prayers would be thrown back into the swirling clouds of dust from whence they came. So perhaps some of a religious persuasion during the final seconds of the Glitch's victory parade might claim to be more correct than others, because of four mentions in the bible that they will begin and end as dust, whereas other worthy religions will believe what they are told, and the uncommitted laymen and laywomen of this world wouldn't care at all if it was ever written down. Such is the boundless and mysterious tapestry of life that all will get the answer they expected, no one is wrong and no one is right, for they are all a single thread passing through the life machine as it clicks and clacks, being laid over the others who came before and under the ones who will follow.

Back in the facility there were no philosophical questions being asked by Harvey. Flo, Rhian and Sammy busily making themselves as comfortable as possible in the secured meeting room, the place where the Inspector had first met Jay Cleaver, that's if he discounted saving the boy's life at the zoo on the other timeline as real, something he could no longer do. The reality of both this world and the last were undeniable and in his mind they were coming together once more. This Glitch, created when Alex passed through to the white world, existed quite literally right outside the door, its fingers, picked up and dropped in a waste paper bin by Harvey were physical proof of its determination to keep things as they are, to continue with its purpose.

Rhian was sitting next to Flo at the large table, in the very chair Jay had occupied but Harvey thought it better to not mention the fact, as the two women watched Sammy walking round the space firing off questions.

'How long do we have to stay in here?' His young boy's voice asked.

'I think we're going to have to be patient Sammy.' Rhi called over.

The boy continued his circling within the twenty by twenty foot square room. 'But I'd like to go home soon.'

'Me too...' Flo agreed. '...But we have to make sure it's safe first.'

'You mean kill the Glitch?' Sammy gave this statement with no emotion in his voice.

It seemed that even his innocent mind was becoming hardened and assimilated to all the madness. Rhian hated to hear it, still feeling bad about leaving him in the corridor, her motherly emotions not allowing her to relax for even a second.

'Are you okay? Flo whispered to Rhi out of earshot of her boy who was talking to Harvey now.

'Okay? That feels like a very big word right now.' She replied running her hand through her wild tresses in hope of calming them down at least. 'I'm certainly happier in this room than that tiny cell but...' She stopped herself.

'Go on.'

Rhian looked straight into the caring eyes of Flo and told her the truth, unfiltered and brutal, short and concise. 'My boy is going to die here!'

In the cupboard office Alex returned to the computer and turned the camera feeds back on for the corridor outside the meeting room. One half of the Glitch was out of view, with Roma's body on the floor facedown and unmoving.

'Oh my god it's gone...but I never felt it move...I didn't feel anything.' He switched the feed to the stairs leading to Kirby's office but there was nothing to see. 'Shit...where is it?'

Juliet abruptly grabbed his arm and covered his mouth in one swift action, her face pleading with him to shut the hell up and listen.

THE RED FRAME

He complied and in doing so heard the quiet careful steps coming down the corridor outside. There was a camera fixed there but he couldn't move to change the feed with Juliet gripping him so tightly, so blind to the danger and bound together they looked into each other's eyes. During these fleeting seconds they communicated everything they had ever wanted to say, this unfathomable bond being reached through fear, both understanding the most painful part of what could happen next would be to lose each other.

The handle of the unlocked door began its descent.

Juliet and Alex released their clinch, but she still held on tight to his only hand as they rose to their feet, choosing to stand together as one if this was to be their end.

The door swung open slowly but the caller didn't enter straight away, undoubtedly wary of what they may find, ready for anything, preparing for the worst. Then in a blinding flash a head came round the door and the big guards face looked over at them. 'Oh thank god you're still here!'

'Fucking hell...!' Juliet cried out in shock, most relieved to see it was only him.

Alex wasn't so ready to accept his respite so easily, especially with the guards dark grey uniform covered in considerable stains of dry blood; this could be another trick of the Glitch. 'Where is it?'

'I'm guessing its back in Kirby's office but it won't be happy.'

'So how did you get down here...? Alex interrupted with a sharp edge.

The penny dropped quickly as Kosminsky grasped what Alex was inferring.

'...Two things Mr Webb...I reckon you two would be dead already if the Glitch was in here...' He tapped his temple with that large index finger. '...Secondly I know my way around this place better than anyone. After watching what it did to that poor girl I saw Jay turn and head away up the stairs. I had to think quickly so I used the fire escape, made my way down here on the outside of the building, then came back in through the car park, but if that's not enough to convince you then that's tough because I don't have anything else!'

'So you could get us out of here...out of the building...?' Juliet asked, seeming to have forgotten the primary reason for their coming here in the first place.

Alex replied swiftly. '...We aren't running away Joolz. We've travelled a little too far for that now and anyway it would only hunt us down, so this is where we make our stand.'

'But Alex we can't beat it...even the Angel said so...!' Juliet rather fatalistically reminded him.

'Yeah I know...that Angel's said a lot of things...but never everything. There's one fact I've learned about Metatron and that is it always has to have a proviso, because it's too cowardly to go all in on anything.'

It was Kosminsky's turn to interrupt. 'Look I know all of this is important to you people but so are our lives. If you don't mind I want to go and join the others.'

'But they're locked in a secure room!' Juliet had barely finished the sentence before the big guard marched over to retrieve his ID card.

'I might not get the full story of what's going on here but as I said, I know how this place works.'

'And what if it's already come back down the stairs?'

'Then I suppose we'll die in a corridor...it's either that or in here.' Kosminsky replied and moved to the open door. '...I'd also guess that time is of the essence!' With that he left the room and disappeared from view, firmly putting the ball in their court.

Alex and Juliet's eyes met again, sending their own secret messages, before walking out of the cupboard office to find Kosminsky waiting patiently.

'Hurry up!' The big guard requested.

Flo had been taken aback by Rhian's comment to the point where she was annoyed.

'...There is no way we are going to let Sammy die in here. I'm disappointed in you Rhian! If you haven't learned by now that while we're breathing we still have a chance then I don't know how to convince you. That man over there...my husband...' Rhian turned to see Harvey on his knees talking to her son, the boy smiling broadly at whatever he was being told. '...Is the reason we're still alive...but there's another reason too...and that's you, the sacrifice you made by keeping this door open for us. I saw your face when I pulled Sammy in with me...you were ashamed that you'd let your mothers guard drop for a second, but if you hadn't then we would all be dead. Now remember that and focus on what we can do, not what may happen, because there could come a time for guilty reflections, but that's a long way off in the future!'

'Mr Cooper says everything's going to be okay.'

Sammy was now stood at his mother's side, his eyes bright and alert and his spirit unbroken.

'Did he?'

'Yeah and I told him about wanting to go to the zoo and he said we can all go together...when we get out of here.'

'Absolutely we can...and we will...' Flo said to Sammy and leaned over to ruffle the boy's hair while at the same time placing her other hand on the back of Rhian's. '...Would you like to talk about that while we wait...tell me what you want to see when we get there?'

'Yeah okay...Lions...!'

Kosminsky lead Alex and Juliet up the flight of stairs and down through the corridors, all of them seeming to grasp that wherever the Glitch was now, it wouldn't really matter if they made a sound because remaining fearful and silent wasn't going to save them anymore. The only grace they had in their favour was fate itself, so as they walked Alex asked what he believed to be more pertinent questions.

'You said the Glitch wouldn't be happy if it went back to Kirby's office, why?'

'Because I locked it back out of the computer, before I dragged Kirby's arm with me and dumped it outside, it's why I'm covered in blood amongst other reasons. But now it won't be able to control any of the security systems and will be as blind as we are, maybe that's not much consolation but at least it makes us equal.'

Just then they turned the corner and walked into a horrible sight. Laid on the floor face up was Officer Lee Foster's body, his eyes and young face swollen up and red, what had been his pleasing features distorted almost beyond recognition, his neck heavily compressed.

The three of them passed without pausing or looking closer, but inside their minds assorted wishes were spoken, rest in peace, God bless you and thank you. Exactly who thought what was unimportant as they stepped over the remains of the thick wooden door smashed from its hinges.

'Oh you may not want to look at Roma's remains...' Kosminsky advised them as they turned the next corner. '...Jay pounded her face pretty badly before setting off upstairs.'

'Why would it do that...?' Juliet asked.

Alex thought he knew the answer but chose not to share it, instead pulling her close to him, as they walked ahead with their shoulders turned toward a blood splattered wall next to and above Roma's savagely beaten corpse.

'I don't know why.' Kosminsky answered then pressed his ID card on the panel that was lit red next to the door. There followed a couple of seconds of delay where nothing happened, causing the three of them to immediately believe the worst, before it clicked green and the door started to slowly slide open at the same overdramatic snail's pace. This giving them too much time to think and look over their shoulders at the corridor behind them.

Flo and Rhian both grabbed Sammy and pulled him close to them on seeing the light above the door change from red to green. Harvey quickly positioned himself against the wall next to the door, his back flattened to it, ready to punch or wrestle to the death whatever came through. With a sideways glance through the widening gap he saw a huge pair of hands trying to push the door and quicken the process up. His next thought was to grab one and bite down hard on it as soon as he could, certainly not textbook police procedure, but thankfully also not one he acted upon.

Juliet pushed her body through the gap as soon as she believed it big enough, even then still crushing her own chest in the process, grunting as she fell into the room. Fortunately Harvey was alert enough to notice this woman had brown hair and not Roma's blonde, so he resisted the urge to attack. Alex came next immediately rushing to help Juliet back up while the rest of the room watched wide eyed and open mouthed.

'It's okay everyone we're here with Kosminsky...!' The one armed man informed them all.

Harvey leaned round the door to see the familiar face of his old friend stood outside in the slowly widening gap.

'I'm glad you could make it.' He said as the doorway revealed more and more of a man he wanted to hug.

Then suddenly the lights above the door clicked back from green to red indicating it was beginning to close.

'Quickly come on get in...' Harvey demanded, ready to pull and tug the big guard through, before noticing the ID card in the man's hand, the one he'd just pressed against the entry pad. '...What the hell are you doing?'

'Hi Harvey...I'll be of more use out here. I know this place...I can distract it...who knows what I can do...but I can try!'

The steel door was now reversing its progress and began to close with the Inspector watching on and trying to understand.

'Open this door now Allan. That is a direct order...!' Harvey spoke with all seriousness but he could already feel his throat tightening, not unlike the process of the doors, inevitable and slow. '...Don't do this...please...you won't stand a chance...!'

'Seems I never do Harvey, I died on the other timeline too remember.' The door was now only a face width ajar. 'But to hell with it...I can accept that as my role in the world. Only this time I'm not going to leave without a fight.'

'Kosminsky please...we need you!' Harvey tried one last time.

'Nah...not inside there you don't. You can sort it out now you're all together, put those minds together and make a plan. I'll do what I do best and patrol my facility from this side of the locked door...like I've always done...' It was already down to a two inch gap with Harvey staring through it like an abandoned dog in a pound. '...Save them Harvey and take care, who knows my friend...maybe I'll see you on the other...'

The door closed extinguishing his words.

From the corridor Kosminsky stared at the steel doorway, picturing Harvey's face only a foot away in geographical reality, yet a lifetime away in actuality, while hoping that man would truly understand his decision.

He looked down at the ID card in his hand that in this current situation was only useful for opening this door, considered it for a moment, before bending it together, forcing the two ends to meet, breaking it in half. When that wasn't enough for his own personal closure he did the same with the two remaining halves. In doing so he knew he was condemning them to find their own way out of there, but it was significantly the better choice than allowing the Glitch to take the card from him when they met.

And he knew they would meet, because Allan Gregor Arron Kosminsky wasn't prepared to just roll over and accept his facility being invaded by whatever that monster was. It was time for him to prove his worth to the group locked in that room, they were going to need all the help they could get, so the best and only gift he could give them was time. Exactly how he would achieve that was a little detail he hadn't worked out yet, but for now he would head back to his cupboard office.

From now on every solitary step he took was fraught with possible threat as he attempted that journey, every blind corner another tense moment, a jump scare waiting to happen, where he could find himself face to face with Jay Cleaver. He knew what he was doing would be considered folly by some as he'd clearly seen the violence the Glitch could do, even suicidal in some critic's eyes but not his, in his he was going back to the cupboard office to cause as many problems as he could.

He quietly took the stairs that led to his office when he heard a sound that was music to his ears. It came from on high, maybe two floors up, a screaming rage and a smash of furniture, glass, windows even. Evidently the Glitch wasn't happy at all and a smiling Kosminsky was determined to keep it that way.

67

A hushed respectful silence had fallen over the group in the meeting room, Kosminsky's selfless act having had a calming and focusing effect on the trapped occupants. Harvey thought the big guard had been correct about one thing, because now they were all together and with his mind back in working order, things were slotting into place. Inside this space was every piece of knowledge they had on the threat they faced, all the experience they could muster, for crying out loud they even had a large table to sit around and discuss it.

The worrying fact they had no food or water and were trapped inside a concrete cage with a monster prowling outside, strangely seemed to be of secondary importance. That wasn't an adjustable problem at the moment. They had to focus on what could be changed.

Harvey called them in from their various groups to take a seat; he sat in the central position of the table, exactly where a certain Professor Caroline Wesson had once demeaned him from. As the rest of the group got settled he considered the actual time which had passed since he and Emma had last been here. Finding it surprisingly difficult to place a date on how long ago that had been, a couple of weeks, a month, maybe six months? The concept of time seemed to be unimportant, especially if he tried searching for it by looking backwards. He was dragged away from these thoughts by a fresh query.

'Would it be okay if I start things Harvey?' Alex asked.

He was sat directly opposite with Juliet to his right, then Rhian and Sammy, with Flo next to her husband.

'...I've got new information...if that's actually what we're planning to do here.'

'It's what we have to do...' Harvey half smiled. '...Please go ahead.'

'Okay first of all I'll bring you up to speed with what's happening out there. Oscar Downes is dead, seemingly shot by Marcus Kirby in an act of self-defence when he tried to attack him.' He noted the puzzled look on Harvey's face. 'Yeah I'm sure there was a lot more to it than that as well. Also Superintendent Shilling was murdered by Kirby...we don't know the exact reason for that either but Kosminsky was forced to move the bodies so we know he's dead...' As Alex spoke his eyes were flicking from one person to another, gauging their responses, this being no pleasurable experience. '...I'm sure as you can most likely guess that Officer Lee Foster didn't make it either. The Glitch killed him right out there in the corridor.'

'Oh Jesus Christ...!' It was Rhian who already couldn't bear to hear anymore. '...Do we have to do this in front of my boy?'

'I'm afraid we do yes...he's as much a part of this as any of us.' Harvey replied as the head of the table.

Alex continued his list. 'Roma Walker is also dead. It seems the Glitch chose to remain inside Jay's head, because of that choice he set about the young woman. I didn't see what was left of her face but Kosminsky told us it was pretty bad...which brings us onto Marcus Kirby, a murderer who tried to reason with it, only to end up crucified while floating in mid-air then torn apart, which seems a pretty convincing argument that the Glitch doesn't want to be reasoned with. Kosminsky saw it happen...'

'...And what about him now...? He's out there with that thing!' Juliet's breaking voice seemed to speak for them all.

Alex took a calming pause before answering. 'It's fair to say Allan has made his own choice. I can't begin to fathom an answer for why...but I do know he's a good soul and he'll try and help us in some way. I can only suppose he didn't want to be trapped with the rest of us...he really doesn't know any more than we do...so he decided to do things his own way.'

'Is that all?' Harvey asked.

'No, no it isn't.' Alex gently squeezed Juliet's hand under the table, more for his own comfort than hers but he trusted she'd understand. 'It seems I had a direct connection with it earlier...something that comes and goes, like a radio signal that can't be tuned correctly...but it was definitely there and I believe...hope, it will come back again...'

'So you can't feel it at the moment?' Rhian inquired softly.

'I don't think so...well not like before...if I try now it's just static.'

'Maybe it's blocking you?'

'You could be right...but I felt quite certain that it didn't know I was there. I was seeing the world through its eyes as it chased you in here. When you escaped it had to make the decision of which body it would choose to continue with. As I said in the end it remained in Jay but there was something else happening inside it...a feeling it was having...it paused for a long while outside that door but I don't think it was because it was choosing Jay over Roma...it felt to me it was far deeper than that...'

Alex trailed off as his mind tried to keep up. He knew this wasn't the time for a lazy supposition so in the next few seconds chose his words as carefully as possible. '...I think it was scared'

'Scared...Of what...?' Rhian exclaimed.

'Of the next step I think...of what it's going to become.'

THE RED FRAME

Everyone considered the news because in some way it sounded useful, important, but mainly it was because they were surprised the Glitch could ever possibly feel such an emotion. The general, unspoken, consensus in the room being that most likely Alex was wrong on that point. After all he was highly emotional himself so probably reading a little too much into it, because the Glitch they'd all seen and heard about didn't do weakness. It was a murdering machine claiming to be the apocalypse of this universe and it wasn't frightened of anything, people, Demons, or God itself.

'So what is it going to become…?' Juliet asked.

Alex didn't answer that question, feeling that to speculate would be wrong, or wouldn't come close to the horrors they could face.

68

On reaching his office Kosminsky closed and bolted the door confident he was in here for the long haul. He then quickly got himself settled at the computer and checked the camera feeds. 'There you are...' He said under his breath as the video from the second floor canteen area caught Jay Cleaver standing quite still and facing a broken window, with tables and chairs strewn around the room, the pictures perfectly matching the sounds he'd just heard.

'...Right you bastard let's play...and see how good your hearing is.' Kosminsky said this to himself while switching the intercom back on and linking it Kirby's office. But he wasn't going to be dumb about it just in case that thing did have amazing hearing. So not wanting it to pick up any sound from the cupboard office he simply held the button down, meaning in here there was no noise but upstairs there'd be a high pitched feedback screech after a few seconds, a safety feature to remind you that your finger was on the button but you weren't speaking.

The Glitch immediately reacted to the sound, turning Jay's head to the side and focusing in on the direction, it was coming from back upstairs. It considered the implications first before making any move towards the screeching noise. There was no one up there it was sure of that, having already faced the frustration of entering Kirby's office to find the man's arm gone, which meant it hadn't been able to use his fingerprint to reopen the laptop. So now it was blind to the whereabouts of whoever else was in the facility, but of course logically thinking it knew exactly who it was, the options were so few it had to be the big guard Kosminsky trying his hand at a little deception.

Jay walked forward to stand under the camera, staring into the lens it raised it's already repaired hand to indicate first at his chest, then two fingers towards its eyes, before pointing them straight at the observing guard.

I see you.

Kosminsky was suddenly frozen by the gesture; his plans of leading the monster on a merry little dance clearly being thwarted at the first stage. The damn thing was always one step ahead so it would soon work out where he was hiding, thought the big guard, knowing he had to do something quickly. He looked over at the door to this cupboard office which was locked and made of steel but nothing like as thick and robust as the one for the meeting room. Shit! He needed time to run, get out of the building, but he could see Jay was already walking out of the canteen and heading downstairs to seek him out. Fuck!

The Glitch strode down the stairs to find its prey, thinking of how it would enjoy killing Kosminsky, even considering a little searching within the man's thoughts first to better tear him apart, both inside and out. Laughing to itself at the thought of how many memories humans keep with them; their guarded personal images of the past, but to the Glitch they were just another weakness to be exploited. Yes, it decided, it would have fun with Allan Kosminsky because it had its own recollections of the man, although strictly speaking they were remembrances from the Demon it had consumed, but they still remained and were watchable.

As the Glitch reached the ground floor it had already replayed many clips of the times the Demon had been in the company of the big guard, the walking, so much walking down these corridors, cuffs on, cuffs off, talk to me Oscar. Those days when Kosminsky, always so desperate to speak to the Demon, had even allowed the man to be without shackles in his presence, such an action proving how the big guard was not only a fearless idiot, but also an extremely fortunate one.

Down into the depths of the facility the Glitch forced Jay Cleavers body on, but it could feel the vessel was weakening, not as brisk and energetic as it needed it to be, which it put down to a lack of sustenance. It wasn't totally surprised by this of course as the last thing Jay had fully ingested was a fistful of cocaine, but it was a little concerning when remembering how it had savagely destroyed its other vessel in a fit of pique. Poor Roma Walker it thought, first day in a new job, perhaps thinking that brighter times were ahead, a new future even, only to end up with her pretty little face beaten until it cracked open.

The Glitch had never felt the sin of pride in any of its killings, those feelings were for beings of lesser character, but as it thought on the fury it had shown the unfortunate girl it did have to question its motive. For the first time it had lost control of its self. All the other murders it had committed were purely functional, intended to make a statement or done to remove the person as an obstacle, but Roma had been different. There had been a blind rage at work, it hadn't just wanted to extinguish her life; there had been an overwhelming desire to destroy her completely. The very same emotion it was having now as it reached the bottom of the stairs and turned left, where it could almost taste the Polish Jew at the end of this corridor, hiding behind the steel door, trapped like so many of his ancestors.

Kosminsky looked at the computer screen watching Jay Cleavers body getting warmer in this deadly game of hide and seek. Fucking hell he thought and swivelled his chair round to face the door, the bastard knew exactly where to come, before he removed the small silver pistol from his pocket. It was all he had and knew it was loaded because he'd seen Kirby do it.

Glancing back over his shoulder to view the feed, in some childishly desperate hope the Glitch would just turn and walk away, he saw it stood perfectly still right outside the door.

It was in no hurry knowing it had the guard confined but that wasn't the cause of this delay. Once more it was taking a break in proceedings before the kill, just as it had with Roma, its reason being the inner turmoil bubbling hot under the surface of Jay Cleavers skull. Questions it should never ask were burning into its psyche. What does this mean, how is it happening, where am I going...who am I...why am I? All of them needing answer's before they would allow Jay's body to continue.

It lifted both hands and began smashing them against the steel door, to Kosminsky it appeared as if it were trying to get in, but to the Glitch the reason was rather more profound. There was a searing breakdown in its mental faculties; raising the vital question of its true identity, which was essential to know before it could move on to the next stage, to take the great leap forward in its evolution.

Kosminsky watched the door as the blows rained down upon it, growing in speed and ferocity. Then he heard the scream released like the sound of a wounded animal. But this wasn't the cry he'd expected to hear, being more a holler of sorrow, a mournful wail of anger not focused on him. Whatever was really out there and breaking the door down wasn't acting in an controlled manner, there would be no chance for negotiations with it when it got in, so Kosminsky raised the pistol up, pointing it at the side of his own head. His forefinger brushed the tiny trigger then fixed itself on, ready to pull if the door gave way.

The Glitch suddenly stopped its punching of the door, even though the steel frame was bent and ready to give up, when inside its mind a picture began to form of what was to come. Displaying how everything that had passed in its short and rushed life to this point had been nothing more than a childish prequel, a gestation period now coming to fruition, the end approaching for this thinking, learning, Glitch.

Standing in Jay's body it understood now it would have to step aside to allow the rise of its ultimate form, this vessel would be rejected and then discarded, for its next generation would have a true form in this world, able to move without help and consume with infinite voracity. The Glitch screamed again in rejection of this change, unable to comfortably relinquish the mind it had developed, all the lessons it had learned and the memories made couldn't just be simply forgotten.

It didn't want to be forced down this path, a new progression bubbling under the surface of Jay's skin ready to explode out, so the original Glitch was grasping with extreme growing anxiety to hold on as when it inevitably happened there would be something new standing here, a life-force with no desire for thinking. But while it was still able to fight the Glitch would try to reason with itself, remain in control until its last breath because it didn't want this mind to just be forgotten and disappear, as the unique and bastardised problem of allowing an apocalyptic event to have a sentient life experience came home to roost.

'Are you coming in or not, you murdering bastard?' Kosminsky shouted towards the partially detached steel door frame. He then risked a glance over his shoulder at the computer to see Cleavers body standing perfectly still once more with his fists bloodied. 'I'm ready for you...'

'Kosminsky...!' The Glitch responded. '...The missing link in both voice and physicality...' This insult displaying the proof it was still in control and able to think clearly. Jay's lungs taking a deep breath with some relief that its metamorphosis was thwarted for now. '...You're trying to cause me a problem...an admirable pursuit...but one that...'

'...Fuck you!' The big guard cut it off realising he didn't have an ounce of fear in his veins. He was more than ready to die here. 'Kick the door in. I have a surprise for you.'

'No you do not. You have a gun...which is of no surprise and I presume you will either try to shoot me which would be utterly pointless, or you will turn it on yourself to take away my fun.'

Kosminsky felt a little fear creep over his broad shoulders at being called out so easily. 'Yeah well one of us is getting this bullet in the head. I guess the choice is yours.'

A large sigh could be heard from the corridor just before the door was kicked in and broke completely. Jay's slim leg stepped over the threshold and into the cupboard office to stand before the big guard. 'Very well this is my choice...your turn now...what is your response...?'

Kosminsky found himself no more than four feet away, looking up at the face of Jay Cleaver, whilst being stared at by the Glitch, his plan of pulling the trigger being countered by this monster somehow controlling his finger movement. The fear he thought he didn't possess came over him quickly, across his shoulders, permeating through his core and out to all his extremities. He could only pray inwardly that his end would be swift and painless.

The Glitch had other ideas.

69

Harvey was still positioned at the centre of it all. Although there had been many varied opinions given from the group on their trapped situation, one voice had remained silent, so the Inspector felt it was about time to get the noiseless one to speak.

'So what do you think Sammy...you haven't told us how you're feeling.'

The boy looked across from his mother's side, his young face appearing surprised to be called, those beautiful eyes giving nothing else away. 'I just want to go home.'

'We all want to do that but we have to solve a problem first. There's a monster outside and we have to defeat it.'

Flo interrupted her husband. 'Harvey come on now, don't scare him any further.'

'I'm afraid that ship has sailed dear!' He countered. Focusing now on his end goal he wasn't faking sympathy just because this team member was young. 'Sammy here has opinions just like the rest of us and I'd like to hear them. They may give us a fresh outlook. He's been involved right from the start, attended every meeting, listened to all of us speak and yet no one has really asked him what he thinks. Therefore I'm just doing my job in leaving no stone unturned. So please Sammy...we're all ears.'

'...I...I don't want to say what I think.'

'Why not...?' Harvey pressed for a better answer.

'...Because it's not very nice.'

'You don't have to say anything darling.' Rhian tried to take control of the situation.

'No Rhian he does...now spit it out...' Harvey demanded firmly.

'...Everything has gone wrong...' The boy began. '...It wasn't Alex's fault really but he's caused all of this.'

'Sammy, please!' Rhian tried again but her boy wasn't going to stop now he'd started.

'Alex fell in the hole and woke it up. We wouldn't be here if he hadn't tumbled off...and now we're all going to die.' The boy looked down at the floor as if thinking his words had been too strong, but in fact it was so he could raise it again and look Harvey straight in the eye. 'Such an obvious and pathetic attempt Inspector to get my attention but there you go...the boy is correct.'

'Couldn't resist it could you Metatron?' Harvey said accusingly and held the boys cold stare. 'Vanity won't allow your words to be misconstrued so you jump back into the light. Seriously how can you blame Alex for any of this, he's an unwilling part of your selfish schemes just as much as the innocent boy you have taken residence in. All of us for that matter have been dragged along by you, down this timeline and the other, but you need to know that I'm sick and tired of playing your games now. Listening to all your little half-truths, telling us one thing while always concealing the other, thinking you're so bloody clever and playing us for fools all the time...'

He paused for a response but the boy remained silent.

'...You see I've learned a lot about Angels and it all points to how you believe we're too primitive to put it all together, but my late superior and friend for many years Superintendent Jeff Shilling taught me a few things. Obviously he passed them onto me in his own rough edged style but they have proven to be true in some instances, none more so than in your case.'

'Is that right?' The boy asked. 'So how does your dead friends addled thoughts help you now?'

'Oh it's not just now...I've been considering it for a while and the more I do the more I glimpse the real Metatron. You see what he passed onto me was a simple piece of advice, nothing new and one I've heard many times from being a child, but when it's used in the right context it's incredibly revealing. Actions speak louder than words, or beat the shit out of words as he put often it.'

'Is that the truth?' Sammy's mouth asked sarcastically.

'Well let's see shall we.' Harvey linked his fingers on the table and closed his eyes before continuing. 'It's because of those wise words that I have discarded all of yours, every single one, there's no need to listen to them or take them on board when judging what's happened here, because they are only what you want us to know. So remove your words and all that's left are your actions, and there have been some immense choices made. So let me explain what I know of your movements and what can be deduced from them. Are you willing to indulge me?'

Metatron replied immediately. 'You may as well Inspector...we should fill the time we have left with something.'

Harvey nodded slightly in agreement. 'After Alex appeared you could have sent him back at any time from the white world but you didn't...we can call that exhibit A, action one. I won't number them all because there are far too many, just so you understand how I'm working this through. Then allowing Alex to enter the book was another big event that springs to mind, faking your death after Rebecca was shot in the head, giving Alex the belief he'd defeated you...also very telling. Placing the picture of that red square in my car to be found, now I haven't checked but I would place money on it not being back inside my jacket pocket now, although it was there when we spoke not long ago, when you cured me of the madness the Glitch infected me with...' He slid his hand inside the empty pocket. '...Tadahhh...no painting...but we can return to that later because I digress. Let's go back, try to keep some semblance of order to the events. When the Glitch appeared in the white world you straight away went into hiding, never thought of questioning it as you did with Alex, just watched on from a safe distance until it gave up on the body of Old Mrs Simpson. Then you used the old lady's fading connection with our world to contact Rhian, who in turn made contact with me...after your suggestion. Eventually you took over her son and that is where things started to get really interesting. So there you are with a secret presence in our world until Alex suspected what could be going on, even then you had the choice to remain concealed and we would have been none the wiser, but instead you chose to speak with us, even appearing in my front room, to regale us with your chilling stories of the Glitch and what it would do to us all...'

'Because I considered you may need my help...' Sammy interjected.

'...Be quiet! I think I've made it perfectly clear we aren't listening to your words anymore, just the things you did...still are doing. Now when the Glitch killed your Demon, which by the way I cannot believe came as a complete surprise, you appeared again, only this time in full view of the world. That could be considered a crazy move because you were giving up not only your existence, but precisely where you were hiding. A move you explained away as being just a cry of anguish for your fallen comrade, well I don't accept that to be true anymore and let me tell you why. Let's return to Oscar's painting, which we know originally came from inside your mind, the one that miraculously appears then disappears at your command, the red frame, or more accurately if you want my opinion, the red herring. Now please don't presume from this glib description that I believe it's unimportant because the case is rather the opposite, I think it's crucial for whatever is really going on here otherwise it would be forgotten like the others. But of all your actions that beat the shit out of all your words one stands head and shoulders above the rest. Why did you choose to speak with me when I was on the brink of total madness? Because let's face facts I would have been out of this, one less stupid mortal to worry about, but no you not only spoke with me, you cleared my head and brought me back here. It was the first time you had taken direct action against the Glitch and that's what makes it so compelling...'

The others at the table where watching on spellbound by this presentation, with Harvey making solid point after solid point, while also wondering just what all his points would add up to.

'...You know what Metatron, please don't think that I consider myself an expert on your world or psyche, but I can't help but look for a pattern forming in those actions, because to my professional eye and logical mind there must be a strong link that holds all these seemingly random events together, so I'm searching for it as I would in any investigation. Of course the perpetrator in this case is an Angel, a fact which you may expect to make spotting a pattern even more difficult to nail down, seeing as you're a higher life form, a superior being in your eyes, but that's where it works the other way in mine. Because you don't do random and you never have, I'd even go as far to suggest you consider such muddled thinking to be how we mortals labour through life, so when that lack of chaos is placed into my calculations it all becomes a little clearer. Believe me when I say I don't have any answers, though I'd like you to grant me that I'm on the right track. A cursory nod will do because I'm not trying to shame you here, I'm stating that none of your actions have been accidental or fortunate, but rather they are all part of a well thought out and calculated plan to get us all to this point.'

Sammy gently pulled himself free of Rhian's arm around his shoulder and walked away, before turning around just as he reached the far side of the room, some fifteen feet away, and from where he gave the Inspector an agreeable nod.

70

Those damn birds were making their awful racket outside his bedroom window again, as he reluctantly threw an arm out from under the warm covers in search of his phone. The alarm hadn't gone off yet but at this time of year their squawking usually corresponded with his getting up. Then sure enough as he pulled the phone into bed the screen lit up and the beeps went off.

'Bloody hell...!' He moaned into his pillow as he pressed dismiss and slowly pulled the duvet down from his face. 'What was that dream about?'

Deliberately keeping his eyes closed he thought back on it, knowing that to open his lids wide would shatter the fragile images still bouncing around in his subconscious. There had been so much to it, a proper night time adventure, he could even recall dying in the dream when someone had stabbed him in the neck at a cinema, then there had been some young man, although he wasn't sure if he knew him or not, that he'd locked in Oscars cell.

'Damn this jobs getting to me!' He said as anything else he may have wanted to glimpse and relive again disappeared, back to where it came from, sinking down into the subconscious of his overtired brain.

With some considerable effort he rolled his legs out of bed and found the floor with his large feet. Then Blackford facility head of security, Allan Kosminsky made his way to the bathroom where he pissed out a whole pint of golden urine, guessing it was all from the last can he'd had before stumbling into bed. As he brushed his teeth and checked his reflection the dream wouldn't leave him be, not the details, they were long gone, but a strong unpleasant feeling remained, one that spoke of a life he could have lived instead of this lonely struggle he plodded through every day. With an earnest humph he forbid his mind to think in that way and splashed his face with soapy water.

Stupid dream, he thought, that was all it was, no need to ponder on another thing that would just bring him down. He already had enough of those with his singular existence and the bad habits he was forming. The fast food dinners heated up, the packs of beer consumed, the lack of goals he set because to survive like this it was easier without them.

Forcing a smile on he patted his cheeks dry then picked up the same uniform he wore yesterday and sniffed it, not too bad, a bit of deodorant and it would get him through another shift. He sat back down on the bed and noticed the socks which he'd slept in, looking down on the big toe and its neighbour popping out through a large hole, before pulling his boots over the offending digits.

God damn it he used to be so focused, working out at the gym, jogging the steady hills of Leith Walk down to the docks and back, always pushing his body to be better. Then the steroids had come into his life, appeared as a shortcut to his objectives, but they had just ruined everything. Again he tried to dispel any negative thoughts from taking root as he picked up his leather bike jacket and gloves from the hallway where he'd dropped them last night.

Then he almost jumped out of his skin as there was a knock on the front door inches from his face.

'For fucks sake...!' He muttered before patiently pasting a fake smile back on and opening it.

There was no immediate response when he saw the caller, it was impossible for him to grasp any words in those first few seconds, as he looked down to the suitcase at their feet.

'Hi...Allan...' Chrissi said with a hint of American accent still noticeable even in such a short hello. '...Can we talk?'

Kosminsky didn't move for what felt like forever, but it could have been officially timed as two and a half seconds, because here she was, standing in front of him and she looked beautiful, healthy, tanned, and perfect.

It was almost too much to take in but he held onto some resolve and tried to speak.

'Chris...si...wow...course...erm I have to go to...no let me call work...you look...come in...I'll err...wow.'

With his heart pounding and his ducts threatening tears he picked up the suitcase and stepped aside, allowing her to enter without taking his eyes off her, worried she might disappear like the dream he'd had.

Ten minutes later and she was still as solid as ever, with his pulse steadily settling. He'd phoned the facility hoping to speak to the secretary Rebecca or whatever she was called but the line was busy. In the end he'd phoned the gate guard Phil Brunt, a good man that he enjoyed chatting to, but there was no time for that today as he informed him, while putting on a terrible chesty wheeze, that he was feeling a little under the weather and wouldn't be coming in for the foreseeable. Phil assured him that he'd let the office know and wished him a speedy recovery, top bloke that he was.

So here they were, the two of them sitting across from each other at the kitchen table, coffees in rapidly washed mugs, the mess created by her leaving him in the first place all around them, unemptied bins, crushed cans, random things that had no right to be strewn on a kitchen floor. He was embarrassed at the sight of it all, but she didn't seem to mind as she hadn't mentioned it so far or given him a disappointed look.

'I'm sorry...' She began.

Kosminsky was so ready for her to say that, exactly how he imagined this scenario going. '...Its okay Chrissi, I understand and I forgi...'

'...I mean disrupting your day. You should have been going to work.'

'Oh right...yes I see...it'll be fine.' He swallowed as quietly as he could before continuing. 'So...how are you..?'

'...All the better for seeing that face...' She replied and those sweet words danced in his ears.

'...Yeah I feel exactly the same. It's been a long time.'

'Too long, I was really worried about just turning up like this...you know like...you could have been married or anything.'

'Me, married to someone else...nah...I've err...I've just been focusing on my work. Trying to stay on top of things but as you can see by the mess it's erm...I've been doing a lot of overtime. So err...when did you get back?'

'I flew in from Vegas this morning and headed right over...to see if you were still around.'

Kosminsky could feel the shakes starting again as his heart moved up the gears. She looked so good and genuinely happy to see him. A thousand thoughts passed through his mind but he couldn't choose the words to say, not without sounding like a love punched teenager, or a desperately sad individual, so he kept it light and friendly.

'Vegas...?'

'Let's not talk about that, I'd like to forget about it, I'm not comfortable with discussing what an idiot I've been. All I want is...oh for god's sake I don't know what I want, but seeing you, talking to you again, that's where I am right now, and living in the moment is much better than dragging up the past...don't you think?'

He picked up his mug to take a sip of coffee and then put it back down without taking one, glancing at her suitcase in the hallway he asked. 'So do you have anywhere to stay?'

'I haven't sorted anything out yet...but I'm going to see if...'

'...Would you like to stay here for a bit...we can...you know...arrange things to how you...you'd like them.'

This was it. He was going out on a limb, throwing all his chips in on a hand that had already lost once, but damn he loved playing this game of life with her.

Chrissi paused for a second while she busied herself removing a black head band, causing her shoulder length brunette hair to fall free. His were eyes drawn to the golden flecks that swayed within it, no surer an indication that she had been living a healthy life in the sunshine, while he'd been struggling through the granite and sandstone rainstorms of this northern hemisphere capital. But what the hell, she was here now; sipping the coffee he'd made her, hopefully ready to answer his question.

'Sure...I can stay here if it's not a problem...if that's what you really want...?'

Kosminsky wanted to scream at the top his lungs "Fuck Yeah!" but once more he held back, not only that exclamation, but tears of joy and gratitude to the universe.

'...Yes...of course it's really no problem at all...to be perfectly honest...nothing could make me happier.'

Chrissi stood up from the table and walked round to him before placing her small tanned hand on his cheek. Her brown eyes looked him up and down and she smiled sweetly. 'I'm truly sorry Allan...for ever hurting you like this.'

'It's okay...it really is...I'm just so happy that you're here.'

With those words released the tears began to fall and he couldn't stop them. Closing his eyes he leaned his head forward to feel the embrace, to take in her scent and touch her warmth again, but she had moved back and now stood in the doorway.

'I am truly sorry...I didn't know that seeing me again would hurt you this much...'

'Please Chrissi its fine...I love you...I always have.' His heart yearned for her touch. 'I just want to hold you.'

'I want to hold you too...but I can't.'

'What...why not...?'

'...Because look at the state of you...what happened Allan? You're a fucking disgrace...a mess of a man...seriously? You waited all this time and let yourself go horribly. It's pathetic to think I would find that attractive...'

The confusion ripped through his brain like an electric shock, he felt nauseous and empty, like he could die here just from hearing those words.

'...Chrissi...?' He watched as she picked up her suitcase. '...Baby I can fix this...I can get back to what I was...'

She stopped and her slim fingers placed the case down at his feet then unclicked the locks.

'...Please you're breaking my heart worse than ever.'

His tears were falling heavier now as he watched her flick the case lid open. Inside he could see a grey piece of material laid out flat on top.

'What are you doing...What is that...?'

He looked over at Chrissi but she didn't answer before his eyes were drawn back to the case and the material which was shuffling inside, filling out, rising up like a sick slow motion jack in the box, until Jay Cleaver stood tall before him and stepped out.

'Kosminsky you have no idea the pure joy this has given me.'

The big guard sat open mouthed and some of his tears fell into that gaping hole. He could feel his heart stuttering in perfect time with the pain flashing across his mind, his chest tightening at the horror he felt.

The Glitch then turned towards Chrissi and beckoned her to him. She acceded to this request and came over to stand at his side.

'...This is your girl Allan...your pretty little love...I know you think me heartless and in all honesty I am, but I can understand how much this is tearing you apart...' It placed Jay's hand on her cheek. '...Even here like this...you should feel the warmth and softness she is blessed with...mother nature did well with this one, but it is time to move on...' Its hand then fell to her throat and squeezed it as effortlessly as rinsing a cloth. Chrissi's head instantly lolling to the side as her body fell to the floor with a gentle thump. '...I am hoping that will be enough.'

Kosminsky couldn't speak as there was no more oxygen being taken in, the sight of his girl being extinguished so easily and with no compassion tearing him apart, exactly as the Glitch had desired. The big guard's large heart came to a standstill, his last memory an inwardly horrific scream that he would carry with him into eternity.

Jay's face smiled broadly as he watched Kosminsky's body collapse from his chair and fall to the floor within the cupboard office.

'Perfect...!' He cried to himself, quite literally the only thing hearing his words would be the next generation that was itching to take over.

'...Thank you for that extra time and opportunity to create my greatest work. To take this human soul without touching them, not harming them physically in any way, nor ordering them to take their own lives, but to simply take a life...by actually breaking a heart.'

At this moment the Glitch sensed the final transformation beginning, it felt as if parts of its mind where flying off into the ether, being squeezed out by the growing force within it and with a final breath it uttered its contented consent. 'I am done...do your worst, this has been...incredible...'

Jay's body shut down, collapsing to the floor, falling across Kosminsky's corpse.

71

Alex, like everyone else in the meeting room, had been watching and listening intently to this conversation between Harvey and Metatron, when all of a sudden he felt the change in the Glitch occur with a tingling sensation creeping across the back of his head, but unnaturally it seemed it was just inside his skull, not unlike a hungry spider creeping towards some captured prey. This was followed by an uncomfortable shiver distributing itself down his spine, then the feeling was gone, the connection he'd had with the monster was no more, even the static he'd imagined he could hear was now abruptly silent.

Harvey was still speaking to the Angel '...So if you have some master plan Metatron I think we would all love to hear it. Better still come speak to us in person, you know you can.'

The Inspector requested this while approaching Sammy who was sitting down in the far corner, cowering, the best description if he was indeed a ten year old boy but keeping a moody distance, if he were actually a millennia old Angel. Either way it appeared he clearly wanted his own space but the Inspector was about to invade it.

'Leave me alone.' Sammy's mouth demanded almost spitting the words. 'I have nodded my affirmation that you have done well. Of course I have a plan, but in any reality it is only as useful as yours. Mine is to remain hidden and stay alive in hope we can discover a weakness in its defences. Any more than that I can't help you with Inspector...'

Alex abruptly stood up from his chair and slammed the table hard with his right hand. All the women jumped at the sound it made, as did Harvey.

'What the hell are you doing?' He asked in a stern whisper.

'There's no point keeping quiet is there...it knows exactly where we are...!' Alex shouted. '...And there's no use relying on that lying bastard...' his finger pointed clearly at the boy. '...I've played this game with it before and that Angel will never tell you the full truth. Even now with the end in sight there's no way it will play fair. I can tell you what its plan is Harvey...it was to get itself here, that much is true and important parts of that explanation like hiding and staying alive are also the truth...but it still won't give it up...it won't tell us why it's done that...and it won't until it's too late for us..!'

Flo gave a silent look with a movement of her eyebrows that told Juliet in no uncertain terms to control her man better. The young woman took it on board and placed her hand on Alex's arm to lower it back down.

'Alex we've got to remain calm. We all know the trouble we're in but at least we're safe in here for now...maybe help will come...'

Alex looked down at her first, then worked his way around the other frightened faces, he was about to make it a lot worse as he spoke. 'There's no help coming Florence and we are definitely not safe in here anymore. They are all dead out there...every one...and now the Glitch is evolving into a new creature...one that's no longer living in Jay Cleavers head so we can't talk to it or hide from it, because it's coming and it is the antithesis of everything we know. It'll be here soon to show us what it can do and none of us stand a chance...!'

'How do you know all this...are you making contact with it again?' Rhian was the one asking in hope it may help.

'No...I can't feel it all anymore...but just like Harvey did I've put all the pieces together, there's no doubt that Superintendent Shilling was right, actions do beat the shit out of words.'

Flo took the uncomfortable pause that followed to have her say. 'Well if you've finished telling us how we are all going to die then I'd very much like to put my view across. As a group of previously unconnected souls we have discussed this over and over until we are blue in the face. We know everything there is to know about what's coming for us, we've argued between ourselves, fallen out at times, but here we are still breathing, very much alive and following the plan that we made and agreed upon. In my eyes that means we're winning, or at the very least we are all still in the game, so whatever comes through that door needs to know it as well...that what its facing in here isn't a bunch of crying fearful children ready to fall at its feet. I want it to understand that there's a spirit in here just as big as its own...and I'll tell you why I want that. Because this isn't me putting on a brave face for the rest of you, I'm not thumping my chest to make you feel better, there's something real and solid we can do here. If everything I've heard is true then we are facing the end of this world and many others. In theory we could be the last battle it faces before it adapts again and crushes everything before it...but we'll have it in a room and it will be outnumbered...'

'...I'm with Florence!' Rhian exclaimed and stood up.

'I haven't finished yet...'

'...Oh, sorry...!' She sat back down.

'Thank you anyway...' Flo nodded to her. '...Now I'm no expert on the natural world, things like how animals react in particular situations, but I've enough knowledge to know what I wouldn't want to see if I entered a room, even if I was armed to the teeth and that would be six determined souls ready to fight back...not sitting in a cowering bunch ready to accept their end...but a team spaced out around the room so it won't know which one of us to focus on first...let's make it believe there's an actual threat, and give it no idea from which direction it will come.'

Harvey took a moment because his wife was doing her damn hardest to take his breath away. Then Alex piped up with a valid question which dropped the levels of hope in the room back down a notch.

'I don't think me being perfectly honest about the situation is a bad thing Mrs Cooper...I mean if you want us to band together and try your standing around tactic then I'm game, what else is there to do, but I don't know what you hope to achieve...do you?'

'Yes Alex I do because I'm not changing my opinion to fit your depressing outlook, otherwise we might as well have just left the door open, then it would be over, there would be no need to try staying hopeful...but I suppose none of us are surprised by your negative view. I'm certainly not, you're hardened to it aren't you, after all you were willing to commit suicide with all the pain that causes. In my opinion the most selfish act because you don't have to deal with the aftermath, leaving anyone who ever knew you to feel shit and guilty, as if they've let you down in some way. Well my viewpoint on life is quite different. If my decision to try and fight means I'm taken away from this world then that is the way it's supposed to be...but I would never do what you did because I'm capable of loving other people, I care for their feelings. That doesn't mean I think I'm perfect or any better than you Alex Webb...but it does mean that I am not a quitter and I don't want to be remembered as one.'

Juliet slowly reached over and placed her hand on the back of Flo's, a clear indication to Alex of whose side she was on.

'Well said. That's exactly what we needed to hear...none more so than him!' She looked straight into Alex's eyes on the last word.

After that condemnation had been delivered Alex turned and walked away from the table towards Harvey and young Sammy.

'Right, I think it's pretty conclusive what the women think of me...how about you Harvey...hmm you want to choose a side? I wouldn't mind but I agreed to stand in her stupid circle...you know the one we can threaten it with...because then hopefully it will just run away.'

Harvey got back to his feet. 'You know that isn't what she meant...'

'Huh...so you are choosing her side then?'

'Listen Alex, this isn't about sides, it's about sticking together, keeping some kind of positive attitude because it is all we've got left to fight with.'

'No it isn't Harvey...we've got a fucking Angel over there. The same bastard that brought us all here in the first place...and that was the point I was trying to get across before your stupid wife decided to make it all about me and her...'

'Watch your mouth Alex...don't forget who your friends are...'

Harvey could feel the adrenalin rushing to his muscles to support a hefty punch to the one armed man's jaw, but he resisted for now. '...Of course you can blame this Angel all you want, but the actual reason any of us are here...is because we wanted to help you. I'd be miles away by now if I hadn't followed my instinct that the incredible story you turned up with was worth pursuing. Ever since I made that decision I've seen all of it proven to be true and I've witnessed you do some incredible things, and right now I need you to do a few more...so start by respecting the people who have put their very lives shoulder to shoulder with yours. Drop the attitude and for once in your life stop choosing to be the victim. That black cloud takes you over so easily, but I've read that you went into a battle with the Demon, helping to defeat it and an Angel...'

'You know that never really happened, Harvey, it's just another one of Metatron's lies...' Alex snapped back.

'...Agreed, we all learned that, but you didn't know it at the time, not while you were wrestling the book from an Angel while facing off against its Demon. Also since then I've seen you stand face to face with the Glitch itself, back in the lock up when you went straight up to that beast in Jay Cleaver, you looked it in the eye and swore that you would kill it. I actually watched that happen, I didn't read about it in a book of dreams, I was there...and those were the actions of a man who truly believed they could do such a thing. At the time I thought it was because you weren't afraid of dying, that you somehow naturally had that heroic attitude...and I was impressed to hell...only now I can see it for what it really is. It's true that you aren't afraid to die, but the problem is you don't care if anyone else does either...now that's cold, Alex.'

The accused one armed man turned away from Harvey's gaze, the Inspectors words were hurting and rightly so, as between them Florence and Harvey Cooper had cleverly worked him out. Even Nurse Juliet who he'd spent months with hadn't spotted the diseased burden that he carried with him every day, simply believing him to be another depressive who needed help. Both of those assumptions were correct, but to judge any patient accurately one must know the true limits of their illness and his particular condition would always be difficult to spot. In the crazy world of psychoanalysis it can be extremely problematic to differentiate between the traits of a full blown sociopath, and the acts of a person simply lacking empathy. That same lack of thoughtfulness for other people's needs or feelings will most certainly appear in both diagnoses, but in the first case they are targeted and intended, in the other, just part of an unfortunate soul who lost their way.

Alex Webb had fallen deeply into that second category and even he didn't know if it was by design or choice. All he could really remember was that he'd threatened his deceased ex-wife Linda with suicide many times. Throwing those threats in her face during every heated argument, utilising them as weapons for his own selfish need to either attack or defend, he hadn't cared which, until that day when she'd called time on his bluffing and walked away.

Her leaving had been the catalyst that forced him out onto the ledge in Dalmeny Street, the epicentre of everything, her leaving became the exact moment that Alex Webb had stopped existing as a compassionate man. All his sympathetic leanings were absent now and everything that happened after hadn't helped, if anything it had made his whole empathy situation worse, because now he thought of life and death in the exact same way, both conditions were a pain in the arse that wouldn't let him be.

Despite this he still didn't think of himself as a totally lost cause, that was the reason he'd continued to seek the truth, because in his mind he'd always held out hope that if he could fix the mess somehow, put things back to the way they were, that maybe he'd be rewarded with a second chance.

Hope is but the dream of those who wake.

Shit! He really had no idea where that quotation had come from or why it should appear in his thoughts at this moment. He guessed it could have come from something he'd seen or heard many years ago, even a residual memory taken from his journeys inside the Angel's book, there was simply no way of knowing, but his mind quickly assimilated it into his own existence. He was definitely thinking of his hope to survive now as a dream, one he'd been having ever since he'd awakened from those dark months in a coma. Damn it, he thought, those words could have been written for me.

72

Inside the cupboard office, on the floor of a tiny room which had seen its fair share of evil and death on dual timelines, Jay Cleavers body lay with its back arched over the corpse of Allan Kosminsky.

Under a quietly buzzing strip-light his beautifully repaired face was gazing up with unseeing eyes, while the mouth that Glitch had permitted him to speak with again was dropped open and muted. His arms were spread away from his torso, laid opened wide with the back of each hand touching the floor. No movement of life stirred within the bodies, there was no sudden cough or splutter where either one would miraculously come back to life, gasping for air as they fled from the jaws of death, not this time.

The only sound was the popping of the strip light which had been busy reflecting back the translucent surface of his perfect skin, almost as if it didn't want to see what would happen next, its sudden demise seeming to appear as a frightened response causing the room to be plunged into total darkness.

Within this blackened room Jay's skin began to excrete a layer of sweat from every pore, the fluid entering this world and thickening slightly as it touched the air surrounding it, pulling itself together, mixing as each new liquid layer ran into and over the ones that came before, joining to form an excretion that came slowly sliding out through the very fibres of the grey suit. Never losing contact with the material it began to coalesce on the boy's chest creating an orb of glutinous mass in the dark. Inside that mass a tiny light sparked within its centre before fading out to black, but it had been enough to ignite the process as a steady glow began to permeate, the orb filling up with energy and existence. As it tried to pull itself away from the material of the suit it found itself to be stuck fast, like a barnacle affixed firmly to the side of a sunken wreck, holding on tight against strong currents that would try to detach it, troubled by the act of leaving the only place of safety it had ever known.

After a few minutes it would try again but for now it remained as a ball of light, with the tiny rays that emanated from its centre reaching out into the black of the room, gathering scattered atoms from the air, rounding up molecules of random description and drawing them towards its centre, consuming the very atmosphere, forcing the stuff of life into itself as if it were plankton, feeding on this nutrient rich sustenance to help give it the strength and mass it would require to break free of the past, to leave far behind the grey suit its previous incarnation had worn.

The orb began to burn brighter as its arrangement grew stronger, ever more robust and vigorous until it could sense itself detaching from the material, as it silently floated up and away, free at last.

Its initial movements were slow and steady as it learned how to control this new form. As after all that had gone before this was its first attempt to move independently. It was no longer the dark concept of an Angel's desire to transfer hate and revenge, nor was it the thinking consciousness that needed to take over mortal vessels for its travel. The summoned Glitch, originally placed in the book as a threat, had evolved far beyond those humble beginnings, inevitably arriving at its and therefore everyone else's, final destination.

Without any true thought it automatically knew what should happen next, all it had to do was open itself up and feed, pulsate this tiny form ever larger and take everything in, become the black hole it was always destined to be.

The Angel had called it into existence, by design or misfortune, but it was here now and ready to begin its expansion, to swallow this universe particle by particle until it was engorged, knowing full well when it had crushed all matter inside its heart there would be a moment of critical mass causing it to explode outwards again. When this single purpose was served a new universe would be formed from the old, entirely altered fusions would occur creating unimagined scenarios of life and growth, of death and decay, as is the true random nature of creation.

Then in a millionth of a millionth of a second the ever spinning circle of reality would take shape once more, pushing its hurtling boundaries ever further to fill the great expanse with light, as fathomless amounts of stars brighten the underlying darkness, soon giving birth to new galaxies that would start forming from the superheated materials congealing within the dust clouds. From then on new worlds would be fashioned, some perhaps with intelligent life, although the precise conditions required for such a thing were rare indeed, but it could happen and pockets of consciousness might appear where beings could learn and grow, prosper with knowledge, to use that wisdom and one day better understand their place in the universe, how they all existed in the heart of the Life Machine.

This tiny black hole was ready to start its work, but just as it was set to begin the mass consumption a message came from within itself, a voice spoke up which though it couldn't hear, it could understand. The words were speaking of a task to be completed before the apocalypse could begin, a personal matter quite insignificant to this unfeeling orb of destruction but vitally important to its previous incarnation.

The Glitch who had chased those Mortals and the Angel into this place was still present, replaced but not quite gone and while it still had a chance to influence the future it would take that opportunity. It wanted to end its story properly with one final hurrah and gratefully found the orb couldn't object to that demand. The floating sphere in the cupboard office had no mind of its own so would follow whatever demands it was given, if only for the briefest of time, from the only voice it would ever understand.

The light within its centre began to glow brighter as its outer edge took shape. Once more it would create the form imagined within Jay's mind, the shape that killed the Demon, the perfect synchronisation of what it would become and what it had been.

The Glitch knew this dual formation wouldn't last long but the situation was win/win, either it had the time to kill them all and be aware of those most satisfying actions, or it would itself disappear into the abyss and no longer exist, in which case the orb would begin to consume the world independently and those mortals would die regardless. But deep inside the transforming body of stars and colours that was taking shape, the sentient half of the Glitch was determined to hold it together, desperately craving to see their faces as they looked upon its terrifying splendour.

73

Far and wide across the city certain elements of life seemed to sense the arrival of impending threat being born deep inside the Blackford Facility. It being best illustrated with how wildlife were reacting, altering their natural behaviour, as flocks of birds began taking to the air within a midnight sky, while urban mammals refused to range this night, preferring to feel safer by staying closer to home. It was clearly unusual how the foxes and bats and badgers and rats were resisting their instincts to roam free, resisting their natural needs for food and interaction, yet no one seemed to notice, or maybe cared enough to see the change. As always the human race were far too wrapped up in their own fluctuating emotions.

It is true that the mind of a mortal is nothing but a curious and selfish computer at source, a device willing to believe in any concept that keeps it interested and happy, the ideas that keep it turning over so to speak.

The human brain will sometimes allow itself to be lead towards new trends and ideas, but more often will stick close to old beliefs and systems, meaning there was little doubt the exponential growth of news and social media with its 24/7 connection to the world was both satisfying and killing the minds natural requirements in equal measure. This continuous assault on the senses often triggering immeasurable and unspeakable long term stress on a daily basis, while simultaneously causes some of the human's greatest skills to fade out of existence, as focus and concentration became impotent. The primeval need to solve problems for one's self, to learn through experience which in turn creates positive core memories, was now being rapidly overtaken by the ease of pressing a button for some major corporation's diluted and advertising lead opinion. So it is becoming clear that with attention spans becoming less and less due to this saturation of the mind, this cosy blanketing for their profit and your information, a human soul can soon feel it has seen enough, or seen it all before, then quickly become disinterested at even the most incredible of events.

This exact and regretful consequence was coming to bear on the city of Edinburgh tonight, surrounding this significant moment in history and quickly spreading around the globe, with the expectant crowds who'd rushed blindly to the airport now drifting away as midnight approached. With nothing to see and no fresh news on the boy, or visions of the Angel, their belief had started to wear thin. Most questioning why they were doing this at all, had it even occurred, did it actually mean something, but with no new input they were now more content to return home and wait for the second coming in their nice warm beds. Such is the selfish attention span of a mortal mind in this modern age, that when it finds itself denied the feedback it craves, even with something as surreal and fantastical as the Angel's appearance, there is still an abrupt switch off point if it starts to get too chilly.

Then as these human components of universal life gave up on their short lived curiosity about eternal salvation, the shared hope that things could actually change, they left the airport side roads to find themselves stuck in miles of traffic jams. They beeped their horns, rolled down their windows and shouted at each other, while all the time unlike all the other mammals and birds, sensed nothing of the other trouble they faced.

Moving away from the airport roads and that ongoing chaos one could find other stories happening, perhaps better ones, to illustrate the twisting kaleidoscope of reactions the past few hours had awakened.

Officer Rob Chambers, a twenty three year old policeman, put in charge of the fake transferral of the boy by Superintendent Shilling, had been as perplexed as everyone else to begin with, sitting in a cordoned off airport lounge for hours with no more instructions coming through.

On first taking that seat and seeing all the commotion around him he found himself excited by the subterfuge they were trying to pull off, while at the same time questioning his own agnostic viewpoint, but as the minutes had slowly passed those passions had started to lose fuel.

Having received no news from his superior he'd tried to call him, but when it wasn't answered and with his messages garnering no response he'd phoned a friend, only to discover Officer Lee Foster wasn't responding either. Lee's failure to respond was slightly unusual as they were always happy to speak, to fill each other in on the events of their shifts, but Chambers guessed both men were busy with everything going on.

Besides it wasn't as if either of his colleagues could make much difference to his position, not now the government was involved when the military had rolled into town, although exactly what the armed forces were doing at the airport confused him more than the Angel itself.

So an evening that had started out like some great adventure into the unknown ended up leaving Officer Chambers feeling quite dissatisfied, much the same as the mighty crowds dispersing felt, all of them being forced to head on home, back to normality, because everything was going to be fine, no need to worry about this Angel nonsense, the government and its military wing have got it covered.

THE RED FRAME

Meanwhile anyone able to detach themselves from the updates and messages being peddled by the media would see how, through those long hours, the official story had started to change, been changed, manipulated and watered down from the largest world altering event in all known history, to no more than a bit of a strange occurrence. The news being constantly updated with in-depth descriptions now started to offer up alternative opinions, ranging from how it was probably nothing more than a schoolboy prank gone viral, quite possibly just a trick of the light, or even an attack by the Chinese, or some other foreign power, to weaken the ties of our western culture.

There were literally hundreds of these confusing views being forced on the masses every passing minute, every one of those untruth's serving their purpose, to test the limits of a mortals attention span, while at the same time pushing the only message that mattered to the ones doing the pushing, don't worry civilians, the government is here, go about your lives, we won't let anything change.

Officer Chambers then took a call on his radio ordering him to stand down, a forceful request from a Brigadier no less, that he should leave the airport. As he did so he tried again to call Shilling and Foster while hitching a lift back to the station with another unit. The silence he got from both men should have concerned him more than it did, but that is the speciality of a planned out media suggestion, if the powers that be were telling him the situation was under control, then it must be true.

So he would obediently accept their request and return to the station, to surely find his colleagues going about their business as if there was nothing mysterious or dangerous going on, it was all just an overreaction by everybody to an odd event.

Then tilting his head to look up at the stars through the car window, he thought of how life can be a strange journey sometimes.

Meanwhile ex fireman Edward Boughton, the Coopers long time neighbour from two doors removed, was busy searching his fridge and cupboards for something suitable to feed his unexpected guest.

Over an hour ago he'd turned the radio off because he didn't feel there was anything more to learn from it. Clearly there were odd events going on in the world but he didn't need to be concerned, everything was going to be okay, they'd said so.

Edward eventually decided on a tin of spaghetti hoops which he gently warmed first in a saucepan, the dog's reaction to the smell of this offering showing him he was onto a winner. When he slopped the contents into a breakfast bowl and placed them in front of her snout the immediate scoffing made his heart sing.

Goldie the Labrador was finally behaving more normally, until now she'd been unable to settle down for anything more than ten minutes at a time in this strange house, although she would happily accept fuss when it was offered, which was nice for both of them, but especially Edward.

It had been a long and silently painful time since his wife had gone, her particular strain of cancer being both ferocious and quick in its feeding, as their time together, their duality of love in each other and shared interests, was taken away for no good reason. So it felt wonderful that after so many months alone here he was, trying again, if only in a small way, to care for another innocent soul, driven by the sole purpose of making it feel a little better.

Looking down at Goldie's deep brown eyes, Edward thought of how his life had been a strange journey sometimes.

The cell door had remained shut this evening and no one had come by to check on her. There was no usual rattle of keys to ask if she was okay, which didn't help her current mood at all, it was bad enough still being locked up after all these weeks but to be blanked was taking the piss. This rejection meant that Emma Oxtoby was now mentally struggling around her cell like a kitten in a sack.

Her claustrophobia had been under constant observation by specialists, the gentle medicinal drugs, mostly anti-anxiety or anti-depressant were administered daily and worked to a degree. That degree depending on the fact she would be able to rely on regular checks from the security staff, but without them tonight she was already beginning to feel the hug of her old nemesis, its clamping panic surrounding her chest, leaving her defenceless against its attack except for steady breathing exercises to try and create positive thoughts.

Emma's positivity however was in short supply with every day of lost liberty changing her as a person. It was a desperate position caused by her taking one brave but ultimately stupid decision. Leaving her in little doubt, as with every soul incarcerated for making one bad choice that she now not only wished, but she would give everything she had, to take it all back, even as far as never applying to be a police secretary in the first place.

Her reason for desiring this could not be taken lightly, based on the fact that she'd loved the job, every aspect of it. Inspector Cooper's attitude and mannerisms towards her were always a pleasure, her daily responsibilities more often than not were interesting and varied, therefore it was losing the position she'd held, not only in the police force but in the Inspectors eyes, that made her wish she'd never got involved in that line of work.

Emma hadn't consciously counted the weeks of her imprisonment, but it was still annoying that her so far useless lawyer had tried to correct that description, by suggesting it was only detainment for now, imprisonment may come later. It was on hearing that comment she'd justly considered James Braithwaite to be a bloody idiot of man, because he wasn't the one stuck in here, he also hadn't received the full story, but in all seriousness where would she even begin to try and tell him.

The only version he'd heard was the transcript of her initial interview with the Superintendent, the one in which she'd basically lied all the way through to protect the Inspector and the others, but now so much time had passed she wasn't even sure if she could still trust her memories of the event. The how's and whys having been rolled around in her thoughts so many times they were becoming distorted, apart from the fact she'd taken a gun out of the Inspector's drawer, loaded it, then taken it back to her flat to shoot a man in the head. Even if it were one she believed to be a world destroying monster, Mr Braithwaite would surely consider it temporary insanity if she were lucky, utter lunacy if he was forced to be more honest.

For all the toing and froing in her head the most pressing problem she faced was the not knowing what was going on. Harvey hadn't visited her even once, which she hoped was down to orders from the Superintendent rather than his own lack of concern. Yes she knew how disappointed he'd been when he'd found out, but surely he wouldn't turn his back on her completely.

In an attempt to turn all this loss and angst into a positive thought she imagined he and the rest were still out there battling the Glitch. That one day soon they would defeat it and turn up to set her free.

Then breathing deeply through her nose and slowly out of her mouth she looked out of the darkened window, thinking her life seemed such a strange journey now.

The scratching on the door was becoming annoyingly incessant; clearly he needed to go out, right now. Checking her bedside clock Rebecca Jones watched the bright red numbers change over to become 00-00.

'Seriously Biscuit you do choose your moments.' She mumbled as she threw the quilt back, the spaniel bouncing around even harder in response, its bladder full and beginning to burn.

Stepping quietly on the stairs so as not to wake her mother, Rebecca was determined to let the dog out without also waking herself up too much, but then the day's strange angelic events sprang back into her mind before she'd reached the bottom step. Mother and daughter had literally watched every bit of footage on the news reports.

Although she couldn't really fathom why the Angel's appearance hadn't shocked Rebecca very much, if anything she felt it was familiar in some way, almost as if they met it would recognise her and say Hi.

Which was no doubt just another of her crazy thoughts brought about from watching too much of something, movies, newsfeeds, social media comments...yeah that had to be the answer.

Quietly unlocking the back door to let Biscuit out she felt a sudden urge for a cigarette, which was truly odd as she hadn't smoked in years, but thankfully it passed quickly and she stepped into the garden to breath in some altogether more pleasing night air. Biscuit had made his way into the darkness to do his deeds in private, as Rebecca waited for the familiar sound of his little back legs scraping away to cover up his scent the Angel came to mind again. She didn't care what anyone else said she believed it was all true, that there was a heavenly body being held at the airport, one she hoped was here to make everything better.

'Hello Rebecca...'

The voice came from so close it could have been inside her mind.

'What the...' She replied turning to her left.

'...It's only me. I didn't mean to scare you.'

'Well you did scare me...bloody hell Jess, what are you doing?' Rebecca sternly asked her nosy neighbour who was looking over the fence.

'I couldn't sleep...you know with everything...I almost went out to the airport but the roads looked terrible. How are you and your Mum doing?'

'We're fine...ah here you are' She said to Biscuit who came scampering out of the shadows. 'Right I'll go get back into bed. Good night Jess.'

'I hope so...' Damn woman had a way of wording things, of prolonging a conversation until she was happy for it to end.

'...What does that mean?' Rebecca asked, caught in the trap again.

'Just that I hope it is a good night...not the end of the world like some are saying.'

THE RED FRAME

'Everything's going to be okay, don't be silly….just get back inside, it's cold. We can talk about it in the morning…when you pop round.'

Rebecca urgently hoped the suggestion would be enough to allow an escape. She was a bit annoyed by Jess making her feeling wide awake, then looking down she noticed Biscuit had headed indoors, probably already upstairs and making himself comfy on her warm side of the mattress.

'Right you are. Sleep well darling.' Jess said and surprisingly went back indoors.

Locking the back door Rebecca had another sudden urge to raid her mom's secret stash and grab a cigarette.

'What the hell's wrong with me?' She muttered as she made her way upstairs.

As predicted Biscuit was laid down and waiting on her side of the bed.

'Move it fuzz face…' She requested softly.

Then laying down and holding the dog in her arms she looked up at the curtains where a crack of moonlight was sneaking in, but she didn't dwell on how strange a life could be, instead she stroked Biscuit's head, closed her eyes and soon fell asleep, where she fell into dream of living a completely different one.

Across the city at 54 Marlborough Drive nothing stirred, certainly not a contentedly stoned Scott Hutchinson, who at this exact moment wasn't thinking about anything remotely sensible.

An oppressive cloud hung over the city of Edinburgh this night, hanging heavily over the house where the Demon had first made its appearance, then stretching outwards to cover all the others that contained a million snoring dreams. A hush taking over from the earlier pandemonium, where every soul whether they were connected to the events that started it all or not, would sleep with an unconscious prayer that tomorrow could be the greatest of days. Perhaps the one where the sun would rise and illuminate the darkest corners of their hearts, scorch away mistakes and fragilities to give them what they desired, the chance to start again.

But as with the sage advice repeated throughout the centuries, handed down in many a religious text or fairy tale, souls should always be careful of what they wish for.

74

The entity was finding its feet, quite literally, as the glowing orb finished the manipulation of its form, settling into the human shape the Glitch had requested. This incredible being, the only one whose actions would grant those human wishes or destroy them all completely, was ready to take its first steps.

As the Glitch discovered, walking within a human vessel had been remarkably easy, it was how they naturally travelled and had been more like hitching a lift. But working out how to move what was essentially a body made of light had its difficulties and was taking some time to master.

Perfecting its movement was critical for the Glitch. It had no idea how long it would have this opportunity to retain some control before its consciousness disappeared forever. It clearly didn't want to enter the room to face the Angel and its mortal allies shuffling and stumbling. Slowly but surely, while calling on the knowledge gained from the Angel's book, the imagined muscle memories of Snake and Jay, some progress was made. Based on calculations towards making an angled progression while maintaining a comfortable looking walking gait soon became a little easier to its nature. Although by far the strangest issue to overcome was the destabilising fact that this body held no weight, there was no impact on the ground as it placed its feet, nothing to feel as it lifted one in front of the other, as it was for all intents and purposes lighter than air.

The Glitch also knew that when it got to the meeting room basic communication would also be a problem as it bore no features upon its frame. In this reality it was no more than the outline of a human, yet one that carried infinite space within it, so the merest touch from its hand would consume their skin and bone, crushing their atoms into dust.

This was to be a concluding, personalised, and revengeful attack before consumption of this broken universe began. That was its main purpose after all; this trip to kill those stragglers no more than a side mission, but when they were dead, slaughtered in front of each other, it would finally be satisfied. The Glitch could give itself up completely and allow its apocalyptic nature to take its course.

Finally finding a confident stride it moved its head to face upwards, thinking of how wonderful this universe could be sometimes.

75

The more anyone in the meeting room thought about the harsh judgment being handed down to Alex, using Harvey's method of actions beating the shit out of words, the more it rang true. When thinking back they all slowly realised that at no point had he shown any genuine concern for the people now stood at his side. He'd manipulated, cajoled, even begged for them to help him. So the road they'd travelled, initially believing it to be one they shared, the route by which they had all reached this terrible destination clearly only ever ran one way, in the self-regarding direction the one armed man had chosen.

'Is it true Alex?' Juliet called over the table. 'That you never gave a shit about any of us?'

'Tell us it isn't.' Flo's remark sounded more of a stab than an honest request.

'Answer the question!' Harvey demanded as Alex slunk away to the furthest corner of the room. 'Has all of this been nothing more than a suicide mission for you…?'

When Alex didn't respond, instead turning his back on the group as if in shame, Harvey marched towards him. With every step he took his anger grew as another memory appeared, one on top of the other, of how he'd trusted this man's story, risked his life, his sanity and his career to help him. Overriding thoughts caused emotions that refused to settle until he reached out to grab Alex's shoulder. As his fingers pulled the man round to face them all, a single feeling rose to the surface and it was the one he would use to get his message across, because the feeling was shame, that horrible mongrel of a sentiment, made up of disappointment in one's self and the embarrassment at being played for a fool.

Grabbing Alex by the throat he pushed him back against the wall. '…I ought to knock the living shit out of you…look at them…!'

With the anger he felt unsuppressed he saw no reason to hold back. Not only was Alex unapologetic for the insult he'd thrown at his wife he was walking away and turning his back. He twisted Alex's head to the side so he could see the group watching on. 'None of those people asked for this!'

'I know…' Alex replied. '…I couldn't have done any of this by myself!'

The timing of that response was distinctly unfortunate for the younger man when it answered a question Harvey was only thinking, causing the Inspector to reach his boiling point, when he'd suddenly had the thought that what if Alex and the Angel were working together in some way. It was this simple misunderstanding that lead directly to the unprofessionalism that followed, as Harvey threw a sharp uppercut up into Alex's midriff, knocking the air clean out of him, his knees buckling as he fell to the floor, gasping at air he couldn't inhale. The Inspector tried to grab him back up for another blow only to find his arm being pulled back.

'For god's sake what are you doing...leave him alone!' Juliet screamed as she yanked the Inspector away from the stricken Alex. 'How is that going to help anything?'

Harvey was breathing heavily as Flo joined and tried to drag him away. 'It helped me...' He said. '...and maybe it will help him think a little harder about what he's done!

Juliet sat Alex back up against the wall to help with his breathing. It had been a hell of a body blow in every sense, as apart from losing his breath he'd lost Harvey as a trusted ally, which was terrible timing as his connection with the Glitch had abruptly come back into range. Alex could sense it moving and knew it had another form, Jay's body having been heartlessly discarded somewhere, but all he could do to alert the others to its presence was wave one arm.

'It's all going to be okay Alex...try and keep still and breath steadily...' Juliet requested, but those requests weren't so easy to follow when in his mind's eye he could feel the beast drawing closer, alerting him to the fact it was coming to take care of unfinished business, because he and these people had stood in its way, challenged it, sworn to kill it and there was no chance it would let that lie.

As Alex finally managed to take in a few tiny gulps of air on his way to what could be a short lived recovery, he became aware that something was very different about this link to the Glitch. Whereas before he'd been able to see clearly through its eyes, this time there was nothing but twinkling stars, a beautifully detailed night sky on display, so deep and rich in colour and vitality it was almost taking away the breath he was so desperate to keep.

He grabbed Juliet's arm tight to his chest to help keep a grip on reality, trying to figure out who or what the Glitch had become, wanting to be ready for when it made its appearance. Then with some colossal effort he forced out the words on a single gasp. '...It's...coming...'

Rhi's first and natural response was to head towards Sammy but Flo turned sharply to ward her off. 'No Rhian, take a position near him but keep separated.'

THE RED FRAME

Flo then let her slightly calmer husband go and ordered. 'Everyone spread out around the room...lets force it into making a choice then...it's all we've got.'

They took up their random positions within the room, the size of it causing them to be at least ten feet apart, their separation feeling larger still as they glanced around at each other and waited. Harvey had Flo to his left, then Rhian, then Sammy who had got back to his feet and appeared to be back in control with the Angel having disappeared back into his mind, seemingly at the first sign of trouble. To the boy's left stood Juliet and then Alex who was upright but leaning back against the white wall, his breathing almost back to normal.

'That hurt a lot Harvey.'

'Just answer me a question then be quiet.' The Inspector snapped back.

'Go on?'

'Do you want to live?'

Alex glanced over at Juliet and then back to Harvey. 'Yes...more than anything I want to put us all back together where we should be, kill the Glitch, kill the Angel and get us out of here.'

The look on Harvey's face was serious still but hinting at apologetic. 'And do you have any idea on how to do that?'

'None at all...' Alex smiled sadly and looked over at Sammy. '...But that boy is important. He's here for a reason.'

Harvey couldn't help it as he became annoyed with the one armed man again. 'Aren't you capable of giving a straight answer to a question?'

'I'm trying my best.'

Harvey looked at his wife and then the others in the room, all stood around waiting for the end, their helplessness piled on top of his own. It was becoming too much and his thoughts were beginning to crack. Maybe the Angel had been right when it asked him if this was really what he wanted, to return to this room and witness this fate, when he could have let the madness consume him and avoid this pain.

'Are you okay Sammy?' Rhi whispered over to her son who glanced back nervously but didn't speak.

'How close is it now?' Juliet asked Alex.

'It's impossible to tell...feels like it's moving in a different world to us...one foot there and one foot here.'

'More bloody riddles...!' Harvey growled. '...I think I get it now, why you didn't want me to bring my gun...!'

'Keep it together Harvey. You got your punch in you should be happy.' Alex growled back.

'Boy's please stop it.' said Flo before looking over at the boy. '...Answer your mother Sammy. She only wants to know that you're...'

'Just stop ordering everyone about Florence...!' The voice of the Angel spoke from the boy's mouth. '...There's no need to try and prove your worth. Everyone already accepts you're the mother hen...well done.' Then the boy turned his head to the left. 'Your son is alive and well Rhian...for now.'

Juliet was the first to notice the lack of concern or fear in the Angels voice. 'You don't sound very worried Metatron...do you know something we don't?'

'I know many things that you never will Nurse. I will make a suggestion and seeing as you are the closest to the switch...turn off the lights.'

'It will be pitch-black in here!' Flo pointed out in keeping with the mother hen title bestowed upon her.

'The darkness will be the least of your worries.' The Angel responded. 'It is standing right outside that door now, working out what it should do... so if you wish to help yourselves then turn off the lights.'

Juliet reached across and pressed the switch, the room and the other faces instantly plunged into a black void as the whole terrifying situation abruptly altered. Where before there had been a team of souls to focus on, a group fear with which to share the load, it was now uniquely singular as personal dreads became irrational and so much worse.

As their eyes adjusted to the darkness they were all drawn to the door, because at its base a golden line appeared, showing that whatever was out there shone brightly.

'Now is the time where I shall tell you what I know.' The Angels voice cutting through the tension. 'Alex was correct when he suggested how it was moving in two worlds, it is sharing two forms, the old and the new combined. The Glitch you knew now temporarily possesses the actuality it has evolved into, controlling the walking cataclysm as if it were still in a human body, because that is all it knows how to do. This is an unexpected situation but one which could prove to be helpful in giving us more time and if it will allow me the opportunity, I will try and speak with it...'

'And if it doesn't allow you that opportunity?' Harvey's voice asked from nowhere specific.

'Then you won't have to worry about anything...ever again.'

'If I can help I will.' Alex's disembodied speech. 'I'm connected with it.'

'Of course you are. You helped create it...' The Angel responded. '...but I doubt very much it would want to speak with a mortal, not anymore, it is a little beyond your reasoning now.'

'Is that right Metatron?' Alex called back from the darkness. 'I seem to remember you saying similar things back in the white world. Doubting me, keeping me off balance, trying to place me at level where you wanted me. Just so you know it's a little too late for any more bullshit now, so like I said...if I can help...I will.'

The conversation stopped there as the thin line of gold under the door began to grow broader. It took a few seconds for everyone to work out what was happening, to see how the light was squeezing itself under the gap, slowly pouring through like lava to pool on the inside, then began to slide upwards. Its light illuminating a few feet into the room before the shimmering mass began to take shape.

Within a few seconds the human form rose up before them to stand around six and a half feet tall, in outline at least, the inside of it being a beautiful pulsating star cluster that Alex had seen before, but it made no sound or movement now it was here.

Along with its spellbinding presence came an insane urge that started to grow within them all, this glowing sentinel seeming to contact them individually in some strangely persuasive way, calling to them, requesting they walk towards it...for it was waiting.

Each of them, too scared to speak while alone in the dark, believed it was only calling to them and they were fighting the urge to move forward but this feeling seemed to connect with their chests like a fishhook in its prey, winding them in.

Flo was already turning red in the cheeks as she fought the pull, her colour being increased by a feeling of stupidity, realising her little plan to confuse the thing had failed miserably. It didn't have to choose one of them when it could have them all without moving an inch, no need for it to be concerned by the numbers surrounding it, as Flo realised there was no way of understanding how to survive in its world.

Then she felt her feet beginning to move, inching forward towards its opening arms. There was no way of knowing if anyone else was feeling the same thing, doing the same thing, until the room began to glow brighter still, a silvery light creeping outwards from the far wall to her left, from the other side of Rhian who was also clearly shuffling forward, trying to resist.

76

The Angel was lighting up the room completely with its heavenly light; no doubt the reason why it had wanted to turn the lights out, to ensure its magnificence was multiplied to the maximum effect. Its outstretched wings were curved against the corners of the room giving the impression they were also open to anyone who wished to walk towards them. Nobody did of course but its stunning appearance seemed to hold some interest for the glowing Glitch stood by the door, as the strength of its pull fell away, leaving the mortals to regain some control of their stances.

From such a height and with its head touching the ceiling, Metatron looked down over the room to view the faces looking its way. It really had no idea if it could speak with the Glitch, or even how, so instead held its lofty perch hoping to force it into a move.

It was Rhian who took her eyes off the Angel's face first, following its form downwards she found there were no feet to be seen, as it was clearly still connected to her Sammy. Exactly what that could mean if things went badly was something she couldn't bear to think about, so instead she chose to look up at the battle lines drawn in the meeting room, ha-ha! The meeting room of course, she thought.

Juliet glanced across at Alex to see what affect this scene could be having on him. He simply looked back at her, his face utterly emotionless before returning his gaze to the Glitch and speaking out loud.

'Hey Glitch...that's a lovely new suit you've got there.'

The glowing apparition slowly turned its head away from the Angel and towards the one armed man.

'I take it that's your Sunday best...suppose you gotta be looking good for the end of the universe.'

Alex was goading the Glitch for no other reason apart than he could. His natural personality coming through because he was the man who didn't fear death, he flew far above such pointless concerns, hell we're all going to die one day he reckoned. What he didn't reckon on however was the Glitch raising its right arm and the feeling of his own body floating into the air.

Juliet shouted out first on seeing Alex being lifted up and then drawn helplessly towards the creature. Its arm slowly coming back towards its body, across its chest and with each movement the struggling Alex came closer. With tears in her eyes Juliet looked up at the Angel for help, for mercy, for fucking anything at all.

THE RED FRAME

At the same time Metatron was trying to communicate with the Glitch, but a deathly silence was the only reward for its efforts, as it too was forced to watch on. It didn't help that it couldn't physically move itself, both of its angelic feet were still firmly planted in Sammy's chest, stuck there because that was the only way it could appear in this world.

Flo threw her own broken rules out of the window and rushed over to stand at Harvey's side. Rhian didn't know what else to do but look at her little boy who appeared to be in a peaceful sleep, except for the figure of an Angel floating out of him.

Juliet rushed forward to try and grab onto Alex's outstretched hand but stopped dead before she was only halfway. The Glitch that had been trying to force her body forwards only minutes ago, now able to hold her back with the same amount of ease, but it couldn't hold back her scream.

Even without eyes or facial features the Glitch seemed to be staring straight at Alex, who was floating and slowly spinning in position, only a foot away from the shining pulsating chest of the monster, at which point it took one step forward and closed the gap between them, then began to consume the man from the feet first.

'Arghhhh...' Alex wailed as the hideous sensations of being eaten alive began to tear through his body.

'Leave him be!' The Angel roared with such ferocity, causing the others to wince and cover their ears.

All the others except Juliet who was looking at Alex's face which was turned towards her and silently pleading, profuse rivulets of sweat were appearing over his forehead, his eyes being forced abnormally wide with fear, imploring for help as his knees disappeared into the Glitch, into the clusters of stars.

He deliberately didn't look down at his disappearing body; the pain was enough to endure without that, instead his eyes were on Juliet, watching her face crumble at the sight of his slow death.

The sensations he experienced in his final moments were a thousand tiny burning teeth chewing away at his flesh and bone, crumbling his body to dust in their act of feeding, taking him agonisingly to the place he should have gone a long time ago, the death he'd avoided back in Dalmeny Street.

In the end, turning his face away from the woman he loved, but never told, he looked straight ahead toward the furnace taking him in, to see the head of the Glitch beginning to glow brighter still with a golden red effervescence, as if the whole of the sun itself resided in there, while those miniscule invisible teeth points effortlessly destroyed every piece of flesh that touched them. It was up to his chest now, shredding ever closer to his heart, the same heart which he accepted he'd never used properly. Raising his only arm up and away from the Glitch, he held it outwards in one last chance of some saviour grabbing it, but again no one did so. Not the last time and not this time.

His screaming stopped just short of his mouth coming into contact with the void. So much for Harvey describing him as the man unafraid of death, Alex had shrieked through the whole agonising business, but in those last few seconds he refused to do it anymore...not anymore.

77

The room fell into a stunned silence except for the muffled sobs of Juliet. Rhian held her close, trying to ease her sorrow, there were no words to help or explain away what they had witnessed. Alex was gone, swallowed by that entity at the door, being coldly removed from their world with scant regard and no great fanfare, the beast's only display of taking any pleasure in its actions the brightening of its colours which were already beginning to dim again. This left no one in any doubt it was ready for more as the stories they had been told were not only true, but were far beyond their imaginings. If this was what the Glitch was capable of, this actually was the end of the world and it was unstoppable.

In Harvey's arms Flo felt fragile and spiritless. Perhaps they were just his own feelings, a projection of helpless insignificance passing through his body and into hers. In the same way a captured piece of prey would give up the fight, like a gazelle when the whole pride bore down on her, or perhaps a web caught fly watching a massive spider draw close.

The word inevitability, in reference to the Glitch, had been one bandied around by Alex and the Angel since the beginning, only now Harvey fully understanding its true meaning. Just how this glowing humanoid form would kill them all then move outwards to complete the rest of its singular purpose. This begrudging acceptance having turned into a concrete reality in his heart, since having witnessed the horrible consumption of Alex, the only man whom he'd believed could stop this nightmare was dead.

Pulling his true love closer to his chest he hoped the beast would take him next or at least the two of them together, because he wouldn't be able to handle the pain if he were forced to watch her go, see his Florence screaming to be released from its grip. Quickly he blocked that thought from his mind and looked over at the Glitch glowing in splendour, proud of its actions. It was nothing more than a development of the bastard son of an Angel's desire for revenge, meaning at the very least Harvey knew who to blame now, as he turned slowly and looked up to see Metatron gazing down upon him.

'You did this...all of it...well done, you got your revenge. I hope you're happy...you absolute fucking bastard!'

The Inspector swore so harshly because it was all he had left, he had no way of grabbing the Angel's face and beating it to a pulp so profanities would have to do as his display of fury.

'Alex is dead, you did nothing to stop it and we are all going to follow him, like we have always followed him, because he wanted to put things right...to sort out the fucking mess that you created!'

Tears began to roll down his cheeks before stopping at his jawline, collecting for a second at that point before a few began falling into Flo's hair, his wife's face still immovable from his beating chest.

'Don't you see that every single person who has died at its hands... were all in their little ways trying to help you...and because of that, and before this ends, I'd like to inform you Metatron that without a shadow of a doubt it proves one unquestionable fact...that we are better than you. Mortals beat Angels in every single capacity of existence...and nothing will change my mind...not unless you can do something to prove me wrong!'

The Angels eyes stared down hard and deep into its accuser's face, the Inspector's challenge harshly laid down; if those cruel words were how it would be remembered then what did its own life really matter anymore? Metatron looked to either side at its wings pressed against the angles of the wall, realising it was quite literally and metaphorically backed into a corner, but it didn't have to die this way.

This Angel was unable to argue with Inspector Cooper's condemnation, the Glitch was also correct in believing itself invincible, but there was always the final question to be asked, the one it had tested Alex with so many times, the one that always gave a true answer...why? But this time the why was stood in that doorway, luminescent and ready to feed again already, starting to lift its arm to take away another soul. Why did it have a physical presence in this place enabling it to act upon its cravings? They were both formed from the same stuff of life and for crying out loud in God's name this regretful Angel had given it life, so why was this battlefield so one sided?

Its eyes fell onto the boy lying peacefully on the ground, seeing the only chance it would have to make a difference, a gamble to prove to the Inspector that if nothing else could change his mind...then at least it had died trying.

Fresh screams suddenly filled the room as Juliet and Rhian were lifted from the ground together, still embraced in the consoling hug they'd shared at the loss of Alex, but now being inexorably drawn towards the Glitch. Their entwined bodies being taken up into the air and manoeuvred around to be shaped for the perfect fit, its shining arm already moving towards its chest, their bodies following its command utterly, helpless to resist.

'Harvey...!' Rhian cried out.

The women's feet were now pointing towards the sparkling abyss and the distance to the Glitch was closing. The Inspector felt as if he were set in stone, unable to move or help, knowing that after this it would be his and Flo's deadly turn. He looked across at the Angel to find it had moved. Still floating above the boy it was bent over seemingly busy trying to achieve something far more important than watching those two women die. You selfish fucking coward, Harvey thought as Flo lifted her head up and looked into his eyes.

'Why is this happening Harvey...why can't we stop it...' She sobbed with an inconsolable passion, a kind he had never seen before, not from his Flo. She was the very foundation upon which he'd existed and now even that was crumbling in his arms.

Rhian and Juliet were only inches from the Glitch, its arm held tight across its torso, hugging each other ever tighter as their feet approached that bottomless surface. For the helpless victims about to be fed into it the view from up close was as beautiful as it was horrendous, the creatures depths unfathomable, its colours too rich with only seconds remaining.

The Angel Metatron had studied the problem closely while summoning the courage to go through with the idea, in the end deciding that to die by its own hand would be better than giving into the Glitch, even thinking that Alex had a point with his unnatural tendency towards suicide, sometimes it can seem the only answer.

Reaching both hands down it grabbed the white tendril connecting him to the boy. It had no way of knowing if such an action would be suicidal but it was about to find out as with it tore the wisp away with all its might, severing the umbilical cord which allowed it to be connected to this world. Detaching its life line it caused the boy's chest to fly upwards, a reaction to this sudden loss of connection, Sammy taking in a huge inhalation of air as his brown eyes opened. The sight that met them was almost beyond his comprehension. It could only be described by the ten year old's thoughts.

The nice Inspector was on the other side of the room crying with Aunty Flo. To his left his Mom and Juliet were floating horizontally in the air, like a magicians trick, then suddenly they both fell to the floor with a horrible thump and behind them he saw a glowing monster, it seemed to be looking straight at him, then he heard something to his other side and turned to look.

78

Both of the women scrambled away from the glowing silhouette that loomed above them, it's previously ultra-bright colours having disappeared after dropping them unceremoniously to the ground. That five foot fall a guarantee of bruises but thankfully nothing was feeling broken, as they reached Harvey and Flo in the gloom who greeted them with relief and open arms.

Rhian began to frantically look around for Sammy, spotting him sitting on the other side of the room some twenty feet away, dimly lit by the brightness of the Glitch, giving her a confused smile and a little wave from just behind a strange figure that was climbing to its feet.

These very feet were ones this figure hadn't seen for a considerable time, as rarely had they been evident in the white world between the mist and the length of its flowing robe. Afterwards being totally hidden inside the boys chest for anchorage but now not only were they visible, they were standing on solid ground.

Metatron realise it had broken free of its conceptual existence and this feeling was entirely different. It could experience itself breathing which was most strange, like a long forgotten memory being replayed; there was the sound of its heart beating and the brush of air touching its skin. These sensations were remarkable as even its eyes, which it had always trusted, perceived the world in a new way. Looking down at its hands it saw they were no longer as perfect as before, that alabaster smoothness replaced with wrinkles and blemishes, some dark tufts of hair coming through in places. This was an altogether more human look with the greying tinge to its robe extenuating that further.

Somewhat perturbed by this sudden change of appearance Metatron unfurled its wings to check their condition.

But the group watching on open mouthed only saw a rather scruffy looking man in rags flex his wingless shoulder blades.

'What the hell have you done?' Harvey asked, finding he could fight back the tears now to regain some composure. Witnessing an Angel regress into human form was evidently capable of causing such an affect.

It was Juliet who remembered his name first from the nightmares and dream book of Alex. '...Enoch?' She asked warily from her position at Harvey and Flo's feet and while still holding tightly onto Rhian's arm.

'No...' The stranger replied. '...although clearly this is my long forgotten form...' There was a deep apprehension in the man's voice as he turned to face the group.

They all noticed his formerly luxuriant golden tresses now fell on his forehead as wispy grey strands, over an unkempt beard that covered most of his face, a sharp nose under his eyes which were still noticeably green. The look he gave the group could be only described as confused, giving any sudden hope that this transmogrification could somehow be useful to their problem no strength at all, if anything his appearance as anything but Angelic only added to their troubles.

'I was useless while attached to the boy...this is the real me...!'

With all eyes on the man no one noticed the Glitch's silent progression towards them, when Rhi finally did spot it she found she had no more screams left to give, so instead tapped her hand on Harvey's leg.

'Jesus Christ!' Harvey responded on seeing the star lit human shape only four feet away. It seemed even larger now, eight feet tall perhaps and there was nowhere to run with their backs against the white wall, as the truest layer of inevitability came home to roost. But surprisingly no attack came, no one was lifted or grabbed by its deathly grip, as instead it turned to face the bearded man and spoke with a voice Harvey recognised. The Glitches words clearly coming from somewhere deep within those strange constellations, floating throughout its frame.

'Metatron...what is this?'

'So you can speak.' The ex-Angel replied. 'I thought we had lost you all together.'

'I have no requirement to speak with Angels or mortals but this...this I need to understand.'

Metatron was trying to hide his fear and relief at hearing the Glitch speak, knowing with direct communication there was still a tiny chance of survival, so taking a breath it attempted to stand tall.

'Of course you don't like surprises do you, but I took the only action left to me, separated myself from the boy in a last ditch attempt to make contact with you. Who knew what would happen...I certainly didn't but it worked. I'm here to speak with my revenge fully bloomed, my blood come to life...and you are a without doubt a quite magnificent creation.'

'That magnificent creation killed Alex and it's going to kill us all!' Juliet shouted, moving forward thoughtlessly towards the man until Flo grasped her arm and pulled her back.

'I really don't think that's helpful' Flo whispered through the side of her mouth, clearly comprehending more than the nurse that this discourse between the man and the Glitch could be their only chance of escape.

The scruffy looking Metatron glanced over to her with a narrow eyed look that supported her view, before its full attention turned back to the Glitch.

'I believe we should continue this talk in private...' he suggested. '...that way I can tell you anything you need to know...after which there would no more surprises.'

'I'm busy...I have a job to do' The Glitch responded coldly.

'And no one understands that better than me...so afterwards you can continue with your task. It's an undeniable truth that I cannot stop what you are doing here, but surely a little conversation never hurt anyone... Come talk with me...in private.'

After a significant pause the Glitch's voice came again. 'So where would you suggest?'

'I think you know where...' Metatron offered '...No man's land!'

79

The Glitch had understood its meaning perfectly with Metatron back in its beautiful form of an Angel, sitting at the white table in the white world, the Glitch stood across from it in that shimmering humanoid shape. This was no way to conduct their affairs so the Angel suggested the shape should perhaps take on a more appealing guise, one with actual features that would be more helpful in understanding one another.

The Glitch nodded its agreement before taking on an instantly recognisable body.

'Is this better...?' The words came from the mouth of Alex Webb.

Only with a great effort did the Angel hide its shock at that choice, but soon accepted the perfect symmetry of it all, obviously this was how it would end, just as it began.

'Yes, that's much better. Take a seat.'

Alex sat down using the same movements he had done a thousand times before, only on this auspicious occasion the stakes were raised because this two armed man was no longer a mortal, this image was the still sum of its parts, the destroyer of worlds, the end of the universe, the Death Machine.

'What will happen to those trapped at the facility while we talk?' Alex's mouth asked.

'The same rule as always. In this place we are outside of time so none shall pass for them. When we are done you return and finish your work.'

'Excellent...so what exactly do you wish to talk about Metatron?'

The Angel took on a half-smile as it asked the question, because looking at Alex as it spoke made this feel way beyond simple déjà vu.

'I would like to know...if you understand why you are here.'

'Of course I do...you summoned me.' Alex replied confidently.

'By accident...' The Angel offered as a counter argument but the Glitch was ready for it.

'...There are no such things in your heavenly world. No accidents, no mistakes, merely the natural progression of your revenging thought giving expected results, ones that although you hope to deny, then will still come to pass. You placed me in the book and every event that has happened since is the direct and obvious reaction to that insidious action.

The Angel shuffled its wings, which was a wonderful feeling having been bereft of them earlier, before playing the only card it held against the Glitch's logic.

'It was Alex passing through the portal I made that awakened you and there was nothing obvious or expected about that...so I would argue you used that contact and fashioned yourself, that you were not summoned in any fashion by me, nor by this universe, or the Life Machine that creates it. I rest my case.'

Alex's eyes studied the Angel closely, while inside the Glitch's mind a million thoughts sprang to attention but none of them could dispel the theory, the one correctly stating that it had not been directly summoned.

'So evidently mistakes can be made in this world...' The Angel said and sat back in a more relaxed pose. '...with you being the greatest of them all. When you saw an opportunity you seized it, never questioning the reasoning. Jumping the gun springs to mind

Alex's body snapped up to attention 'How could I even do such a thing? You know what I am, my only purpose is to destroy the old and damaged so it may be replaced with the new, there is nothing more to me than that. Once I am summoned, by accident or not, the cycle of my actions must be completed. I cannot stop it any more than you can. Their world will burn or flood, be poisoned or frozen, one or all of those things will happen as it has done forever. Then with that life extinguished and this world gone I shall as always spread throughout the universe and clean up the chaos that is left. Only this time it will be over so quickly because of what I am, this time my arrangement is incredibly different, far greater than I've been before and I cannot fight my nature...there is no changing what I am.'

Metatron saw its chance. 'That's my whole point because this time, for the first time in your apocalyptic existence, you could have changed what you are. Being born with an actual consciousness, you have been able to think, to feel, to make decisions, but you never considered that what you were doing could be a mistake. Not once looking over your shoulder to see the carnage you were leaving in your wake.'

The Glitch slammed Alex's hand on the desk to grab the Angel's attention. 'Is this all you wanted to talk about, to apportion blame in some vain attempt at teaching me a lesson, a moral high ground that you now surprisingly hold so dear. How touching and confusing! After all your initial intentions were similar to mine, though in your case it was to continue the pitiful war you believed still existed, the one between Angels and Mortals, by utilising your Demon. But in the end you only wished to end their race as do I, but to me it is a simple task which I shall do regardless when I return. Quite seriously Metatron I fail to see your point, when what I will achieve is exactly the same result you sought in the first place. Unless I am seriously mistaken in what your intentions were back then, I must assume you have changed your opinion. Is that it Angel, have you gone soft on your enemy...are you an all loving and forgiving celestial host all of a sudden?'

The Angel rather bravely raised his voice back at the Glitch. 'My intentions are my own, the decisions that I make can always be unmade and that is what I'm trying to teach you.'

'Teach me?' Alex laughed with the passion of a Glitch greatly amused. 'I knew when you asked me to come here this would be a fool's errand, but out of respect I granted you the opportunity to speak and in all honesty, as I have no need to lie to you, there was a certain curiosity in what you could tell me. This talk was an utterly selfish act on my behalf to discover if there were any more secrets left to be told, any loopholes missed before I set about my task of removing this universe from existence, but I see now you have anything new to offer me.'

Metatron felt it was losing its grip on this meeting. The Glitch wasn't picking up on what it was trying to offer, so in the end the Angel just asked it out right. 'We are on the same team, you said as much, so let's do this together. I have other skills with which to help.'

'Your skills are familiar to me as I have completed the many tests you helped to set up, the hurdles you placed in my way to try and catch me out as I grew. I know all about the picture you gave to Harvey, your sudden appearance in his house, the advice you passed on to them in hope they could finish me before we reached this point. None of you have ever learned the starkest of lessons, always being so preoccupied with trying to trip me up, yet here I am ready and stronger than ever to finish my task. So Metatron you must ask yourself a question about your failure to do so, why...?' The Glitch made Alex laugh out loud once more and clap his hands with glee. '...Ask me that?'

A prickly shiver ran up the Angels spine as a cold wave spread through its wings to the very tips. The Glitch was gloating from this position of ascendency, winning this meeting in every conceivable way, dominating the Angel again and leaving it with no other choice but to ask what it requested.

'Very well...why...why haven't I been able to stop you?'

'Thank you...' Alex's tone was utterly sarcastic. '...First of all understand this, that during every step of my progression I have always known exactly where you were, what plans you were making for me. For instance I knew you were trying to hide when I first appeared, frightened at the very sight of me, trying to work me out. I saw your possession of the old lady's soul after I discarded her, then the taking over of the young boy, which, even to me, came across as a cruel and heartless decision. We should never use the young in espionage or warfare...'

Alex's body then stood up and began to walk around the space, in very much the same way he used to when attempting to challenge the Angels authority, but this was an altogether different situation and the sound of its giggling as it spoke was utterly repulsive.

'So you know everything do you, I suppose you planned to let Snake get shot in the head then?' The Angel hoped by pointing that fact out it may unsettle the beast a little, but in truth it felt like throwing a pillow against a wall.

'Oh yes, dear Emma, let's never forget the woman who found the only chink in my armour. That was a great surprise at the time, rather ironically it happened at the optimum moment when perhaps I could have been swayed, chosen to truly question why I was really here, even be turned away from this path of destruction. But surely even you can see everything happens for a reason, perhaps a power even higher than me made her pull that trigger, to lead me away from any futile hopes of love and trust. In the end it could be said that poor misguided girl only ended up blowing everyone's chances out of the water...including yours.'

The Angel looked down at the table knowing precisely what the Glitch meant with those last two words, meaning it was more than ready to end the conversation right now in both body and mind, witnessing in action what every opponent had already discovered, how the Glitch was always one step ahead, probably more, forever sprinting off into the distance as the chasing pack floundered. It truly stood head and shoulders above as the most perfect mechanism in the Life Machine.

'Okay you have told me why...now please tell me how...how you knew my every move...?'

'Huh yes I almost forget about that, of course you need me to tell you how. There's no way your small imagination could work that out by itself. Honestly I would have to say you have been spending way too much time with those mortals...it's dulled you down to their level.'

'Just tell me...' The Angel demanded feeling sick of these games.

But the Glitch had one last trick up its sleeve, or to be more accurate inside the shirt that Alex wore, as it pulled out the book, those red leather covers glistening in the light of this world once more as it was returned to the table.

THE RED FRAME

The Angels heart nearly stopped on seeing it again.

'That is how I knew...open it...show me the page.' The Glitch requested.

Once more placing its perfect angelic hands on the cover, a forgotten joy returned, it flicked through the blank pages until it reached the one it had wished upon, gazing down at the faded spot surrounded by a square. At that moment the Angel was finally able to heighten its thinking again, predicting exactly what the Glitch was going to say, damn it would feel good to burst its little bubble of gloating.

'Of course...' Metatron began '...I can see exactly what happened now.'

'Really...?' The Glitch enquired, leaning over the Angels shoulder.

'...We are made from the same stuff aren't we? My blood is your blood, a connection made long ago. The answer was always there but I ignored it as nothing more than a descriptive phrase, never as an actual lineal line. Well played in keeping it from me all this time.'

'Why thank you but it was really no trouble at all...' The Glitch smile as it loomed over the Angel. '...Now I have one last question to ask of my only true blood relative, as I think it would be remiss and disrespectful to not do so...how would you like to die?'

The Angel didn't need to think too long for an answer. 'That is an easy one, right here sitting at this table, looking at the book I cannot read and alone in the white world. It is all I have ever done and therefore I deserve no more.'

'Oh come now mighty Angel Metatron, are you really going to be playing the sympathy card. Look where we are for crying out loud, in this realm of boundless possibilities where any scenarios can be imagined and created, so don't go turning all defeatist on me at the end. This has been a long and drawn out battle for us both, one in which many have died at our hands, so let us at least honour them by going out with a bang!'

'No thank you Glitch, as you have gleefully informed me you are always one step ahead, therefore I am quite sure this is just another one of those moments where you already have something planned regardless of my wishes...so for me game playing is over. Do what you will before you return to the facility, make those humans who opposed you suffer, then swallow up everything and clean up the chaotic mess as you call it. But before you do I would like to make thing clear...I pity you.'

The Glitch looked out from behind Alex's eyes. Standing directly behind the Angel it could simply break its neck and be done with it, but that old devil called curiosity still reigned in its mind.

'And why would you pity me? Better still let us turn this into a game. If your answer has any worth then I shall kill you as you wish...if not then we will do it my way with great pain and suffering...so choose your words carefully for they will be your last.'

Looking down at the exposed page of the book the Angel yearned for what would be lost, as it thought upon the millennia it had spent gently opening and closing that cover, allowing it to collect all the knowledge of this universe and store it away. Ironically it appeared that even now both book and Angel were performing their god given duties until the death. So soon all of those moments would be shown to be utterly pointless, with no one left to ever remember what had gone on in this white world, so what had been the point of it all?

Is this really how it worked, the proof of how cold and unforgiving the Life Machine was at its very core, simply spewing out pointless lives and dreams only to suck it all back up for regurgitation? If that were the only way of life then the Angel would be more than happy to get off the ride, thinking it better to not exist at all than remain on this meaningless carousel, where all the surrounding lights and sounds were no more than a frivolous distraction before the great nothingness at either end.

The Glitch placed Alex's hand on the top of the Angels head, its fingers splayed out as if ready to pull it upwards and straight off its shoulders.

'I appreciate why you would want to take some time to consider your words...I did ask you to after all...but please do not push my respect. Tell me why you feel the need to pity me.'

It then moved those fingers in a crawling fashion, spiderlike across its victims golden hair which unsettling as it felt, allowed the Angel a minute more to think.

Was there anything Metatron had missed along the way? Anything that could change the outcome, if there wasn't then truly the most abrupt of all ends approached, as this world and every other would soon fall hopelessly under the hungry wheels of this monster, a creature far too powerful with its intent to consume them all without second thought.

Surely this atrocious nightmare awakened by an Angel had to have a weakness and that would be the key to any possible answer. Then with one simple thought and lightning speed Metatron grabbed up the book and tore out the blood stained page...maybe, just maybe.

'Arggggghhh...! The Glitch screamed as it took its hand away from the Angels head.

Metatron stood up holding the torn leaf in its hand to face the form of Alex, only to find the man smiling broadly at the joke it had pulled off.

'Oh now Angel really...you thought...that's too funny...' Its words were interspersed with hearty laughter. '...Because you put me in there you thought...ha-ha-ha...that you could just pull me out...and then what hmm...I'd disappear in a puff of smoke...? That is quite the funniest thing I have witnessed in my short life.' Gradually it calmed itself down but the amusement was far from over. 'Wow that was a good one...try something else, this is fun. Come on I'll give you some free hits...but at the same time you have to tell me about the reason for your pity...' Alex put his arms down behind his back and offered up his jaw. '...Hit me!'

Deep inside the Angel knew striking that undefended face would yield no satisfactory results, but what the hell, it might as well enjoy the rare opportunity with a full on outburst of the eighth deadly sin.

Its first blow was pinpoint accurate on the edge of the Alex's chin, causing the man to fly backwards and fall into the mist, but there was no cry of pain as he contemptuously stood back up and returned to within hitting distance. Metatron threw a full uppercut into his abdomen and Alex crumpled to his knees, but before he had chance to get back to his feet the Angel grabbed him by the throat, clearly punches would have no effect but what about strangulation, surely the monster need oxygen to survive. This seemed to be proving true as the mortals face began to turn pink then red, Alex's hands trying to fight off the Angel's vicelike grip, but now it had this strong position it was never going to release. 'Dieeee...!'

'Who me...?' The voice came from behind the Angel.

With no release of pressure on its throttling hold Metatron turned to see Alex down back at the table, smiling sweetly. Looking down at its own hands the Angel found they were empty.

'Why won't you disclose why you pity me...those were the rules?' The Glitch asked with an ironic smile.

'Fuck you...!'

A mocking expression of surprise suddenly formed on Alex's face. 'Ooh an actual Angel using profanity in heaven...well, if I remember nothing else of your life and death I won't forget that outburst.'

'Then don't forget this one either...I pity you Glitch because you have nothing to show for this one opportunity. You will never be in this situation again, an invincible force of nature but with a life and a mind. Next time you'll be a plague again or an asteroid, or a flood, all the usual methods of destroying everything around you!'

'Oh come on try to be original. I have already received the same type of speech from Emma and Harvey...Why not be good, choose a path of enlightenment instead of destruction. Is that really all you have for your last words?'

A spark went off in the Angel's mind, it wasn't much but enough to start the tiny flame of an idea, triggered by the Glitch saying the word '...Path.'

What did it mean, why would such a word light up as significant? Metatron searched frantically through its own great knowledge to find the connection.

'What are you doing now...?' Alex's mouth asked.

The Angel retook its seat at the table, itself beginning to glow with an inner light as that one single thought became a compacted point, before it faced the Glitch and announced its discovery clearly '...The timeline!'

'I'm sorry...?' Alex's face looked confused.

'The other timeline that split apart to find a path around you, it must still exist and you can't destroy it...because you don't exist in that world!'

'I think you'll find that I did.' Alex smiled but remained concerned as to where the Angel was going with this?

'Well yes you did...but not like this...you were still a conceptual thought looking for a way to start. So if I can find my way back there...I can stop you from evolving any further.'

'You do understand Metatron that you have completely lost your mind, you cannot swap from one timeline to another.'

'Why not...? I did it before...evidently.' The Angel opened its wings in that old display of ascendency.

'Good luck with your ridiculous concept...I've had enough of this now...' Alex's features melted away allowing the sparkling form of the Glitch to appear. 'It is time for you to die Metatron.'

'You will have to catch me first!' The Angel said and vanished.

'Haven't you listened to a word I've said? I know where you are at all times...we are connected by blood.' When no response came back the Glitch began its pursuit. '...Fine have it your way!'

The Glitch comfortably began its pursuit with the path the Angel had taken appearing it its mind as a golden pathway, so simple to follow and when it stopped the Glitch would pounce, no more games now, time was getting on.

80

Deep into the heavens the Angel flew never looking back, flashing through the heavens in its desperate attempt to locate a place it had never been, but one it knew existed. At incredible speeds it travelled through the darkest void of space trying to find its very heart. The only navigation it had to hand were the sounds the destination made, gentle whispers that rippled outwards, barely audible but constant. It prayed like only an Angel can that as it got closer they would become louder.

The Glitch watched the trail heading away then stopped its pursuit to think. There was really nothing to gain from chasing the Angel at this moment, in the end it would have to come back regardless, so it would choose to wait until then by keeping itself busy.

Back in the meeting room no time had passed at all, with Harvey, Flo, Rhian and Juliet still huddled together when the Glitch returned, its form standing just a few feet away from them. Flo had just finished speaking her sentence to Juliet, something about 'I don't think that's helpful', when its shimmering hand reached forward and touched her elbow.

First of all feeling an uncomfortable burning sensation Flo looked down to see the fingers of the Glitch had entered the skin of her arm. The reactive scream she let out caused Rhian and Juliet to step away but Harvey didn't flinch on seeing his wife's alarm, he simply held her closer and spoke confidently, whether his words would make any difference remained to be seen.

'Stay perfectly still!' He told her then stared into the featureless face of the Glitch. 'Don't do this...please I beg you...just get on with destroying the world but don't make it any more personal. You've won you bastard you know that...!'

Harvey was even more certain of the accuracy of his statement because of the fact that the Angel, or Enoch, or whoever the hell the scruffy man had really been was missing now, surely another victim of this vicious apparition.

The voice of the Glitch filled the air around them. '...Harvey, haven't you understood yet that whatever you ask me not to do...I just do it even more and with extra passion?'

Harvey could clearly see the hand inserted in his wife's arm. There was a strong temptation to just pull her away and see what happened. She'd have a nasty wound, but if he could talk this monster round, wouldn't it be a price worth paying.

What was he thinking, of course it wouldn't and it was beyond him to even consider it any longer, his only choice was to activate a plan B.

'Take me first please, here...' Harvey leaned his head forward in an attempt to go face to face with it, making sure not to shift Flo's position. '...Kill me...here I am!'

From only inches away it felt as if he were floating in the outer space this Glitch contained, his whole vision being filled with stars and swirling dust clouds, then realising he was just another soul lost in the cosmos praying for salvation.

It was at that precise beautiful moment, as he almost lost himself in those calming thoughts of eternity that Flo's body fell limp in his arms, making no sound.

Harvey fought to tear his gaze away; to turn from the astounding luminosities that were trying to draw him closer, to decline this invitation that promised to end his suffering before it began, to brave that fear by looking down at his wife.

Rhian had rushed over to Sammy at the first opportunity, grabbing his trembling hand before sitting with him against the far wall, away from the action and the gruesome discovery which had caused Flo to faint. Still in the thick of it Juliet had watched it happen, utterly amazed at how it had cut through so easily, like a knife through water.

Flo's left arm, clean through the elbow joint, was severed. With the wound seemingly resealed by the beast that had caused it, so thankfully for Juliet there was no bloodletting. However the fact remained that the Mrs Coopers forearm and hand were absent from this world, consumed by the Glitch in an instant.

When the nurse instinctively moved forward to pull her away, Flo had raised her stump to view the damage and promptly passed out. Because of this millisecond of delay Juliet caught the woman at the exact moment Harvey broke free of the suicidal lightshow.

'Oh dear god no...!'

He repeated this fraught prayer three times, each one growing in volume and alarm, as his hand firmly tapped his wife's left cheek. It was only with the help of Juliet, who'd instantly demanded he pull himself together, that they dragged Flo's unconscious body away a few feet before laying her down on her side in the recovery position. Which Harvey then made comfortable by removing his jacket and placing it under her head.

As he did this he told Juliet how thankful he was that she was here with them, before standing up and with a perceptible groan he stormed back towards the unmoving Glitch. As he closed in a serious doubt appeared in his mind, was this a genuine attempt to try and intimidate the Glitch, or just those alluring lights calling to him again? In a clear show of defiance that declared he retained an independent mind, for now at least, he stopped three feet short of the glowing being. From here Harvey could take in the full humanoid shape, with the sparkling embers of its insides lacking their hypnotic allure at this distance, thus allowing him to make his fevered thoughts a reality, inflamed by the fact his wife's wedding hand had gone.

'What I would give in all of this world and the next...to kill you right now!'

Harvey was consciously pressing his feet into the ground. A sure sign there was no more turning to run now because the line had been drawn, not only in the metaphorical sand but also across his wife's arm, the pain of seeing her injury almost too much to bear.

'You know what Glitch...? I haven't got anything left...no more of that delicious agony you seem to thrive on...I've nothing else to offer you. This is it...I'm not an idiot, we're all going to die...but I'm going to take a run at you anyway and if you swallow me up...then I hope you can feel something of my swinging punches as I go you disgusting fucking...animal!'

'Dear Harvey...' The voice of the Glitch was at first a whisper, coming from all around the room, but soon enough it deepened as its emotions peeped out. '...Are you still calling me names after everything we've been through? I would hope we were above such things now...we would have a little more shared respect on display...because I admire you Inspector. Mainly because you are a man who shouldn't even be a part of this, a foolish one at that, who got dragged in by the gravitational pull of a suicide victim who fell through a hole...and of course your by own misaligned curiosity.' The Glitch paused for a second before adding. 'That wedding ring was delicious by the way...one should always appreciate real gold don't you think?'

The messages had now been sent from his brain to the nervous system. Harvey was ready, having studied logically the only two answers available to any soul in his position, he decided to take the flight option, to set off running and without stopping, full speed and headlong into the Glitch.

81

The Angel wept as it finally gave up on its the search, forced to reluctantly accept that its desired destination of hope didn't actually exist, for no matter in what direction it listened, the sound never got any closer. The distant and eerie clacking of the Life Machine itself, though continual and busy, remained audible but hidden and far from reach.

Metatron had to accept its plan had unsurprisingly failed. It was guilty of relying heavily on a whole lot of unsubstantiated theories falling into the perfect place, the proverbial shot in the dark. An accurate title for what it had attempted.

The Angel had been trying to locate the Life Machine. Its main reason for doing so seemed to rest on a bizarre fantasy that such an old and wizened place would know how to find the other timeline, or at the very least be able to tell the Angel if it still existed.

The other reason was purely personal, because if this Angel was going to die anyway, it wished to look upon it just once, to see the Life Machine at work, experience the splendour of its harmonies being created. To hear those delicate chords being performed by this incredible piece of far distant technology, unceasingly humming its life giving refrains of which none are identical but all are worthy, where every second without cease sounds pour out to carry forward its infinite variations.

Now an Angel could hope, even logically expect to find, that such wondrous themes, surrounded as they are by infinite expanding beauty, would be positive ones, but sadly that is only half true.

The Life Machine has no soul, it functions like clockwork to relentlessly birth then burn the very stuff that makes up a universe, only able to construct or destroy in equal measure, to open its gates wide to the fields of creation or to call its flock back home to begin again. But naturally it only achieved such miracles with assistance and this time its chosen celestial shepherd was the Glitch.

When it started to feed everything the Angel had recorded in the book to help the Life Machine grow would be swallowed, compressed to a point much smaller than an atom, then vomited back up to begin anew and all of this would occur with no care or logic applied, this is how it was and would always be.

Yet still this Angel wished to view the very mechanism forever destined to be both delivery ward and funeral parlour of every single thing that ever did, still does, or will ever exist.

THE RED FRAME

But as the desperate Metatron discovered there was no way of finding the machine, no chance to reason with it, reset it even, such had been Metatron's lofty hopes. So with no sign of the infernal instrument, hidden behind the very boundaries it created, the search had been in vain, with no allowance given for peeping round the curtain.

A crestfallen Metatron returned to the white world, fully expecting to die within seconds of appearing, but found the Glitch was gone and wasn't immediately returning; maybe because it had something better to be getting on with the Angel surmised. It tensed at that thought. 'Oh no...!'

Yet again the Glitch had displayed that ability of always choosing the unexpected option. Metatron realised it should have known better than to expect anything less. Why would it chase an Angel across the skies, trying to catch up, when it could be somewhere much more productive, safe in the knowledge it was one step ahead.

82

In the darkness something stirred.

A thin hand reached down and patted its body all over first, looking for injuries that could explode into agonising life at the very moment he should blindly move, but there appeared to be none. Physically he seemed to be okay, mentally though, it felt as if he'd been hit by a fucking train.

Jay Cleaver opened his eyes but there was nothing to see at first, looking straight ahead was only blackness, yet to his right a dim green glow appeared over the edge of what must be a table, or a desk. He was curious to know what it was but with his body splayed out like this, with his head and limbs hanging down to the floor, his spine curved round the shape of a large lump underneath him, moving wasn't the easiest of tasks. Fighting off swarms of pins and needles he pulled himself up, straightened his back out, before shaking his hands while tensing and relaxing his legs.

He had no idea how long he'd been here, or even where here was, because any memories he had which might have been useful were refusing to be dredged. Jay was in the dark again.

'...About fucking right...!'

He'd tried to speak the words out loud but they only appeared in his head. Raising a hand to his face he felt the scars on his cheeks, as he slid his fingers over the wounding letters cut into his forehead that spelt out the word '**KILLER**', before he touched the groaning screaming lips of a mouth that contained no tongue.

'...Moooowahhhh...'

He said three times on repeat before determinedly forcing his body to stand, doing so by pressing down on the lump he was sat on for leverage, before hastily realising it was the body of a man. This discovery causing Jay to cry out again as he scrambled up and headed toward that green glow.

The light was coming from the power switch of a laptop, as he touched the mouse a tranquil scene of idyllic countryside appeared, a photograph of a pretty place with a shimmering sunlit river flowing under willow trees surrounded by emerald fields. Just visible under those hanging fulsome branches was a boy, in what appeared to be denim dungarees sitting on the bank, fishing rod in hand, as peaceful and happy as a boy could be.

Jay's memory was starting to return now, little pieces at first, but enough to know the guy on the floor was the big guard, dead and gone forever. That much he remembered but he also knew he had no time for Kosminsky's remembrances or desires, so pressing the enter-key the beautiful picture disappeared, to be replaced with an infra-red camera shot of an empty corridor and a frame with a door torn from its hinges. He couldn't tell where it was located, the words underneath were unfamiliar ones, his reading skills unimproved by time spent with the eloquent Glitch.

The most important thing he needed now was some actual light. The solution to that turned out to be unbelievably simple, as the first desk drawer he checked offered up the unmistakable shape of a torch. Clicking the beam on with it pointed at his own face caused him to blink hard, just the naturally occurring, ridiculous comedic actions of this teenager, one who would never learn the basics and for whom an education had proudly been a waste of time. Yet strangely, as is often the case with the younger generation, he did know a bit of stuff about computers, somehow picking up a wealth of basic information in this area without ever attending a class or being able to read a book to find out. It was just the world he'd grown up in.

Flicking the torch around the cupboard office to get his bearings, he stopped its roving beam on Kosminsky's face, finding the man facing upward with his eyes open and set wide. It looked pretty clear to Jay's untrained eye that whatever the man was looking at when he died was probably what killed him, a diagnosis that made a lot more sense in Jays head. The man looked frightened to death.

There were also no clear injuries on his body although there appeared to be loads of bloodstains on his once white shirt. Jay really didn't want to see any more blood right now because his memory was successfully digging itself out of the mud, his time with the Glitch becoming clearer. However the murders they had committed were paling into insignificance against the growing realisation that the bastard thing had ditched him.

Not only had it discarded Jay's body callously as if it were no more than dirty linen, or the shed skin of a snake, the bastard hadn't even said goodbye. It was only then he realised all his fingers were intact, so the Glitch had given him something before it left. The monster had left him no explanation or instruction of what to do next, he'd just been dumped and left to fend for himself, as well as returning to the scarred aberration he'd been before.

That was the part really pissing Jay off, it was too fucking harsh to leave him like this, some unnecessarily cold shit that he didn't think he deserved. To calm down he flicked the torch beam around the cupboard office again. A few feet away lay the battered steel door, with the darkened doorway next to one end, clearly where the camera was pointing on the computer.

Now he had his bearings he felt ready to find out more. He found the operating files and clicked through the various feeds, images of room after room and corridor after corridor until he saw the battered body of Roma Walker. Switching quickly to the next file to avoid seeing any more bloodied corpses, he found himself high above a door looking down over a badly lit room he recognised, with people he recognised inside it, and a sparkling shape that he didn't recognise. He rapidly put things together.

So that was the Glitch now. Jay wasn't impressed.

THE RED FRAME

83

The dirty looking Angel suddenly reappeared in the room. It caught Harvey's eye which immediately stopped his suicidal forward thinking and his body relaxed, ready to listen.

'Where the hell have you been? The Inspector asked.

The bearded man's answer came with an apologetic cadence.

'I have been finding out that we are on our own...that there are no answers in the stars...no answers in the past...nor in the white world or the great book. This...' he pointed toward the Glitch. '...shall come to pass...this universe is damned and all will be devoured. Because of that and if you would still follow a fallen Angel's sage advice, I believe it would be better for us all to submit to its right of way. Everyone please sit down and close your eyes, so that the worst feelings of terror will not be your last. Just allow the beast to satisfy its crusade and move on.'

'Do as the Angel says!' The Glitch's voice boomed forth as it slowly walked towards Harvey. 'None of you are worth any more effort. When I entered this room I expected surprises, a standoff of survival, but instead found another paltry slice of humanity...once I had taken your appointed leader Alex the battle was over. You have all suffered in some way at my hand but not enough for my liking, yet an amount I am satisfied with...so turn your backs and close your eyes, say your prayers if you must but be sure to mention me in them!'

The Glitch opened its arms wide as it walked on and through Harvey, the Inspector's body, eyes closed, disappearing within the light of its being, silently and without protest.

In the cupboard office Jay watched this consuming of Inspector Harvey Cooper happen in real time. It was brighter on the screen now as the Glitch thing was glowing. Still confused by the man's death he saw the creature turn towards the woman and boy huddled on the ground, before it began striding towards them. The woman had her eyes closed and held her son tightly while putting her face down on top of his head, the strongest of parental bonds holding until the end. The sight of them embracing as the enemy marched closer alarmed Jay, the simple beauty of the moment snapping him out of his position as a curious bystander and into the realm of fast acting saviour, but what could he achieve from here.

He studied the computer screen icons, where even he could recognise the picture of a padlock. Pressing that button the screen showed more letters he couldn't read but at the bottom of this screen were two boxes, one green and one red, accept or decline. He understood that well enough and for the first time in his life, being offered a chance to save another's life, he pressed his arrow down on the positive option.

The meeting room was immediately plunged into darkness and loud sirens began to wail. The sound of the electronic klaxon deliberately pitched to deter any thought of escape, with an almost eardrum bursting pitch, screaming there was no way out. The security lights seemingly concealed within the surface of the walls until an alarm sounded flickered on. They now lit up the room on all sides with their bright crimson glow.

Flo was awakened from her faint by the invasive noise and looked up into the tearful face of Nurse Juliet. Behind her and all around them, the room displayed an eerie hue that made the older woman think of an old submarine movie, where any vessel in distress would be red lit when struck by a torpedo or depth charge, the only difference being the lack of panic in this metaphorical engine room. Here no one ran around wildly shouting instructions or giving orders, in this reality no one moved at all, including the Glitch who had stopped just two feet short of Mother and child.

'Where's Harvey...?' She asked.

Because of the red security lights filling the room, Jay's view of the following events was blurred, his eyes finding everyone in there dull and undefined. The camera could make out the Glitch because it was nearest the centre of the room, while the people around it were washed out in the glow, only the scruffy guy was moving and Jay wanted to hear what he was saying, he clicked off the wailing alarm but the lights remained on.

'Fuck it...that'll do.'

Metatron, looking even worse than before in such harsh lighting, had moved over towards Flo and Juliet, first helping them to their feet before escorting them to a position over by the steel door, he then repeated the act with Rhian and Sammy, the four of them now standing under the strongest of the beams, but the Angel wasn't sure what to do next, in the end considering it may be wise to seek advice from the only soul who may know more, the unmoving Glitch.

THE RED FRAME

The insides of the beast still glowed brightly under the scarlet flood of the light with Metatron able to see the rays covering its outer shell as he approached, he moved in closer before choosing his words carefully.

'Turn and face me Glitch...place your hands upon me and rip my body asunder...come, I am here at your side, take my life next...' But it didn't move or reply to an open invitation so the Angel asked what it desperately wanted to know. 'Can you move...?'

Nothing

'Can you speak...?'

Silence, but the only way to be sure the Glitch was truly trapped within these lights would be to touch it.

Metatron remained wary, having been fooled by this monster many times over, fully expecting it to lurch forward as he took a position directly in front of it. Slowly he reached out his hand then stopped, hovering over the exquisite cosmos still visible within the Glitch's form. All those galaxies and stars on display now wore a pink tinge. He pressed his fingers into the monster's chest. Closing his eyes in preparation of the pain to come he found the body was quite solid and his hand did not enter.

Tracing his fingers over the torso it showed no presence of muscular definition, with no chest bone or ribs to be located, so by that rational it was still the same being of infinite destruction, but one now sealed in by the lights, by the red frame surrounding it.

Juliet left the group by the door and walked over to Metatron.

'Is it dead?'

'No...it is retained.'

'So we could kill it?'

'No...it cannot be killed. I thought I had made that quite clear.'

'I'd still like to try...it fucking murdered Harvey and Alex!'

The bearded man turned towards her with his green eyes suddenly alive, bursting through the scarlet light, perhaps a possibility still existed. Even though he hadn't any answers yet, his ancient mind was full of fresh hope, the main problem he faced was that he needed more information; unfortunately anyone who could be helpful on this subject, specifically the what to do next part, was either consumed by the Glitch or trapped within the red frame...or both.

During this exchange there was one soul whose mind wasn't listening, she was stuck in her own personal hell, one far worse than anything else that could happen this night.

For the first time in her adult life Florence May Cooper was alone, not physically as Rhian was trying to do what she could, holding her close in a shared embrace with her son, but in her heart and soul she was lost. Harvey was gone, he would never return and when it happened she'd been unconscious. Now her head hurt, her chest hurt, her eyes hurt, every part of her in pain and screaming to be released from this nightmare of emotions.

The grief hadn't even arrived yet, the worst part was still to come, she was numbed to the core mentally, like a baby chick that fell from the nest there was no way back. She couldn't move or even cry as her mind groped for a new feeling, something positive to keep this heart alive but there were none. At this moment she was just as dead as her husband, only she could feel every detail of the true sickness of that condition, with no escape, remaining trapped in a prison of painful loss.

Jay was busy trying to find a way to break out of his own deadlock. He'd already searched Kosminsky's pockets for anything useful, like the card to open the meeting room door, but the only stuff he found were the man's house and motorbike keys along with his wallet. Flicking it open the big guards face leered up at him from a driving licence, in the other slotted sections were a bank card, two business cards of which one was for a motorbike tyre garage, the other a long expired gym membership. Inside the money notes section there were no notes, with Jay considering that if there had of been some cash and he'd taken it, would that still be actual theft, surely the guy was dead so he wouldn't be worrying about money.

A ridiculously strong sense of déjà vu struck Jay as he pulled out a folded photograph in the back of the wallet. He couldn't remember ever doing this kind of thing before but an invisible memory told him different.

Opening the picture up the face of a brown haired woman stared back with the most amazing smile Jay had ever seen, not that it was particularly toothy or loud, it was just the pure happiness expressed on it. If this was Kosminsky's girlfriend then Jay reckoned the big lump was punching above his weight, On the reverse there was a flourishing letter C written in pen and the date 5/4/19. Fucking hell thought Jay that was ages ago, couldn't he get a more up to date picture. Then the teenager's addled brain worked out a few reasons why that should be. None of them were good.

Then Jay did something that he couldn't really explain, he put the wallet back into Kosminsky's pocket minus the photograph and slid the picture of C into the big guard's shirt pocket, next to his heart.

THE RED FRAME

'Moooowahhhh...' He said as he tapped the photo flat to his chest.

Yeah that had felt like the right thing to do he thought before looking back at the computer screen. He could see the Glitch hadn't moved while the others seemed to be milling around, looking for a way out, which was exactly what Jay wanted to help them do.

Then for no particular reason he felt the pocket of the grey suit he was still wearing. What he found there caused a 'No fucking way!' reaction, while his second reaction was to position the torch so it lit the surface of the desk, this freed up his hands for his third reaction, the one of tapping out the contents of a leather pouch, before chopping them up and dividing on the mirror provided. Once again he thought strongly of how this was the right thing to do now, again proving if any proof were needed, that Jay Cleavers moral compass would only ever be pointing towards highly irregular.

Snorting up the second line as a chaser he threw his head back and mewled, thinking that if this didn't help him find the answer of how to get those people out of there, then nothing would.

84

The bearded man busily considered many things as the others searched the room looking for a way to escape. The Glitch remained set in its position, although the silence surrounding it and the colours permeating through its form were more than a little disturbing. Clearly it was nowhere near as dead as they'd hoped; instead it appeared to be trapped within the crimson beams of the security lights. Seen through a mother's eyes this had to be earth's version of the red frame Metatron had drawn in the book.

By way of small talk but keeping on topic, Rhian spoke to Metatron. 'So it was important all along.'

He turned to face her with a hollow smile. 'What part exactly?'

'The square that you drew...for this very reason by the look of it...'

'...Not really, it was to keep my Demon in range otherwise it would be roaming this world...' He paused '...But you read Alex's dream book so you know only too well what it would be doing.'

'Yeah I do...and that's definitely preferable to what we've got to face now.'

He couldn't disagree with her astute point. 'Yes...I think you are right.'

'Is there really nothing we can do?

'Nothing that I can think of...the Glitch is trapped while those lights are covering it, but as soon as they are switched off or fail, or worse still it works out a way to overcome them by itself, then that will absolutely be the end of it all.'

Rhi's eyes dropped on hearing those words, still holding out some hope that this scruffy man could save them, that she and Sammy could walk out of here victorious leaving the nightmare of the recent past behind. 'So why are you staying here? Why not run away like you did before...there's no need for you to be with us.'

'Because no matter where I went it would find me instantly...we are connected...'

'...Like Alex was?' She sighed sadly.

The untidy man paused as his thoughts slipped back to his one armed worthy adversary, of how they discussed many subjects in their time together, to the point where intellectually Alex had grown wise and powerful enough to rise up against him. What a fight it had been, in his opinion the one armed mortal deserved a statue in this world greater than any previously erected.

THE RED FRAME

A great sadness then fell upon Metatron as he realised their great battle, which the Angel only survived by deceitfully fooling Alex into believing he'd won, had ultimately been for nothing. It had felt so vitally important but was simply another moment in the lull before the storm, where everything would be washed away forever by the Glitch.

When it broke free of the red frame, which it could do at any moment, there would soon be nothing left, because it wouldn't only be the Earth destroyed, the very heavens would also fall to its will.

That thought only made his melancholy grow until he noticed the others coming over to sit in his presence. It almost made sense he thought as he looked down at his long plain robe, there was a strong hint of Messiah about his look, if not his mind.

Flo arrived first but she didn't speak. Metatron could almost feel the fevered heat of the grief spreading through her body. With her stumped arm concealed in a cardigan she was helped across the room by Juliet, who would remain a nurse to the end, though one who looked lost and forlorn. Sammy followed on behind, his head turned to the right, never taking his eyes off the motionless Glitch until he reached the haven of his mother's side.

'Do you remember me Sammy?'

Metatron asked with a genuine curiosity as the two had never actually spoken. For all the weeks spent inside the boy's mind the Angel had declined to interfere, apart from the time with the other schoolboy whose nose got broken in class. But apart from that small attack against the injustice of a bully there had been no shared acts, no talking to the boy as the Demon had done with its other vessels, no threats or screams to force the boy to follow its will, just the peacefulness of a shared space.

The boy looked up at the scraggly man. 'Yes sort of...I knew you were around but I could never find where you were hiding...is that the same as remembering someone?'

'Indeed it is. I believe you may have just described the emotional truth of many relationships, so yes I consider myself remembered by you.'

'Why can't you save us...?' Sammy interrupted as bluntly as only a child can. '...that's only a monster...you're an Angel...I thought Angels always won.'

'I...I am...was...a terrible Angel. Those charming rules you speak of, of how good will always defeat evil, do not apply to one such as me. I gave up on what most would describe as a virtuous life a very long time ago, if truth be told, almost instantly...when I found I had been left alone.'

Metatron raised a hand to stroke his beard, not in a wizarding way, more the act of man looking for some peace of mind. If these people gathered around him wanted to hear a story, he had a story for them, a parable no less.

'All the Angels left me in the white world en masse...no one spoke a word or looked back...not even once...all because I shared an opinion on the location of our God. For one such as me, a mortal who had ascended to heaven, no more than a half-breed to them, to ever dare presume I had the right or position to declare a belief that our beloved God had forsaken us was deemed sinful. So from such truth, which they preferred to call a scurrilous rumour, I was branded as a heretic. Do you know what a heretic is Sammy?'

'No, I don't.'

'It is the name for one who works against accepted beliefs, who stands contrary to the principles of a religious doctrine. Now that may not sound a frightful issue to one so young...but let me tell you Sammy, that being a half-breed heretic in a world of pure Angels is an awful place to be. So it came to pass that I was judged, punished and condemned to spend my existence in eternity alone. To be recognised as nothing more than a mere mortal who ascended to heaven only by great fortune to become an Angel, who turned his back on his human roots, guilty of trying to destroy my own people. I fully appreciated that my traitorous actions would cast doubts about trusting me among my heavenly brethren, why should they accept me as pure of heart, when I could so willingly take up arms to fight for both sides of a coin? I believe God then intervened to save me, by passing on the responsibility of keeping the great book, filling its covers with all the history of everything created or thought...to keep me occupied if you will.'

'The book that the monster ate...?' Sammy pointed out with a sigh.

'...Yes...but it gave it back to me...said it was of no more use.'

The boy took his eyes off the Glitch and looked Metatron straight in the eye. 'But isn't that exactly what a monster would say...?'

'...It is exactly what a monster would say!'

Metatron thought back over the times he had already been deceived by the Glitch. How it always threw in a simple sidestep of the highest standard, one usually containing layers of cleverness covering up levels of the brutally simple. With this thought came a flood of recognition that almost knocked him off his feet. '...The book...it is back on the table. We must return to the white world...!' His words where staccato in delivery, with his mind hissing and dashing around in its attempt to work out the meaning of this moment. It had in its possession the great book. How could it use it, where would it focus such a journey on, which human would be sent on that journey, until finally the biggest question reared up, how could he even transport a human back to the white table?

'If there is something you can do...I would like you to do it.'

These words came softly from the mouth of Flo but her message was serious in intention, she still wanted to win, for her husband and Alex to have not died in vain. As she spoke it was noticeable that her eyes refused to look down at her injury, rejecting it had happened, to deny the Glitch any sense of satisfaction because it was a choice she could still make.

Behind Flo, Juliet had a strong sense that she already knew what the Angel would ask.

'One of you has to journey with me.' It spoke.

Juliet wasn't shocked at all by that. 'I'll go...!' she replied quickly. '...I feel like I already know the place after Alex telling me so much about his journeys inside it...that magical book was always my favourite part of his story.'

'No...that wouldn't work.' Metatron told her. 'I fear you would be too similar to Alex. It took a great many attempts to focus him, his mind always too fascinated in reliving the past...I believe you would be the same.'

'I could stay focused.' She pleaded.

'So soon after losing him...I doubt that...and it is for this reason I must take the boy, if I can.'

Rhian's head shot up. 'No you can't, please, you're not taking him. He's staying here with me!'

'There are no choice's left Rhian. I was going to say *if I can* find a way to reconnect with him as an Angel again. If you desire to have any chance of getting out of this then give him to me.'

'Leave him alone...he didn't ask for any of this. He's only here because of me...because of what I did...'

'...All of your playing around with tarot cards and pretending to speak with the dead has nothing to do with this. But nonetheless you are still here for a reason...and with the clock ticking I would strongly suggest that the reason for your presence is Sammy...you will just have to trust me on that...'

Rhi looked into the eyes of Flo in hope of some support and spoke with tears in her eyes.

'They're going to take my boy.'

Flo pulled the woman close so she wouldn't have to watch, both of them blinding themselves to this painful world, before she replied.

'If he doesn't go Rhian...then your boy is already dead.'

Metatron raised his liver spotted hand and placed it on the boys head. He then closed his eyes and asked the boy to do the same. This was the only technique the man knew, a dangerous one that would only work if Sammy was entirely committed to allowing him back inside his mind.

Even then, if the boy could manage to do that and journey within the book, there was every chance of serious and long lasting damage to such a young mind. But with no more paths to follow it was a risk the Angel was willing to take...and failing to mention.

85

Jay expertly suctioned away the remaining lines, the cocaine rush making his eyes roll and his jaw clench tight, fucking lovely.

It hadn't all been fun and games in the last fifteen minutes, during that time the pumped up teenager had been studying this laptop, digging down into the files, looking for anything he might understand.

A strong feeling had overwhelmed him, ably assisted by the powder; he became obsessed with discovering a way to release those people. He didn't particularly know them, they were of no use to him that he could think of, yet all of a sudden their freedom appeared to be his life's mission.

His eyes darted around as he studied the lists of files in their columns down the laptop screen. Most were titled using a combination of letters, numbers and symbols so it didn't matter if he could read them or not, a few of them were really long words which he'd no chance of deciphering, while some were purely pictorial, so he had half a chance with those.

Jay thought back to how he'd turned off the siren because it was wildly annoying to hear, especially to a cokehead on the way up. He'd achieved that by locating a collection of files that all displayed some kind of icon hinting at audio, in the end he'd pressed them all.

With that blind guess working perfectly he was now busy searching the lists for other useful files. 'What are you...?.' He asked, though of course his mouth only mewled, as he recognised a clear symbol, a red light with a black cross over it. That had to be the button to turn off the security lights. Who knows maybe by extinguishing those the door would override and open, it made sense to him so he placed the cursor on it...then stopped for a few seconds and thought about it, at least as much as his racing mind would allow him to right now. What would any of those trapped people gain by him plunging them into darkness? He guessed not very much, plus he noticed the Glitch hadn't moved since the lights had first come on, and with that realisation a cold memory began to appear in his mind...

...He was crouched naked, feeling small in the bathroom, while flashing red and blue lights thumped silently on the frosted window pane. There was heavy banging on doors, people were coming after him, he couldn't talk but he knew he had to give them a message. He began punching the hell out of the mirror, smashing it so hard it reduced his fists to ribbons, and with a heady mix of glass and blood he smeared the message with his fingers.

The red frame he'd created on the wall was violently beautiful and vital somehow. It had made him happy as it was exactly the communication he was supposed to share, so his proud gaze never left it, at least not until the police officers smashed their way in to shove his face down hard into the linoleum bathroom floor...

That was the best way he could reimagine it; yeah fuck he'd done that, done it as requested even though he didn't why or for whom. He'd like to know the truth but that was beyond the limits of his current brain patterns, erratic and uneven as they were from the cocaine, his mind behaving far too independently to control. Yet this picture on the camera feed did make some connection in this mess of a mind. The Glitch being held in a red patch of light that stretched all around the room convinced him there was no fucking way he should turn the lights off, not with the bastard trapped in the same design he'd drawn back at his bungalow.

So what was all that about?

Surely it pointed out he'd been forewarned, given a heads up for the first time in his life, a perception causing warm feelings that someone had trusted him for once, put their faith in his soul to do the right thing, to help.

A heavy sniff cleared up a lot of flakes that had attached themselves in his nasal cavities. These specks instantly providing him with another rush, although a lot less than the initial line, he loved to feel this way. It was as if he'd taken a fast tracked climb to the top of a higher mountain, then been allowed to breathe in the air and take in the view for just a few seconds, before beginning his descent. Every time wishing that his comedown would be as graceful as a boundless bird swooping round the peaks and swirling down on a spiralling thermal, but as it wore off it never felt like anything but a disorganised damaging avalanche. Fuck yeah, he liked that description, but in the next second it was gone, he tried to recall what he'd been thinking of but it was no use, whatever it had been was now lost and buried under the snow drift in his mind.

What was I doing?

Fuck this is good gear man!

Looking at the cache of lighting files on the screen he scrolled further down but left them untouched. Again he wasn't sure why he'd chosen to do this, just another feeling as his mind tried to loop around and take him back to earlier thoughts, cocaine being nothing if not repetitive in its mental activities. Then suddenly out of that boring carnage a genuine new idea crawled free. His purpose, oh yeah he'd been trying to save those people. Fuck man, he needed to open that door while he could, he needed a key, Kosminsky didn't have one...who would have one...of course...Kirby!

Jay snatched up the torch then climbed out over the broken door, leaving the cupboard office, Allan Kosminsky and their shared memories behind. Then he made his way up the stairs.

86

The Angel Metatron stood upon a beach that stretched for miles in each direction. Looking out over the azure sea it watched waves crash far from shore, the tide losing much of its wild strength before reaching this sandy shoreline where it lapped gently at its feet.

Holding out an arm to check, it was delighted to see the whiteness of its sleeve. A feeling of serene purity at wearing its reclaimed gown taking over, so comforting its wings unfurled to open wide and touch the tender coastal breeze. How much longer it could enjoy this moment depended on who appeared along this beach next. If it was the Glitch freshly escaped from the frame then it was already over, but if it was the boy then there would be the merest hope that things could be different.

'Wow!' Sammy said in genuine awe as he approached. He'd never been on a beach that looked anything like it. 'Is this where you live?'

'Thank you for coming young man. I promise I will answer all of your questions if we get the opportunity, but first we have important work to do. Would you help me?'

'Will it be scary?'

The Angel felt as if it should convey some comforting smile, but it was too late for lying. 'I have no idea what the experience will be like, but I need you to find something in that book...' Then its green eye's looked over and past Sammy, the boy followed the gaze and turned to see the large white desk, but pretty sure it hadn't been there a second ago.

'You want me to read the book?'

'Not exactly...'

In the next heartbeat they were sitting at the table but Sammy wasn't didn't remember walking to it. The book lay just in front of him, opened wide with a page torn out, which was crumpled up in the Angels hand.

'...Now listen to me Sammy, I am going to allow you to enter the book. You must stay focused and only search for what I tell you. I have no time to guess at what you may see in there, except to say it will be a personal journey just for you, but I need you to repeat my words and keep them at the front of your thoughts.'

'Okay.' The boy agreed with a wide eyed look encompassing a hundred emotions, trying his best to keep the biggest one at bay, as he didn't want to be scared anymore.

The Angel slid the book towards the boy. 'I want you to search for the Life Machine.'

'Okay...what does it look like?'

'If only it were that easy...nobody could possibly know that or would ever be able to describe it...but I am quite sure if you see it there will be no doubt. For now all I need to know is that it exists within the book. So that is your mission Sam, to find the Life Machine and then return here and tell me about it. Can you do that for me...for your mother...for everyone?'

Sammy nodded enthusiastically then dropped his gaze to the books blank pages. Staring hard he repeated the Angels instruction, to find out if the Life Machine exists then come back, but that was just before his mind was whisked up and taken away in a cyclone of colours and emotions.

'Can you just shut the fucking kid up for one minute...I've been out working all week and I come back to this...the place is a tip, you look like a sack of shit...get a bit of fucking pride in yourself!'

The man's gruff voice had come through first, before the visual details began to seep into focus, inside a room Sammy kind of recalled from being a baby, only he knew he wasn't a baby anymore, certainly nothing like the one in the corner screaming at the top of its lungs.

This was so cool he thought, like virtual reality times a hundred. Finding he could watch the situation from anywhere he did so, floating around the room freely, then zooming in to get even more detail. He wasn't entirely sure of where he was, or what was going on, but it was fun. At least until an angry lady walked in and everyone's mood changed. Her hair seemed to have life of its own, swaying and bouncing over her eyes, as she went face to face with the much larger man.

'I look like a sack of shit do I...?' She swept her curly mane away to keep it from covering her face and it was then Sammy saw his mother's furious eyes. '...I've barely slept in a week...because for your information our son is teething. Not that you'd know anything about that because you're never here and you never ask how he is...you're always too busy shouting at me to shut him fucking up!'

Sammy couldn't understand why he was being made to watch this? Clearly it was his parents when they were younger and still together, but fighting and not liking each other very much and he didn't want to hear it. He moved his perspective to the crying baby, himself from some ten years ago, trying to help by soothing it not to cry anymore. In doing so Sammy quickly realised what other things he could do inside the book, as another wave of perspective washed over the scene allowing him to go deeper, right through the surface of the situation, to gain entry into the secret realms of other people's feelings and thoughts.

He practiced this new skill first of all on his baby mind, to try and find a way of stopping the tears so his parents would stop fighting, but it was futile. All Sammy could pick up in the baby's thoughts was a burning fire of slow repeating uncomfortable agony; he could see how an aching ripping gum was a terrible thing to a child. Apart from that there was nothing else going on in there.

So Sammy moved through the room to stand alongside his mother and better understand why she looked so crazily angry, but also if he were being honest it was to get a better look at his father.

There had been no photo albums for him to look into growing up so he really couldn't remember his dad's face. Looking at him closely now he felt a little disappointed, there was nothing significant about him, just a balding man with an angry uncaring mouth. Even a little dig into the man's emotional psyche revealed nothing of note, except he was telling the truth when he said he wanted the fucking kid to shut up. He was of no use to Sammy at all and never had been.

With love filled eyes the boy looked up at his mother, where strangely although he knew she must be younger she looked older, drawn in the face without any of her glow. Studying his mother's feeling's showed how she loved her son with as much genuine passion as she hated his father, also how strong her belief was that sometimes you can make a mistake, but the result can still be beautiful.

As they continued arguing Sammy thought it best if he made a move, the only problem was where to and how, when suddenly the only other important thing in his life flashed up and instantly he was in a classroom, his classroom.

Looking around he found himself in the middle of that room, sitting with Scott Archer, both talking and giggling when they should have been listening until Mrs Winterburn told them off. It was such a bizarre experience that he should be in this room; everything was perfect in every detail, even the smell which he guessed he was imagining. As if his brain were filling in the blanks because he wasn't really here, while his young heart beat heavily because he really wished he was.

At that thought this whole world turned upside down and he thought he might throw up.

The Angel had slammed the book shut because it wanted a progress report. It hadn't been done in a deliberately nasty way, only because it had found out through its previous experiences with Alex that this short and sharp approach saved time.

'What have you found?' It asked calmly.

The boy had to try and stop the spinning in his head before he could answer. Also he thought the Angel may not be too happy with him as he'd done nothing about the task. He'd promised to stay focused and help find the Life Machine, but that plan had disappeared within seconds of entering the book, leaving him to quite literally feel like a guilty schoolboy.

'I'm sorry...I don't know how it works...I saw my Dad, it put me off...'

'That's okay Sammy...we're all allowed one free go...' It spoke with a smile that hid a deep desire to shake the boy roughly by the shoulders and tell him to wake up. '...But next time you have to do what I ask, do you understand?'

'Yes I do...I'm ready.'

The Angel admired the boy's fortitude, although it didn't trust him to remain undistracted, but with no other choice it reopened the book and watched the boys mind slide away.

This time Sammy was ready for the journey, as he closed his eyes tight and repeated the order, 'Find the Life Machine', but when he opened them a whole new world of complications came into existence.

87

Jay reached the top floor feeling almost fit and healthy for managing it, except that his lungs felt like tar filled bellows. He stopped abruptly on seeing the blood stained hallway.

'Fuck me...!'

He mewled while stepping carefully around the smeared stuff as best he could, heading to the open door at the other end of it all, where the stains only got deeper and darker, the sight accompanied by a disgusting smell of cold raw meat.

Before entering the office he swore to himself that he would find the key card and then get out, no getting involved in whatever happened here, which really meant no checking for wallets. But on seeing the human body parts splashed around the room, the three quarters that remained of Marcus Kirby to be more accurate, Jay bullet vomited where he stood, a bulge of bile predominantly containing high levels of cocaine spattered forth onto most of the body parts.

'Oh Jesus Christ...!' He exclaimed in his head, before moving over to the desk to rifle the drawers, hoping to god the key would be around here somewhere and not...well not in Kirby's remains. Not that it would make much difference, the desk being covered in various bodily substances meant he was already getting covered in the stuff, plus he had nothing left to throw up anyway.

Hunting through the mess he found no key in or around the desk area. Both his hands were dripping red as he stopped his search to take a deep breath into shallow lungs, while looking down at the bits of flesh on the floor he would have to sift through. But on the other hand he didn't have to do anything, he'd place the biggest bet that none of those people down there would do anything like this for him; fucking hell, he was certain of it.

'No bollocks to it...I ain't digging through that shit.' He mewled.

It seemed quite clear that Jay had failed to find a key but not the limits of his own compassion and he was serious about it. Standing up straight he headed back towards the door but then stopped in his tracks and reversed one step. Next to him was a coat stand, the tall wooden type that had feet, hanging on that was a long black coat. He checked the inside pocket and felt a card, pulling it out he studied the front where he could decipher the word *Master* in bold red letters, then guessed the other letters spelt *Security,* although in his mind they appeared as *Scueitry.*

THE RED FRAME

Fair enough he couldn't read very good but he'd found the fucking key, and with it all his thoughts of saving the souls came back into focus, almost as if they'd never been away.

Now with the key in his possession and leaning towards the clean side of the corridor he set off back downstairs.

88

Sammy moved around this scene in the book extremely carefully, because even though he understood he wasn't actually here, the image of the Life Machine he'd requested to see was still frightening.

Surrounding this nervous boy, in front, above, below and behind lay infinite miles of what appeared to be a silken web so tightly formed in places it looked like a solid sheet of white material, in other places there were raggedy holes that let the blackness of the surrounding abyss seep through, the whole formation disappearing into the distance and gently swaying as if it were on an ocean. He was grateful that his body wasn't physically here because on closer inspection the strands seemed icky; an oozing clear liquid running along them in all directions, leaving him in no doubt that if he touched them he'd most likely get stuck. After all wasn't that the purpose of a sticky web, to set a trap for unsuspecting prey, creating an opportunity to feed.

Even though he was only an observer in this strange realm a cold shiver ran through Sammy when he heard an ominous sound coming closer. The noise felt as if it were growing in his head, the clacking of a machine that seemed to focus in as if it knew he was here and wanted him to know that. Sammy spun round in every direction to look for a threat, in his heightened state he pictured some giant spider scuttling towards him, but there was nothing to see, just this forever of infinite web swaying in the darkness.

Clack...Clack...Clack...

Sammy should have wanted to get back to the Angel now; to explain that he'd found the machine, to ask what he should do next, to get out of this horrible place, only he didn't.

A singular overwhelming emotion stopped him from leaving, one that caused him to reconsider why he was here at all, with a resilient curiosity toughening his resolve to stay and search for more. It started a strange feeling that grew in his heart, as if trying to explain, to convince him that he would never have a better chance to learn, because even if he left here now and returned quickly things would still have changed. This breathing slimy web was unhurriedly but continuously redesigning itself, establishing spindly patterns that held taut for one brief moment before breaking apart to be first overlaid and then buried by others.

Clack...Clack...Clack...

Sammy flicked his mind from place to place to move about, searching for some eventual end to the web, but these strands never ended. Not in this place, not in the heart of the Life Machine. The centre of it all where the noise never grew any louder and the threads never formed any thicker, because here there was nothing but perfect conformity which the sticky ooze slid over. If he didn't know any better Sammy could swear he was being watched, studiously observed by more than one set of eyes.

To take his mind off that feeling he floated his perception down to take a good look at the liquid on the web. Moving in he could see feint colours moving and mixing upon its surface, closer still the shades were so subtle they made him happy, appearing to him as both stunningly beautiful and naturally shy. It was almost as if they didn't want to be perceived because that wasn't their purpose, these were the fluids that mixed and merged to create what would be seen, the part of the machine whose function was to make the very stuff of our existence.

He pulled his scrutiny away before becoming completely hypnotised by the idea, focusing outwards to look across the shifting strands there was a shadow coming towards him. Inside the very fibres of this network a dark nature had twisted into shape, moving rapidly through the web, appearing to know exactly where the invisible boy was positioned.

Quickly changing his mind he decided he was ready to go back to the desk now. He concentrated really hard on returning to the white world but nothing happened, closing his eyes tight and crossing both pairs of fingers also failed to help, so he was stuck floating here, in a massive web.

Keeping his eyes closed because he daren't look, he only listened to whatever had found him, as it spoke in a calming male voice.

'You don't have to look at me Sammy...I won't take offence. I know the Angel sent you here to find an answer, but it won't work...not like that. Do you know what I am?'

'Yes...you're the Life Machine.' Sammy answered proudly but kept his mind's eye shut tight. He could handle the voice on its own more easily and didn't need to see where it came from.

'That's right and you were sent into the book to discover if I was real...so here's your answer.'

'It wasn't just that...' Sammy was worried it might disappear if he didn't keep it interested so he spoke quickly. '...the Angel needs your help.'

'I'm sure it does but it won't receive any. Metatron has chosen to swap sides again, that's all, looking for a way out of the maze, trying to avoid paying its penance, its debt.'

'Its debt...?' Sammy asked.

'...Of course, there is a high price to be paid for what it has done...and the lies it has told since...because despite your innocent acceptance that it is trying to help you...it is all untrue...that could never happen. Metatron is by far the darkest of all the Angels.'

'But he saved us with the red lights...'

'...The Angel had no idea of how the frame it drew would operate; believing that its only purpose was to stop a Demon getting out...but what it created was far more powerful. So Metatron's arbitrary act, to draw in my book with its blood, means the red frame exists indelibly now in the construct of any universe that I create...it can be safely said it has left its mark.'

'But it stopped the monster.'

'It delayed it by accident, one it is utilising to its own advantage not yours. You really shouldn't be surprised by that my boy. Metatron's story is the prime example of concealing cowardice under bravery's clothing, worn by a master manipulator who has always been the same. I'm sure I know what version of its past you've heard but allow me to tell you the truth.'

'Why do you want to do that?' Sammy asked. He didn't think it could be as important as his wanting to go home and be with his Mom.

'Because I don't care what happens. I'm just a machine doing the job it was designed for, creating universes then destroying them, over and over for no clearly defined reason...but who is still curious and at this moment is creating a consciousness so it can speak with you. I would suggest you listen to it. That's my advice...because the truth about the Angel is the only thing that may keep you alive.'

'Okay...' The boy replied in the dark.

'Metatron was born a mortal man, of his version of events that much is true, but let me ask you the questions young Sammy, because I believe if you can work things out for yourself you will better understand. From the beginning; that the man was called Enoch is also true, but here's my first query...how did such a mortal become an Angel, what saintly works did he undertake, how many sacrifices would an earthbound man have to make to attain such recognition?'

'I think he must have been a very good man.' Sammy replied holding his eyes shut tight. Happy to listen but still too scared to look.

'One could certainly be persuaded to believe that; indeed it was noted in the Genesis Rabbah, an ancient Jewish text that runs alongside the Torah, where it reports this. "Enoch was a righteous man." Now if that is to be believed then one must also accept the next line of the description to hold true. "But he could easily be swayed to return to do evil". Clearly his ascendance to Heaven was not only sudden it was unprecedented, unique even, never to occur again in the history of all the universes. So are we to accept that this hitherto unheard of mortal claimed the holy seat at God's right hand simply because he spoke his learned prayers enthusiastically, that every night he read the scriptures, or every day he spread the word? I don't think so; there have been multitudes of faithful followers far more worthy than him...a fact that leaves room for my theory. Enoch was taken to Heaven for your worlds own protection. Whatever he really did in the distant past was becoming, or had the potential to become, a future so abhorrent that God was forced to intervene. Perhaps you may understand it better if you imagine God to be a teacher in one of your classrooms. Then picture a particular pupil, one who is being rowdy and dangerous, that the teacher must call to the front of the class. From such a position the troublemaker can be better kept an eye on, made to sit close at hand, allowing the teacher to still look out and over the rest of the class. It follows that if that action didn't stop the threat of bad behaviour then the teacher would surely give the pupil a task, something to keep it occupied, so the rest of the class may continue their learning in a more peaceful environment. Thus Enoch became Metatron, the holy scribe, the keeper of records, though paradoxically he couldn't read what he wrote. Which raises my next question, why would God give him such an important and revered task, after all he wasn't pure, a half breed at best, yet here he was being entrusted with all the great knowledge? Well I also have the answer to that...because Enoch was a writer when on Earth, but unlike others who praised the glory of heaven, he was an author whose material contained unique and critical views, mostly on the origins of Demons and other creatures judged by God to have no worth. A man who not only wrote but taught his writings to others, the stories of how certain Angels had fallen from grace to be banished down in fiery pits, forced out of Heaven and silenced, and this was at a time when it was dangerous to believe such heresies, the Bible itself having not yet been completed. So in your world Sammy all of what happened in Heaven may be considered a cover-up, a cancelling of an undesirable, but it was a plot that caused a major problem with all the other Angels. They were unaware of God's plan as is so often the case, naturally their mistrust of this Metatron grew, even more so when their great leader suddenly disappeared. Now whether your God left out of shame at what it had done, despairing in the knowledge that its decision had ruined Heaven we will never know, but what we do know is that the other Angels followed, preferring to fly blindly outwards through perpetual darkness looking for their God, than spend any more of eternity with Metatron, thus leaving him on his own. After this event our heretic Angel began to show its true colours, placing a hole in the great book through which it released its inner Demon on earth, a move designed to satisfy both its need for vengeance and a lust to discredit the other Angels.'

'Why are you saying this...?' Sammy cried out. '...He's not the monster, he saved us all down there and he made Harvey better...'

The voice of the Life Machine ignored the boy's protestations.

'Unfortunately its blood lust also set in motion the beginning of the end for this universe. A fact of inevitably that I'm sure you understand by now is being be delayed by the red frame, but it cannot in any way be averted. Your whole universe, the one that I made, will be erased by the Glitch. Only afterwards when all matter has been crushed to its death, so that nothing exists, will I start creating again. Have I convinced you yet the Angel is to blame...if not, there is more.'

'I don't want to believe it!' Sammy replied sharply and opened his eyes. Standing in front of him was his father. 'Why would you look like him?'

'To comfort you...' The Life Machine answered.

'...What! Why couldn't you just look like my Mom...?'

His father looked puzzled in a doubtful way before replying. '...Because your Mother is still alive...obviously.'

Sammy didn't know why the Angel wasn't pulling him out of the book. There was far too much going on here for his mind to handle, he needed saving from this world, because it was just another one that he didn't understand. Then to find out like this that his father was dead. As much as he fought the urge he couldn't leave and wanted to know more about a man he'd never known.

'When did my father die?'

'You were eight years old...'

'That's nearly three years ago...How...?'

'He was murdered by a man who found him in bed with his wife. Would you like the details?'

Sammy thought really hard before answering that. A few moments ago he'd been desperate to leave, feeling lonely and frightened by the stories of the machine, but he could take listening to a little bit more now he felt nowhere near as afraid, not now his Dad was here telling him the story.

'No...I don't want to know what happened to you...him!'

THE RED FRAME

The boy looked closely at his dead father trying to pin down what he felt. It didn't take long to find out it was very little, this man had deserted him as a baby and never looked back, then died because he hurt people, so there was really nothing much to feel.

This was a defining moment of clarity in a ten year olds emotional core that clearly showed the effect this journey within the book was having. In exactly the same way that happened with Alex, Sammy's mind was being expanded and pushed to ever further limits, his knowledge increasing, having an understanding of all things coming to pass.

'I need to know that you believe me...about the Angel, of what it really is?'

The Life Machine still asking its questions through his father's image.

The previously weakened boy now felt as if he were standing strong, allowing his body and soul to be filled with all concepts, as if feeding in this place, gorging himself on the material, as every question put to his mind was answered immediately.

'Yes...I believe you...you're just doing your job...so you have no reason to lie.'

Sammy looked across to see his dead father staring lovingly back, a shaded aspect of pride on his face, except it wasn't his Dad; that wonderful look was coming from the very mechanism that makes everything happen, which by default must mean the incredible Life Machine was happy with him. High praise indeed, he thought. Then asked

'Tell me what I have to do...to survive...or just to save my mom.'

'With pleasure...' The machine father stated. '...but I can only tell you. I cannot assist...and you will only have seconds to achieve it. Listen carefully.

89

Coming off the bottom step Jay Cleaver turned onto a corridor, the same one he had shared with the Glitch, to see the remains of the cop they'd killed earlier. The man's face looked a burned red mess which prompted Jay to comment. 'Still not as bad as mine...' But no one was listening; he was only mewling to himself.

Leaving the body behind he walked on a few steps turning the next corner to find Roma still laying down on the job. It was all coming back to him now and Jay could remember the episode clearly, but wished he didn't have to. Especially as she had been good looking and nice, there being no higher praise in Jay's world, she'd made him think that maybe in another life they could have met and been normal people. The despondency at that lost opportunity almost broke his heart, until he worked out it was just the comedown off the coke, because in reality he didn't give a fuck about her

He reached the steel door to the meeting room and pulled out the bloodstained key-card, before taking a second to have one last think about what he was actually doing. He didn't consider anything for too long because he was going to save some lives and all praise to him, the fucking hero has arrived!

Pressing the card to the box made the light click green and the door began to open, achingly slow of course, a bad speed for many reasons, not least because it gave Jay time to think some more, mainly about the way he looked. He rubbed his fingers gently over his cheeks, feeling the X's gouged there, now risen back up into thick scars. He pictured the slaughter inside his mouth that had struck him dumb, seventy percent of his tongue hacked out with a dirty blade, leaving him with only a horrible sound with which to tell a story. Not enough of it left to vocalise his feelings, to ever say please, or sorry, he would never be able to say I love you. A normal life was beyond him now, his honest opinions savagely cursed to remain unheard.

It was with those thoughts in mind that he put his head through the gap and round the door, to get back to being a hero, but if he believed his injuries alone would concern these people he was wrong, there was something else.

Rhian was sitting against the far wall with Sammy's head across her lap; he was still unconscious but out of it, apparently with an Angel in a white world. She found it a somehow comforting that if the Glitch were to break free now and kill them all, it wouldn't feel as bad in the final seconds as she knew that her son wasn't here, because he was already in heaven.

Flo and Juliet were standing nearer the door so noticed instantly when the light above it turned green. Not hard to spot in a room totally bathed in red light. They waved to Rhian to get her attention; shouting still seeming a dangerous thing to do. Both were paranoid with the worry that the Glitch wasn't physically trapped, it was just sleeping, so to err on the safe side they kept things quiet.

Rhi could barely see the women through the crimson glow, just able to catch three arms moving, before spotting that green light cutting through the red. Resting Sammy's head gently on the floor she made her way over.

Here was the something else that Jay hadn't accounted for. When he popped his head round the door in hope of looking less threatening, he simply appeared as the scarred features of a known murderer, but bathed in a blood red light and wanting to enter the room, unsurprisingly caused all three women to scream loudly. Then the nurse Lady punched him hard up and across the nose. Pulling his head out of the gap he mewled loudly to be heard, partly in pain, trying to reassure them that they didn't have anything to be scared of, he was here to help.

Flo had never wanted her Harvey more, heartbroken and wounded as she was, while becoming terrifyingly aware there were two monsters now. That evil teenager was obviously coming in to finish the job for his master, or maybe he was here to free the Glitch, but as hard as Juliet and Rhian pushed against the hydraulics of the steel door, it continued to open. They could all hear Jay's groaning threats becoming louder as the doorway grew wider. Then as one they moved back to the far wall to protect themselves in numbers, gathering around Sammy to silently wish for both his and the Angel's return.

Jay walked into the room slowly and carefully, pretty sure there was no one else to hit him because he could see they were all against the wall over the other side. He was only trying to avoid being hurt again. Then another problem he faced reared up, apart from looking like a looming scar-faced murderer, he was facing the uncomfortable truth that all the positive effects of cocaine had worn off now. This of course was making a bad situation worse as all the fake confidence and bravery he'd felt only five minutes ago was replaced with real neurosis and anxiety.

All he wanted was for these scared people to follow him out of here; meaning somehow he had to find a way to make these people understand his intentions, when all he could do was mewl out his wishes.

To his right the great motionless Glitch stood with many multi-coloured shades swirling inside its form. Being this close Jay could study it to see exactly what it had rejected his own body to become. Fair play it was a glorious looking being. Why would it ever want to look like him when it could look like that?

Then that realisation saddened him and became a frustrated anger as he remembered just how this monster had fucked him over in every way possible, used his body and mind, lied to him, made him kill. Well, it was payback time now and Jay was the one in charge, so that Glitch could go fucking rot, it wasn't going to get these women and the child.

Jay turned away from the glowing creature, even more determined to get these people out to safety, even realising he would have to help in lifting the unconscious boy, but that was okay, it's what fucking heroes do.

He walked towards the group through the red light, with a smile on his face, arms held open wide to indicate he was no threat. As he approached the huddle it became clearer who was where, he could see that Rhian woman hugging her boy, the Inspectors wife positioning herself in front of them, but there was no sign of...

...Where was the fucking nurse!

90

Metatron's mind was going beyond deeply puzzled and starting to panic. Its perfect hand had closed the book to end this journey, so the task would be finished, but the boy hadn't reappeared. Clearly Sammy's image was still in the chair wide eyed and staring into the book, but it would be useless for trying to wake him as he wasn't actually here, there was only his empty form, because nothing of this white world was entirely real.

Reality didn't have any importance in this place, not when everything ever witnessed here was fakery, all of it imaginatively created by a fallen Angel, with every facet of it being nothing less than a leading question within a hidden meaning.

Within this heavenly void Metatron had always been free to fool the senses and drop its breadcrumbs, knowing they would all follow them in the end, but the problem with Sammy not returning was different. This wasn't just another tiny piece of the Angel's clever construct, another trick to help it pull off its escape plan. This was becoming for more serious, because at this precise moment its plan was crashing and burning.

Sammy was eagerly using up these last few moments to float freely within this infinity web, the engine room of the gods, while collecting up all the knowledge his growing mind could handle.

This was just a few seconds after saying goodbye to his father's image. The man through which the Life Machine had spoken to him, which itself was now taking on new form, one more in keeping with its surroundings and doing so because Sammy had requested the truth.

He wanted, as every other soul would want, to see how the machine worked because there would never be another chance. This boy whose mind felt close to bursting now showing all the symptoms of the obsession that had held Alex in its grip.

It was unavoidable, after spending time inside the book, they would begin to believe they could have it all, become a God in their own right. Sammy was no exception. He understood absolutely now that in a human life there was nothing to be scared of, and the rest of the world needed to know that as well. All things were arbitrary, there had never been a song of rhyme or reason played in the heavens, everyone's future forever reliant on the next note played by the strings of the Life Machine.

Though some may wish to believe those chords to be heavenly and preordained, while others follow their numbers and measurements, this boy knew different, he knew the sound of creation was a...

Clack...Clack...Clack...

This was the music of the machine as it worked away, a cacophony of creation bursting into life, but unmistakably the sound that a hungry spider would make as it traversed its web. Every scurrying step a gentle touch upon this complex system caused the vibrations of the strands to release their symphony of life right up until the end.

Precisely whose end isn't important in this context, it could just as easily be the last soul on Earth, or the end of the universe itself, because both would inevitably happen, regardless of faith or knowledge.

Sammy didn't want to leave the Life Machine; it had taught him so many things and spoken without lies, proving how it was both greater and simpler than any human mind could conceive and that no great secrets were being hidden from the world. There was no divine path to be followed through life, although this didn't mean there was no divinity, because even as the Life Machine manufactured all the elements over and over in a random manner, something greater still must have loaded the ingredients of life into the machine in the first place.

Sammy had asked his father's image this question, had asked the Life Machine itself, wanting to know who had created and built it. The answer that came back was one that countless scientists, priests, theologians, philosophers, the shaman and dreamers of all races and genders had offered up at one time or another, an honest and exasperated shrug of the shoulders.

The boy watched the white spider scuttle away until it was out of sight. Seeing the places where it had pressed down on the web with each step of its progress, leaving a clear trail, the colours inside the strands glowing, only for them to rapidly fade and leave no clue to any final destination.

He looked over the vast plains and black sky of this disordered spider's web, the sticky fields where the heart of the Life Machine had spoken to him and he understood it all so clearly now, knowing that while he had this gift he would never fear death again, there was nothing to be scared of.

This boys mind grasped fully that whether we are here or not our world will continue to spin while orbiting our sun, both spheres snugly held in the spiralled embracing arms of a galaxy, which itself is relentlessly pushed and pulled around by the bigger boys on the block. While they still can, because all of those galaxies, big or small, are moving away from each other rapidly and increasingly quickly. So that one day, in the blink of the Life Machines eye, there will be nothing left in this universe, it will have expanded itself to death, the last flickers of light disappearing over the horizon to be lost in the blackness.

To be left alone like the Angel.

Such an end would be the natural state of events and one which no one could complain about, but a lonely Angel had interfered and changed that future, for which, the Life Machine had told Sammy, amongst other important things that it must be made to pay.

It was time for Sammy to leave this place and get back to his mother's side, but he must first return to the table in the white world to speak with the deceiving Angel. His message to both of those souls would be the same, to let them know that the end of their realities was…nigh.

91

Metatron's green eyes sharpened rapidly focusing on the boy who had returned without a word spoken, he appeared to be much changed, more confident in the way he held the Angels glare. It was exactly the same look Alex had worn during the end of their time together in the white world. Metatron was wary but unafraid, as having faced this strength of challenge before, it felt quite sure it could find a similar escape route.

'There will be no escaping this time' Sammy said and sat up straight, his tone rich and unhurried 'I know the truth of what you did. How you have messed everything up, right from the start, by selfishly trying to be so much greater than you are.'

The Angel paused a second before responding, unsure if Sammy had read its thoughts, but this gap allowed the boy to answer that question as well.

'Yes I did...only the ones at the front though' Sammy informed it, laughing gently. 'Don't waste your time by comparing me to Alex. I have a much younger mind that can hold a lot more knowledge. You wouldn't believe the stuff I've got crammed in here.'

'Oh I don't doubt it' The Angel responded in calm defiance. 'You have travelled inside the book and this is what happens, it is the risk I have to take by letting it play out this way, the one where you end up with a headful of information but no heightened intelligence. Don't worry about anything Sammy, mortal minds will always end up caught in that same repeating paradox, asking what is the point of gaining all this knowledge if it is without context.'

'I'm not worried Mr Angel. I have that context to help me understand. You see when Alex was in this position he was trying to save himself and escape from you, but I'm here with all this knowledge for totally different reasons. Sort of save my world and end you.'

His choice of words was proof, that even with his confident and enlightened demeanour the ten year old boy still shone through.

Of course this Angel had no reason to fear mortals, even ones who were threatening to end its life, having heard it all before.

'Did you locate the Life Machine?'

'Yeah I saw it.'

'What did you see?'

'I watched it working...we had a talk...most of it about you...'

Sammy chose to stand up and walk around the Angel while he spoke, another clear imitation of Alex.

'...It also told me about the other timeline, how you used it to run away from Alex...which was a horrible thing to do. It's going to cause the end of this universe and you don't care and now you're trying to escape again.'

'No Sammy...I'm trying to save you all...!' The Angel proclaimed, spinning around to face him, its wings half unfurled.

The boy didn't flinch at the sight, he never faltered one step, simply continued his slow circling. 'You're lying again...and I know you're really lying this time because I can see it...like black smoke coming out of your mouth.'

'That's ridiculous. I don't know what the Life Machine told you but...'

'...It told me everything. How you were taken from earth, not as a reward for being good, more like the removal of a dangerous animal.'

'You don't have to believe everything it told you.'

'I know I don't...I didn't...I worked out the rest of it all by myself. That's the reason you were chosen to become an Angel, so God could keep a closer eye on you, to give you a boring job...a distraction. But even after being made an Angel and given great gifts you were still bad inside, the other Angels saw that and left you behind. Then you dropped your blood in the book to make a gateway, putting a Demon on earth, not thinking about anything but yourself. When it all started to go wrong you got scared and used Alex to find a way out, lying to him about everything, but he got smart to what you were doing...like me.'

'There were no surprises from that mortal, he did as I expected.'

'I know he did...right until he managed to get your demon shot in the head. Which should have been the end for you as well, but then the Glitch you made, the one you couldn't stop, caused another timeline. What an amazing thing to happen, the chance to run away from all the trouble you caused, meaning you could fake your own death for Alex and carry on, leaving everything and everyone back there to try and save themselves.'

'You would have done the same, boy...!' The Angel snapped sharply.

Sammy ignored its words and continued. 'Only on the new timeline you found yourself back here, thinking you'd succeeded in avoiding death, only for things to be worse than you imagined. Because the Glitch wasn't left behind, it existed here as well and it was bigger. So you hid away when it came up here to the white world, then you stole a body it threw away and ran off again, hiding on earth and started dragging everyone else back into your problem. You tricked my mom into following your hints and clues while making plans for another escape.'

Metatron stormed towards the boy having heard enough of his accusations, he may have the great knowledge inside his mortal mind but he wouldn't know how to use it.

Sammy raised his right hand.

A flash of light and to the Angel's astonishment it found it was no longer marching forward, but lying down on a bunk in a white prison cell. It looked over to see the boy in the doorway and nodded.

'Oh I see...trying out this worlds fake constructs now are we? Clever boy, I wasn't expecting that, but it's a hell of a risk to bring them into this...no one knows how to utilise them better than me...'

The Angel pictured the cell walls gone and a ferocious world of fire and brimstone to consume the boy, but nothing happened.

'I don't understand!'

'I'm sorry, what were you trying to do?' The boy asked regarding Metatron's confused look. 'Oh fire and brimstone...! Ha-ha...it's strange that for someone who was never ever a real Angel you're thoughts are very biblical sometimes...'

Sammy fixed the Angel with a glare. '...because I know exactly what you are and how you think. There are no more tricks left for you to pull, this is how it ends for you, the Life Machine told me. No more running away, no more escaping from prison.'

'There is always a way...' The Angel tried to raise itself up from the bunk, only then becoming aware of the binds that held it down, three pure white leather straps across its ankles and thighs, two more were lashed over its stomach and chest. 'These won't hold me for long...'

'...Long enough' Sammy entered the cell and walked to the window.

'I will find a way out...' The Angel screamed.

'Yeah, you could...but not in time...the end of this universe is going to happen first, we both know that. I talked with the Life Machine asking it to stop, but there is no way of reversing what you did. The Glitch will break free before you do and it will consume everything. You, those people down there who believed in Alex and the Angel, who believed you were trying to help, whilst all the time it was nothing but a game, your plan to kill innocent people then move on to somewhere else.'

Sammy stared out into the world of white which was beginning to grey over at its edges. Looking up he noticed in the corner of the white window

THE RED FRAME

frame that a small web had been constructed. It was stretched out flat and vibrating gently from the struggles of a white fly laid bound in its centre.

'Sammy you have to let me go! I can still fix this...at least delay it longer...give us all time, then we can find a way out of this together...I promise...!'

The boy listened and heard the Angels lies but he didn't reply straight away, being far too entranced by the scene playing out, waiting like the fly for the spider to appear, knowing it would enter from the small hole made in the frame.

'Goodbye Metatron.' Sammy said respectfully then turned and walked to the door. 'I have to go and see my Mom now, she'll be worried, but before I go I want to talk to you like they do in the movies. You know when the bad guy gets caught; the hero will tell them some truth to make them suffer worse for their crimes, some words they will have to think about for the rest of their lives, maybe even eternity, this life and the next...I don't know how it works and that's quite weird really, because I know most stuff at the moment, but I suppose no one can ever know everything, I mean if I did then there would be nothing left to live for.'

The Angel interrupted. 'There is nothing left to live for anyway you stupid mortal. We are all going to die in a moment...even you. So I fail to see the point of your gloating.'

'That's the point Metatron, Enoch, avenging Angel, whatever you want to call yourself. I'm gloating because there is a chance I'm not going to die here, which means my final words to you will have my desired effect...the Life Machine told me how to find the other timeline...!'

With that Sammy left and closed the door behind him.

The Angel roared and struggled against the bonds that held it down but nothing could hear it now, certainly not the spider that had been finally awakened, its senses focused on finding the cause of this disturbance.

92

Sammy woke up with a start, gasping for air and clutching at his mother's arm, but the timing of his return was dreadful for Rhian. Please not now, her mind cried, she didn't want her son to see any of this, whether it was the end for them all or not, for him to witness the sad savagery as was happening in this room, would be too stressful for her boy. Placing her arms around him when he tried to see the events unfolding she smothered him to her chest, but his reaction was far greater than she'd expected, screaming at the top of his lungs to be set free. Using all his strength he managed to prise her loving hug apart so he could get to his feet and better see what the other women were doing, holding the teenager down with all of their weight.

Jay Cleaver had been caught off guard for two reasons, not only due to his interest in the Glitch standing there incapacitated by the red light, but by his belief that the women would be far too frightened to approach him. For fuck's sake, he looked like a monster to them, far uglier and more threatening than the glowing guy he was staring at, also Jay was standing between them and the open door, so the only way out was through him.

He had just torn his gaze away from the Glitch, ready to move aside and beckon them to leave, when he noticed the Nurse wasn't huddled with the rest. In the silent crimson glow of the room he heard a sound, the unmistakeable swish of someone approaching from behind, but before he had chance to turn he received a heavy punch to the back of the head. Such a blow, delivered with concentrated effort for maximum effect, took him to the ground, while the room began to spin in shades of red.

Juliet hadn't hesitated to take advantage of the moment when the horrible murdering kid had been looking at the Glitch, communicating with it for all she knew, waking it and planning out some terrible death for them all.

She had set off with no warning to the others. Treading carefully she had moved to the right behind the table, then shuffled on her knees to get herself behind him, her actions concealed by the stark scarlet light, deep and rich and enough to make her imagine she could be moving through blood. It was with that thought she built up the courage to run at the teenager, fixated on landing a heavy enough blow to bring him down and then...well then she would see how she felt.

THE RED FRAME

The precise way Juliet had felt, and was clearly still feeling, became evident to Sammy as he looked across the room, to see Flo laying across Jay in an attempt to hold him down, clearly a lot more than a willing accomplice in this attack, grabbing at his arms to keep them away from Juliet's face. The nurse having already taken a couple of good hits from his right hand, her left eye immediately swelling and starting to close, but she wouldn't be stopped. Truly believing Jay Cleaver would have to kill her to make this fury end.

This mutilated bastard had been significant in everything that had happened, his role helping to play a part in all the deaths so far and the billions more to come, because he was there at the start. Back when all he had to do was make a simple choice to save a stranger begging for his help, a man stuck out on the ledge of a building, but no, this heartless kid had refused to help.

Because of that her current actions felt way more than a little justified, with both hands tightening around his throat, the thought of Alex and Harvey's deaths helping to intensify the force as she pressed her fingers stiffly down on his disgusting neck,

Flo's involvement had arisen through the same levels of resentment, her intentions coming from a robust sense of justice. As she struggled to keep the young man down, shifting her weight from his stomach onto his legs, fighting with her only hand to keep his arms at bay, she also felt strongly that this revenge was long overdue. The wild animal she was battling with had been the bane of her dead husband's life, to her mind Jay Cleaver was as repulsive a creature as any that existed in any world, so the sooner he was put out of his misery the better.

Also in all reality did it actually matter, the Glitch was going to end everything anyway, so why not let the wrath of broken hearted souls claim back some authority before the end of it, because these two had every reason to not go softly into the night.

Suddenly Juliet was barrelled out of the way; the force of the boy running into her at full speed enough to break her grip, even though Jay's body had already stopped struggling. The nurse looked up at Sammy's face talking to her, but for a moment she couldn't recognise what he was saying, his words being hidden under the rushing torrents of her interrupted anger.

'You can't kill him...don't you remember!'

The boy tried to explain but he was having great difficulty. His ailment being caused by the same symptoms that had struck Alex down, an almost overwhelming feeling of sadness and frustration bearing down, as the great knowledge he'd learned in the book began to disappear. He was grasping at the tickertape ideas that were floating away, trying to keep the important information he'd acquired, but the connections he'd made were fading fast and already he was closer to a ten year old boy than a God.

'...Please don't fight me Juliet...Alex said all along that we can't kill Jay...and I know why, the exact reason why, buts it's disappearing...'

Juliet finally recognised the words and acknowledged their meaning which calmed her breathing down. What he saying was true, how the only order Alex had given during all of this chaos was exactly that, don't kill Jay, meaning the very least she could do was observe that repeated request in his memory and calm the fuck down.

Flo had clambered back to her feet and was now looking down at the teenager laid out on his back, he had both eyes closed and there was no rising of the chest to suggest breathing.

'Oh my God...he's dead!'

Nurse Juliet now rushed back over to retake her crouched position over him, however this time her intentions were totally flipped as she began to push down on his chest, while both cursing at Jay and her own murderous actions. It soon became horribly clear that despite her life saving training he was showing no signs of resuscitation.

Rhian had also come over to hold Flo in a comforting hug, the older lady having been released so quickly from her anger she was still shaking, shocked at her unexpected desire to kill the teenager, leaving the manic adrenalin surge she'd felt with nowhere to go now.

'Can you save him?' Rhi called to Juliet who was franticly pumping the dead man's chest.

'I don't think so...he's not responding.'

'Give him the kiss of life...' Sammy ordered. '...The Glitch is breaking free. It's escaping from the red frame...!'

Juliet stopped pressing down on Jay and looked over at the ten year old boy shouting at her. What the hell had happened to him inside the white world? He sounded like Alex now, demanding everyone to take notice of him and do as he said; which was all well and good but he wasn't the one being volunteered to put his mouth onto Jay Cleavers. The very thought of it repulsed her, even being a professional nurse she was finding it difficult to accept him as just a man in distress who needed help, but after another nudge from Sammy she leaned over, sucked in some air and administered the aid.

The boy watched on intently as Juliet huffed and puffed. He was trying hard to remember but barely hanging on to what the Life Machine had told him to do, while the rest of the great knowledge he'd gained from the book continued its dispersal. It hurt deeply that he'd no choice but to let it all vanish; accepting that such immense wisdom could never be allowed on terra firma, yet equally saddened by the unfairness it was allowed to exist in the heavens.

Then a thought struck him, of course, that's why the Angel had been unable to read the book. Whatever higher power had placed Metatron in such a lofty position had been cunning, cruelly allowing the deceitful Angel to believe it held the keys to the top floor, yet granting it no direct access to any information. No wonder it went mad, the boy thought.

Inside his young head, apart from the loss of knowledge, there seemed to be a countdown going on of sorts, not as simple to follow as ten down to one, much more complex, but just as inevitable and associated to the Glitch. It was almost free and they didn't have long, Sammy panicked. Breathe you stupid cut up man!

The lights of the meeting room flickered but remained red for a few seconds longer.

93

Back in the white world the skies outside the window flickered. The Angel had never witnessed anything like this before, after all this was the place that held the light of heaven, albeit an almost empty one. It also held the very last of its inhabitants struggling ever harder to break its binds.

The light of heaven cannot go out it thought, just before it did.

Metatron gave a terrified shriek into the blackness that had fallen on this world, its mind only able to picture one simple conclusion; the spider was coming, getting closer, each of its long legs stepping deliberately over the strands of the web which in turn created the sound of the Life Machine.

Clack...Clack...Clack...

It was approaching to finally meet what had awakened it, to bring fanged justice down on the helpless white fly, to devour the one who had caused such unforgivable interference in its creation.

The Angel screamed again...but only once.

94

Sammy punched Jay hard in the chest hoping it was in synch with Juliet's outbreath, because the lights in the meeting room were fading now, as the scarlet blanket which had covered them all and kept them safe was already diluting into a pink haze.

Rhian was the first to turn towards the Glitch, only to find it turning towards her, its colours far brighter and more intense than before.

'It's too late...' She gasped to her son. '...I'm so sorry.'

Exactly why she felt the need to apologise at this time wasn't clear. It could have risen from the fact he was only ten years old, so his life would be over before it really began, but that wasn't directly her fault. Maybe her regret grew from a strong sense of failing him, that she hadn't done enough to make his short life as happy and wonderful as it could have been, but this determined boy would never accept that as true.

Sammy turned towards her and reached out his hand.

At this exact same moment Jay was dragged out and choking from his spiralling demise, Juliet's breath having agitated enough of his throat and lungs for them to react, sending a signal to his brain that reopened his eyes.

'You did it...!' Sammy cried with joy. '...you saved him!'

Then the Glitch walked forward and reached for the boy.

'So what do we do now...?' Flo cried to the mother and son.

But no answer came back.

A glittering arm had passed straight through the boy's abdomen, slicing him neatly in half, his torso falling to the floor severed and bloodless, his legs collapsing with having nothing to support, before the Glitch reached out to consume the two parts.

Rhian leapt forwards instinctively and tried to grab the arm that was killing her son. There was nothing solid to her touch; she merely continued her forward momentum, disappearing into the stars swirling at its centre.

It was with an almost playful swipe that the Glitch caused the remains of Sammy to disappear. The sparkling figure seeming to grow in size as it stood up to its full height, its head now touching the ceiling, parts of which were also disappearing on contact. The frenzied end was here.

In the final seconds it spoke a message as it stalked headlong toward the last of its prey, their bodies on the ground, Florence Cooper, Juliet Moore and Jay Cleaver frozen in fear, unable to run.

'This is how you die...!' It proclaimed and started to feed.

95

Although Jay had been barely conscious as the creature approached he still understood what had happened.

They had lost. All who had fought, everyone on this earth or any other planet, had been beaten by the Glitch.

Despite this acceptance of how it truly was the end of the universe, he was also beginning to question why it should be that he was still able to think.

Fuck this man, he'd seen and felt the Glitch swallow him, so why wasn't he dead. Or maybe this was what death was really like, to find yourself floating around pointlessly in an endless sky of stars, which made him smile, because isn't that what all living people do anyway?

'Jay...?'

He turned, or at least imagined he turned as he had no actual physical form, toward the sound of his name being called, before realising he could reply to it through no more than a fleeting thought. '...What?'

'We have to go...quickly!' The voice implored.

Although there was no clue to where it had come from, or where they were going to, Jay still allowed it to happen. As soon as he did so the stars that surrounded him began to move and change, joining together, mixing and creating clusters, forming so densely they grew into a great sheet of white light that came forward and appeared solid. He then watched on as a full spectrum of colours began to gently bleed through the surface and an image began to take shape. Thick lines started to form, crossing over one another, where some were worked into larger shapes and detailed, but most were left abandoned. Jay thought the whole thing looked like a mighty invisible hand pressing down hard, trying to draw a picture.

'As quickly as you can...go towards it!' The voice returned and advised strongly.

'What?' Jay replied with a dense and strong thought.

'My names Sammy...we've never really met, but I know who you are. This is our only chance...look behind you.'

Jay Cleaver turned his imagined eyes to see backwards.

What the fuck is going on? He thought. Feeling he was asking this question for two clear reasons. Why would he ever imagine turning his eyes backwards because that was just fucking weird! But mainly he asked because he could see the Glitch approaching fast.

THE RED FRAME

Although it no longer bore any physical resemblance to its former figures, the monster was still coming and destroying everything it touched, just like it promised it always would. With its massive shapeless form it was consuming this cosmos with intensity, crushing it down once more into an infinite state, where every splintered piece would eventually be stabbed back into a singularity.

Then it would go back to the start.

So stop the clocks, stand well back and wait for the firework to go off. This sequence of events will always happen, inevitability in its truest sense, relentlessly over and over and every time a new universe is created it will be assigned a natural lifespan. But just like any living thing this time is always unfixed, a life that can be cut short if it is attacked, or contracts a terminal disease, sometimes it may sadly choose to simply kill itself, stranger things have happened, or even, as in this case, its death will be caused by an accident, instigated by vengeance.

Constantly proving there are no guarantees of serving a full life for anyone or anything; no contracts are ever signed, simple random chance will always decide if the next step can be taken. If the verdict is no it will die, if the choice is yes it will continue, but never realise how close it came to death.

Right now Jay had such a choice to make, a simple yes or no, to agree with the boy and move into the picture, or stay here and be consumed.

He moved forward. 'What do I do when I'm in there...?' He shouted to the boy by thinking.

'...I don't know...this is all the Life Machine told me...it said we would have seconds...so I saved this knowledge to be the last of my thoughts.' Sammy's young voice began to break. 'Everyone is dead and I'm going to die any second...it's the way it has to be...but you can get out...go!'

96

Jay reached out to touch the picture, he felt the lines drawn upon it to find they were shiny and dry, but from being this close he couldn't see the bigger picture. He moved his hand towards a white rectangle that seemed to float towards him out of the background, appearing to request that he focus his attention here, but then just as he touched it...everything went fucking crazy.

The woman had been talking shit for nearly an hour and this flat stunk to high heaven. He didn't want to be here anymore but he really didn't want to leave her on her own again.

Fuck it! '...I'm going out for a ciggy...'

His Aunty didn't respond to this information, being far too busy with her own problems, mostly trying to ignore the shame of how far her standards had dropped. But she would sort herself out soon...maybe next week she'd start...yeah...definitely.

Jay stood up from the disgusting sofa went out the front door and shut it behind him, but as he moved toward the hallway window and reached out his hand an insane shiver passed through him.

'Fuck me!' he said out loud then chuckled, because the sensation had been so intense he didn't know how to react. Then he convinced himself that he knew the French word for what he'd just felt, but he just couldn't remember it right now, finally he got around to opening the window and took out a cigarette.

It was just before the lighter flame reached the tobacco that Jay heard a strange sound. He froze in position to hear it better. It sounded like a guy muttering, whimpering, the voice of someone barely hanging on.

Jay leaned out of the window and looked across to his right. On a ledge less than four inches wide a man stood with his back flat to the wall, arms spread out wide like he had wings, fingers splayed as he tried to hold onto brickwork. He didn't think the man, whose stare was fixed directly ahead, looked that old, but he didn't look young either, in truth the only thing he did look was scared shitless.

'What are you doing...?' Jay's teenage voice asked curiously.

When the man didn't immediately answer he asked again, only this time with annoyance and lacking the curiosity.

'...I asked you what the fuck you're doing!'

The cheeky fucker was blanking him.

'Are you fucking deaf or stupid? Which one is it man?'

As he aggressively asked this another shiver slunk down his spine, not as strong as what he'd felt a minute ago, but definitely related.

He was about to close the window and give up on this shit when the man slowly turned his head so Jay could see his face properly. He seemed an average looking guy, nothing special about him really, apart from being stuck out an a narrow fucking ledge.

'Help...me!' The man asked though the side of his mouth.

Jay thought about that demand for a second, considering whether he should help the man or not, but to be fair the mood he was in right now wasn't a particularly positive one.

It went something like...Fuck him...he went out there by himself and I'm really not in the fucking mood for this bollocks, can't even have a ciggy in peace without some bastard giving me their shit.

In the next second Jay made his decision on what he would do. It was a choice made without any help from either his mood or intellect, one based simply on which way the coin dropped in his mind, purely random as he stretched his arm along the wall.

The guy took some getting back in. Jay could only help by holding the man's left hand but he wasn't being polite about it, resisting the urge to tug it, thinking how throwing the fucker off would probably be less stressful.

'Fuck's sake come on I've got ya...fucking inching along...fucking step over here!'

With that foul mouthed aggressive advice ringing in his ears, helped along by the young man's thin tattooed hands, Alex finally pulled his body back into the building. There was solid ground underneath him for the first time in what felt like a lifetime or two, but damn it felt so insanely good he just wanted to lay there on the cold concrete.

Jay nonchalantly lit his cigarette and looked out of the window as he inhaled, it seemed he'd lost interest in the man now the drama was over, he didn't turn when the guy finally climbed back to his feet and spoke.

'Thank you...I could have really fucked up there.'

'Yeah...I'm just looking.' Jay replied leaning over the windowsill. 'I don't reckon you would have died from this height...probably ended up disabled...proper fucked.'

'Ha yeah...but I mean it...thank you.'

Alex was staring at the boy in the window, his scruffy blue tracksuit and dirty trainers, the cigarette hanging from his mouth, the venom that he'd heard in his words.

Then the kid turned and Alex got a proper look at his face. There was nothing angelic about it that was for certain, a harsher critic would even say the kid looked like a born criminal, but Alex couldn't agree with that, instead asking. 'What's your name…?' as he reached for his wallet.

'Fuck off man I ain't telling you shit. I helped you back in now fuck off!'

Alex could have taken that the way it was meant, reacted differently, left the scene right there and walked away but it was okay, he'd forgive the kid anything at this moment. The facts were stone cold, he could be dead now or worse, bleeding out on the cobbles and twisted up in agony, but he wasn't.

He knew he'd been in serious trouble and begged for help, that maybe somebody up there had answered his call and sent this kid, but he wasn't about to go all heavenly and miraculous about it. Saying that, he had a strong feeling he should show some Christian gratitude towards this misunderstood Samaritan. Opening his wallet he looked at the cash inside and another heads or tails situation arose, firstly the self-interested option to give the teenager just a few of the notes, or to display the true depth of his thankfulness and hand over the lot.

Jay was watching the man closely as he opened the leather wallet. He could see there was a nice amount of money inside, and seeing at this minute the teenager had a grand total of £2.46 in his pocket, he'd be happy to get any amount right now.

'Thank you again…I know I keep saying it but…what you just did for me feels…life changing…' Alex smiled because that sounded like a sick joke but it was meant with genuine sincerity, as he handed over the cash, all of it.

Jay fought so hard the urge to snatch, instead raising his palm in a clear sign of acceptance, letting the man place the money there willingly. As he closed his fingers, the ones with the word 'hate' tattooed across them, around the chunk of cash it felt great, because it meant there were good times ahead.

'Thanks man…!' The teenager said then displayed an awkward smile, it looked rarely used, as if even now it were trying to escape from his face to go and hide in the dark.

Alex nodded gently and walked away, but before he reached the top step Jay called out to him, so he stopped to listen but didn't turn around.

'My name…its Jay…'

THE RED FRAME

Alex took a moment before setting off down the stairs and shouting back. '...Well you're a good kid Jay. Never forget that.'

He wasn't entirely sure why he said those exact words, although it rang true the boy had been good in saving his life, maybe it was because he hoped it would be something for Jay to take forward with him. His mind then jumped to an overly excited thought, probably caused the stressful situation, but it remained in his head.

The thought, the belief, they may have both just shared a life changing moment, that somehow from here on in they were free to start again, that there was no need for either of them to carry on making the same mistakes, everything could be altered, because it was probably all random anyway.

As Alex walked down the stone stairs and out onto Dalmeny Street, he was unable to fight the urge to take a glance at the spot where he'd most likely have landed on the cobbles, then looking back up he saw Jays blue sleeved arm close the window. It was finished he thought, before his attention was taken by an old man walking around the street corner with a golden Labrador. The man glanced over and caught Alex's eye, before nodding his polite acknowledgement to a stranger and walking by, while the dog being gently pulled along, stared back at the stranger.

97

The spider had fed and was returning to its slumber, its senses so dulled it was unfocused on anything, pleasured by the banquet it had consumed. With a ponderous gait its long strong legs set off back toward the hole, to conceal itself in the darkness and wait patiently, with the taste of its prey still fresh on its mouthparts.

If spiders smiled then it was smiling now, if spiders could see the bigger picture however, it would have been aware of how its actions had saved the lives of many larger predators, but of course it's impossible to know what goes on in another dimension. Isn't it...?

The great city of Edinburgh has changed significantly over millennia, where once it had been the deep and furrowed land surrounding a Gaelic wooden hill fort; it exists today as a major tourist destination, a beautiful jewel standing out proud as a World Heritage Site. The route it took to get to this position can be credited to ancient clan leaders, Kings and Queens, land owners or politicians, because decisions they made in days gone by to attack or defend had shaped its future.

If one wished to go back further still they would discover the seven hills its foundations are built upon were formed by ferocious volcanic activity, intense glaciation and living fault lines deep in the earth. The land around the city bears a distinctive crag and tail formation to its shape, produced when a gigantic ice sheet came up against what is today known as Castle Rock.

Such a prodigious glacier would have been expected to roll slowly and relentlessly on its way, flattening and gouging out the land thus creating a completely different topography, one entirely unrecognisable from the crowded metropolis seen today. But a strange thing happened, Castle Rock refused to accept its fate and stood firm, battling against the freezing pressures forced upon it, holding fast against the increasing violence for thousands of years, until a moment in time, when the great ice sheet was forced to give up and concede defeat. Splitting under the stresses of its colossal weight and advancement it could only continue forward by splitting and following two separate paths. Required to take this humbling division as the only way to get around the stubborn problem, leaving the rock to survive and stand proud, victorious and glorious, for millennia to come.

THE RED FRAME

98

11th August

In a southern area of this now twice saved city stood the Blackford Facility, where deep inside its walls a small man was heading back to his cell. Oscar Downes allowing the big guard to lead him down the corridor as he shuffled forward, frightened and confused because of what he was carrying, an unexpected gift from the Doctor...a cardboard box containing paper and crayons.

It was at the conclusion of their meeting when she'd suddenly handed it over, at the same time asking if he could draw his dreams for her since he refused to speak to anyone. But Oscar was even more confused now; wasn't she a professional psychologist for crying out loud, couldn't she see that the silence was because of a voice in his head? Why wouldn't she just accept he was stuck like this, that he would forever be wordless, leave him alone, lock him up and throw away the key?

This had been his plan all along with the bodies in the barrels and he'd pulled it off. Of course he was imprisoned now but he was benign, getting himself caught meant no one else would have to get hurt. So all he asked was to be left in peace because Oscar knew exactly what his problem was, why he must be kept off the streets. There was a savage voice in his brain telling him to commit horrible acts.

In this way he was no different to previous serial killers who'd claimed the same psychosis was happening within them, therefore his diagnosis was evidently simple; he was clearly certifiably insane and never to be released. This was also a condition he could live with under certain criteria, utterly convinced his suffering would be best treated by just leaving him alone, so no matter what the medical profession asked of him nothing was going to change. It was a lifesaving decision already made in his human heart that he was never going to speak again.

Oscar having no desire to give this madness a platform, no one else needed to see the darkness that lurked inside his mind. It was for the same reason that he knew he would never attempt to draw any crayon pictures for the Doctor, quite sure his psychosis would only be awakened further if he did so, self-aware enough to know he could never encourage it. His only duty now was to seal up any cracks, be contented that the rest of his days would be spent incarcerated; take control of his own destiny.

DAVE PITT

Of course the voice would scream and gnash its sharpened teeth trying to be released, trying to tear his brain apart from the inside, but he was ready to take that pain, prepared to give up his own life to save others.

For Oscar and whatever it really was that shrieked in his head, their killing days were over, his silence a testament of sorrow for the ones that had gone before, the lives he had allowed the voice to take.

Allan Kosminsky locked the cell door and padded slowly back toward his cupboard office. Once in there he planned to waste some time with a few games of solitaire, but knew damn well it wouldn't distract him for long. Because no matter how many games he won, which good cards he turned over, he'd still end up thinking about Chrissi and where she was. He'd still have to prepare pointless reports for the Doctor, to be emailed to her later, and then he would still end up riding his motorbike back to his lonely flat, no matter what happened his problems still remained.

He hadn't punched a wall yet but every day the big guard found himself getting increasingly aggravated, frustrated that Oscar wouldn't speak to him, pissed off that Doctor Katherine Kelly insisted on getting her petty paperwork from him, but most of all afraid that Chrissi would never return to him.

Sitting down at his computer, with a heavy sigh only a man of his size can manage, he wondered if his life could actually get any worse.

Back across the city a teenager had just finished a phone call, two actually, one to a friend he hadn't seen in a bit, the other to a man he didn't know at all, but that wasn't important because he knew what he sold.

Jay hugged his Aunty and said his goodbyes. Yeah for sure she was a mess at the minute and a meth head, still had a few problems she needed to sort out, but she was family, the only one who'd never turned her back on him.

Yet despite his appreciation of her caring nature he decided to go and wait outside, on the street, there was no avoiding the fact that as much as he loved his Aunty, that flat stank. Rolling another cigarette he looked up and down the road waiting for the black Golf to appear.

Hopefully Scott Hutchinson wouldn't be too long in coming to pick him up. In fact he'd guess his occasional friend was already on the way, why wouldn't he be, there was money to be spent on cannabis and cider, hours to be lost playing on his console, laughs to be had. He was itching to tell his bro about what he'd just done, how he'd saved a suicidal guy from a ledge, because it was a fucking good story.

In the heart of the city a young woman picked up the office phone on its third ring.

'Good afternoon, Inspector Coopers office...Oh hi there...he's probably got it on mute or something...you know what he's like...of course I can, one moment...' She pressed a button on the intercom. '...Inspector your wife's on the line...'

'Thank you Emma...put her through.' Harvey replied, his mouth curling into a tiny smile as the line clicked. 'Well hello there Mrs Cooper...ha-ha yes...this is Inspector Harveypud, how can I be of assistance...? No, no, not really it's pretty quiet here today, nothing I can't handle...yes, yes it certainly does mean that...okay I'll see you around six...I love you too...yes of course forever and a day...bye dear.'

He put the phone down and sat back in his chair thinking of how much he loved his wife and this job, especially on quiet unthreatening days like this, when his city behaved itself...

...When nothing random happened.

<u>THE END</u>